A FATAL NECESSITY

Also by Marjorie Eccles

The Herbert Reardon mysteries

BROKEN MUSIC
A DANGEROUS DECEIT *
HEIRS AND ASSIGNS *
THE PROPERTY OF LIES *
DARKNESS BEYOND *

Novels

THE SHAPE OF SAND
SHADOWS OF LIES
LAST NOCTURNE
THE CUCKOO'S CHILD *
AFTER CLARE *
THE FIREBIRD'S FEATHER *
AGAINST THE LIGHT *

A FATAL NECESSITY

Marjorie Eccles

First world edition published in Great Britain and the USA in 2025
by Severn House, an imprint of Canongate Books Ltd,
14 High Street, Edinburgh EH1 1TE.

Paperback edition first published in Great Britain and the USA in 2025
by Severn House, an imprint of Canongate Books Ltd.

severnhouse.com

Cover and jacket design by Jem Butcher Design

British Library Cataloguing-in-Publication Data
A CIP catalogue record for this title is available from the British Library.

ISBN-13: 978-1-4483-1600-7 (cased)
ISBN-13: 978-1-4483-1809-4 (paper)
ISBN-13: 978-1-4483-1601-4 (e-book)

All Severn House titles are printed on acid-free paper.

Typeset by Palimpsest Book Production Ltd.,
Falkirk, Stirlingshire, Scotland.
Printed and bound in Great Britain by
CPI Group (UK) Ltd, Croydon CR0 4YY

The manufacturer's authorised representative in the EU for product safety is Authorised Rep Compliance Ltd, 71 Lower Baggot Street, Dublin D02 P593 Ireland (arccompliance.com)

Praise for the Herbert Reardon historical mysteries

"Draw[s] on the world of Agatha Christie"
Booklist on *Darkness Beyond*

"Eccles combines a steady police procedural with a tense family drama that hits all the right notes"
Kirkus Reviews on *Darkness Beyond*

"Eccles' entertaining historical mystery series combines nicely rendered period detail along with a complex murder and a completely unexpected ending"
Booklist on *The Property of Lies*

"Entertaining . . . The clues are clearly presented, but the ending will still come as a surprise"
Publishers Weekly on *The Property of Lies*

"Will delight fans of the TV series *Downton Abbey* and authors Simon Brett and Kate Kingsbury"
Library Journal Starred Review of *Heirs and Assigns*

"Reminiscent of an Agatha Christie novel, this delightful British country-house mystery features a clever plot, captivating characters, and authentic period detail"
Booklist on *Heirs and Assigns*

About the author

Marjorie Eccles was born in Yorkshire and spent much of her childhood there and on the Northumbrian coast. She is the author of many crime novels, including the Gil Mayo police procedurals, which were adapted for television by the BBC; several Edwardian mysteries; and the DI Herbert Reardon historical mystery series. She has one grown-up son and now lives in Buckinghamshire.

TEMPLEWOOD, WORCESTERSHIRE, 1935

PART ONE

PROLOGUE

It really is the most beautiful day, heavenly as only a shining May morning can be. Hard to believe that only this morning she'd opened her eyes to dreary, wet London rooftops and the early traffic grind building up below. It doesn't matter. Here she is now, happy to be back home, at Templewood.

They've had showers in the night here, too. The grass is still wet, and raindrops glitter on the swooping lower branches of the sequoia, taller than Sophy can estimate, older than she knows. Its long, sharp shadow lies over the lawn that slopes away from the house, the ridges in its corky bark almost visible, even from here. Against a cloudless sky the flowering cherry glows palest pink.

Doing nothing, waiting for Papa, is making her nervous. It's nearly one o'clock – surely he's had time to wash and change by now? He'd arrived just minutes after the Malpas chauffeur had deposited Sophy and Gizi here before returning Dee and her mother home to Falquonroy. At the thought of what she has to say to Papa, Sophy's stomach does a plunge and she almost wishes herself back in London – almost, though not really. Not at all, in fact. There's an uneasy feeling about London nowadays. A sort of waiting. Restless people rushing about with anxious faces, as if there's a train they might miss. Newsboys at every corner shouting dismal tidings of rising unemployment, industrial disputes, more strikes and lockouts – when they're not shouting about Herr Hitler and Germany, or Mussolini and Abyssinia, that is . . . No, definitely not London.

Where is he, for goodness' sake?

Fidgeting with the papers on the table doesn't help. The local rag never has much to offer and the *Daily Mail*, mistakenly delivered yet again, along with Gizi's *Vogue*, sits unopened. It isn't a paper allowed to make an appearance at Templewood, not since the inflammatory headline '*Hurrah for the Blackshirts!*'

appeared last year. She shoves it aside, picks up the magazine and inserts herself into what space is left on the cushioned window seat. Juno isn't allowed there in theory, but she's a very old, much-loved dog and knows what she can get away with. Sophy scratches between the dog's ears with one hand and opens *Vogue* with the other. Impossibly beautiful models, a smoke-brown silk coat and skirt with sable collar and cuffs by Schiaparelli – simply divine, as Gizi's sure to say when she sees it. She pulls a face, tosses the magazine aside and stands up to fling one of the big windows open wider.

Away in the flower beds flanking the drive, Emilie's fat little bulldog puppy is enjoying a new game, following old Garbutt and trying to dig up each of the young bedding plants (which Garbutt alone loves) as they go in. But Towser's antics bring the smile back to Sophy's face and for a minute she almost forgets she won't be here anyway when the plants offend with their eye-dazzling blaze in the summer. Nor, she reminds herself, will she see the cherry tree turning its gorgeous coppery red in autumn. She turns abruptly away. There's a price to pay for everything.

Garbutt, exasperated, at last gets creakily from his knees and somehow manages to grab the little dog and haul him away. He's getting old, and the garden he considers his own domain is becoming too much for him, even with the help from his grandson, when he's here.

The sun pours into the room, dappling the dark polished floorboards and the faded oriental rugs. A slanting shaft of buttery gold lights the smiling face of Mama in its gilt frame. What would she have said to Sophy's decision? She thinks – hopes – she might have approved.

At that moment, she hears footsteps cross the hall, and the door opens. And then comes Papa's bombshell . . .

'So, there it is, Sophy. My wife has left me.'

For a second or two she thinks she's misheard, but she hasn't. He stands there, stock still. He could have been a marble statue, his classic, distinguished profile set and grey. He holds two letters between finger and thumb, as if they're contagious, the one type-written on a business letterhead, the other scrawled in purple ink on the lavender writing paper Emilie always uses, deckle-edged, scented with Parma violet. Their stepmother is many things, but rarely subtle. Not even in the manner of her departure, it seems.

She has run away with Rex Surtees, the architect who has designed the new house, the building of which – when it eventually gets underway – he himself was supposed to have been overseeing.

'Oh, Pa!' Sophy says, and he doesn't even notice. That says something – he considers the use of 'Pa' very sloppy, and Sophy suspects he'd really prefer 'Father'. It suits him to let people who don't know him think him stuffy and old fashioned, as befits his calling. Just now he doesn't even raise his brows at how she'd addressed him, maybe because for once in his life he seems unable to find anything to say. He's used to the sound of his own voice and usually rather likes it. Beautiful and rounded, much admired and a useful attribute when he's in court. An actor's voice, as Granny says. All judges, Judge Eliot C. Waring not excluded, tend to have something of the actor in them.

'You'll let the others know, Sophy?' he finds it possible to say eventually.

Me?

But she can't bring herself to utter the protest out loud. Not when her immediate reaction to what he's just told her has been only for herself. Hitting her like a fist in the solar plexus – not just because of how sorry she is for him, but because of what it's going to mean to *her.* It's guilt that shames her into agreeing. 'Yes, Papa, of course I will.' He's had a shock of the worst kind any husband might ever expect, after all. The least she can do is to save him from having to repeat it all over again.

This is a moment when she really should hug him, but he's still holding himself stiffly aloof. An unlikely Napoleon, he stands with his hand to his heart, but it's no theatrical pose, only a momentary one, his hand on its way to sliding the letters back into his breast pocket.

In the end he's the one to make the first gesture, touching her shoulder gently, brushing her forehead with a brief kiss. He suddenly thinks better of his request and says he will write to Sam himself. This at least is a relief, though Sophy wishes her brother was here, and not so far away in Berlin. 'And on second thoughts I believe it will be better for me to speak to Alexei, too,' he adds. An even greater relief. Her cousin's reactions to anything at the moment, never mind this, are unpredictable.

He looks about to say more, but then he shakes his head, pats her shoulder and goes to his study, shutting the door quietly but conclusively behind him. As he turns away, she sees on his face a look she can't immediately identify, until with something of a shock she recognizes it as a sort of sad acceptance.

She might have known Papa, of all people, wouldn't really have been fooled by what she sees now as those mock spats between Surtees and Emilie over the moderations to his austere, modern design for the new house (a cosy corner here, an inglenook there, cute suggestions by Emilie which had the architect throwing up his hands in mock horror). Play-acting like that, a cover for what was really going on between the two of them, surely wouldn't have got past Papa for long. And Sophy realizes that although he is hurt – no doubt of that – he isn't drowned in grief as he had been when Mama had died so suddenly and tragically, that perhaps it's his self-esteem which is suffering more. Who, after all, except the two intimately involved in it, knows the true state of a marriage?

ONE

The first time any of them saw Emilie, she was without a hat. In *Scarborough*, in March! They were there because of Sophy. And perhaps because of Papa, too. Since Mama had died, nearly eighteen months before, he'd been so sad, and Granny's suggestion to take his daughters on holiday had maybe been in the hopes of cheering him up, too. Sophy was thirteen and had been making a slow recovery from chickenpox, and Dr Fentiman, who was a Dalesman from Yorkshire, had patriotically recommended Scarborough and its invigorating North Sea air. The weather was dry, but so cold they could only think that Yorkshire people were a hardier breed than the rest of humanity.

They were staying at the Grand Hotel, a mammoth edifice perched high above the South Bay with rooms overlooking the North Sea. Each morning, in a bid to warm up, the two girls would dash down the cliff path towards the almost deserted promenade, leaving Papa to follow more circumspectly and join them for their brisk walk from one end of the bay to the other.

And then, one windy day, but at last one with a glimpse of spring, there was this woman, losing her hat. Straw it was, totally unsuitable for the time of year, never mind how sunny this particular day might be. It had been blown off in the stiff breeze coming from the sea, no doubt because she'd been too impatient to take the trouble to anchor it securely to her mane of thick, unfashionably long, red-blonde hair. She was chasing after it, laughing as it eluded her, her curls escaping the pins and falling down her back. It was because she wasn't looking where she was going that she ran full tilt into Papa – and only stopped herself from falling by clutching his lapels to steady herself.

For a moment their eyes met, and they were locked together like lovers, then he stepped back, removed her hands and fastidiously brushed down his jacket as if he'd been clutched by some sticky-fingered child.

'Oh, goodness, I'm sorry! My hat . . . Oh, please! I'm so sorry.' She didn't look in the least sorry. She was still laughing.

Between them the girls at last managed to capture the hat, battered and bedraggled by then from being blown along the promenade and on to the beach, trodden on by a heedless boy running after a ball.

'Oh well, not much of a loss, anyway, is it?' remarked Gizi. Fifteen years old, she was the self-appointed fashion expert in the family. Sophy handed the hat over to its owner with a very odd feeling, almost of recognition, as if she had seen this lady somewhere before. Perhaps she had. Once seen, Mrs Emilie Logan was not someone easily forgotten and Scarborough, out of season, wasn't packed with holidaymakers in search of warmth and sunshine, so they were among the select few who daily frequented the promenade. The locals knew better than to subject themselves to the dire wind that seemed to blow straight across the sea from Siberia and tended to keep to the sheltered streets and shops behind the sea front.

The guests at the Grand were few at that time of year and the Warings were the only family staying there. The vast dining room so far had been occupied by gloomy old men sitting over a bottle of claret, and sometimes a book, and pairs of maiden ladies taking advantage of winter rates. They dined early and that evening, as they were leaving the dining room, they noticed new guests being shown to a table. One of them was an elderly lady leaning heavily on the arm of the other, younger woman – she of the rebellious hat. Her hair, which they had last seen blowing all over the place, had been done up in smooth waves and though her clothes were modest – a quiet lilac dress and an insignificant little fur cape around her shoulders – there was something about her that drew all eyes.

When she saw them, she gave them her brilliant smile. Papa inclined his head and made some polite remark about the fate of the hat. After that it was natural that the family and the two women should fall into conversation when they encountered each other about the place, and that the younger woman would sometimes be invited by Papa to share their table when her older companion was unwell and kept to her room.

They learnt that she was a widow, which made the girls feel

sorry for her, imagining her passing her days in widowed solitude, mourning her dead husband, just as Papa still mourned Mama. Then the holiday ended, they went home and soon forgot her as they started the new term at school.

Nothing could have amazed them more when, six months later, Papa announced he was to marry again, and that their new stepmother was to be none other than Mrs Logan, the pretty widow smelling of violets whom they'd met in Scarborough. The circumstances of where and how the acquaintance had been renewed, and developed to the point where they agreed to marry, were not vouchsafed to the girls.

The idea of Papa being married again, even to someone they'd initially admired, came as an unwished-for shock. Both girls still missed their beautiful, happy mother, who had died in a tragic accident. One moment she'd been singing to herself as she arranged lilies in a huge vase which stood on a chest at the head of the wide, shallow stairs, the next she was lying on the floor of the hall, her head and limbs at an awkward angle, the scissors still clutched in her hand, the smashed vase pouring water down the stairs. It was assumed she had stepped back and stood on part of a thick, succulent lily stem she had just cut off and slipped to her death.

The idea of Emilie took some getting used to. She had certainly lifted Papa from the wretchedness that had consumed him. He'd once more become their handsome and urbane father, and she had shown herself agreeable to the girls as the smiling, amusing and romantic person they remembered. But perhaps both sides soon tired of trying so hard, because after a while she seemed more ordinary and perhaps just a little . . . well, not like Mama, as Gizi said sniffily. She had particularly found it difficult to offer anything more than the cool politeness Papa demanded towards the woman who was now their stepmother. Sam, of course – sunny-natured Sam who got on with everyone – was just beginning at Oxford, and then working abroad, so he didn't really have much to do with her, except when he came home for the vacations.

As for Sophy . . . Emilie was easy to get on with, as long as you didn't try to see her as a substitute mother. And yet it was difficult to get close. She was something of an enigma – outspoken and sometimes tactless, amusing and full of life when she wanted to be, which wasn't always. Those blue, almost violet eyes of hers made her look pretty when she laughed, but you never felt you really knew which way she might jump, though she was usually good-tempered and fun, especially after a glass or two of wine, and when in company she could sparkle and amuse.

TWO

As soon as Papa's study door closed, Sophy sped upstairs to find Gizi in her bedroom. She was packing, the gramophone switched on, and humming to 'Love Is Just Around the Corner'.

Sophy gasped out what had happened.

'What? Emilie, skedaddled? With Surtees? *Quelle horreur!*' Not shocked – rather amused in fact – Gizi's comments were made in much the same way as she'd once disparaged that ruined hat in Scarborough, as if the loss of either was equally trifling. 'And she left a letter? What did it say?'

'You don't imagine Pa let me read it? I haven't the foggiest!'

'I suppose not.' Gizi shrugged and carried on folding a peach satin camisole trimmed with café-au-lait lace, laying it neatly in the case, and added a pair of matching French knickers. Packing, as always, was an absorbing occupation for Gizi, even though she and Sophy had only just returned from two weeks in London. Sophy herself hadn't even *un*packed yet. It was only for Falquonroy, for heaven's sake, the home of their friends and neighbours, the Malpas family across the valley. Nothing more than a Saturday-to-Monday visit, but as well as Gizi's small case, there was another half-filled one standing on the floor.

'But Sophy darling, do think!' she said after a moment, in the affected drawl she'd picked up lately (which she was careful not to use in front of Papa, who considered it yet another assault on the English language). 'The good news is that's the last Pa will hear of the Shoebox.'

The Shoebox was the name it amused her to call the new house, which was to be built on the one-and-a-half-acre clearing where an old cottage in a spinney had once stood, just beyond Templewood's kitchen garden and the orchard. Mother Foxley, a wise woman, or witch (depending on what potions she dispensed) and her cottage were long gone, and Emilie had said, 'We don't want the old crone coming back to haunt us. We'll just call the new house The Spinney.' It was still known to the locals as Old Foxley's.

'And imagine,' Gizi went on now, 'how much money it's going to save him.'

She reached for a pair of silk stockings, rolled them neatly into a ball and tucked it into the toe of a soft slipper. Small and slim as a reed, Gizi moved like a dancer. She wore her bobbed, shiny black hair smooth and unwaved, with a fringe, dramatic against her pale, creamy skin. High cheekbones, elfin features and almond-shaped, greenish-hazel eyes tended to give her a slightly fey impression, although nothing about her could be further from the truth.

Finally, having satisfied herself that she'd missed nothing out, she snapped the case shut, hefted it off the bed and then, without looking, reached behind to stop the gramophone. The needle screeched and Bing Crosby wheezed and groaned to a dying halt long before he'd got as far as his cuddle around the corner. Pulling a face, Gizi said, 'Oh, come on, sweetie, don't tell me you haven't worked that out!'

She meant that the Shoebox wouldn't need to be built now. So far, owing to Emilie wanting all those changes to the design, progress hadn't gone much further than the clearing of the site. With a sudden lift of the heart, Sophy realized that everything could now stay as it had been.

Emilie had never made any secret of finding Templewood old-fashioned and too big, its confusion of rooms too many, the furnishings hopelessly out of date, though one could understand the aversion to inheriting another woman's domain. It was a rambling old place, certainly. Mama's beloved old home, the village of Temple Atwode's manor house, where she'd been born and lived all her life. It had been given to her and Pa as a wedding present from Granny Lychfield, by then a widow, who had moved into the former home farm, only a step and a jump away, where she still lived with her devoted maid, Agnes, as old as she was.

Although Papa rarely denied Emilie anything, he had put his foot down about changing the least thing in the house when he married her. He even insisted on Mama's portrait remaining on the wall in the big sitting room.

Everything had stayed the same, comfortable and well cared

for – Maitland had seen to that. The only thing missing nowadays was her lovely flower arrangements. No one could do them as she had done, except Gizi, when she could be bothered. A few months ago, however, Papa had agreed to – or perhaps it would have been more correct to say he hadn't objected to – Emilie's wish for a new house altogether.

The architectural practice in which Rex Surtees was a junior partner had been selected, and Surtees had been appointed to design the house and oversee the work personally. He seemed to see himself as a rising star, with ideas rooted in a desire to make a name for himself by designing clean, crisp and austere modern buildings to rival anything the Bauhaus could come up with.

What would happen to Templewood when the house was finished was a question which had dogged Sophy for months. The idea that Pa might be taking it for granted they would all move in there with him and Emilie had given her nightmares.

Until the letter had arrived for her.

It crackled now in her skirt pocket, the proposition for her future which had suddenly, amazingly, offered possibilities. The brother of her dearest schoolfriend, Jane Gilchrist, had recently borrowed money from his father and taken over a small gallery in Highgate which sold pictures and small antiques – of unparalleled dullness, according to Jane, but which had still sold rather well under the gallery's previous owners. Piers was fired with the idea of changing all that and selling modern paintings, avant-garde sculptures and *objets d'art* from upcoming artists, most of them his friends. He wanted an assistant, who needed only to look decorative and be nice to the customers, and if Sophy was still as intent on leaving home as Jane had told him, then she was welcome to the job, he'd said airily – as the offer to share Jane's flat nearby had been. Jane had warned Sophy that Piers wasn't very practical and the venture (not his first, by any means) would be run on a shoestring. Sophy hadn't, until yesterday, made up her mind to take the job. She was now glad she hadn't mentioned it to anyone, not even Granny. Nor Gizi, who would certainly have turned up her nose at it. She had been unsure about Pa. True, it would put an end to his not-too-subtle hints that there were better things she could do with her life than scribble away in exercise books, but he might persuade her, by one of his reasonably thought-out arguments, that this new idea wasn't a compelling way to envisage her future, either.

Sophy sometimes thought Papa wished she was more like Gizi, who was possessed of an absolute certainty as to her future. It was her stated intention to marry a lord. Not, as yet, any specific lord, and maybe not an actual lord ever, but certainly a man with a title, or expectations. She'd set her sights on it. And if Gizi decided on something, it was unthinkable she wouldn't get it. The trouble was, most of the top-drawer young chaps in the set she and Dee were currently running around with were penniless (or believed themselves so, which was not to say they were precisely poverty-stricken), and Gizi was not the heiress they were seeking, who would enable them to hold on to what was left of their crumbling ancient estates and to support their current lifestyles, rather than actually working to do so. Someone like Dee was who they were looking for, someone with a father like Sir Julius Malpas, never mind that he was a *nouveau riche*, and a Jew to boot. Or that Dee herself, although pretty and good-natured, was silly and a bit empty-headed. At least she knew which knife and fork to use and how to dress well. Toby Shefford, at least, had evidently decided that was enough for him. They'd just become engaged. It was the reason for the party tomorrow.

Having finished her packing, Gizi lit a cigarette, swung her legs on to the bed and propped herself against the pillows. 'Sure you won't change your mind, darling, and stay over at Falquonroy?'

'Absolutely not. I'll be there for the party tomorrow, of course, but I'd already excused myself from staying overnight.' It would be ridiculous to say that Pa needed at least one daughter with him, but that's how it felt. 'I'll come home with Pa as arranged. It's all fixed up. Sir Julius has seen to it.'

'Oh, then of course, if he says so . . .'

'Gizi!'

But Gizi merely raised her eyebrows.

Sir Julius *was* high-handed sometimes, it was true. His abrupt manner of speaking could easily give the impression that orders were being issued. All the same, anything he was responsible for always meant it went without a hitch. It must have been how he'd run the several large and successful engineering companies which had earned him his knighthood, made the fortune which had enabled him to buy and restore Falquonroy Park, and was no doubt how he operated the business concerns he still occupied himself with in his retirement.

'Anyway, do you think Pa will still go to the party?' Gizi asked.

'Of course he will.' He would do everything he could, Sophy was sure, to avoid creating a sensation by revealing that his wife had decamped. Sooner or later – probably sooner – the true state of affairs would become public knowledge, of course, but meanwhile she knew Pa would find some diplomatic excuse to account for Emilie's absence tomorrow night. 'He won't dodge the invitation.'

'Oh, it goes without saying that he'll be awfully brave, I'm sure . . . so you don't *have* to come home, just to be with him, do you?'

Gizi believed everyone had a right to do exactly as they wished, and she said it with the impatience she used all the time lately. Sophy threw her sister a sharp look. Chic, as always, from her scarlet mouth to the tips of her woven, strappy white sandals. Her seafoam-green crepe de chine dress was bias-cut and clung in all the right places, showing off her slim figure. Slim? She'd always been slight, lightly boned, but she was beginning to look positively thin. Maitland was always telling her she needed to stop smoking and eat more. Does she see what she's doing to herself, Sophy wondered. 'I know I don't *have* to come home, but I will, all the same,' she said stubbornly.

Gizi narrowed her eyes and for several moments squinted at Sophy through a cigarette haze in a way that said she was preparing to speak with sisterly candour. 'You know, sweetie pie, I do so absolutely hate to say this, but I'm so afraid you're in danger of becoming something of a wet blanket. Well, you are, darling – admit!'

Sophy flushed but didn't think it deserved an answer. She turned away and picked up the new hat tossed on to the bed – one item from the mad shopping sprees Gizi had indulged in during the last two weeks in the capital. It had been so hectic. Besides the shopping, there had been tea dances, matinees, evening parties, the newest musical comedies to see, more dances, nightclubs . . . Sophy needed to breathe.

Meant for later in the season, the hat was ivory velour felt, and in place of a feather had a spiral of cleverly wired and twisted black silk, secured to the turned back narrow brim by a sparkly black brooch. To avoid Gizi's scrutiny, she took the hat to the dressing table, sat down and plonked it on her own head, turning this way and that. It was the sort of hat that ought to be fun to wear. As it was, her slippery hair poked out messily and when she tried to tuck it back it looked worse.

She wasn't going to be allowed to get away without answering. Gizi swung her legs off the bed and came to stand behind her, enveloping her in a smoky floral fragrance of Joy and tobacco.

'Oh, Muffin,' she said more gently, as their glances met in the looking glass, 'what's wrong with you lately?'

The old childish nickname touched Sophy. She wafted away the smoke curling from the cigarette that was getting in her eyes and making them sting, reached into her pocket for her glasses and snatched the hat off, putting it on the dressing table. Gizi's hands pressed on her shoulders as she started to get up.

'No, just listen to me for one second! You're nearly twenty-one and you do absolutely nothing but sit about and dream, or scribble away in those dreary old notebooks. Maitland's right, you're away with the fairies most of the time! You won't join in like you used to. You'll be thirty before you know where you are! How do you ever expect to meet anyone?'

She meant *meet someone who'll marry you and take you away and give you a more exciting life.* For a moment Sophy thought about telling her of her escape plan. Except that Gizi wouldn't see it as escape. Anyway, Sophy wasn't sure that was how she could see it now, either. Things had changed dramatically in the last hour. It was surely ridiculous to feel that Papa would need her to stay here and support him, yet something inside her did a miserable, downward plunge, a sigh for lost freedom.

'For heaven's sake,' Gizi was going on, 'there's another life out there and you're . . . you're . . .'

'Practically an old maid,' Sophy finished. The comments had stung.

'You said it, darling! But oh, Sophy! You used to be such fun.' And just for a moment, Sophy did miss the parties, dancing the night away, shopping for frivolous new clothes, and all the other fun things she might regularly enjoy, if she shared more often, as she was urged to do, the time Gizi and Dee spent at the Malpas townhouse in Mount Street, chaperoned, of course, by Lady Malpas. But it wasn't what she longed for, positively not what Gizi had at the moment: a life devoted entirely to mindless diversions, when she'd once been so different. And that not so long ago, either.

'Oh, ducky, I've made you cry,' Gizi exclaimed. 'Do dry your eyes and take no notice of me.'

'I'm not crying. It's your cigarette.'

Gizi obligingly stubbed it out. 'Take your specs off,' she ordered, then picked up the discarded hat and put it on Sophy's head again, tilting it seductively forward and sideways, tweaking it to dip over her eyes and dampening a finger to induce a tiny kiss-curl to peep out. 'There you are! I have to say it suits you so much better than me. It's yours if you want it.'

There was a certain family resemblance between them, though Sophy knew she would never be a stunner like Gizi. Her eyes were not sparkling hazel green but ordinary brown – and her hair was *definitely* mousy, and yet . . . she had to admit the frivolous hat now did something for her. If she'd been Gizi, she would have had a copy of that Schiaparelli outfit in *Vogue* made to go with it as well. A little laugh escaped her as she took it off again.

Gizi shrugged and went back to the bed. 'Do have another think, darling, about the weekend. You don't know what you'll be missing. It's bound to be hilarious. Everyone will be there – Marigold and Boo, and we'll have to put up with Stumpy Hetherington, I suppose, though he's such a scream when he wants to be. Toby will be there, of course. And Fitz,' she added.

Her smile was dazzling. Sophy couldn't imagine why. The Honourable Gerald Lancelot Henry FitzAlban never brought a smile to *her* face. One more reason, she decided, not to change her mind about staying as a house guest if he was to be there.

Rather obviously, Gizi changed the subject. 'How is Lex taking the news?' For all her apparent indifference, it didn't appear that the upheaval Emilie's leaving would cause in the Waring family had been dismissed entirely from her mind.

'Pa's going to tell him, but he's off somewhere with Catchpole.'

'Poor boy.' It wasn't clear whether that was for having Catchpole for company or for Emilie's departure – which he was going to take badly, Sophy thought with a sudden pang. The two of them, he and Emilie, had rather oddly hit it off.

Alexei had come to live with them when his mother, their own mother's younger sister, had died a few months after giving birth to him, whereupon Costas Kyriakou, his Greek father, had departed back to his own country, never to be seen again. But Mama had opened her arms wide and the squalling, angry baby had become the youngest addition to the Waring family. Now sixteen, he'd grown to be as handsome as his father reputedly had been: straight nose, dark, thickly lashed eyes and black curls lying close and flat, a young Greek god. He was neither a loving nor an easy child – you could never tell what he was thinking – and this hadn't changed as he'd grown older. He was seen as 'difficult', but the main thing about Lex was that he was also very clever. Which was why it had been an absolute astonishment to the girls when he'd been expelled from his school three months ago, for reasons unspecified, at least to them.

Sophy sensed a cold, silent fury about this; she didn't dare ask him for details, but she couldn't help feeling sorry for him. He'd been led to believe he had a bright future ahead of him and he evidently saw being expelled from Westingbury, where the teaching was supposed to be first class and where he'd always shone, as an injustice and an insult. A private tutor had been engaged to continue cramming him for entrance to Cambridge, though Brad Catchpole didn't appear to be one of Pa's more astute choices. He was a plump, dull young man, given to wearing flannel bags and tweed jackets with leather patches on the elbows, who never said much and tended to blush when spoken to. A frightful bore, in Gizi's opinion.

A crunching noise sounded on the gravel outside. For a wild moment, Sophy thought: Emilie – she's changed her mind and come back! But a glance out of the window showed it was only Maitland.

She'd been the first person the girls had looked for when they arrived home, and were told she'd gone shopping, cycling through Temple Atwode to the Maxstead road, where she would leave her bicycle behind a hedge and take the bus into Folbury to give her meat and grocery orders for the following week.

Sophy watched from the window as she lifted her shopping from her bicycle basket. She was their old nurse, so long in exile from her native Western Isles that her Scottish accent had almost deserted her, except in moments of extreme annoyance, or stress. There wasn't anything she didn't know about Templewood and its inhabitants. It suddenly struck Sophy that she might even know more than Pa did – or was prepared to tell them – about Emilie's departure.

THREE

Alexei lay flat on his stomach by the edge of the pool in the cool, dark clearing, chin on his hands, supported by his raised elbows. His head hung inches over the water. Above him, bright arrows of sunlight pierced the young foliage of a slender silver birch, throwing dappled patterns on to the water. Nothing moved here in this remote part of the garden, though he thought he'd earlier spotted a muntjac deer watching him from under the shade of the surrounding trees, unmoving, at one with the soft silence which surrounded it.

He could see his own distorted, fairground-mirror reflection wavering between a clump of yellow flag and the spreading pads of a water lily. He lowered his elbows until his nose just felt the cool touch of the water. The smell of underwater vegetation, secret home to frogs, tadpoles and newts, rose to his nostrils. How far down could you push your face without drowning? And how long would it take, he wondered, before the instant when you knew it was too late to stop?

These moments in his life came to him when he did things outside his own volition, testing himself, knowing he shouldn't, but unable to prevent himself responding to the impulse. He never knew what made him act like that any more than other people knew. The devil himself was in him sometimes, they said. They – authority, whoever that happened to be at the time – had always predicted a bad end for him, something Alexei himself had no reason to disagree with, but he hadn't anticipated it coming so soon. For the first time in his life, he was afraid he'd gone too far. He stared through the water into a dark, inescapable future.

He'd been lying by the pond for nearly an hour, ever since that terrible ten minutes with his uncle. As it came back to him, he lowered his face again, this time right into the water. He opened his eyes. If he held his breath long enough, everything would go away. What she had done. What *he* had done . . . or not done. Oh, God! It felt as though all his life he had been moving inevitably towards this. His senses began to swim.

The moment shattered when he felt his hair grasped, as if his scalp was being torn off. Water went up his nose, he swallowed some and began to choke and splutter. An enormous clutch on the back of his shirt dragged him bodily backwards, and he was thrown, landing on his back, the breath knocked out of him, then he was rolled on to his side, his face scraping the ground. He coughed, agonizingly, retched up water, coughed and spluttered again and again and finally, with a struggle, sat up, his chest pumping like a steam engine.

'What the hell do you think you're doing, you bloody little fool?'

Brad Catchpole's wire-rimmed glasses were askew, his sparse sandy hair was all over the place, his plump face was scarlet, but with rage, not effort. Alexei, for all he was slim, was tall and no lightweight, but Catchpole had lifted him as easily as though he were nothing.

He found he could breathe again, just. He was all right. Apart, that was, from the burning sensation in his nose, his throat and his chest, and also his watering eyes . . . as though he was *crying*, for God's sake! But he found he could, with an effort, speak. And he wasn't even wet, except for his head and shoulders. 'Keep your hair on, Catters,' he croaked. 'Wasn't trying to do away with myself.'

Catchpole too had now collapsed on to the ground, his back against a tree, his knees drawn up. The furious colour had drained from his face, and it was back to its usual porridge hue. His hair was still plastered to his damp forehead, but he didn't look ridiculous. Generally as mild as milk, he looked like a man who was striving hard to keep his temper. But he said nothing more. He didn't have to.

Why the devil did he pull me back? I wouldn't have minded dying, were the thoughts that ran through Lex's mind, which he knew was rubbish. Of course he would. In spite of what he was going to have to face up to: the fact that she'd gone, for good, and that it was his fault. Because of him, because he'd allowed himself to be taken in. Emilie had spun him a lie and he'd believed her, when all the time she'd been intending to go off with that puffed-up fool, Surtees. Oh, God, life without Emilie! She had been so much a part of his existence. After his Aunt Isobel had died, no one else had seemed to bother with him. Sam was so much older and mostly away anyway, and the girls were . . . girls. Emilie, on the other hand, genuinely seemed to like being with him. She could make him laugh . . . and she could actually beat him at tennis. They talked, and she was willing to listen. To hear what he was *really* saying. Not even Uncle Eliot, with all his experience and judgemental skills, could do that. He would listen with patient understanding, but he expected contrition: it was imperative that Alexei should learn to exercise self-control and be willing to accept the consequences of his actions, he told him gravely. Emilie, on the other hand, had been sorry for him and saw that he couldn't help being driven to doing what he did. And now she was gone, with no one to take her place.

Catchpole stood up and began to walk away, saying, rather wearily, 'Come on. Let's get you into a dry shirt before anyone sees you.' In spite of himself, Alexei admired the way he'd mastered his temper.

After a moment, he struggled to his feet and followed. They walked back to the house and, as they rounded the corner, they saw the sit-up-and-beg bicycle parked against the wall by the old stables. 'Oh, Lord, Maitland's back!' Alexei said, and fled.

FOUR

Sunday morning found Sophy sitting at the desk in her room, nibbling the end of her fountain pen, her mind far from the waiting pages in front of her. *Last night*, she wrote, then stopped. Gazed out of the window at a view as familiar as her own face: the woods on the opposite slope of the valley, and the distant roofs rising just above the treetops like some magical, imaginary castle in a fairytale illustration: Falquonroy Park.

It wasn't like that, of course.

Generally spoken of as an imposing pile with a long and honourable tradition, Falquonroy had for centuries been owned by the family said to be descended from a powerful crusading nobleman who had come over with William the Conqueror. Now, the last heir of the Falquonroys lay in an unknown grave somewhere in Normandy, returned to his ancestors, killed in the Great War. The estate had been broken up, much of the land sold and the mansion itself had been in danger of being demolished. Forbidding, crumbling, with icy draughts sweeping along its corridors and the ghosts of Falquonroys long gone said to haunt its forgotten, echoing rooms.

Sophy didn't remember how old she was when they heard the estate had been bought by Sir Julius Malpas, a wealthy Birmingham industrialist, and that he intended to restore it and live in it with his wife and their daughter, but she did remember the stir the news caused in and around Temple Atwode. She and Gizi were especially excited when they heard Dee was a girl of their own age: Falquonroy was scarcely half a mile away across the valley, even nearer to their own house than the village, where there were hardly any children to play with. There had scarcely been a day since they came when they hadn't seen Dee at some point.

Outside, Falquonroy didn't look substantially different from what it must have done a couple of centuries ago, but inside, it was now unrecognizable. Central heating and bathrooms installed, carpets laid, a lot of what Sam called 'staggery' staring down, snooty and glassy-eyed, from the walls in the great hall, where the portraits inherited from the Falquonroys had been regilded and rehung, along with one each of Sir Julius and Lady Malpas, and one of Dee looking angelic at the age of five or thereabouts. The furniture was expensive and comfortable, and the dogs were kept out of the principal rooms. It was all very grand, and certainly warmer than it must ever have been in all those past centuries, if slightly off-key in some way that it was hard to put a finger on.

The truth was Falquonroy was in fact still little more than a grand façade, though no one would believe that unless they went exploring, which of course most visitors did not. Behind the doors which shut off the greater part were corridors leading to locked and empty rooms, stairs roped off, going nowhere. An icy chill hung over its yet-unrestored rooms, a memory of its ancient, sometimes bloody history. Ghosts of Crusaders, the Knights Templar who had given their name to the village, dashing Cavaliers and heroes of Waterloo were all said to walk its precincts.

Sophy tried to pull her attention back to what she'd begun, but her mind didn't seem to be on it.

Grandpa Lychfield had been the only one, apart from Sophy herself, who always knew she was destined to be a writer. He died when she was eleven, but he had loved to read the stories she wrote, and it was he who'd encouraged her to keep what he called a journal as well. 'Like your great-grandmother, the other Sophia, my mother. Like her, you notice things about people, and that's what a writer needs. She never wrote books, alas, but there were dozens of her journals left when she died. Such a pity nobody thought to keep them – what a story they would have told!'

If only they had! Sophy agreed, garnering every scrap she could of her great-grandmother's romantic life. Gizella Szophia had been born in Budapest, a member of one of those turbulent, aristocratic families with a dark Central European history. There she'd met and fallen in love with Amyas Lychfield, Sophy's great-grandpapa, then a dashing English army subaltern. She'd given up everything to marry and live a peripatetic army life with him, until finally, his military career over, they and their children had settled back in England at his ancestral home, Templewood.

Sophy knew she hadn't inherited Gizella Szophia's looks; she'd been a beauty, dark and passionate and intense. Gizi had been the favoured one there, as well as receiving her first name, while Sophy had the second. (And Sam was really Sándor, though no one, not even Pa, ever called him that.) Szophia had, however, perhaps passed on something else other than her second name, Sophy told herself, but she sighed, trying not to think of Jane's letter.

Two stories published by a magazine very few people had ever heard of didn't yet amount to anything. And as for the detective novel she was attempting to write – the sort Mrs Christie wrote, perhaps – well, she wasn't getting much further with that than the first vague notion. The trouble was she didn't know just *what* it was she needed, to order and make sense of all those thoughts and ideas tumbling about inside her. Except perhaps what Sam called wider horizons, and what she herself thought of as space. Independence. She felt she knew nothing of life outside Templewood and glimpses into the sort of world Gizi wanted to inhabit, which she herself despised. She longed to be different from what she was – wiser, more *interesting*. She had thought time away from Templewood might do that.

Don't think about it now, just write! She took a breath, picked up her pen. And once started, the words began to flow.

The party wasn't a big one by Falquonroy standards. Most of the guests were young, with just a handful of older people – family friends like Papa and Granny Lychfield, Dr and Mrs Fentiman, Mr Meredith the rector – and, alas, the Thorpe-Bassetts, who live about five miles away. Vernon Thorpe-Bassett, our local MP (known to the Waring family as The Hound) had accepted the invitation, I suppose, because he finds it expedient to be on good terms with his constituents, especially when they are well-heeled. He's smooth, with a politician's handclasp and a wide smile that doesn't match. His wife is a quiet woman who has been trained to be pleasant. I suppose their invitation had to include their insufferable daughter, Pamela, though she's no friend of Dee's (or Gizi's – or mine, for that matter) since our schooldays at

Maxstead. Pamela the Perfect Prefect. Blonde and very tall, attractive in a haughty, horsey way; she was sitting next to Fitz, dazzling him with her smile. Well, rather her than me. Even though my companion on one side was Dee's fiancé, Toby Shefford.

Poor Deedie – imagine spending the rest of one's life with such a man. Very good looking in a dishevelled, sulkymouthed sort of way, tall and athletic – but so boring! He's patently interested in nothing other than the games he seems to spend his life playing. He was a captain of games at his public school, and he still plays rugby, tennis and squash, as well as golf. And of course he fences, though not at present: he badly sprained his knee when he slipped on the piste when recently engaged in something he calls a fifteen-touch bout. Fencing is all the rage nowadays, like everything else Sir Oswald Mosley does.

Mosley . . . his name's everywhere. They say he's an impassioned and persuasive speaker, a charismatic leader – God to his followers – who might have been prime minister had he not chosen to form his own new party: the British Union of Fascists, better known as the Blackshirts. Gizi says he's handsome as the Devil, and no woman is safe from him. I've never met him and have no desire to. I don't even want to think about any man who is considered a danger to women. Even Toby's better than that. Whatever his faults, he doesn't pretend to be some sort of Lothario.

I suspect I'm being beastly about Toby. I hope, but can't quite believe, that his affection for Deedie isn't connected to the Malpas money. He's always hard up and he doesn't have any hope of coming into anything himself as far as I can gather, and yet Dee's wearing an emerald the size of a pigeon's egg on her engagement finger. Who paid for that, I wonder.

Does it matter? She was rosy with excitement and happiness last night, and looked extremely pretty with her thick, wavy black hair and big dark eyes, wearing a beautiful, expensive silk dress, the same colour as the stone in her ring. She's always been plump, and I'd guess she'll look exactly like her mother in twenty years, matronly and grey-haired and with the same pleasant, round face. She's a sweet girl, and maybe one day she'll grow to have as much common sense as her mother, who runs

Falquonroy as if she's always been used to such a grand lifestyle, though Granny Lychfield, her greatest friend, thinks she's uneasy with her title and would be more comfortable to have stayed as plain Mrs Malpas.

The evening had hardly started and although I'm not exactly known for being short of something to say, Toby and I had already come to a conversational roadblock. He was being even more than usually dull last night, forever losing the thread of whatever conversation I tried to start and staring into space, and he was drinking an awful lot. His bow tie was slightly askew, and his boiled shirt front was losing its starch. The wine hadn't loosened his tongue, though. I was sure he was the sort of man who is interested in dogs, so in desperation I started to tell him about Towser, and how he'd been one of a litter of bulldog puppies destined for dogfighting by a gang of vicious morons, until they were caught and prosecuted. Pa had been the judge in the case and when he heard that the puppies were to be put down, had offered to take one as a present for Emilie.

'I say, that was pretty decent of him!' Toby roused himself and threw an approving glance at Pa, though his admiration appeared to be more for the acquisition of such a dog rather than for Pa's altruism. 'A bullpup? Nothing to equal 'em! Ugly little brutes, one has to say, but jolly brilliant fighters, what?'

'Only when they're bred to be,' I answered coldly. Anyone who cares anything about dogs knows that it's their looks, poor things, and their inability ever to give up which have given bulldogs a bad reputation. At the moment, Towser is a joyous little bundle of happiness with a sweet nature that will hopefully be his for the rest his life.

But Toby looked at me without any understanding. 'Well, if that's how you see it. But you'll never take the spirit and the fight out of him, and you shouldn't try.' He took another long swig of his wine, and lost interest in me, a woman who'd no business criticizing such manly pursuits. But no sooner had this crossed my mind than he threw me a smile that totally disarmed me.

Perhaps I'd better try harder with him. He might be nicer than I think. Luckily for both of us, Lady Malpas, on his other side, claimed him at that point.

The meal over, the engaged pair toasted and congratulated, the company separated, the older contingent taking themselves off to the drawing room, we younger ones to the big room that leads off the conservatory. Someone began to improvise on the piano, then the carpet was rolled up, the gramophone turned on and people began to dance. The party soon became very gay and rather noisy. One person not dancing was stiff-kneed Toby. After a mandatory attempt at a shuffle with Deedie he was let off and sat back, getting quietly drunk. I avoided him (Toby when sober was bad enough) and had another energetic hop around with Stumpy Hetherington, who always makes me laugh but has sweaty palms and a tight grip, as if one might try to escape.

Afterwards, I flopped down on to a sofa, when someone immediately thrust a glass of what I hoped was lemonade into my hand. When they moved away, I found myself looking straight across the room at Fitz, who was . . . I almost wrote sprawled, but Fitz never sprawls . . . sitting relaxed, cool and collected, at ease in an armchair, toying with a glass of wine.

He was immaculate as usual in his well-tailored evening clothes, tall and elegantly slim, smooth fairish hair, a face which most people would call handsome, and that charming smile that makes me shiver. His gaze wasn't turned in my direction, but towards Gizi, who was looking exceptional tonight in a gold, backless silk dress with a halter neckline, and had as usual attracted a crowd around her, mostly men. At that moment, laughing at something someone had just said, she turned her head and caught Fitz's intent look. He lazily raised his glass. The smile left her face, and something passed between them that stirred in me a feeling I didn't want to analyse at that moment. But it raised the goosebumps on my arms and made me shiver slightly, despite the heat of the room.

I told myself it was nothing. The goosepimples left me, and the hot feeling returned. My new shoes had begun to pinch. The party had turned out to be enjoyable, but Pa wasn't yet in evidence, ready for home. Holding my lemonade, I wandered out into the conservatory, which was sure to be cooler. It was unlit, except for a pair of standard lamps, leaving the ends of the long room in darkness. I hoped I wouldn't be disturbing any couple who'd slipped out there, but I seemed to be alone. I threw myself down into a cushioned basket chair and held the cold glass to my forehead.

The conservatory was Lady Malpas's territory. She had green fingers, like Granny. It was the great interest which drew them together, and among the palms, ferns and exotic flora, the scent of lilies and stephanotis massed in pots mingled headily with the smell of cool damp earth and greenery.

A door at the far end opened and someone came in.

'Not feeling indisposed, I hope, Sophy?'

Sir Julius had evidently felt the same need as I had for a breath of air, though he had come into the conservatory through one of the normally locked doors which led to the unfinished part of the house. He was as usual smoking a cigar and the aroma of rich tobacco almost overlaid the heavy exotic scent of the lilies.

Despite what a lot of people think about him, I'm disposed to like Deedie's father very much, and I can understand why he and Pa have become such friends. He doesn't smile much, and has an abrupt manner of speaking which can seem a bit intimidating. He doesn't give way to anyone or allow his family to be put down by those who raise their eyebrows at the owners of Falquonroy. He may not have been born with a silver spoon in his mouth, but he has made his own way in the world to his present semi-retired status: he owns at least three factories that I know of, and very profitable concerns they're reputed to be, mostly through having supplied heavy engineering during the war.

'No, I was just feeling a bit hot.' I answered his question.

'Your papa will be ready to leave shortly, I believe, if it's not too early for you. I hope you've enjoyed your evening. Too bad about Emilie's cold.'

I started to get up, ready to go and find him.

Sir Julius put a hand on my arm. 'No rush. He's still saying goodnights to everyone, apologizing for letting me take him away from the company. I must follow his good example.' He seemed in no hurry to do this and, switching on another lamp, he sat in the chair next to mine. 'I'm afraid I dragged him away for a little tour of the house. We've been comparing our experience of architects.'

I wouldn't have thought Pa would have told even Sir Julius yet that the building of The Spinney was now unlikely to go ahead – nor the reason why. I soon saw, however, as Sir Julius went on, that it was nothing of the kind. He told me they'd been inspecting the unfinished part of the house. He had, he said, decided to resume the abandoned work of restoration and repair. 'Lady Malpas doesn't care for living in a half-ruined house,' he confessed with a slight smile, 'and it's very likely we shall shortly be having a number of visitors, so we shall need more accommodation.'

After Dee was married, there would only be the two of them living in this great house, and there would be far less entertaining and hospitality, at present mostly done for Dee's sake. He didn't offer any further explanation about his changed intentions for Falquonroy, however, and though I was intrigued, I could hardly ask for one. Surely there were enough guest rooms already – look how many people would be staying tonight, for instance. How many visitors was he expecting, for goodness' sake, and who might they be? A royal progress?

At that point Lady Malpas joined us. 'There you are, Julius. And Sophy, my dear! Your papa's waiting for you. I hope you've had a good evening?'

I sprang up and thanked her, and she kissed my cheek, then took her husband's arm. 'Come and say goodnight to Eliot, Julius.'

Well, it had gone better than Sophy had dared to hope. And now, this morning, thinking it over as she closed her journal and stowed it safely away in a drawer, satisfied that the party had been recorded, she felt it was a source of congratulation that she'd managed to go through the whole time without speaking to FitzAlban at all, apart from hello and farewell.

She was just about to run a comb through her hair before going down to breakfast when the door opened abruptly and in the mirror Maitland was reflected, standing stock still in the doorway.

Sophy swung round. Before she could ask what was wrong, Maitland said in a very strange voice, 'Sophy. Towser, he—'

Oh heavens, he'd had an accident! Been run over . . . he was dead! He was only a puppy, not properly trained yet . . . someone had left him alone in the garden and he'd run out into the normally so-quiet road outside and been killed by a farm tractor or something. He . . .

At that moment, Towser bounded in and rushed up to Sophy, greeting her as if he hadn't seen her only an hour before when she'd slipped downstairs to give him his breakfast. She bent down and scooped him up, four months old and already as solid as a suet pudding, and looked into his funny little face as he enthusiastically tried to lick hers. She could feel his heart thudding, almost as much as she now realized her own was. 'What's the matter, Maitland?'

'It's Mrs Waring.' And then Maitland rushed on, her face twisted. 'She didnae run away, after all. Towser found her, and . . . Och, Sophy, she's dead.'

PART TWO

FIVE

The hamlet of Temple Atwode was only a few miles from the busy market town of Folbury, but it might have been on another continent. Where Folbury had crowded streets, shops, municipal swimming baths and a public library, not to mention factory areas that probed murky fingers into the market town from the Birmingham sprawl, this place simply had silence . . . and trees, trees and more trees. Hundreds of peaceful acres of beech, oak and ash surrounded it. Deer could occasionally be glimpsed in clearings, rabbits scuttled away from approaching cars and the roadside hedgerows foamed with cow parsley.

Today, however, on this sunny Sunday morning, Detective Chief Inspector Herbert Reardon (Bert to his friends) wasn't entirely in the best of moods to appreciate this or any other sort of landscape. He sat back in the passenger seat, willing only idle, random thoughts to drift through his mind, hoping that would concentrate his subconscious on what was to come.

A small cloud passed across the sun – another shower on the way, April weather rather than May, but great at least for the new roses which had just gone in at number nine, The Avenue. Now *there* was a random thought! He gave a grunt that might, despite himself, have been a laugh. He, a professed non-gardener? He'd merely done the good-husband duty and dug over the hitherto neglected plot at the back of their house, happy to leave the rest to Ellen. Even happier, to tell the truth, that making a garden was absorbing all his wife's spare energy. Was this because she might direct it otherwise, once she heard of this new investigation? Perish the thought! Her keenness to help was something he'd had reason to be grateful for in the past, he reminded himself. But he still felt she was better employed keeping her energies to her new preoccupation with the garden, as well as her teaching job in the girls' boarding school at Maxstead – a village, incidentally, only a mile or two from where they were now headed.

Temple Atwode wasn't in fact as remote as it might seem. It

was one of several other surrounding villages, though surely the smallest; it took less than a heartbeat to drive right through it when a minute later the narrow green tunnel of the road opened out. A few cottages, a little Norman church, with one solitary worshipper making her way between the yews to the church for morning service. Not even big enough to possess its own pub, though in one of the cottages was a front window that suggested it might also have another existence as a tiny shop. All of it a far cry from bustling Folbury and the hospital where Reardon's DS and right-hand man, Joe Gilmour, was presently lying with his leg in traction.

A marble. Gilmour had stepped on a *marble*, of all things, near the swings in the recreation ground where he'd taken his little daughter, Ellie. Sending him sliding several yards before he crashed to the ground and then realized he couldn't get up. An ignominious accident which had cost him a fractured femur and didn't even have the heroics of being caused by chasing some evildoer. To make it worse, Ellie had chortled at the time, thinking he was doing acrobatics to entertain her. A bloody marble! The result was doing nothing for Joe's self-esteem, or his normally equable disposition. Or Reardon's for that matter, whose first question when this new case had come in had been who the devil was to replace his right-hand man?

One of his two most capable DCs was the possible answer. But Gargrave? Not on your nelly! He wasn't a serious possibility, or even a possibility at all. An ex-pat Yorkshireman, a good detective, ambitious but with too good an opinion of his own capabilities. Pickersgill, then? Serious, steady, slow but sure, and without a trace of imagination?

He needn't have worried. His detective superintendent, Knott, already had a directive in place – quite possibly issuing from further up the chain of command – that this new young chap, now occupying Gilmour's place in the driving seat, would be sent to Folbury to assist him on this case.

'Jago?' Reardon had repeated. 'That young Cornishman?' He had nothing personally against the previously London-based detective sergeant, except that he would almost certainly be another of Knott's own breed, a product of the new-fangled thinking to update the Force. In his twenties, he was university educated, bright as a button and pushy, fast-track promoted and on the lookout for further advancement.

'He's an excellent officer,' Knott had said sharply, well aware of Reardon's doubts, but offering no choice. 'I wouldn't saddle you with anyone who wasn't, you know that.'

Well, Reardon didn't doubt that. There was no love lost between him and his super, but Knott was no fool. This new case was high profile, and he had his own carefully nourished reputation to think about. 'As things are at the moment, I can spare him,' he'd continued. 'Events seem to have quietened down in – er – in his direction. Understand what I'm saying, Reardon?'

An unusual moment of accord had passed between the two men. Yes, Reardon understood, or thought he did. You had to ask yourself why a young Scotland Yard detective sergeant with obvious prospects should have been sent to work here in the Midlands, presently a place of struggle and strife, like industrial areas all over the country.

Knott had smoothed back hair that was already smooth as butter, examined his immaculate fingernails and confirmed the assumptions Reardon had already made.

This young chap, Jago, was among other Scotland Yard officers who had been 'volunteered' to trouble spots across the country, to cities like Liverpool, Manchester and Birmingham, where Sir Oswald Mosley was presently wooing the disaffected with promises of stronger government, freedom from poverty, jobs for all, fair wages. A Better Britain! If ruled by him and his British Union of Fascists. As long as you weren't a communist, or a Jew.

These officers were not precisely intended to work undercover, more for 'information gathering' as Knott had put it . . . meaning their remit was to find out what they could and keep a wary eye out for any indications of impending trouble without making it too obvious.

'I'm surprised London could spare them,' Reardon said, 'considering what's happening down there.'

London's East End was in turmoil. What the police there were having to cope with made the Birmingham BUF rallies look like playground scuffles, the large population of Jews, communists and red-hot socialists, all of them with their own agenda, waging war against Mosley's Blackshirts. While Ramsay MacDonald, the prime minister, and his coalition government were asleep, according to what the *Daily Mail* said and most of the nation believed.

'Ours not to reason why, Reardon.' It was as far as Knott would allow himself to go in criticizing higher authority, but his feathers had evidently been ruffled. He obviously felt he had been overridden. As if he wasn't being given credit for having his finger firmly on the pulse of what was happening on his own turf.

The truth was that here in the West Midlands, recent Blackshirt rallies at Bingley Hall and the Rag Market, and the mayhem resulting from them, had caused public outrage. Support from people who had enough troubles of their own without the intervention of Mosley's bully boys stirring up more hadn't been forthcoming. But although ad-hoc recruitment meetings for the party still kept cropping up all over the place, if more in hope than expectation, the belligerence, for the moment, had more or less settled into the odd skirmish.

'To tell the truth, Reardon,' Knott said with an unexpected change of direction, 'I don't believe DS Jago's time here has lived up to his expectations so far. He's been working well under his own capacities – not that he hasn't done an excellent job – and it's making him . . . restive. Frankly, I don't need that sort of aggravation. Giving him something else to think about for a while won't do anyone any harm.'

So here he was now, Detective Sergeant Thomas Jago. Loose-limbed and long-legged, with a pronounced Cornish burr, a level glance, intelligent eyes under straight, heavy dark brows. Thankfully not the smart-arse Reardon had expected. Quick-witted but seemingly amiable and easy-going. He looked fit, with enough about him to suggest he could be tough if needed.

Toughness, though, wasn't necessarily a quality to recommend itself in what was to come. Tact and diplomacy were more to the point, as Knott hadn't been slow to remind Reardon. 'Delicate situation,' he'd said. 'Needs handling with kid gloves. I know you're capable of that; it's why I asked you.'

Soft soap never got anywhere with Reardon. But good grief, Judge Waring! Not the most formidable of judges – not always, at any rate – but being in charge of an investigation into the case of *any* judge whose wife had just been found dead in suspicious circumstances was hardly something to be devoutly wished for.

Reardon fingered his scar, a wartime souvenir that ran down his left cheek, an unconscious habit he had when he was perplexed or thinking hard. He leant back in his seat and closed his eyes. Making the best of it wasn't something he was good at, but it was what he'd have to do.

SIX

A few hours before, DS Tom Jago had been champing at the bit, cursing yet again what was only supposed to have been a short, sharp interlude in his working life: spying on the BUF activities in the Midlands. He privately regarded this as a Boy's Own Paper lark thought up by some bright spark in the upper echelons. But refusing the temporary secondment hadn't been an option if he wanted that transfer to the Murder Squad . . . and he did want it. His work as a detective sergeant in Scotland Yard so far had convinced him that was the way he wanted his career to go. The move had not, however, turned out as expected. The local Blackshirts were presently keeping a low profile and he'd been kicking his heels, sent hither and yon by Knott, who didn't seem to know what to do with him.

Then DS Joe Gilmour at Folbury had had his lucky accident. Lucky for Tom Jago, anyway. And here he was now, about to be involved in the real job of detecting a murder once more, working under Reardon, whom he'd already decided would be a very different proposition to Knott. He'd heard good things about the chief inspector, at the moment asleep beside him.

He drew to a halt but before he'd had time to wake him by saying, 'Looks as though we're here, sir,' Reardon's eyes had flown open and he was halfway out of the car, not asleep at all.

It was just a clearing in the woods, coming shortly after they'd passed the house called Templewood belonging to Judge Waring: large and low-built, with a red-tiled roof and many gables, standing back from the road on a slight rise. Here, the narrow road was made even more so by the presence of a couple of parked cars and a bicycle propped against the hedge.

One of the cars, Reardon noted, belonged to Kay Dysart, the police doctor. The bicycle was police-issue, so Police Constable Ted Shay, the Maxstead village bobby, must also be here. It went without saying that Temple Atwode wasn't big enough to possess its own arm of the law.

Sure enough, it was Shay. He and a smaller, older man were standing next to each other in what appeared to be a shocked silence. The cleared, open space in front of them had the appearance of a building site, though little work seemed to have been done as yet, other than marking out whatever was to be erected there with posts, stakes and string lines. There was no evidence of machinery, tools or building materials. Sloping towards the road, the site was surrounded by woodland separating it from its neighbours: on the one side, Templewood's orchard, and on the other a grey stone dwelling house, just visible through a bluebell copse.

Several yards from the opening, Kay Dysart was kneeling beside the body. She raised a hand in salute to the newcomers and called out that she was nearly finished.

'Morning, Shay.'

'Morning, sir.' The constable, big, burly, grey-haired and broad-spoken, was someone Reardon knew to be a sensible and reliable officer, with years of experience in one of the busy urban divisions of the Dudley region, but now cruising on towards retirement in the quieter waters of village policing. Introductions were made all round, the other man being named as Fentiman, the local doctor.

A grizzled man with a kindly, jowled face and horn-rimmed spectacles, Fentiman extended a hand, explaining that he had been called out when the body – Mrs Waring, he was sorry to say, whom he had known well – had been found. 'Though there was nothing I nor anyone else could have done by the time the boy found her. Bad business.'

'Boy?' The woman's body, according to the information Reardon had been given, had been found in time-honoured fashion by a man walking his dog.

'Manner of speaking. Martin Garbutt's still a boy to me.' He paused, intercepting the look passing between Reardon and the sergeant. 'You know Martin, Inspector?'

'He's local?' Reardon asked quickly, side-stepping a direct answer.

'Born and bred. Staying with his grandfather just now, I suppose – Ezra Garbutt is Judge Waring's gardener. Martin thinks a lot of the old man and he's often back here.' It was his turn to exchange a look with Shay, then to direct another at Reardon. 'Look here, Inspector, Martin wouldn't do a thing like this, if that's what you're thinking. He's a hothead, bit of a Bolshie and all that, I'll admit, but he's not capable of this, I assure you.'

'That's right,' Shay said. Martin Garbutt was obviously known to him, too. 'Besides, if he had, he'd be miles away by now, not finding the body.'

Reardon didn't query the logic of this or point out that he wouldn't be the first killer to 'find' his victim, seeking to establish his innocence. He looked around while they waited. 'What's being built here?'

'A house. Eventually. For . . . er . . . for Judge Waring.'

It wouldn't have been anywhere Reardon would have chosen to live. The woods surrounding the field gave the place a dark, closed-in, slightly miserable feeling, despite the haze of bluebells spreading themselves and their perfume below the slender trunks of birches in the little adjoining copse.

'I believe they're due to start digging the foundations any time now. It's been a slow job so far; they had to clear a lot of young trees, and then there were hitches.'

'What hitches?'

'Oh, nothing much.' The doctor looked slightly uncomfortable, as if he'd spoken out of turn. 'Just changes of plan and so on, I gather.'

'They do say the place is haunted,' Shay said unexpectedly. 'On account of the old witch, Mother Foxley, that once lived here. They say she cursed it.'

'Rubbish, Ted! I'm surprised at you.' The doctor's response was sharp.

'All according, Doc,' Shay remarked enigmatically, Black Country to his back teeth.

Fentiman rolled his eyes. But there *was* something, not just the presence of death. Despite his scorn of such maudlin feelings, for a brief moment Reardon fancied he felt a cold finger touch the back of his neck.

There had been showers during the night and although the soil was the local red, sandy stuff which absorbed rain like blotting paper and dried out quickly, footprints and maybe other significant traces of what had happened might have been made and now destroyed. *Might* have been? Almost certainly, the evidence was already compromised by other people walking over the ground.

At that moment the police doctor joined them, having completed her examination and packed her bag.

'You can take a look at her now,' she said. 'No surprises. She's been strangled, poor lady.' And before he could ask, she went on: 'Two to three days since . . . or as far as I'm prepared to say. The autopsy will give us more.'

Kay Dysart and her husband the pathologist were on friendly terms with Reardon and his wife. She was a competent, caring doctor who took this part of her work, examining people who were already dead, with as much care, attention and respect as she gave to the living. Her habitual abrupt tone softened as she reassured him on what was always the first consideration when a female body was found. 'She's fully clothed, and otherwise undisturbed.'

'She's been dead two or three days, and no one's reported her missing?'

Behind him, Shay coughed. 'Maybe these might explain that, sir.' He indicated a spot behind where he and Fentiman had been standing. Like forgotten items on a station platform, two pieces of matching luggage stood forlornly there, a large suitcase and a considerably smaller dressing case. 'Going away somewhere, looks like. Or coming back?'

Either way, what had the dead woman and her luggage been doing here at all, in this spot of all places? 'Let's have a look.'

The cases were expensive, custom-made, in tan shagreen leather with brass locks and clasps, personalized with elaborately worked initials E.W. stamped in gold. Mindful of the new precepts they were all now obliged to follow, Reardon pulled on rubber gloves before unsnapping the clasp of the larger case and finding it tidily packed with enough clothes for a seemingly lengthy stay, though you could never tell with women. He opened the dressing case.

'How lovely!' Dysart exclaimed. Practical and unfussily dressed as she herself always was, a woman working in a man's world, she was feminine enough not to scorn pretty things. And this one was pretty as they came. A dressing case, exquisitely fitted out with everything a lady might need when travelling: brushes and combs, a mirror affixed to the lid, spaces for an ebony and silver manicure set, scent atomisers and various cut-glass, gold-lidded bottles and jars filled with creams and powders. Obviously expensive, though the gold might be pinchbeck.

Reardon snapped the case shut and finally walked with Jago to where the body of Mrs Waring lay on the grass.

As a policeman he was all too familiar with such sights, and it was a long time since he'd been a young rookie constable and had actually thrown up at the sight of a mutilated corpse, but he still had to steel himself. Yet he knew it would be a sad day if he were never sickened, or felt no anger, or took the waste of a human life for granted.

Before he actually looked at the victim, he took note of what surrounded her body. There were footprints. Too many, likely to be those of the young fellow, Martin Garbutt, who'd seen her first, and others which would have to be eliminated: those of Dr Fentiman, PC Shay, Dysart and God knew who else. Plus a scrabble of pawprints and a flurry of red soil thrown up by the dog who'd found her. He stood with the questions to which he would need answers already forming in his mind. Why *here*, he asked himself again. Not to say why had she been murdered at all? Who had hated her enough to do this to her? Though not, of course, a question of *who is she?* He already knew she was Emilie, the wife of Judge Waring.

When he did look, his first impression was that she was the tidiest corpse he'd seen in a long while, lying neatly on her back, feet together and her hands folded across her breast, a disconcerting parody of some pious medieval saint on a tomb. A peaceable, relaxed position which only underlined the horror of a death which must have been anything but. Her face was now swollen and ugly, although not to the extent it had rendered her unrecognizable to those who had known her, in life, it seemed. Insect and rodent activity had already begun. Bizarrely, her folded hands were still encased in expensive, supple kid gloves. Something else also struck Reardon as odd, out of place, which he couldn't yet put a finger on, but it was something definitely out of kilter.

He took a step back. A clatter of wings sounded as a pair of wood pigeons rattled indignantly out of the copse behind him. A honeysuckle climbing a nearby sapling, reaching for the light, brushed his shoulder. Its fragrant scent, mingled with that of the bluebells, still failed to conceal the sweet stench of death.

'She was like this when you found her, Kay?' Reardon asked the doctor, who had followed them back.

'Yes. I'm only here to confirm life is extinct, you know, and I tried not to disturb her too much when I examined her. I can tell you it was the scarf she was strangled with – it's a long one and – see – she's wearing it wound round her neck with the ends free. Whoever it was put a lot of weight into pulling it tight.' She hesitated, about to add something else, but decided not to. 'She couldn't have put up much of a struggle, though. She's smallish and slight; wouldn't have had a chance.'

Reardon wondered how the assailant could have come near enough to grasp both ends and pull the scarf tight enough to choke the life out of her. The idea of anyone approaching without being observed, in this place where there was no cover, didn't hold much water. She must have known, and not been afraid of, her assailant.

'How old would you say she was?'

'Late thirties, forty, at a near guess.'

Reardon's hurried assembly of the basic facts before setting out had told him she had been the judge's second wife, so it didn't surprise him that she had been a good deal younger than the judge himself must be. Mrs Eliot Waring, Emilie. The name, the way it was spelt . . . was it foreign, or merely a prettified variation of the more prosaic Emily?

Looking rather jauntily at odds with the expensively understated costume she wore was a gold and diamanté brooch in the shape of a treble clef pinned to her lapel, which was rather showy. Matching earrings. Very stylish shoes, just soft leather with three-inch stacked heels and squared-off toes. Her clothes were already drying after the intermittent showers of the last day or two and it was possible to see that her grey, fine wool walking costume – fitted jacket, straight skirt with kick pleats – was of excellent quality. Under it she wore a lavender silk blouse. The light silk scarf whose ends had been pulled tightly together to make the thin, deadly garotte which had taken her life was a pin-spotted violet.

'Where's her hat?' asked Jago. Her hair, worn longer than most women wore it now, was perhaps the most distinctive thing about her: a spread of light red-gold, plenty of it, with a natural wave the rain hadn't spoiled, that seemed to say how vibrant it – and perhaps Emilie herself – had been in life. 'And her handbag?'

'Good questions.'

That was it, of course: the missing hat was the inconsistency which had struck Reardon, though it only partly explained the intuitive prickling sensation he had that things weren't adding up. No lady would set out, dressed as she was and obviously intending to travel, without her hat any more than without her handbag – indispensable to any woman if his own wife was to go by. He couldn't imagine Ellen setting off anywhere, suitcases packed, without hers.

He stood looking down at the body, more questions gathering in his mind. What could possibly have brought Emilie here, equipped for travelling, not more than a couple of hundred yards or so away from her own home? Had she, this poor woman, happily packed her suitcase, envisaging a nice holiday with friends, or perhaps looking forward to a spell away from the duties demanded of the wife of one of the most eminent judges in the county? Not knowing that it was to be her last day on earth. And again, why this odd place, if not to meet someone? Even perhaps, a tryst with a lover?

Jago had moved off to make a quick circuit round the edges of the site, searching for the missing items. A short while later he came back, having located neither. They still might turn up in the more intensive search made when the forensic people arrived – photographer, fingerprint man, sketch-maker – the whole caboodle of scientific investigation, without which any murder enquiry nowadays was considered incomplete. The suitcase and dressing case would be taken away to be unpacked and examined in a more suitable place, but they'd been carefully packed and there was an undisturbed look about them.

Nothing about this death suggested it could be the result of a random attack, except perhaps the currently missing handbag, yet the chances of some complete stranger happening upon her and killing her in this remote spot for the sake of that were, he felt, practically nil.

All the same, enquiries would have to be made, and this was where Shay's local knowledge could come in useful. Maxstead didn't have a police station as such, any more than Temple Atwode did, but it did have a police presence and the house where he lived. Shay would know where to ask about any strangers likely to have been seen, anything unusual that had been noticed . . . if there was anyone in any of these small communities likely to go off the rails, or even if there was someone who might have reason to want the judge's wife dead.

He spoke to Shay and told him he would send someone out to help him. 'You can direct them where to go, get them knocking on doors. You know the drill.'

The constable's heavy face split into a grin. Clearly the advantages of a quiet life, having time to grow vegetables in his back garden and take a snooze after lunch, didn't entirely compensate for the rough and tumble stimulus of the Black Country constabulary duties he'd left behind, where there was never a quiet moment and you never knew what the villains would be up to next, to keep you on your toes.

SEVEN

Ezra Garbutt, Templewood's old gardener, lived alone in a tiny, low-roofed cottage within the grounds of the old house. Apparently always known as the bothy, it had a separate entrance straight from the road and sat in a corner of the walled kitchen garden – in itself separated from the main garden by a high brick wall with a wooden door.

A battered and dusty motorcycle was propped up against the side wall. Reardon gave it an appraising glance. A BSA, like his own beloved bike, now languishing in his garden shed, alas, in deference to its owner's grudgingly acknowledged maturity, only taken out for a token outing now and then.

Dr Fentiman had offered the information that the old man wasn't without family, most of whom lived either in Temple Atwode or one of the surrounding villages. One of them was with him now, and he was the one they wanted to talk to.

The door stood wide open, and Martin Garbutt and his grandfather were seated at a bare table with pint mugs of tea in front of them when Reardon and Jago knocked and were called in to enter. The old man's hands around his mug were work-stained and gnarled with arthritis, but he looked otherwise hale and hearty, his reddish skin scoured and leathery through working outdoors in all weathers. Martin was a darkly handsome young fellow, with the look of one who has to shave twice a day. Thick brows that came together, sharp eyes and jaws clamped tight in a determined fierceness. Fentiman might not have been exaggerating his bolshiness.

Reardon introduced himself and Jago. Both the Garbutts nodded in acknowledgement, but neither rose to their feet or offered a seat, though in fact apart from the chairs on which they sat there was only a sagging sofa, and that was burdened by a dubious pile-up of blankets and a lumpy-looking pillow without a case, just the striped ticking. The room was claustrophobically small – there was a sink with one cold tap in the corner – and though it looked basically clean, was hopelessly messy in the way of two men living without a woman to keep them in order.

The old man said, 'It's Mrs Waring then.'

'Yes, I'm afraid so.' Reardon turned to Martin. 'You recognized her, when your dog found her?'

'He's not mine. He's Mrs Waring's new pup.'

'How come he was with you?'

'I was exercising him. Needed to stretch my legs this morning – there's not much room, sleeping on Grandad's sofa here. The dog was in the garden with Sophy, and I offered to take him with me.'

'Sophy?'

'The judge's daughter; the youngest.'

They were friends then, though maybe the use of the first name was just one of the ways the Martin Garbutts of this world demonstrated their belief in equality for everyone. It wasn't something Reardon would argue with.

'You'd have had him on the lead, of course?'

'Until we came to Old Foxley's. He started pulling, wanted to go in, so I let him have his way. I could tell summat was up right off. He went mad at what he'd found. I tried to get it off him, but he wouldn't give it up. When I saw what it was . . . and saw her lying there . . . I'm not squeamish, but I felt sick, I can tell you.'

'What was it?' Jago asked.

'What?'

'What was it the dog wouldn't give up?'

'Oh, that. Just her hat.'

'Where is it now?'

He looked taken aback for a second or two before saying offhandedly, 'Oh, me and Prue burnt it in the kitchen stove. Carried it home like a trophy, the dog did, before he would drop it.'

'You shouldn't have done that – burnt it.'

'Why not? Wasn't much good to anybody after that little bugger had had his teeth into it.'

'Who's Prue?' Reardon asked before Jago could say more.

'Housemaid over at the house,' he answered shortly, glowering and jerking his head in the direction of the main house, evidently fed up with the questioning and looking dangerously out of temper.

'Prue's my granddaughter, Martin's cousin,' the old man intervened. His eyes were sharp on his grandson, as if warning him to be careful. 'She's a good girl and she wouldn't have wanted them to see the mistress's hat, not after Towser had been at it.'

'And what about her handbag?' Jago asked. 'You didn't burn that, too, I hope?'

The young fellow sprang up, knocking his chair back. His mug went over, spilling what tea was left in it. 'What handbag? What are you suggesting? You saying I pinched a handbag from a dead woman?'

'Take it easy,' Reardon said. 'It's missing, that's all, and we only want to know where it is.'

'Well, I don't bloody know.' He sat down and threw a dark look at Jago.

'All right, that seems clear enough. It's all we need from you for now, except for a few personal details.'

Reardon hoped that supplying the answers would give him a chance to cool off a bit, but he was too much on the defensive, ready to take more umbrage. His colour had risen dangerously, and his scowl deepened as Jago opened his notebook. 'Why? What do you need that for? Why me? I didn't kill her, for God's sake! Why would I? I hardly knew the woman!'

'Just for the record.'

This was met with another scowl. 'Get on with it, then.'

Jago noted down the answers he gave: Martin Garbutt, aged twenty-eight. Currently unemployed, he stated defiantly. 'Like a lot more of the great British public. And a fat lot the bloody government cares about that!'

'Address?' Jago ignored the beginning of what promised to be a tirade.

'I'm here as long as Grandad'll have me.' Translated, Reardon guessed this was where he bunked whenever he was hard up, or maybe when he needed to be out of the way for some time.

'How long have you been staying here?'

'Since Tuesday, if that's anything to do with you.' It was indeed, if he'd been here when Emilie Waring had been killed.

'Don't go away without leaving an address,' he was told by Jago before they left.

Once the car had left the bothy and before it was turned into the main entrance to Templewood itself, Reardon told Jago to stop. There was something he wanted to say, but before he could begin, Jago pre-empted him. 'That was way out of order, sir. I shouldn't have said what I did, about the handbag, it just came out. I can't think what made me say it. Except that he was putting my back up.'

Jago raked his hand through his hair. It was cut regulation short but had an unruly curl that immediately sprang up and resisted his efforts to smooth it down. He was looking furious with himself, as well he might.

'Yes, it was, and you shouldn't.' Reardon could do without that sort of aggravation from his new sergeant. Well, he was new, and probably feeling he had to assert himself, but if he was inclined to jump in like that, he'd need an eye kept on him. 'Fair enough. Only don't do it again.' It was, after all, the sort of remark he might have made himself at one time.

He was rewarded by a relieved grin that reminded him of Tolly, his Jack Russell, when he'd received a forgiving pat on the head after he'd misbehaved. 'Tell me something, Sergeant – Garbutt's name came as no surprise to you when the doctor mentioned him. Come across him before, have you?'

'Not personally, but it was a name I've seen listed more than once since I started here, and it rang a bell.'

'That's what I assumed. And why doesn't it surprise me? Do I need to ask his politics? Apart from him not being a Blackshirt.'

Jago grinned again. 'Well, if memory serves me right . . .'

Without having to think too much, he reeled off a string of offences . . . bound over to keep the peace after agitating about unemployment; tub-thumping for the Independent Labour Party in the Bullring in Brum; haranguing workers outside factory gates; supporting strikes – 'like those women who came out at the Lucas factory, and that council-house rent strike, that sort of thing. As for Blackshirts . . .' Jago puffed out his lips. 'He's caused uproar more than once at their rallies. Three months in Winson Green, in fact, after Bingley Hall.'

'Winson Green? And who sent him down?'

'Not Judge Waring, in my recollection. Even if it was, it hardly justifies murdering his wife, does it?'

'Not for any sane person. So, let's hope Garbutt's not as wild as he seems. All right, let's get going.'

'What's he like . . . the judge, I mean?' Jago asked as he started the engine.

'Well, he's not the sort to scare the pants off everyone. Reputation for fairness, but by no means a pushover. Severe when necessary . . . very. He gave a punishing sentence the last time we met in court, in fact.'

'He knows you, then?'

'Unlikely he'll remember me.'

The car turned smoothly through open gates and then the manor house, surrounded by its charming garden, was fully before them, serene and settled, looking what it was – a house that had slept through centuries of untroubled ownership. There was a wide, sloping lawn and a magnificent hundred-foot conifer, that Reardon vaguely thought might be a redwood, swooping graceful branches to the ground. Surprising in such a garden. A mistake, perhaps, on the part of some misguided Victorian who had planted this un-English tree in a quintessentially English garden, as Victorians did. Yet it looked superb, a punctuation mark behind the mixed border of shrubs, flowering plants and the pink blossom of a flowering cherry tree.

EIGHT

They were admitted by a rosy-cheeked, energetic young woman, no doubt Prue, Garbutt's granddaughter. She was solemn faced, although she looked as if cheerfulness would sit more naturally with her. Leaving them in a spacious, low-ceilinged room with wide windows that overlooked the garden, she went to inform the judge of their arrival.

Jago prowled around the room while they waited. It was agreeable, comfortable, obviously well lived in. Newspapers and books lay around and an aged golden retriever bitch lay stretched out on the cushioned window seat, unmoving except for a thump of the tail when Reardon went to stroke her. On the wall opposite the window, a large portrait hung in a prominent place, a dark-haired woman with a good-tempered face who looked very much at home here, despite the fact that she had probably died some time since: the first Mrs Waring, Reardon speculated . . . who, in different circumstances, had also met with an early and tragic death.

Jago was eyeing with some respect a very small upright piano which held pride of place at the other end of the room. It was beautifully inlaid and polished, with an intricately carved front and ornate candle sconces. The numerous photographs on a silk runner spread along its top, country house style, interested Reardon more. Family snapshots, he guessed, mainly of two girls and a boy, taken at various ages, but also one or two of the same woman in the portrait opposite the window. There didn't appear to be any that might have been of Emilie, the judge's second wife.

Jago was still admiring the instrument.

'What is it? A harpsichord?' Reardon asked.

'It's a cottage piano, quite old. It was my mother's.' The answer came from a young woman who had come into the room, followed by another. Behind them came a butler bearing a tray set with cups and saucers. No, not a butler. Judge Waring himself.

Performing this domestic task, divested of his wig and robes of office, the big Pooh-Bah looked more approachable but had lost none of his dignity, nor his acumen; he immediately proved Reardon wrong about not being remembered.

'We have met before once or twice, I believe, Chief Inspector Reardon – in particular, the Aston murder, hmm?' he said after setting down the tray and offering his hand.

Impressive, given how long ago that particular case had been, and the number which must have been through his hands since, and considering how brief was the connection with the police giving evidence in the witness box. On the other hand, he'd addressed Reardon with his recently acquired title of *chief* inspector: he had done his homework.

He waved them to seats and introduced the two young women as his daughters. The elder one, Gizi – an unusual name for an unusual young woman, small and slim, pale-skinned, with a black fringe like Cleopatra – was wearing a scarlet lipstick with nails painted to match, and looking very *à la mode* in a dress the colour of young leaves. She smiled, sat down easily and crossed her legs, in a way that said she expected to be looked at.

The attractions of the other daughter, Sophy, were less immediately obvious. She had heavy, shiny brown hair that parted at the nape of her neck when she bent her head while pouring the tea. Clear, watchful brown eyes, and a mouth which turned up at the corners in the same way as the woman in the portrait – attributes which, Reardon noted with amusement, Jago wasn't failing to appreciate, distracting his gaze from the more obvious charms of her sister.

The cup of tea passed over was hardly the paint-stripping brew Reardon favoured – it was far too weak for his taste – but at least it wasn't Earl Grey, or any other fancy stuff. Once it had been dispensed, the younger girl sat next to her father on the sofa and Reardon cleared his throat, ready to begin. Thankfully, he was to be spared the job most hated by any police officer. The family didn't need to be told that a loved one had been found dead, and in this case, brutally murdered. Someone else had already done that.

But probing into a family's private life – never easy for either side – was necessary. Particularly so in this case. *Tread softly*,

Knott had cautioned. As if Reardon needed reminding that judges of all kinds were accustomed to being regarded with due deference and could be acerbic – and worse – if they were not. Reardon hadn't forgotten, but pulling back had never been his style.

As it happened, it was the judge himself who took the initiative, after the condolences Reardon offered for the loss of his wife in such circumstances. 'Thank you. It has indeed been a shock to us all – the sort no one ever envisages.'

Devastating, it must have been – but if so, Waring wasn't allowing it to show, except perhaps for the occasional, barely discernible tic at the corner of his mouth. 'We'll do our best to find out what happened, sir.'

'I don't have any doubt of that. However, there are certain facts I must make you aware of before you start your investigations.' He paused, and the look he gave was guarded, reserved. 'Things which in other circumstances I would prefer to keep within the family, you understand. Matters which are very personal and,' he added carefully, 'extremely painful.'

Personal and painful? The murder of his wife could hardly be otherwise, but there was more to it than that and Reardon could see the dilemma: a judge's view of such tragic events was generally from the other side, but now Judge Waring's own personal circumstances would necessarily be open to question, and he had seen enough dirty washing done in court to be appalled at the thought of seeing his own washed in public. *If* that was what it was going to amount to, which Reardon was by now very much afraid it might.

Waring was still talking. Both daughters were apparently wise enough to know not to interrupt their father, who was giving forth with a typically concise summing up. He had been away from home last week, he said, sitting at the Worcester Assizes; his daughters, too, had been away in London, where they had spent the previous two weeks. They had all, coincidentally, arrived home at pretty much the same time, around lunchtime early Friday afternoon, when Waring had found a letter from his wife, a devastating letter which said that she had quitted the matrimonial home, clearly with no intention of returning. At that point he stopped to take a deep drink of his cooling tea, a frown of annoyance appearing as the cup gave a small but decided rattle when he put it down on its saucer. But he went on steadily. 'It may also provide the explanation as to why she had her luggage with her when she was found.' Again, he paused. Sophy replenished his cup and pushed it across to him, but he didn't seem to notice. 'You will need to read this, Chief Inspector, to understand.' He withdrew a folded paper from his inside breast pocket and passed it over.

Reardon knew instinctively what he was about to see (both he and the judge had viewed plenty of these letters in their time) and he could have wished that Waring had kept this one to himself. He opened it and then found it was not at all what he had expected. This was not the personal letter his wife had left, but a typewritten missive sent by a Wolverhampton firm styling themselves as an architectural design and construction company. The letter was a withdrawal from their agreement with Judge Waring for the building of a house to be known as The Spinney. The decision to terminate the contract was, apparently, due to persistent disagreements over changes to the original plans with the member of the firm responsible for designing and overseeing the proposed building. Waring allowed Reardon to pass the letter to Jago before continuing. 'As you see, the architect in question, Mr Rex Surtees, is now working, or will shortly be working, in the south of France.' He paused, then added, deliberately dry, 'You will draw your own conclusions, of course, but I think you will agree that I have good reason to believe the letters – the one you have just read and one my wife left me – didn't happen to arrive by chance. It follows they had decided to go off together . . . my wife and Mr Surtees.'

If he really did believe that the one thing inevitably led to the other, the judge's normally clear thought processes had been suspended by the shock, or else there had been more in his wife's private letter to lead him to think so. There was no telling what was going on inside a man's head – and least of all, his heart – and the judge had unquestionably had a double shock: for two days he had been imagining his wife running off to France with her lover, while, as he'd now learnt, she had all that time been lying dead, not more than a few hundred yards away.

'Thank you for being so frank with me, Judge. I realize how distressing this must be. I'm afraid, however, there are still a few questions of a personal nature . . .'

'Yes, yes, of course,' Waring agreed, albeit as if he had already said enough to make the situation abundantly clear. There was a touch of impatience, much as he might have said to a long-winded defence counsel. '*Shall we not waste any more time, and get on with the evidence?*'

Reardon said carefully, 'What do you know of this man, Surtees?'

'The architect? Not enough, apparently! But I had little to do with him. After we'd engaged him and the initial plans had been discussed, I left matters mostly to my wife. It was to be her house, after all. It was what she wanted.'

As an answer, it left a lot to be desired, but Reardon let it pass. 'I realize this may be difficult, but I have to ask . . . perhaps you and your wife, sir, hadn't lately been on such good terms?'

'There was nothing at all, Chief Inspector, to indicate anything untoward between us until I saw her letter. I must allow now, after reading it, that some . . . association had been going on between her and that man, but until then, as far as I was aware, our relationship was as good as it always had been.'

Reardon admired his self-control. Perhaps the years of keeping an impartial view of any situation had made it second nature.

'What about her relationships with other people? Can you think of anyone, anyone at all, she might have upset, had differences or quarrels with?'

'Goodness, no!' the younger girl, Sophy, put in quickly, speaking for the first time. At the same moment, her sister muttered something under her breath, of which Reardon only caught the tail-end, but which sounded uncommonly like '. . . count on it.'

Her father turned to look at her and, though he said nothing, Reardon understood that he himself wasn't the only one who knew that on occasion, being subjected to the scrutiny of Judge Waring, the most hardened offender could tremble, awaiting judgement. His own daughter's cheeks took on two spots of colour. Abruptly, she abandoned her seat and walked to the window, where she stood with her arms folded across her chest, her slender back to the room.

A few words with Miss Gizi alone, away from her father, would not come amiss, Reardon decided.

When the judge spoke again, however, it was quietly and

without emphasis, as if his daughter had said nothing. 'If there had been anything or anyone troubling her, if she had had enemies, Chief Inspector,' he said quietly, 'I would have known. She was my wife.'

'Your second wife, I understand. May I ask how long you have been married?'

'Seven years. She was a widow when we met, living as a companion to an elderly lady, whom she'd been with for many years.'

'Is there anything we should know of her previous marriage?'

'Only that it was unhappy. It pained her to speak about it, or indeed of anything at all about her previous life, so I never pressed her.'

The judge must know there were still a lot of questions to answer, but he stood up suddenly. 'If that's all you need from me at present, you must excuse me . . . there is someone I must see. My daughters will help you with anything further you need to ask.' He and his younger daughter exchanged a look, and she gave a nod.

He seemed to think no more explanation was needed for his abrupt departure, and perhaps there wasn't. The man must be distraught, and if there was any danger of him breaking down, he evidently had no intention of it happening before his daughters and the police.

'Thank you, Judge Waring, for being so frank. You will be available if we need to speak to you further?' It was posed as a question but they both knew it was not.

NINE

Sophy felt the tension ease palpably when Papa left. She'd never seen him like this before. Not grieving in the same way as when Mama died, nor when he had believed Emilie had run away with Surtees, although the two situations could hardly be compared, could they?

'You won't object to answering a few questions?' The chief inspector spoke as if they had any option. No, none at all, she told him, speaking for Gizi as well, who seemed to have taken a Trappist vow of silence since she'd displeased Pa by that stupid remark she'd made.

In all likelihood, she was feeling bad about how she'd let that slip, but Sophy had seen the way the chief inspector's eyes had followed her to the window. The police were going to want a lot more information than they'd been given so far. Which would be difficult, if not impossible, seeing how much in the dark they all were about Emilie's past life, before they knew her. But these two detectives at least seemed to be friendly enough. *Seemed* being the operative word. The chief inspector, the one with the old scar puckering one side of his face – a sign he'd fought in the war, Sophy guessed – was the sort you'd recognize instantly as a policeman, plain clothes or otherwise: short hair, clean-shaven, solid, but with steady eyes that missed nothing.

And the sergeant . . . well. Unlike the inspector, he wasn't at all what you'd expect. He too was tall and well-built, his dark hair also cut short, though not looking at all disciplined. A clever, mobile face, a mouth from which she guessed good humour wasn't often missing. Grey eyes that showed pinpoints of light when he smiled, and sometimes when he didn't. But there was too much sharp intelligence about him to think he'd be easily deceived.

'Thank you. Let's start with you all being away from home. Presumably, the servants were still here, Miss Waring?' Reardon asked her.

'Yes, they were, but you can't go on calling us both Miss Waring. It's Sophy and Gizi.'

He nodded and smiled.

'Maitland and Prue were here, of course. And Alexei.'

She explained about Alexei, that he was their cousin who lived here with them, and that his tutor, a man by the name of Brad Catchpole, was also living here at present.

'Prue is your maid, the one who showed us in? And . . . Maitland?'

'Oh, she's our housekeeper, I suppose you'd call her. She used to be our nanny, but she stayed on after Mama died. She's part of the family now.'

'Which of them saw your stepmother last?'

'You'll have to ask them, but Prue says she took Emilie some supper to her snug on Thursday evening and it seems no one saw her after that.'

'Her snug?'

'The room where she did a bit of painting and reading and so on.'

'How was it no one remarked on her absence the following morning?' the sergeant asked.

'Oh, she never bothered much with breakfast. She rarely went to bed before midnight and then she'd sleep late. Quite often she didn't appear downstairs until just before lunch, so no one would have thought anything of it, especially if it was one of her days at Falquonroy.'

'That's Falquonroy Park, the big house across the valley?'

'Yes. She'd been spending an awful lot of time there recently, helping out. I suppose she might have had lunch there.'

'In what way was she helping?'

Sophy considered. Masses of useless stuff had been found in the old house when the Malpas family had bought it – furniture too big to move, probably built in situ, unidentifiable old portraits of people long gone, and heaps of stuff left in attics. The library, with its complement of dusty old tomes, had been left untouched until Sir Julius had recently decided it was time it was sorted out. She said, 'I think Sir Julius might have roped her in to help him sort out the books in the old library. He's quite good at that . . . organizing people, I mean.' She'd said that without thinking, but not looking at Gizi.

'So . . . she wasn't seen again after her supper was taken to her on Thursday until Martin Garbutt found her this morning?'

'That's what they're all saying.'

This at last prompted Gizi to open her mouth again. Her head went up. 'Actually, if we're being precise, it was Towser who found her, not Martin.' Her voice was sharp, as if that mattered.

'The little bulldog? Yes, of course it was. Mr Garbutt told us he'd offered to take him for a run. Does he often do that?'

Gizi shrugged, again leaving it to Sophy to answer.

'No. But he likes dogs and when he saw me in the garden before breakfast, with Towser, he offered to take him for a run. I was quite pleased because I still wasn't properly awake . . . We'd all been out the night before to a dinner party over at Falquonroy, you see. We hadn't got to bed until the early hours, and we were rather late up this morning . . . at least I was. My sister wasn't here. She was to have stayed at Falquonroy until Monday.'

She felt she was babbling aimlessly, and the sergeant, taking notes, probably thought them a heartless family, gallivanting at parties, accepting that their stepmother running off was in fact nothing which should interfere with their social lives. She didn't feel up to explaining that Dee's party was important to her, and they hadn't wanted to spoil it. Perhaps she was doing the sergeant an injustice anyway and he admired them for brazening out what was bound to be regarded as a scandal. She ploughed on. 'Towser woke me up this morning, needing to be let out, so I took him downstairs as soon as I woke. That was when Martin offered.'

'He sleeps in her room,' Gizi said, adding with a short laugh, 'Towser, I mean.'

The young policeman's lips twitched and Sophy was annoyed to find herself saying, 'Well, he cried for his mother, poor little thing, when we first had him, and it's become a habit. Martin was setting out for a walk and Towser was mad to go with him.'

'Known him long, have you . . . Martin?' Reardon asked.

'Forever,' Gizi answered shortly.

'We used to play together when we were children,' Sophy explained. 'Prue, too, whenever they came to see Garbutt . . . They're cousins, you know, and he's their grandad.'

She almost expected to be challenged, but she thought he

seemed to like this, something to be chalked up in Pa's favour, letting them play with the servants' children. Which was almost laughable. Such attitudes had never featured around Templewood. They'd all grown up together – Sam, herself and Gizi, Martin Garbutt and Prue, and Dee when she came to live at Falquonroy.

Prue, even then, was a tall, robust girl of immense energy and cheerfulness. She used to come with her mother, Garbutt's daughter, when she came over from Sawbry, the next village, to visit Garbutt and 'sort him out' as she said. While the sorting was being done, Prue usually joined the girls in their games, while Sam and Martin, if they were there too, would go off and do boy things together. What Sophy remembered most was Prue taking her turn on the rocking horse in the schoolroom, making it rock so hard they feared it would come loose from its springs and they'd fly across the room together.

Later, when they'd all grown up and had begun to go their different ways, and a new maid happened to be needed at Templewood, it was Prue who asked for the job, saying it was a way to keep an eye on her grandad. She was bright, and Sophy had imagined her destined for something better than domestic service, but the arrangement had worked perfectly. Prue and Maitland got on like a house on fire and, as a family, they all loved her and were very pleased to have her around the place.

As for Martin . . . he thought a lot about old Garbutt, and Martin was still the apple of Garbutt's eye, despite his bad reputation. Old Ezra excused him because his father was killed in the war and he and his mother had been left in fearfully poor circumstances, until she too died when Martin was eleven. He then lived with Prue and her mother until he was old enough to take an apprenticeship with BSA in Birmingham, and that was when the trouble had started. He had lodgings in Sparkhill with a landlord who was an ardent, radical socialist and it didn't take Martin long to absorb his ideas. He'd always been that way inclined, and his upbringing had left him bitter about what he regarded as injustices and inequalities, until it had become a way of life for him to take sides and speak up for anyone he regarded as downtrodden. As Sam said, he hadn't got the sense to keep his head below the parapet and, inevitably, trouble followed him like wasps after jam. It was rotten luck that he was here at the moment, and that he was the one who'd found Emilie's body. He was bound to be of interest to the police.

Reardon didn't, however, pursue the subject of Martin. He went back to his notes and the night Emilie left the house. 'Mrs Waring would have needed transport from here to the spot where she was found. But no one heard her leave?'

'They wouldn't. Their rooms all happen to be at the back of the house – Maitland and Prue, as well as Alexei and Catchpole.'

'Maybe she just walked. It's not that far.'

'I don't think so,' the sergeant answered Gizi. 'Not in those ridiculous shoes, with those heavy suitcases, and a handbag – though that, by the way, appears to be missing. She would have her handbag with her, wouldn't she?'

'Of course she would. Absolutely.'

'What was it like?'

'Depends which one it was,' Sophy said doubtfully. 'She had a lot of bags.'

But Gizi was ready with that one. 'What shoes – what *ridiculous* shoes – did you say she was wearing?'

Unfazed by the sarcasm, Sergeant Jago did his best to describe them, and Gizi nodded.

'Tan calf-leather clutch bag, then, about so,' she said promptly, her hands describing a shape about nine by six, 'with a gold frame and clasp. Custom made. Papa gave it to her last Christmas, to go with those shoes.'

'Well done! But that makes it even less credible to believe she walked there by herself. Not with a bag she had to clamp under arm, balancing a case in either hand, one of them really heavy, wearing those – er – those shoes.'

'I suppose it's not beyond the bounds of credibility,' Gizi answered with that annoying lift of her eyebrows, 'that she might have put the bag in the case, out of the way?'

'I wonder why we didn't think of that?' Gizi didn't bother to answer.

But why, Sophy wanted to ask, why *there*, at The Spinney, of all places? No one would arrange to meet their lover on a building site, surely? Well, possibly, if it was Surtees she'd been expecting to take her away. Who'd arrived and then . . . strangled her?

Surtees? In spite of the sun pouring into the room, Sophy felt a shiver run down her spine.

'What sort of person was she, your stepmother?' Reardon asked suddenly. 'I mean, how did she get on with people?'

How did you answer a question like that? And yet, it stirred something in Sophy she wasn't expecting. As if the shock of what had happened was at last beginning to wear off and being replaced by a rush of emotion she hadn't foreseen . . . something like real sadness and a realization of what had actually happened. *Emilie was gone. For good.* Mixed images chased each other in her mind. Herself, teasing Emilie about the number of romantic novels she read (which she always took in good part, it had to be said). Her kindness to poor Alexei when he was sent home from Westingbury and looked like death warmed up. Long winter nights when she'd gather everyone together as a family and persuade them into playing cards, or even *charades*! Summer evenings when she and Papa would stroll around the garden, arm in arm. The smile that lit his face when she came into a room . . .

Emilie was gone, horribly dead. And a lump in Sophy's throat said how much she was going to miss her. None of this she could articulate to the police.

'Perhaps there's a photograph of Mrs Waring you could let us have?' Sergeant Jago was asking.

'What? Oh, oh yes, I suppose so, somewhere.' A lurch of her stomach told her why he was asking. They wanted to know what Emilie had looked like when she was alive, not as she must have looked when they had seen her . . . dead.

'There's that one on the piano,' Gizi said. She made no move to get it, so Sophy stood up and walked over to peer among the assorted frames grouped there. After shuffling them about a bit, she came back empty-handed.

'Someone must have moved it; it's not there.'

It didn't take much guessing to know who that someone might have been. Who else but Pa? Not wanting reminders of Emilie lying around now that she was dead . . . although that was hardly consistent with the other portrait on the wall over there, the one of Mama he insisted on keeping – and not, Sophy was sure, just because it had been painted by someone well known who happened to be a friend of his: Harold Knight, in fact, husband of the more famous Dame Laura, but highly regarded in his own right for the sensitive portraits he painted.

'Don't worry about it. I'm more interested in what she was like as a person,' Reardon asked again. 'How did you get on with her?'

'She was . . . kind.' Sophy realized how lame that sounded, even though it was actually true. 'She made our father very happy,' she added, knowing that was true also, and looking directly at Gizi, who said nothing.

The door opened and Prue came in. 'Oh, sorry, I didn't know you were still here,' she said to the policemen and started to back out. 'I'll come back for the tray later.'

'No, please, don't let us stop you.' The inspector beckoned her in and watched as she began to gather the empty cups. 'You were the one to see Mrs Waring last, I believe, Prue? It is Prue, isn't it?'

She gave him a sharp look. 'Yes, I took her supper to the snug. She said she was busy, so she'd have it there.' She looked for the sugar bowl and moved the cups until she found a space for it on the tray. 'She'd been busy, all right! The room was actually tidy.'

'Was that unusual?'

She rolled her eyes. He couldn't know just how incredible that was, Sophy thought, Emilie being one of the untidiest people on the planet. In person, she was always neat as a new pin, but the little room where she spent so much of her time had to be seen to be believed . . . books, papers, the materials for her painting and drawing, the novels she loved to read, were scattered as if a high wind had passed through. Sophy was not overly neat and tidy herself, unlike Gizi, whose possessions, as well as her clothes, were always in immaculate order, but she thought Emilie's room worse even than Sam's when he lived at home, and that said something. If Emilie's room was tidy, cleared of all the tat that normally surrounded her, it was certainly proof she'd had no intention of ever returning.

'She'd been clearing things out, I reckon,' Prue said. 'Not before time, either. I think she'd been burning stuff. There was a big fire in the grate, though it was a warm night, and the room was really hot.'

'Did you notice anything unusual about Mrs Waring herself?' Reardon pressed. 'Was she agitated, upset, anything like that?'

'No, she just said thank you and that she'd put the tray outside the door when she'd finished her supper – salmon salad and a lemon mousse it was, the weather being so warm. She used to do that – put her tray out if she ate there. She didn't like to be disturbed when she was busy.'

'Any idea what she was so busy with?'

'Reading, drawing – how should I know? Letter-writing, maybe. She wrote a lot of letters – she'd sometimes ask me to post them for her.'

'Did you notice the addresses?' Jago asked.

She threw him a withering look. 'Nothing to do with me, her private correspondence, was it? I didn't look. Some of the envelopes had a lot of stamps on, though. I couldn't help seeing that.'

'Extra postage perhaps, because the letters were very large, or heavy?'

'No, they were the usual size. I just happened to notice there were a lot of stamps on some of them.'

'What about her suitcases?' Reardon asked.

'They'd have been in her bedroom, not the snug, wouldn't they?'

'Perhaps you can show us this snug of hers, Prue.'

'All right.'

She picked the tray up and Jago stepped forward to open the door for her.

Reardon thanked the other two young women for their help and said they would be in touch, then they followed Prue out.

TEN

Having deposited the tray on a table outside the door, Prue led the way upstairs to Emilie's room. Keeping up with her brisk clip, Reardon had the feeling there was more he might have obtained from the sisters, had he pressed them. But these were only the first steps in the investigation, necessarily cautious ones, while those concerned were still shocked and upset, possibly on the defensive, when too many questions could very easily put their backs up and prove counterproductive. Picking up the trail before it went cold was a vital part of any investigation, but the trail here had been cooling for several days. He was still keen to get this essential spadework under his belt as quickly as possible, and get down to framing the direction the enquiry should take moving forward.

They'd barely reached the top of the stairs when an older woman emerged from a door off the landing, clasping a pile of table linen. 'Prue?'

'Just showing these gentlemen to Mrs Waring's snug, Maitland.'

'I'll do that. You go back to the kitchen and keep an eye on the oven – and take these with you, there's a good girl.' She thrust a bundle of tablecloths at Prue, who clattered off down the stairs again with a whisk of skirts.

'Quietly, girl!' To Reardon, she said, 'Come with me.'

'Don't disturb yourself, if you're busy – Miss Maitland, I believe? Just point us in the right direction and we'll find the way.'

'I doubt it,' she answered. 'You need a road map to find your way around if you don't know this house.' A spark of humour lit a pair of steady grey eyes. 'And you can call me Maitland, like everyone else.'

She was a tall, pleasant-looking woman with sandy hair going a little grey and a fresh complexion. Late forties, he guessed. He noted a slight Scottish accent. 'And I daresay you'll be wanting to talk to me.'

'That's right.'

'Then you'd better come away downstairs again while we do.'

The two officers filed back obediently behind her down the stairs, into a small, comfortable sitting room with a slightly open door on one side revealing a glimpse of a white counterpane. Clearly these were her own private quarters and were as neat and tidy as the woman herself. The room was filled with the scent from a handful of lilies of the valley in a little silver vase, standing on a small oval table. Other flat surfaces, and indeed half of one wall, was given over to photographs of the Waring family, parents and children, taken at various ages. Several of them featured other children too, prominent among them a pretty, dark-haired, dark-eyed little girl, and two others Reardon had no difficulty in identifying as Martin Garbutt and his cousin Prue.

The housekeeper answered their questions readily, but she'd nothing new to add to what they'd been told so far about the last time Emilie had been seen. 'So, what had she been doing during the day – Thursday, I mean?' Reardon asked.

'I don't really remember seeing much of her that day. Maybe she went out, but if so I don't know where.'

'How did you get on with her? '

'Well enough.' She hesitated. 'To be honest, I can't say I really knew her.'

'Yet you lived in the same house. You'd known her since she and Judge Waring married?'

'That doesn't mean I *knew* her. I'd stayed on after the mistress died, you see, but when the judge remarried, I decided it was time for me to retire. But his new wife had no interest in running the house and was happy enough to let me do it, so I gave up the idea of leaving. It suited us both, though it wasn't like when the mistress was alive.'

Clearly there had only ever been one mistress for her, a predictable problem for second wives, no doubt. And while she'd been speaking, Maitland's eyes flickered involuntarily towards a photograph of Judge Waring in full colourful dress, complete with wig, robe and bands, in prime position on the mantelpiece. Perhaps there was no need to query her true reason for staying.

'Don't mistake me, Chief Inspector,' she went on, rather sharply, 'there was no bad feeling. We rubbed along well enough.

She was always pleasant, and very kind, but she wasn't really all that close to any of us, you know. Except perhaps the boy,' she said almost as an afterthought.

Reardon's mind flew to Martin Garbutt again, and he offered Martin's name, but she was referring to the cousin who also lived at Templewood. 'I mean Lex, Alexei. They got on well, the two of them. He'd do anything for her. She seemed to understand him, which is more than most of us do. Though goodness knows, he needs understanding, especially since he . . . since he left his school, Westingbury.'

She, as well as Emilie, obviously had affection for this boy. 'He's a clever wee lad, you know, Lex. Off to Cambridge he is, if he can pass the examination – which he can, if he has a mind to, according to that Catchpole.' A little sniff accompanied the tutor's name.

'How old is Alexei?'

'Sixteen. He's been with us since his mother died just after he was born. You mustn't be too hard on him. He's still only a boy.'

'What makes you think we should have any reason to be hard on him?'

She sighed. 'Oh, he's a difficult one, I'm afraid. You'll see. But he's not bad, just sometimes gives the wrong impression if you don't know him.'

At that moment, the difficult one was walking away from Templewood, heading back along the narrow road towards Temple Atwode. His hands were stuck deep in his pockets, his shoulders hunched. He felt to be carrying the enormity of his misery, as he had ever since Emilie's disappearance, grown so much heavier now with the numb sense of guilt which had been sitting on him like a ton weight since the terrible news of her death.

Half an hour earlier, in the old schoolroom he and Catchpole were using, he had shoved his Thucydides aside and scraped his chair back. The Greek wars had no interest for him at the moment, compared with the one he was waging with himself. 'I've had enough of this for today,' he told Catchpole. 'I'm going for a walk.'

His tutor looked up, his round face kindly, patently

suppressing any momentary annoyance he might have felt, in the way that always infuriated Alexei. 'Yes, we could do with a break, Lex.'

'Alone,' Lex said gracelessly. Then he saw the hurt expression as the tutor pushed his glasses up, and added, 'Thanks.' He hadn't meant to snub, but the fact was Catchpole's concern drove Lex wild, the way he couldn't leave him alone for a minute.

He just didn't understand anything about Alexei, not as Emilie had, nowhere near. Nor did anyone else, for that matter. She alone had understood how much life at Templewood stifled him. She had appreciated and sympathized with his secret, his burning ambition . . . which was to travel to Greece and find his father, a wild idea everyone in the family would have actively discouraged and his uncle would have actually forbidden. 'But Cambridge first,' Emilie said. 'You simply can't throw a chance like that away, Lex; it's not something everyone's privileged to enjoy. It's only another few years, after you've waited so long. Promise me?'

And he had promised, because deep down he knew she was right. And because for so long he'd been hoping and preparing for Cambridge. His degree would be his passport to Greece, which was as much a constant vision on his horizon as the Acropolis in Athens. Greece and all it symbolized was why he was hoping to read classics and archaeology at Cambridge, hopefully leading to a job afterwards which would take him to Greece, and with any luck to his father. He knew it would be a disaster for him to relinquish his chance when it was at last within his grasp. Another thing: Cambridge would also be an antidote to his failure at Westingbury, a salve for the shame of it, which still smarted. And yet, he had almost thrown it all away.

Today he desperately needed to escape, not only from Catchpole, but from the police too. He knew they'd want to speak to him. He'd have to face them sooner or later, but he'd every intention of avoiding them for as long as possible.

He was halfway along the normally silent road to the village when the unusual sound of a vehicle approaching, coming too fast along the narrow road, made him take a quick step to one side. Within seconds, a shiny red Lagonda sports car drew level and whooshed past, but then came to a sudden halt a little further along, sending up a shower of dirt and gravel from the stony surface of the road as the brakes were hastily applied.

'Walking, Lex? Would you like a lift?' the driver stuck his head out to call. Someone else Lex didn't want to see – FitzAlban, that fellow his cousins and Dee Malpas hung around with and seemed to admire so much, but who, for many reasons, made Lex feel uneasy, especially now. FitzAlban leant across and threw the passenger door open. 'Hop in.'

'Er – no thanks,' Alexei called back, while looking enviously at the flashy motor, a red exotic dragon breathing out waves of heat and power. Feelings rose in him that he couldn't stop. If he had something like this, he would get in, put his foot down and drive as far and as fast as he could, until he reached the end of the world . . . or ran out of petrol . . . or fell asleep at the wheel and there was . . . nothing. Oblivion. Well, that was what he wanted, wasn't it? The trouble, as always, was knowing that he could never carry such intentions through, however constantly he might test himself to try and prove that he could, if necessary. 'I'm only going as far as the village.'

He was actually making for the tiny little front-room shop in Temple Atwode, hoping they'd have cigarettes, which they might not. What they stocked was only what they had space for at the time, mainly basic necessities such as sugar and tea, matches and so on, and it was merely a matter of luck what you might find there. He didn't think FitzAlban was the type to disapprove of him smoking, like the rest of them did, but he didn't think it necessary to mention he was in search of cigarettes.

'Hop in anyway,' FitzAlban said, as Alexei's slow footstep dragged nearer. 'I'd like a word.'

After a moment's hesitation – no, he wouldn't be ordered about by this fellow! – he hopped in and sank into the armchair comfort of the sighing leather seat. He stared at the polished wood dashboard, fascinated by the complex array of dials, and for several minutes he was in danger of being carried away, forgetting he didn't like FitzAlban, as the man demonstrated his own enthusiasm and his knowledge of the inner workings and mechanics of the motor, its performance, its reputation for brilliant acceleration, its successes in speed trials . . . 'They're going to win at Le Mans next month, mark my words,' he said. 'I'm hoping to be able to go and watch.' He drew a slim silver cigarette case and a lighter from his inside breast pocket and offered the case with a smile. Sobranies!

Alexei took one, FitzAlban likewise. They lit up and smoked in silence for a while. Once or twice Lex, hugging his misery to himself, thought of the relief he would feel if he said what was on his mind, but each time he thought better of it.

'You're wanting to know if I did what you asked,' FitzAlban remarked eventually.

The man was a mind reader. Lex wanted to show nonchalance, but he knew he had to be careful that he didn't forget the promises he'd made to himself. He said, as casually as he could manage, 'Well, did you?'

'A gentleman never goes back on his promise.'

You may be an Honourable, but are you a gentleman?

FitzAlban laughed, as if the words had been spoken aloud, then quickly sobered. 'I'm very sorry about what's happened to Mrs Waring, Lex. You must be feeling blue. You were very attached to her, weren't you?'

Lex felt himself flushing scarlet, despite himself. 'What if I was?' he asked truculently, his voice as well as his flaming cheeks in danger of betraying him. 'She was . . . very nice,' he managed to say at last. Damning with faint praise, a base denial, given what he'd felt for Emilie. He reached for the door and pushed it open. 'I have to go. Thank you for the cigarette.'

'My pleasure.' FitzAlban's hand hovered over the starter switch, then, smiling, he removed it to the door pocket beside him and drew out a new, unopened packet of the same brand. 'Here, take this.' And as Lex hesitated, he added, 'A token of my good intent.'

He couldn't really refuse the offer. The best he'd been hoping for at the little shop was a green paper packet of five Woodbines – and anyway, he remembered suddenly that it was Sunday and it wouldn't be open. He turned back to Templewood as the car started up, but when it had disappeared, his legs seemed to give way beneath him, and he threw himself down on the grass verge. He suspected – he *knew* – exactly what FitzAlban had done, or omitted to do, which came to the same thing, and he hadn't had the courage to face him with it. The man's narrow, smiling face with its sleepy eyes came back to him, and for a long time he sat there, tracing a resemblance in the dust with a broken stick he picked up, then scrabbling it out savagely.

ELEVEN

The housekeeper may have been exaggerating, saying they would need a map to locate Emilie's snug, but it wouldn't have been easy to find, had she not led the way. As happens with very old houses, Templewood had been altered and added to in haphazard ways over the centuries, resulting in low ceilings and different floor levels, unexpected flights of stairs, and sudden glimpses of the garden from unpredictably sited windows. When they reached the snug, Maitland opened the door. 'Her bedroom's further along there if you want it.' Pointing to another door at the end of the corridor, she left them to it.

The room overlooked that part of the garden which backed on to the brick wall separating it from the kitchen garden: not much of a view, and it wasn't much of a room either. Small, utilitarian, with a black iron fireplace, and not enhanced by decades-old, putty-grey wallpaper patterned with sad bunches of dark grapes, against which hung three or four melancholy charcoal sketches, amateurishly framed in passe-partout. A small desk held an Imperial typewriter under its dust cover, an easel was propped in a corner and a large square deal table occupied the centre of the room, all of them empty. There was a couch by the window draped with a haphazard collection of unmatched shawls and cushions, and bookshelves lined another wall, not empty at all, but packed with an extensive selection of romantic novels, most of them with lurid titles and dust jackets to match.

Reardon stood and let his gaze roam around, while Jago opened cupboards and drawers, finding nothing but a small stack of stationery of one kind or another: pens and pencils, envelopes, a packet of carbon paper, a stack of typing paper. There was also some fancy, lavender-coloured notepaper and a bottle of violet ink.

Reardon considered the large heap of blackened paper in the grate. 'Whatever she kept in the cupboards seems to have ended up here.' Reaching for the poker, he gingerly touched the flakes, which immediately disintegrated into nothing but a flurry of grey dust. Whatever had been burnt there had been destroyed beyond hope of retrieval. Perhaps it had been her artwork she'd destroyed. There was no evidence of it, unless she was the creator of those charcoal sketches Jago was studying.

'My wife says you have to *read* pictures to understand what the artist's getting at,' he remarked, staring at them. 'Give me a book, any day.'

'I think she's right,' Jago said, 'but I don't know about reading these. They actually remind me a bit of home . . . Cornwall, Bodmin Moor? Stormy skies, rocks. But no wheal chimneys, and no stormy seas, either. Bleak though, aren't they?'

Bleak was hardly the word. It would be interesting to know why Emilie had found it necessary to surround herself with something so depressing, Reardon thought as they left the room and moved on to the one Maitland had pointed out as her bedroom.

A glimpse into the one adjoining it as they passed showed it to be spick and span, nothing out of place, a man's room, conventionally furnished and as lacking in character as a hotel bedroom. A camel-hair dressing gown was neatly folded across the bed and a pair of men's slippers stood on the floor.

Emilie's own room didn't take long to search. It was light and pretty, good furniture and with as little evidence of that muddle and disorder to which she had allegedly been prone as her snug had shown. Someone had maybe tidied it; the bed was already stripped of all but its creamy silk coverlet; the room's only clutter was the array of bottles and jars on the dressing table.

The coats, suits, dresses and furs she had left behind in the two wardrobes held the intimate, lingering scent of Parma violets, as did the silk underwear in the drawers. Reardon closed the last one, feeling sightly grubby, overly intrusive as he always did on a search like this, though it had to be done.

'She'd forgotten her reading glasses,' Jago said, waving a pair of tortoiseshell-framed spectacles he'd picked up from the bedside table, where several more romantic novels sat waiting to be read.

'She could have had a spare pair in that handbag we haven't yet found,' Reardon answered absently. 'Look at this.' He was holding a photo frame he'd found in a drawer containing nothing else but stockings. It was a pretty thing, polished pewter, art-nouveau style, leaves and stems curling in a whiplash design.

'The photo missing from the piano?' Jago asked before he saw it was simply a frame, with an empty space where the photograph should have been.

Prue, when asked, said yes, she recognized the frame. It had always been part of the clutter on the dressing table. She thought the now-missing picture in it had been that of a young woman, but not of anyone she knew.

From the tennis court behind the house came the plunk of tennis balls on racquets, suggesting Alexei might be found there. A Sunday lunch smell was drifting from the kitchen. Would the family be able to face roast beef and Yorkshire pudding today, Jago wondered, thinking *he* might. 'The housekeeper said there's sandwiches if we'd like them,' he suggested.

But Reardon only said, 'First things first. We'll catch something later.'

One more thing to learn about his new boss: food wasn't a priority with him when he was on a job. Jago's stomach rumbled, just the same.

At that moment a car came into view, its soft top down, roaring up the drive at speed, where it came to a gravel-showering halt. The car was so dusty its colour wasn't easily discernible, though it might have been green, and from it an equally dusty and very large young man of about Jago's age extracted himself and his long legs from the car by stages. Once out, he straightened up, stretched an arm into the back for a canvas holdall from among the assortment of luggage piled there, slung it and his jacket over his shoulder and turned to walk into the house. It was only then that the sight of the two men brought him to a sudden standstill. A second or two of startled incomprehension before his face split into a wide, delighted grin. 'Well, stone the crows!' The bag was dropped, his arms extended. 'What the heck are you doing here, me 'andsome?'

'Hell's teeth!' muttered Jago under his breath. He ought to have known this might happen. But he couldn't prevent a huge, answering grin in response to the bear hug he was then given.

TWELVE

After the first shock of seeing her brother barge through the front door, Sophy could almost have believed he'd been conjured up through some wishful thinking on her part. Since that was impossible, he had to be here, didn't he, in response to the letter Pa had said he would write when he'd believed Emilie had absconded? Almost immediately she realized that even if that letter had been posted, it couldn't possibly have reached Sam in Berlin, never mind the time it would have taken for him to drive the hundreds of miles here. Likewise, if Pa had telephoned . . .

Well, never mind how, he *was* here. It was uncanny, but oh, the joy that he should have arrived at such a time, just when he was needed! She screamed with delight and flew into his arms. But his first words bewildered her: 'What's going on? What's old Jago doing here?'

'What? You know Sergeant Jago?'

'Better than his own mother, after three years at Christ Church! I knew he'd joined the police, but I hardly expected to find him here. Why wouldn't he tell me what was going on?' He looked at her sharply. 'Sophy?'

So then she had to tell him. Poor Sam, to be welcomed with such news! She wished Gizi had been here to help her, but she was over at Falquonroy again, poring over wedding plans with Deedie.

He'd been driving so long he was nearly dead on his feet, he said, having had only the necessary stops for food and sleep. No wonder he looked all in. Yet he insisted on hearing everything, and Sophy was so absolutely relieved to have someone to *really* talk to about what was presently turning their lives upside down that she let it all pour out. Sam was the sensible one of the family, the oldest of the three siblings, the grown-up one, the one who never appeared to take anything seriously but always knew exactly what to do and what he wanted from life, who made his own decisions and stuck to them.

He was as dumbfounded as any of them had been, hearing the explanation, which was not the answer he could have anticipated as to why his friend Jago was here at Templewood. Sophy wasn't prepared for his reaction. He sat and listened silently to the whole appalling story and then dropped his head in his hands, saying nothing.

He looked up at last. 'Emilie? Dear God, why Emilie?'

Fear suddenly churned inside Sophy as she saw his ravaged face and remembered that although he'd been away, Oxford and so on, for much of the time since Pa had married Emilie, she and Sam had been very chummy whenever they had met. She pushed a preposterous idea firmly away. Sam got on with everyone; he had that sort of nature. Instead, she demanded to know what had brought him home and how long he was here for.

All she got was a non-committal shrug, as if all that didn't really matter now, his face still shocked at what he'd heard. She noticed the dust of the journey in the laughter lines around his eyes, which she saw with alarm now looked more like worry lines. His thick, fair hair was dusty as well, and surely those weren't grey hairs at his temple? Grey hair . . . Sam? He was twenty-seven! 'I won't be going back to Germany, Sophy,' he said suddenly. 'I don't work for the bank any longer.'

If a thunderbolt had struck her she couldn't have been more stunned. '*What?* What's happened?'

He'd always been happy and satisfied with the way his chosen career was progressing, hadn't he? Even one as boring to her as banking. He had, as Pa was fond of saying, excellent prospects, and his position was already well established. He'd been directly recruited by the bank on graduating from Oxford and whisked off to a position at their branch in Berlin, to be groomed for a more important one, probably in London. They had all been so proud of him.

Questions boiled inside her, but he shook his head. 'Can we talk about it later? All I want at the moment is something to eat, a bath and to sleep forever. But I have to see Pa first.'

'No, you don't, you're in no state. And anyway, he's over at Granny's at the moment so he doesn't know you're here yet.' Sophy knew Granny was the person Pa had told the police he must see . . . she would have to be told about Emilie being found and she was always the one any of them, including Pa, went to when they wanted advice or were in trouble. He'd been there for ages and there was still no sign of him.

'Go and get a quick bath, then into bed and I'll bring you something to eat.'

Sam wasn't going to object, but he said, 'Must have knocked Pa for a six, poor old sod. Sorry, Sis, language!' She could see he was now also worried that his own problems, whatever they might turn out to be, weren't going to help the situation. 'And what about the others? How's Gizi taking all this?'

'Oh, you know Gizi.'

'Only too well.' Their eyes met and he lifted his shoulders. The years between him and Sophy had grown less of a barrier to understanding one another as Sophy grew older. Once it had been Sam and Gizi who'd had a natural affinity, but it had lapsed; they hadn't been seeing eye to eye since they'd grown up and their paths diverged. 'She's not still running around with that blighter FitzAlban, I hope?'

'I'm afraid so.'

'She's off her chump. He's a bloody—!' He bit off what he'd been going to say, but he didn't apologize this time for swearing.

'She doesn't think so. And he's terribly rich, rolling in it. Plus, he'll have a title one day.'

'When it's too late for her to back off. What about . . .?' Again, he broke off, blowing out his lips. 'Well, I'll see her as soon as I'm in better shape – and Lex, too, poor little worm – he must be shattered.'

He went to get his bath and Sophy made for the kitchen, prepared for the curiosity there his arrival would certainly have caused. Diverting it was going to take some doing. But Maitland soon realized from her unaccustomed silence there was nothing yet that Sophy could or wanted to say, shook her head at Prue and didn't press her. She then relieved Sophy of the bread knife as she attempted to slice a new-baked loaf and herself made a thick beef sandwich from the joint which should have been eaten for lunch. She added plenty of mustard, just the way Sam liked it, and placed a large tankard of cold beer on the tray.

He was already looking better when Sophy took the food to

his room, clean and tidy after a quick bath, with his damp hair brushed back. In his striped pyjamas, he looked like a little boy ready for bed. The room was already Sam's again, his bag opened and ransacked, clothes thrown off and left just where they'd landed. She cleared a chair and sat down while he sat on the edge of the bed, the tray balanced on his knees while he ate ravenously, as if he hadn't had food for weeks, too busy eating the sandwich to speak. Finally, she took the tray, he swung his legs back and leant against the pillows while he finished his beer. 'Lord, that's better!'

'All right, now get some sleep.'

She was dying to know everything he had to tell her (not least about DS Jago and whatever there was to know about him), but she could also see she'd get no proper sense from him if he didn't sleep first and get his mind clear of whatever had been happening to him, plus the situation he'd been greeted with when he arrived here. Drowsiness, helped by the beer, was beginning to get the better of him, but he still seemed to feel the need to offer some excuse for inflicting the disruption his unexpected arrival had caused. His voice was slurred as he said, 'Sorry to dump myself on you all like this, Muffin, but everything blew up suddenly. I had to leave the bank.'

'What?' *Had* to leave? 'Sam, you haven't been . . . sacked?' Totally incredible as the idea seemed – ludicrous even, not to say slightly frightening – Sophy couldn't think of any other reason why he – steady, reliable, predictable Sam – should suddenly have left the brilliant career he was carving out for himself.

He gave a wry laugh. 'I've sacked myself. I've quit.'

'*What?*' She was running out of incredulous expressions.

'Give me a minute and I'll tell you about it.' But he could scarcely keep his eyes open. Despite his best efforts, his eyelids were drooping and in less than a minute, he was fast asleep.

She eased the pillows behind him into a lower position and he didn't stir. The eiderdown was folded across the end of the bed, and she lifted it gently over him, pulled the curtains across the window and left him in the darkened room.

* * *

Leaving the little travel-battered car where it was, Sam had disappeared indoors, while Jago berated himself for not anticipating such a meeting. But what the devil was Sam doing here, complicating an already tricky situation, when he should have been safe in Berlin? Safe in Berlin? Now *that* was a contradiction in terms, nowadays, wasn't it?

'So, who is he then, the young fellow in the Rolls?' Reardon asked when Jago caught up with him. He had stepped back and carried on walking towards the tennis court, leaving the two of them to their exuberant greeting.

'It's a German Opel, and he's Sam Waring – the judge's son. We were at Oxford together.'

'Oh, Oxford, is it?'

No, that's not it! Jago wanted to shout, hearing the echo of his own father's good-natured irony. It wasn't always easy for people like Reardon – very like his father, from the same sort of solid, working-class upbringing, he guessed – to understand how such a friendship as his and Sam's had begun, and lasted. Their backgrounds couldn't have been more different, but right from their first meeting they'd enjoyed a blokey relationship, exchanging cheerful insults about Sam's posh establishment forbears and Jago's tin-mining ancestors, his Cornish accent. Since leaving Oxford, they'd gone their different ways and hadn't seen each other for some time, but Jago hoped – no, he knew – that the time they'd spent together, the shared enthusiasms and ideals which had driven and excited them and cemented their relationship in their student days and beyond hadn't disappeared. He didn't feel up to explaining all this to Reardon, though he knew his reply was lame.

'By rights, he should be in Berlin – that's where he lives. Works for the German branch of a British bank; that's why I was taken aback see him here. I'd no idea he'd be around.' He hesitated, looking distinctly uncomfortable. 'Won't be a problem, will it, sir?'

'What won't be?' Reardon asked, deliberately obtuse.

'Oh, Sam and me, knowing each other . . .'

Reardon saw the dilemma reflected on his young colleague's face. They were so self-assured, these smart young chaps, before finding that nothing in their advanced education prepared them for what they had to face in the real world of policing. Despite his rapid progress in Scotland Yard, Jago was not as confident as he would like it to appear. Reardon could appreciate his present problem: conflict of interest was a very grey area. How much of a friendship was that with the judge's son? 'Well, we'll need to clear it with the super,' he said.

'I already told Mr Knott I knew Sam when I discovered the victim was Judge Waring's wife . . . and he knows I'd never met the rest of the family. I'd no idea Sam would be here . . .' Nor did Knott, presumably. 'And he didn't seem to think it would be a problem. It . . . er . . . won't, will it?'

After a moment, Reardon said, 'Only if you let it. Which you won't, of course.'

When Lex had returned from his quest for cigarettes and that encounter with FitzAlban, he'd felt he must do something, anything, to let off steam, and smashing a ball across a net had been the best thing he could think of. It had simply never occurred to him that inviting Catchpole to join him in a knockabout on the tennis court was in no way a recompense the tutor would appreciate for his pupil's earlier behaviour. Catchpole did in fact make no objections, but Lex's attempts to keep the ball thwacking hard enough between them were defeated by his opponent's limp returns.

Reardon let the tennis players carry on, waiting until one or other should notice they had an audience – which wouldn't be long, he anticipated, given the lack of commitment on either side. Neither player appeared to have their hearts or minds on what they were doing. The boy had the advantage over his stocky tutor in that he was taller, lighter and quicker on his feet; he moved gracefully but he wasn't keeping his eye on the ball and his opponent's returns were lackadaisical and frequently missed.

It was Catchpole who saw them first and called out something to his partner. There was no hesitation from either about abandoning the game. They came over immediately and threw down their racquets when they reached the two officers, who were standing beside a large ash tree, its emergent foliage providing enough of a canopy to give some shade over a rough rustic table and several chairs set about for spectators.

The tutor was demonstrably not the athletic type. The way he slumped into a chair and pulled a handkerchief out to wipe the perspiration off his forehead showed his relief that the game was over. The boy, Alexei, looked scarcely out of breath. Scorning the chairs, he leant back nonchalantly against the tree trunk, feet crossed, arms folded, trying his best to assume a superior air.

He looked older than sixteen, well on the way to becoming one of those good-looking types women fell for like a ton of bricks . . . when he had filled out, his skin had cleared of the slight rash of adolescent acne and he'd gained more control of his coltish limbs.

'You are going to find out who did it, aren't you?' he demanded truculently, though still not able to hide the anxiety in his eyes as he looked at Reardon.

'We hope so. If everyone cooperates and helps us, we will.'

'I suppose that means you're going to ask a whole lot of stupid questions.'

Reardon had decided the one to kick off this interview should be Jago. His own youth wasn't as far behind him as Reardon's; Alexei might respond more readily to someone nearer his own age, and besides, Reardon wanted to see how the sergeant shaped up to it.

'It's usually the way we conduct an enquiry,' he told the boy, 'but there won't be many questions, and I hope you won't find them stupid. Come and sit down, please.' After a moment's hesitation, Alexei obeyed.

Jago began by taking the two of them together, Alexei and the tutor, through the events of Thursday and the days running up to it. Not surprisingly, nothing other than what they'd already been told emerged. Neither had noticed any unusual activity around Templewood, nor seen any strangers all week, in fact. Nothing to excite alarm or even curiosity.

Reardon approved Jago's brisk approach. It was the right way to go about it. You were at the mercy of your hormones at Alexei's age and sympathy might have been too much for the boy if he had really been as attached to Emilie as the housekeeper had said. As it was, the annoying superciliousness he'd tried to put on was not quite holding up, revealing the schoolboy he still was and the vulnerability he couldn't hide. He had to blink and turn away when Jago went on to say that he understood he and Mrs Waring had been good friends.

'Is that what they've told you? Well, we were, and why not?' His unreliable voice went up an octave. 'There's no law against that, is there?'

'Not that I know of. So, I suppose she told you she was going away, and why?'

He flushed and said rudely, 'Then you suppose wrong! She didn't have to tell me everything.'

'I thought perhaps she might have asked for your help with her luggage. It was heavy, two cases. It was found with her down at The Spinney and she'd have had difficulty managing on her own.'

'A taxi driver would have helped.'

'It's not really likely she'd order a taxi to take her only as far as the building site, is it?'

Alexei said, 'Oh God, what does it matter now how she got there?'

His olive skin had paled so that it had an almost greenish undertone. The acne pimples looked angry and all at once he stood up, so forcefully the wooden chair he'd been sitting on fell over. He thrust it out of his way, then turned and loped towards the path that led back to the house, almost stumbling, clumsy as he hadn't been on the court, and disappeared around the corner.

The tutor half rose too, ready to go after him, then changed his mind and sat down again.

'That's right, let him, go, Mr Catchpole,' Reardon said, looking thoughtfully after the disappearing figure. 'We don't need him any more at the moment.'

Catchpole eased himself back into the chair. 'This has been a big shock to him. He really was extremely attached to Mrs Waring. She was always so kind to him.'

'His mother died when he was a baby, didn't she?' Jago said.

'She did, but it was nothing like that. Mrs Waring wasn't the maternal type, and Lex didn't see her as a mother figure, if that's the way you're thinking. He just feels things a bit too intensely . . . a young man, his age, you know how it can be.'

The tutor's heavy, doughy face and the round glasses which kept slipping down his nose and having to be pushed back tended to give him a vacant look. Yet he presumably had the academic qualifications that allowed him to prepare someone for university entrance.

'Are you suggesting he fancied himself in love with her? It can happen with an older woman,' Jago said.

'No, not . . . not precisely. Or perhaps he was, a little, without being aware of it. It was just a stage he was going through, that was all, you know? He'll be all right once he's got over the shock, finds his feet again.'

'And Mrs Waring? Was she aware of how he felt, do you think?'

'Who can say?' He added flatly, 'I'm afraid I didn't know Emilie well enough to answer that.'

Despite the attempt to sound offhand, for a moment there he had looked, as he spoke . . . well, stricken was the word that came to mind. And he had just used Mrs Waring's first name. Maybe young Lex wasn't the only one who, consciously or not, had inappropriate feelings for the judge's wife.

THIRTEEN

'What sort of advice?' Ellen finished slicing tomatoes and picked up a cucumber.

'Sorry, what did you say?' Reardon turned from the window, where he'd been staring out, hands in pockets, as soft, gentle rain fell on the garden. It wasn't the new flowerbeds he'd been looking at for inspiration though; he'd hardly seen them.

'You asked ten minutes ago for the benefit of my expert opinion. Which particular expertise would you like? Cooking or gardening?'

That was the trouble with converts, Reardon thought, returning her teasing smile and dragging his mind away from what was preoccupying him. They became blinkered to everything else. Not that he'd any complaints – the garden, neglected before they'd moved into this old house, once a lodge to the now-demolished mansion it had served, had responded marvellously under that newly acquired enthusiasm – and Ellen tried so hard with her cooking, something that didn't come naturally to her. Yesterday's dinner had been a very tasty roast chicken, the remains of which seemed destined to accompany tonight's salad, he noted glumly. He wasn't yet won over by lettuce and watercress, though he ate them dutifully.

'Or maybe French grammar?' Ellen added, listing her main accomplishment as she put the chicken salads on the table, and they sat down to eat.

'Neither – or not directly. Cast your mind back to some of your former pupils.' He picked up his beer and took a drink.

Since it was this new investigation of his he'd previously been talking about, Ellen didn't need to ask which pupils. The judge's daughters had been educated at Maxstead, the expensive girls' boarding school where she taught French on a part-time basis, so she'd seen the question coming. 'The Waring girls, you mean? Oh dear, it must be so awful for them.'

'I dare say. Neither has given much away so far. What was

your opinion of them? It can't be long since they left school, so I don't suppose they've changed all that much.'

He knew she enjoyed the discussions they had about his cases. His work interested her, she was open-minded, a good sounding board, and he valued her opinions. What was called the woman's angle (which he saw as common sense and the ability to see things in a fresh perspective, no matter what their sex) had proved useful in the past. Never mind that she was in fact a great advocate of women police officers as detectives – why not? she asked – and although he too supported the idea, in theory the notion that she might want to become one herself had once haunted him. Not for long. She was too committed to her real work of teaching, especially as it left enough time for other pursuits – her newly acquired gardening skill, for instance, and her friendship with Maisie, Joe Gilmour's wife, and above all the time she could give to her godchild, their little daughter, Ellie. At the moment, she had other concerns too: the head teacher at Maxstead had arranged a student exchange with girls from Paris, a cultural necessity in Miss Henshall's opinion, and the arrangements associated with it were keeping Ellen well occupied.

Reardon picked up and contemplated the bottle of salad cream, thought better of it, and poked around hopefully for chicken stuffing on his plate while she said, 'You can't be thinking those girls have anything to do with . . . with the murder?'

'Everyone's on the suspect list yet, but no, not really. They were away from home when it happened in any case.'

She gave his question some thought for a moment or two. 'Well, I didn't teach either for long. Gizella – Gizi – was at the point of leaving when I started at Maxstead and Sophy left soon after . . . there's not much more than a year between them. The surprise was that Sophy didn't stay on and get to university as Miss Henshall hoped she would.'

'Why was that?'

'I don't know. Unless she simply followed her sister's example. She was a quiet girl, and I did sometimes wonder if she allowed herself to be in Gizi's shadow.'

'But she must have been bright, with a university prospect in view?' The Sophy he'd met hadn't seemed particularly quiet. She'd shown a quick intelligence, and it didn't seem to him she was the sort to be in anyone's shadow. Perhaps she'd altered, grown up, or simply been stimulated to talk more freely by the shocking event that had occurred in the Waring household. He had sensed an enquiring mind and had decided early on that she had a good head on her shoulders.

'Well, she was brighter than Gizi,' Ellen said, 'or that feather-headed Dee Malpas, her friend, certainly. Those two couldn't wait to be grown up and leave school. It wouldn't surprise me if they're running around now fancying themselves as what the papers used to call the Bright Young Things.' She became thoughtful. 'Actually, take back what I said about Gizi. I think she was smarter than she appeared, though she would have done anything rather than show it. Girls at that age can be so tiresome, their heads full of rubbish. She wasn't academically inclined, that's true, but she was clever enough.' She paused with a piece of cucumber on the end of her fork. 'Or tricky, perhaps.'

'The girls must have been in their early adolescence when their mother died.'

'They got a nice stepmother.'

'How do you know she was nice? Did you meet her?'

'Once or twice, at parent dos and so on, and she seemed so, then. Superficial judgement, of course. I only spoke to her in passing.'

'It seems to be the general opinion of Emilie Waring. Nice enough, but no one seems to have known what she was really like, or known anything about her before she became the judge's wife. Not even the judge himself.' He repeated what Waring had said, how he'd respected his new wife's privacy and so on, and her disinclination to talk to him about her previous existence, his acceptance of that.

'That's really weird. When two people meet and fall in love, don't they want to know everything about each other, however trivial or silly? Not just starry-eyed youngsters. Even you and I did.'

'Yes, even old codgers like us.'

'Not so much of the old!' They laughed and he reached for her hand and squeezed it. The warm current of love and understanding passing between them brought with it a deeper empathy for Judge Waring's situation than Reardon had been able to summon up so far.

'How can you love someone who has had a whole life you know nothing about?' Ellen persisted. 'That's so sad. It makes you think she'd something really awful to hide.'

'Some people are naturally secretive.'

'That's true. But you'll be going to see this lady that Mrs Waring was companion to, of course,' Ellen said thoughtfully. 'She might have something to say.'

'Not immediately; we have others to see first. Miss Oates is a maiden lady. They must have led a quiet, simple life.'

'Miss Henshall,' Ellen said, 'is a maiden lady, but life with her is rarely quiet, and never simple.'

Reardon grinned. But he raised his glass to his wife. As usual, she had a point.

FOURTEEN

Sophy hadn't slept for her usual eight hours. Instead of feeling rested and full of energy, she woke to another lovely morning with a niggling headache and memory snatches of uncoordinated, hazy but nevertheless frightening dreams. Perhaps she ought to break the habit of writing up her journal before sleeping. Last night, it had seemed the only way to try and make sense of the awful day yesterday . . . Black Sunday!

She washed and dressed hurriedly. No one was about downstairs. She ate a piece of toast, swallowed some tea and wandered out into the garden with Juno padding arthritically after her. Towser's frisky presence wasn't in evidence. Very likely he was with Prue, getting under her feet, but she wouldn't send him away. She spoiled him rotten and Towser knew when he was on to a good thing.

Then, across the lawn she saw them standing by the wooden door which led into the kitchen garden and the bothy: Gizi, Sam and Martin Garbutt. They didn't see her, too deep in a furious argument – furious on Gizi's side, at least. The two men were saying little or nothing. Martin was scowling, both hands stuck deep into his trouser pockets, kicking the gravel at his feet. As Sophy watched, she saw Sam reach out to his sister, but she shook his hand off angrily.

Yesterday, having returned from her afternoon with Dee and hearing that Sam was home again, she'd hardly been able to restrain herself from going upstairs to hug him, dying to hear everything he had to tell. It was only when Pa, though he was equally anxious to see Sam, had stopped her, saying, 'Let the boy have his sleep out,' that she'd desisted. Yet now, here they were, facing each other like two cats with their backs up. He hadn't been home five minutes and they'd managed to infuriate each other. And Martin?

Snatches of Gizi's angry words came clearly across the lawn. '. . . nothing to do with you . . . time you let me lead my own life, don't you think?' And then she was storming away with her head in the air, swishing Towser's lead against the plants as she walked, heedless of incurring Garbutt's wrath, and calling for Towser, who was surely in luck . . . since when had Gizi ever taken him for a walk? He came bounding round the corner, but she suddenly changed her mind, threw the lead down and marched indoors. She was not far from tears, and Gizi never cried.

The little bulldog ran after her towards the door and then gave up, having spotted something more interesting on top of a pile of prickly pyracantha clippings in Garbutt's wheelbarrow – a gardening glove he maybe thought was a rat.

The two men stood looking after Gizi. They spoke for a minute or two, then Sam clapped a hand on Martin's shoulder before they separated, Martin going back towards the bothy and Sam, having spotted Sophy, coming forward to join her. He stopped for a few minutes, pretending to tussle Towser's prize from him, until even Towser had at last had enough and called it a day, relinquishing the glove and trotting off back to the kitchen.

Sam joined Sophy where she sat on the swing that Pa had once fixed up by the goldfish pool, wide enough for two, and now made comfortable with cushions. 'What was all that about, Sam?' As if she didn't know.

'Oh, just me and Gizi . . . you know. She's – oh, I don't know, Sophy, I just wish she was as sensible as you.'

Sophy bit her lip. *Sensible. Me? Since when?* Too late, she wished she'd pretended not to have noticed the argument. The last thing Sam would want to do at the moment was carry on talking about the company Gizi kept. She was sure that's what it had been about – especially since Martin had been there, too.

In any case, Sam was looking a bit bruised. She guessed he'd already spoken to Pa. He had never before given their father the slightest cause for concern. Poor Pa! This new worry on top of the other shocks he had already had. 'Sam . . .' she began.

'I'm sorry, I can't talk now, Sophy, I must be off.' He checked his watch. 'I should be over at the Park by now, to see Sir Julius. It's important.'

Sam had never had much to do with Sir Julius, except as a friend of Pa's. What could be so important that he had to rush off and see him now, for goodness' sake? 'Oh, right,' she said.

'Sorry!' But something in her face made him hesitate. Suddenly he drew up one of the garden chairs and straddled it, facing her. He seemed to have belatedly remembered the promise he'd given her yesterday, to tell her just why he'd left Berlin, and decided after all that Sir Julius could wait for a bit.

He sat still for several minutes, wondering where to begin. 'How much do you know of the situation over there in Germany, Sophy?' he asked eventually, watching her carefully. So much had happened. The world had begun to turn upside down since he'd first gone there to work, and he had no idea how much she knew of what was going on.

'Well, only what one reads in the newspapers – Herr Hitler and what he's supposed to be doing, and those frightful rumours . . .'

'*Supposed* to be doing? *Rumours?* Well, that's what I might have thought they were once. Until I lived there . . . But not now, Sophy.'

She felt a strange cold shiver of premonition, but she switched to face him and prepared to listen.

When he had been offered a four-year placement in the Berlin branch of the prestigious private London bank he'd worked for since leaving university, Sam had jumped at it. Initially a lowly position, the prospects dangled before him were tempting. And perhaps as much as the job itself was the chance to get his thinking clear and experience for himself what the political situation was over there in Germany, a subject guaranteed to inflame hot-headed student opinions throughout his university years.

All his life, he'd been encouraged to take an interest in what was happening in the world, but the arguments and endless beer-fuelled discussions, loudly disputed in smoke-filled rooms until the small hours, had left him uncertain as to how much to believe about the ever more alarming reports trickling out from Germany. When the job offer came, he saw it as an opportunity to find out just what the National Socialist Party, the Nazis, now in power under their new Chancellor, Adolf Hitler (whom they were already calling their Führer, their leader) were promising to do for their country, what that might mean for the rest of Europe, and not least Britain. Germany, so they were proclaiming, was beating the economic slump that had affected the whole world after the Great War. It was now a nation on the up and up. The Nazi regime alone had brought this about. Germany was happy, healthy, educated, its disastrous unemployment problem on the way to being overcome.

First impressions of Berlin were mixed. Fresh from England, he'd been excited by the atmosphere generated in the dazzling, cosmopolitan capital. Like all big cities, it had its acceptable and non-acceptable faces, but while deploring its run-down, working-class areas, he could admire the wide boulevards and squares, the imposing buildings, spacious parks, elegant department stores of central Berlin. More than that, there was music and entertainment wherever you went, the city thronged with vibrant life, spilling out on to the pavement cafés, while at the same time the public buildings everywhere triumphantly flaunted the red banners and black swastikas of the ruling Nazi party. Warning reminders of its intention to take over and demand compliance and obedience from every walk of life.

His employers had found gloomy rooms for him on the second floor of a barrack-like block of apartments well behind the affluence of the Kurfürstendamm, complete with a huge, tiled stove that gave out waves of oppressive heat, and furnished with dark and solid furniture in danger of sinking through the floor under the weight of its own over-elaborate decoration. A middle-aged woman with dark, liquid eyes who had worked for the previous owners of the flat came in daily and made his bed, kept the place ferociously clean and left him a cooked meal.

Not that he stayed in to eat very often. Many of the younger staff at the bank were English like himself, seeing their jobs, as Sam did, as a step forward to the City careers they hoped to have back in London. A number of Germans were also employed as translators and so on, who were friendly and sociable. Often, rather than go back to his dreary rooms and dine alone on what Fraulein Keppel had left for him, he would join a mixed group visiting one of the many bars or beer cellars, where he ate sausages, sauerkraut and dumplings, and tried out the different kinds of beer – often paying for it with a hangover the next morning. His new friends also introduced him to a sophisticated café life he hadn't known existed – including nightclubs where exceedingly risqué cabarets appeared every night, where he tried not to demonstrate shock or British prudery at the racy shows openly performed.

'Do you remember the Fraulein Keppel I wrote about in my letters?' he asked Sophy now.

'The woman who cooked for you and never spoke?'

'That's the one.'

He had sometimes wondered what Fraulein Keppel had thought of the untouched meals he often forgot to dispose of in the stove, but since she spoke no word of English and his German at that point was not up to finding credible excuses, he didn't pursue it. She had never given any indication that she'd noticed. He scarcely saw her anyway, and when he did, he had indeed found her the most silent woman he had ever met. 'Yes, well, let me tell you something else about her, Sophy.'

He reached into his pocket, brought out cigarettes and lit one. 'All right,' he began,.'It was one evening in late November, when I came home from work . . .'

He remembered the annoyance he'd felt, finding his rooms in the same chaotic state he'd left them in that morning. He'd anticipated a quiet evening for once, writing letters home, but the stove had gone out, it was bitterly cold, and no meal was waiting for him. Nor even one of the stilted notes Fraulein Keppel occasionally left. Disgruntled, he prepared to go out and find somewhere to eat.

He was locking his door when his neighbour, Frau Foch, appeared with a string bag bulging with shopping. Without much hope, he asked her if she could throw any light on the situation with Fraulein Keppel. She was a big, heavily built woman with shoulders like a navvy, little piggy eyes and thin, straw-coloured plaits wound tightly round her head. He couldn't see that the two women would have had much in common, but he knew by now that all the inhabitants of the apartments spied on each other in order to report to the authorities any suspicious activity or violation of Nazi Party regulations. She told him she knew nothing. 'Well, she is *Jüdische*.' She shrugged, as if this explained everything, and perhaps it did.

'It doesn't do to be Jewish over there, Sophy,' he said, knowing how hopelessly inadequate, almost meaningless that was, not even beginning to explain the dangers of the situation that existed in pursuit of the Nazis' antisemitic aims. So bad, it was no longer unusual for anyone suspected of having Jewish blood to disappear, even to be picked off the streets at random and sent to forced labour camps, for their families to hear nothing more of them, even when they had done nothing wrong at all. He thought it might be quite possible that he would never again see Fraulein Keppel, harmless as she had seemed to him, and he never did.

That same night, after questioning the neighbour about her, he had gone out in search of his supper and found himself in the midst of a street rumpus, where young brown-shirted boys in Hitler Youth uniforms were throwing stones and bricks through the windows of shops owned by Jews while armed police looked the other way. Perhaps it was a coincidence that this had happened on the same day that Fraulein Keppel had disappeared. On the other hand, it could be part of just another neighbourhood round-up and harassment.

Outraged, dodging bricks and flying glass as best he could, Sam beat a hasty retreat. There was nothing he could have done to help, he told himself, but he still felt he had been a coward, and the unanswered letters from England, which had been lying like a lead weight on his conscience, reproached him even more.

Watching him as he spoke, Sophy sensed he had by no means told her everything yet. 'What are you going to do, now you've left the bank?'

'Oh, I'll find something.' Trying to sound as though finding another way to resume the career he'd thrown to the winds would be the easiest thing in the world. 'I don't know what, but it doesn't matter. Whatever I do won't be for long. Sooner or later it'll end up with me enlisting in the army, or the RAF, I guess.' He went on gently, 'There's going to be a war. You know that, Sophy? Nothing's going to stop it.'

She was shocked. 'Surely it won't come to that!' But she knew her protest was token. You couldn't avoid the subject that was on everyone's mind, if not their lips, yet the possibility was too horrific to admit openly. Better to exist in the hopes that it wouldn't happen, to carry on laughing at the newspaper lampooning of Herr Hitler as a shrieking madman or a figure of fun . . . wasn't it?

'It's what the Nazis want, Sophy – war. What they are preparing for, unlike us.' Seeing her troubled face, he tried to explain: 'They're building aeroplanes, you know – ships, submarines. It's how they're solving their unemployment problem. Work in munitions factories, rearmaments, all for Hitler's ambitions to conquer the whole of Europe – and maybe Britain.'

What was he saying? That what was happening in Germany, what he'd just described, could happen here? This was not the mild, easy-going brother she'd always known. The passion he showed was such that she couldn't, just then, think of an answer. 'That's why you came home?'

'Partly.' His eyes didn't meet hers and she knew suddenly the reason was a girl, or a woman. There always had been one, somewhere in Sam's life. Never short of some admiring female willing to hang on his every word, and adroit at avoiding being caught by any of them, it had been a family joke.

'You've met someone! Oh, Sam! She isn't . . . she's not German, is she?'

'What, a fat fräulein with plaits and a dirndl? Give me credit!'

The exchange lightened the atmosphere. She laughed, and he did too, though not very convincingly.

He gave another quick glance at his watch. 'Look, I'll tell you more about it all later, Sophy, when I've time. I'm afraid I really do have to go now.'

This time he did leave. Sophy stared thoughtfully after the dusty Opel as it chugged its way down the drive. She watched a tiny greenfinch land on the very end of one of the low, swooping branches of the sequoia facing her. Even its tiny weight caused a slight tip, but the little bird hung on, back and forth, as happy as a child on a swing. She wished she felt the same.

She suspected what she'd just heard from Sam was only the very tip of a huge iceberg. Herr Hitler was no longer a joke – if he ever had been – and now, the likelihood of what was happening across the sea in Germany happening here no longer felt so remote. She closed her eyes in an effort to shut the thought out.

But what came to her was what she had actually seen happening less than two weeks ago: young men marching through the streets of London, their arms raised in a fascist salute, wearing black, tunic-style shirts, peaked caps, jodhpurs and glossy jackboots.

They looked handsome, tough and very smart, and Gizi's face had blazed with admiration; her eyes shone.

Well, a disciplined band of marching men in uniform was always a stirring sight. They were being cheered on by people in the streets. Women were smiling, some even blowing kisses . . . until everything erupted. Until rough men in the watching crowds, now waving red communist flags, had sought to break up the march, brandishing weapons: glass bottles, knuckle dusters, bare fists. And even Gizi's admiration had dwindled when the marching men's burly young bodyguards appeared with their truncheons, along with the arrival of the police, who had been standing by to break up what had quickly become a riot. Even Gizi had been willing to flee then.

Before he left for his meeting with Sir Julius, Sam said, 'We must look after her, Sophy. Gizi, I mean. She thinks she knows what she's doing but she's playing with fire.'

FIFTEEN

It wasn't the way Reardon would have chosen to begin a murder investigation, but there wasn't much choice when you were faced with a worst-case scenario like this one: a body already three days dead, no witnesses to interview, no weapon involved. No motive, as yet. A death in a quietly undisturbed part of the world where there were no neighbours or even passers-by to have seen anything. The only thing to do was to press on with talking to people who had known the victim. Hoping they'd remember something, let something drop . . . maybe something they hadn't known they knew.

The morning began with what the super, Knott, liked to call a briefing, as if they were in the armed forces. Whatever the meeting of those gathered in the main office, smoking and drinking tea or coffee, was called for, and however much he was itching to get off and see the man Surtees, Reardon still felt he owed it to his small team to bring them up to speed with as much as they'd found so far.

He kept an eye on them as he spoke, and decided Knott could have been cannier over Joe Gilmour's temporary replacement than he'd given him credit for. Jealousy between grown men wasn't unknown, and Gargrave being aggrieved and sulky at seeing his obvious potential ignored, or Pickersgill feeling hurt that he'd had his nose pushed out, was something Reardon didn't need. But Jago's arrival didn't appear to have upset anyone. He had an easy manner, and no one had shown outward curiosity when he was introduced, whatever they thought. They knew he'd been working in London, but nowadays with so many political and industrial disturbances and upheavals all over the country, resulting in mini battlegrounds, officers were just as likely to be sent anywhere that extra clout was needed.

After he'd passed on what information they'd gained so far, with a brisk order to carry on with what they had been working on, while keeping themselves ready to down tools if necessary, Reardon sent everyone back to their desks.

There wasn't much conversation in the car as Jago took the main road out of Folbury, leaving behind the green countryside that stretched out on the far side of the town, the castle ruins and the stone-built beacon on its steep hill, overlooking the bustling streets like some benign medieval saint on a church façade. Very soon they were well into the industrial Black Country, crossing the umpteen bridges spanning the network of canals and waterways serving the factories and workplaces built up around them. They made fairly good progress, one of the few motorcars wedged in among the mass of large, lumbering vehicles transporting goods and materials to and from the steel and iron works, the rolling mills and other heavy industries that were sending their murky emissions to darken today's already grey sky.

Jago swerved to avoid getting caught behind a tram, and Reardon's pencil slipped. 'Sorry, sir!'

'That's OK.' Reardon had been attempting to deal with the backlog of routine work he'd picked up off his desk, trying to read the pile of folders on his knee as best he could. They were nearly there now, and he closed the files. He was normally a terrible passenger, Joe Gilmour being the only one he sat easily beside, and not always then, so it was just as well DS Jago had so far proved to be a competent driver, as smooth as the state of the roads allowed, and one moreover who was content to let him get on with his work, not feeling the need to fill every minute with aimless chat.

As it happened, the reason Jago was happy to be quiet and not have to make conversation with his new boss was mainly because he was too busy with his own thoughts. The exchange over the telephone early that morning when he had rung Sam Waring to suggest a meeting had been brief, but slightly unsettling. There had been no time to say all the things he had wanted to say when they'd met the day before, and Sam had sounded decidedly preoccupied too. They'd arranged to meet that night, when Sam said he'd explain everything.

It was raining steadily by the time they reached the town centre. Driving down Darlington Street, Reardon kept an eye out for the turning which should lead to where Farraday Associates had their offices.

This turned out to be a short, terraced street of late-Victorian vintage: tall, narrow properties now given over to commercial premises and offices of a mostly unspecified nature. The façade of Farradays was as shabby as the rest, a building which Reardon assumed to be their administration offices, the practical side of the architecture and building enterprise premises being located elsewhere. They were not yet open, so they sat waiting in the parked car.

The rain showed no sign of abating. The windows were steaming up as the time stretched out. A terrier of uncertain parentage trotted purposefully by, wet through and intent on its own concerns. A flyer for Wolverhampton Wanderers' latest fixture, when Wolves would be at home, displaying its gold and black colours, flapped wetly on a telegraph pole. 'Out of date,' Reardon remarked, nodding towards it. 'You interested in football? Molineux Stadium's just over yonder.'

'Rugby's more my game.' It was a diplomatic evasion. Jago wasn't particularly interested in either.

'Mine, too, when I was younger. No time to play now . . . or more like anno domini catching up, if I'm honest.'

Really? Jago threw an amused glance at the chief inspector. Middle-aged, certainly, his thick black hair streaked with a few strands of grey, good looking if you didn't count the scar. But still fit as a flea.

'We used to have a good team at Dudley,' he was saying, 'back in the day . . . Hold on, here we go!'

Somewhere nearby, a church clock was striking a sonorous nine and, on the dot, a man with an umbrella had appeared and was now inserting a key into the lock at Farradays. Two or three others came along and followed him in. Another ten minutes for them to settle in and then they made a dash for it.

The reception area was an eye-opener, a different world from what the dingy exterior would lead you to expect; inside it was state-of-the-art, modern, light and airy. A superior lady receptionist with plucked eyebrows and heavy make-up stood by the desk, adjusting three stems of white hot-house lilies into a large black vase on the counter.

Reardon gave his name and asked for Surtees. The offices had been closed all weekend and he apologized for not having an appointment, but omitted to mention they were from the police. The receptionist gave up the attempt at the flowers and pushed the vase to one side, giving both men a wide, engaging smile.

'Orroight, I'll see if he can see you.' She had a built-in Black Country twang and a voice like a frog. Like the lilies, which on closer inspection could be seen to be artificial, the appearance was all façade. But the smile was genuine enough. She waved them to a smart black leather sofa and picked up the telephone.

The man who greeted them a few minutes later was the same man who had opened up the offices. The initial impression was of someone trying to achieve the gravitas his years denied. He was wearing gold-rimmed spectacles, a sober grey suit and a stiff white collar. His brown hair was brushed smoothly back and parted as if with a knife.

'Rex Surtees,' he introduced himself, extending a long and shapely hand that might have belonged to a pianist or an artist – which as an architect he was, in a way, Reardon conceded. The handshake was firm and cool, and the smile revealed a gold tooth. 'You wished to see me?' He spoke quickly, precisely, with the vowels of southern England.

'First, let me tell you we're police officers,' Reardon said. They gave their names and ranks, showed their identities. Surtees looked startled but made no comment and led them into an adjoining small room with comfortable seats and a low table on which cups and saucers were arranged, ready for potential clients.

Reardon had ascertained before coming that there were two other partners in the practice, and that Surtees was the junior one. Looking at him more closely, he reassessed the man's age. Surtees was one of those young-old men whose age could go either way, but he guessed he was not far off forty.

In what was evidently a well-trained routine, the receptionist appeared within minutes, bearing a coffee pot and a plate of bourbon biscuits. Surtees said, 'Thank you, Miss Cox,' then indicated she could leave and himself proceeded to dispense the coffee into elegant white porcelain cups, his hands moving very neatly and precisely. For a moment, Reardon had a vision of those long fingers grasping the ends of a silk scarf, twisting and pulling it tighter and tighter . . .

'What can I do for you?' the architect asked when they were settled.

'We'd like to speak to you about Mrs Waring, and the house that you designed at Temple Atwode – to be called The Spinney, I believe.'

'What?' Surtees stared, then gave an exasperated sigh. 'Oh Lord, I thought that was all settled. But I might have known there'd be trouble! Found some loophole, has he, His Honour the judge? Thinks we can't back off? I must say that surprises me. I would have thought he'd be as keen as we were to chuck the whole idea. It was getting to be a waste of everyone's time and—'

'Mr Surtees, it's not about any arguments or whatever differences you might have had with Judge Waring. He's not about to contest you or your firm's decision, as far as I'm aware.'

Surtees looked relieved. 'He isn't? Then that's just as well. I'm sorry the house never got off the ground, if you'll excuse the pun. It's a damn good design, you know, but it was getting to be a pain in the neck, more trouble than it was worth. I'm almost ready to leave for the south of France to oversee another house there. Hopefully with a less demanding client.'

'So we've been given to understand. But I'm afraid you may have to postpone your departure.'

'Postpone? What are you talking about? What's happened?'

Reardon told him that they were here because they were enquiring into the circumstances of Emilie Waring's death.

It was a moment before Surtees found himself able to speak. 'What? Emilie, dead? What happened? Oh God, I'm sorry, so sorry. She was . . . I liked her, and we got on so well. Was it an accident?' He stopped. The colour had drained from his face. 'There's something else, isn't there?' His glance travelled from one to the other and after a moment, perhaps remembering they were policemen, he said, quietly, 'How did she die?'

Reardon let Jago tell the simple facts while he studied Surtees' reaction. To say that he appeared shocked was an understatement, and when it came to where she was found he looked stunned.

Recovering himself, he said at last, 'I'm sorrier than I can say to hear all this, but what has it to do with me?'

'You don't deny you were very friendly with her?'

'I've said so, haven't I? Well, friendly up to a point. We used to fool around a bit, have a giggle together. But she could be, well, I'm sorry, but she could be irritating, too, you know . . . changing her mind. One day this, the next day that. In fact, I sometimes wondered if she wanted the new house at all or if she just wanted to get away from Templewood. Not much fun there – not for her, anyway. The girls didn't like her – all right, one of them didn't – and as for Waring . . . well, he's a judge, isn't he?' There was no doubting his opinion of Waring as nothing but a dry old stick.

'She left a note with her husband to say she was leaving him.'

'Leaving him? Leaving the judge? I don't believe it!'

'When she was found on the building site, at The Spinney, she had her suitcases with her. What do you imagine that might tell us, knowing how friendly you were, coupled with the letter her husband had received from your firm, saying you were going away, too?'

Astonishment set him back for several seconds, then as realization took hold, he flushed to the roots of his hair, looking for all the world like a guilty schoolboy . . . No, Reardon corrected himself. It wasn't guilt, it was embarrassment. Rex Surtees seemed more put out at being thought to have planned to run away with Emilie Waring than he was afraid of being accused of her murder.

'Where were you on Thursday night, Mr Surtees?'

'Me? Thursday? Well, I was at home, I suppose. Yes, yes, I was.'

'Anyone with you, to prove that?'

'I live alone. I was actually getting my things together, preparing for going over to France.'

'It's not much more than half an hour's drive to Temple Atwode.'

'That's true, but I don't have a car any more. I won't be needing it in the foreseeable future, so I sold it, only a few days ago, as it happens. I'll buy another one when I get home from France.'

'You'll have the name of the garage you sold it to?' Jago asked.

Surtees' eyes flickered. 'I didn't sell it to a garage. I sold it to a friend.'

Jago waited, pencil poised.

'You're going to check up on me!' Pointing a finger at the notebook, Surtees gave every show of indignant outrage, but not enough, when he saw Jago was serious, to stop him giving the name of the man who had purchased the car. 'Ewan McAllister,' he said grudgingly. 'But you'll be lucky if you catch him. He and his wife are off in the car to the Scottish Highlands any time now to visit her mother. And look here, I'm getting rather fed up with this! I've told you how things were. Are you suggesting I had a reason for killing a nice woman like Emilie? For killing anyone, if it comes to that?'

No reason, perhaps, Jago remarked to Reardon as they prepared to drive back, except a passing notion that Surtees might have given Emilie the wrong impression, leading her to believe, rightly or wrongly, that he was in love with her. 'But no, he wouldn't be, would he?'

'No,' Reardon said after a moment, 'I don't think he would.'

'All the same, she mightn't have believed him,' Jago suggested tentatively, 'and taken the decision into her own hands, decided to pack her bags and persuade him to let her join him when he went to France.'

True enough. Emilie, for all they knew, might have been the sort of easily persuadable woman who could convince herself of anything.

'She could have telephoned him to meet her at The Spinney,' Jago persisted. 'All right, it's a stretch, I know, but there was something he was keeping back.'

Reardon hadn't particularly liked the man. There was more than a touch of complacency about him, and he felt the same sense as Jago did of something being withheld. He threw out a suggestion of his own. 'He could have borrowed his car back again from his friend on Thursday.'

'You think so?' It was Jago's turn to be sceptical, but he nodded and promised to see it was checked as soon as possible.

'We can do better than that. You got this McAllister's details, didn't you? It's a long shot, but while we are in the area we'll chance it that he isn't already halfway to the Highlands, and do the checking now.'

They drove to the address they'd been given, a semi-detached house in the Fallings Park area, but it seemed the information Surtees had given them had been correct. As they waited for a reply to their knock, the next-door neighbour came out from behind her twitching curtains and told them the McAllisters had left for Scotland that morning.

'And what else did you get from the nosy neighbour?' Reardon asked as they drove off. While he had been returning to the car, Jago had hung back to say something else to the woman.

Jago's wide smile made him look like a schoolboy who had taken the wind out of his master's sails by coming up with the right answer. 'She may be nosy, but the McAllisters trust her. As well as a key for emergencies, I thought they might have left the mother's address with her – and they have. It's in Fort William.'

'Reckon the police up there speak English yet, so far over the border?'

Jago grinned again. 'I'll find out soon enough when I get on to them.'

SIXTEEN

Sam arrived at The Shire first that night and was sitting in a corner of the bar with a pint of Brew XI ready for Jago when he should walk in.

Folbury's only hotel had undergone alterations and reconstruction since he was last here and was now well on the way to becoming upmarket. Just at that moment it was noisy as a zoo at feeding time. The town worthies were gathering in a space created off the main reception area, the men in best suits, the women in long frocks, bare-armed, sporting all the jewellery they could lay their hands on. Some civic function or other it must be, some firm or club's annual dinner. Waitresses were circulating with trays of drinks and canapés; the manager hovered, making sure things went smoothly, and a haze of cigar smoke, perfume and alcohol drifted across to where Sam sat waiting.

The Shire probably wasn't the best choice for a meeting, but it was better than a more intimate, cosy pub where they might easily be overheard. It didn't matter – on this particular evening they wouldn't have been overheard anyway, just supposing anyone else might be interested in what they were saying. Even the hired pianist, doing his best with selections from *Anything Goes*, was not having much chance against the volume of noise being generated from the assembled dinner guests.

When he saw Jago standing in the doorway, Sam stood up and waved until he was spotted. Jago made his way over and, almost before he sat down, began to make his apologies for what might have seemed a brush-off at their earlier encounter outside Templewood.

Sam waved them aside. Sophy had soon made Jago's reluctance to talk in front of his boss clear enough when she'd explained the reason why the police were at Templewood. Sam had understood his erstwhile boon companion's aversion to poking his nose into the intimate details of his, Sam's, family . . . having to ask about Emilie's relationship with Pa, for God's sake! Questions about Emilie, now dead.

Embarrassing for him, to say the least. But he was a policeman after all. What interested Sam more was why Jago, whom he'd understood was based in London, was here in Folbury at all.

'Long story,' Jago told him, neatly turning the question by adding, with a searching look at him, 'I thought you were supposed to be in Berlin?' He had sensed a difference in Sam immediately, something etched on his face, the look behind his eyes, unreadable at the moment.

'Even longer story, I suspect,' Sam answered. In the event, however, it didn't take him long to loosen up. 'OK, Tom. Pin your ears back. Though I don't reckon it's going to be that much of a surprise to you, Berlin and all that.'

That at least turned out to be true. Curiosity about the political situation in Europe was, as Jago knew, partly what had induced Sam to take the job in Berlin when it had been offered in the first place. He listened carefully as his friend rapidly repeated the story he'd already told Sophy, about that evening when he found Fraulein Keppel had disappeared.

At last Sam stopped to draw breath and to take a pull of his beer. He looked round then, as if suddenly realizing how quiet it had grown. The conversational hubbub in the background had died away; the guests for whatever function it was had been summoned for their dinner, the pianist had packed up and gone home. So intent on his story, Sam hadn't noticed how loud his voice sounded in the new silence – but this wasn't Germany, where what he was saying would almost certainly have been overheard and reported to those in authority. There was no one else around except the man behind the bar, too busy polishing glasses to be interested. All the same, he now lowered his voice. 'Another pint, Tom?'

'I'll get them.' Jago went to the bar and came back in a few minutes with their beers and two packets of Smith's crisps. Sam raised his glass. 'Mud in your eye!'

Sam began again. After Fraulein Keppel, the realities of what it meant to live in a Germany ruled by the Nazis had become impossible for him to ignore. The incident had opened his eyes, but an inner warning not to get involved had still held him back from acknowledging that he himself might have obligations to hold out a helping hand to those suffering such injustices. Trying to ignore those letters from home, he had shut his eyes and ears and carried on with what had become his normal life. But something had to change, and it did.

He had previously met and immediately become good friends with a man named Max Loehmann, a journalist working for the liberal newspaper *Berliner Tageblatt*, familiarly known as the BT. Max was in his late thirties, witty, amusing and certainly more cynical than Sam's fellow workers at the bank. He led a slightly secretive existence: as a journalist his contacts were numerous and varied, embracing people in all walks of life, but he gave little away, except that his brand of cynicism underlined what Sam now knew to be the truth behind the propaganda continually put out by the Nazis.

And it was Max, too, who introduced him to other aspects of life in Berlin other than beer cellars and nightclubs. He lived with his younger, widowed sister, Rosa, and her two little boys, showing them tenderness and concern, trying to make up for their dead father. Sam became a frequent visitor to their home. He had been earmarking money for moving to another apartment after Fraulein Keppel's disappearance, not being able to stomach the suspicion that it had been confiscated from its previous, almost certainly Jewish, owners before being sold to the bank he worked for. Instead, he splashed out his entire savings and bought the chunky little Opel, second-hand. At weekends, he and Max would drive out into the countryside, to the pine-scented forests and lakes around Berlin, picnicking and taking walks, excursions in which Rosa and the two little boys, Jakob and Dieter, were included more often than not. Jago couldn't help noticing how Sam's eyes lit up when he talked about them, and about Rosa, her courage and fortitude and the way she was coping without a husband.

In addition to these family picnics, Sam and Max visited museums, theatres and art galleries together, and once the Staatsoper where they heard Wagner's *Lohengrin*, one of the few operas to have the Ministry of Public Enlightenment and Propaganda's seal of approval.

'You appreciate good music, yes?' Max enquired after the

performance. Sam, who had inherited his mother's love of it, said he did. The next week Max announced he had obtained invitations to a musical soirée to be held that Sunday afternoon, when a noted ensemble had been engaged to entertain a dozen or so selected friends.

The venue turned out to be the home of a cultured, middle-aged university professor of music and his wife. It was a luxurious and tastefully furnished house in one of the quiet, residential parts of Berlin, with a spacious music room overlooking a serene and beautiful garden. The music initially performed was the usual fare: Schumann, Bach, Schubert, but after the Trout Quintet and an interval for refreshments came an unprogrammed piece.

Experiencing for the first time Arnold Schoenberg's Third Quartet, music until then unfamiliar to him, was a revelation to Sam – atonal, haunting and somewhat disturbing. But even as he joined the appreciative applause of the discriminating audience, he knew everyone there was playing a risky game – the musicians daring to perform the music, their hosts and Max himself. 'Out of favour, Schoenberg, you see?' Sam said now to Jago. 'Along with Mahler, Mendelssohn . . . to name but two.'

Jago tore open his crisp packet, dug out and unscrewed the twist of blue paper and sprinkled salt over the contents, then shook the bag. 'Because they're Jewish.'

'Yes.' As a Jew, Schoenberg – this exciting, modern composer – was deemed 'degenerate', the Nazis' favourite word, and proscribed by them. Along with other musicians, writers and artists, alive or dead, who didn't conform to the required stereotype, who were dismissed from their posts, their homes confiscated, the art they created destroyed, the books they wrote burned. What would his little sister, Sophy, who herself had dreams of becoming a writer, have had to say about that?

By that time, Sam had no illusions left about how dangerous it was to be known in Germany as an 'undesirable', which was to say being either physically or mentally disabled, a gypsy, homosexual, a communist or a Slav. But above all, being born a Jew.

'Max kept quiet about his origins,' he went on. For one thing, his position on the *BT* wasn't by any means totally secure. He was too radical by far, his articles and his views were sometimes too outspoken, even for such a liberal paper, which in any case was already in disfavour for its criticism of the Nazis. 'You had to be there to know what it was like.'

Sam closed his eyes briefly, seeing again the blatant swastikas festooning every building; the parades of goose-stepping men and youths; the stiffly raised right arm salute and the constant 'Heil Hitlers' which must accompany every exchange between people to avoid suspicion.

'Why didn't you chuck it in and come home before now?'

'I wanted to, believe me, I wanted to. But I couldn't. What it was ... . well, I'd been getting letters from home that I couldn't ignore any longer but' – he hesitated – 'there were other reasons why I had to stay on.'

So that was it: Sam's ever-active conscience that wouldn't leave him alone, even though it might be dangerous for him. But there was more to it, that Sam didn't yet want to talk about – with no prizes for guessing it was something to do with that man Loehmann's sister, Rosa, either.

PART THREE

SEVENTEEN

Reardon found Jago waiting to grab him when he reached Market Street the following morning. 'A word, sir?'

'In my office, then.'

Jago gave three inward cheers as he spotted the tray full of mugs which was just arriving, borne in the hands of DC Jeavons, the newest addition to Folbury's CID. He picked up the fearful-looking one that could only be Reardon's. It hadn't taken him long to suss out that the chief was at his best with a large mug of the tarry liquid he called tea. He took a mug for himself and followed the DCI into the cramped glassed-in cubicle that passed for his office and set the mugs on a corner of the desk.

Reardon signalled to him to find some space to sit, and he finally found it among the overspill of papers on the already cluttered windowsill. As an office, the place was a joke. Long since outgrown its purposes, the whole police station, attached as it was to the old Victorian town hall, was scheduled for reconstruction. Discussed endlessly, but never materializing – allegedly due to lack of funds – only the promise remained, like the smile on the face of the Cheshire Cat. By now, it had become an accepted fact of life. No one believed in miracles.

Reardon drank his tea while Jago reported what Sam had told him of all that had happened since he'd gone to work in Germany, ending with that concert and what he'd learnt there, which had finally awakened Sam to the fact that he couldn't ignore those appeals from Sir Julius Malpas (backed up by Emilie) any longer.

These letters were not confined to family matters like those from his sisters. They had been concerned with those Jewish families who were trying to leave Germany and find safety in another country, even though it meant selling everything they possessed, leaving their homeland and all they loved. The procedure was fraught with uncertainty, delays and frustrations, impossible waits that could take weeks, months, even years. It was a two-way process, involving sponsorship by those in the host countries willing to take them, and only made possible by the untiring efforts of Sir Julius and other like-minded people.

'And Emilie was helping to do this, of course, not sorting library books,' Reardon said.

'You don't sound surprised.'

'It follows. Sir Julius is a charitable man. He's well respected for it around here. Known to work on all those Jewish refugee committees and so on.'

'Yes,' Jago said, 'but there's something else. Emilie also wrote to Sam that she had a worrying decision to make about someone or something she'd come across. Not specified. Something damaging to do with that business, you think?'

Reardon considered. 'I dare say she must have handled a lot of sensitive information, family stuff that someone might not have wanted to be made public. But important enough to warrant killing her? We'd better talk to Sir Julius today, after we've been to Templewood. I want to catch Judge Waring before he sets off for the day.' He didn't say why.

This time he elected to do the driving himself. 'I'll drop you off at the village, Sergeant. See if you can catch anyone PC Shay didn't find at home yesterday.'

Jago agreed amiably, not offended at his demotion to door-stepping. After any serious incident, early contact needed to be made with anyone who might have information, however trivial it might seem, before memory faded, or played its tricks, and already too much time had passed since Thursday, the last time Emilie Waring had been seen.

Yesterday's overcast skies had given way to a fitful day, but the rain was holding off as they started out and a burst of sunshine lit their approach to Temple Atwode.

There was no more sign of life in the hamlet than when they'd first passed through, apart from a line of nappies pegged out behind one of the cottages, and Jago was no luckier than Shay had been at catching those who hadn't been at home the day before. They were at work, he was told by the harassed young mother at the house where the nappies hung out, and she knew nothing. Thursday? She'd had her hands full all day, and although she'd been up half the night with the little one, poor mite, she wouldn't have heard anything above the screams of a teething baby.

Out of luck, Jago left the houses behind. As he set off on the short distance to join the chief inspector at Templewood, the surrounding silence was disrupted by the noise of a vehicle approaching at some speed from that direction. The red, open-topped sports car with a long nose, sunlight setting the glass of its headlamps glittering, slowed hardly at all as it came nearer. Jago hastily moved to the road edge. As the car drew alongside, he saw the four people in it: a man and a girl in the back, her abundant dark hair blowing all around her face, both of them laughing. The driver had his elbow jutting out, but he kept his eyes ahead, only his aristocratic, beaky profile visible. As they whooshed past, the passenger next to him in the front seat turned and waved a hand. Blowing wildly behind Gizi Waring was the long scarf wound around her neck, worn in the identical way her stepmother had been wearing hers when she was killed.

Jago stared after the disappearing car while wafting its exhaust fumes away. Was she totally insensitive? Unthinking, or perhaps simply defiant?

He was still thinking of her as he walked up Templewood's drive, and didn't immediately notice the man on the bench by the entrance to the kitchen garden. When he did, he saw it was the younger Garbutt, and that he was in a towering rage. Hands dug deep into his pockets, his legs stretched out in front of him, he was grinding the heel of his boot deep into the gravel, and by the expression on his face he was probably grinding his teeth just as ferociously. When he saw Jago, he jumped up, turned his back and in two strides was heading through the kitchen garden gate towards the bothy.

Jago continued on to the front door and rang the bell. While he was waiting for an answer, he heard the sound of a motorbike starting up, ripping down to the bothy's entrance and roaring off into the distance. Martin, going in the opposite direction to the one the driver of the sports car had been taking.

Reardon was talking to Judge Waring and his younger daughter, Sophy, when Jago was shown into the large living room. The judge was looking pale and strained but otherwise as immaculately turned out as a judge should be, ready for departure, his briefcase tucked under his arm. Prepared, as Reardon had predicted, to honour whatever his commitments were that day.

The DCI nodded to Jago and carried on with what he'd been telling the judge: that they had seen Surtees, and that he'd denied any suggestion of he and Mrs Waring being anything but friends. 'He says he'd told Mrs Waring he was off to France at any time on another commission, and he ridiculed the idea of them going away together.'

'Did you expect anything else?' asked the judge. He gave a pointed glance at the clock on the mantelpiece, but Reardon wasn't ready to let him go just yet.

'We've almost finished speaking to everyone your wife appeared to have been in contact with recently, but so far we haven't been able to discover anything which might approach a motive for what's happened to her.'

'That would come as no surprise to anyone who knew her. She led a quiet life, no question of enemies. She wasn't,' he said flatly, 'the sort of person to make them.'

He wanted her to be seen as a conventional wife, leading the conventional existence of a well-to-do country lady. Which to all intents and purposes was just what she seemed to have been. But that didn't define in any way who Emilie Waring was.

'What about her friends?' he had asked her stepdaughters when they had first spoken.

'I don't think she had any,' Sophy had replied and then flushed with embarrassment. 'Oh, goodness, that sounds . . . What I mean is, she was friendly with everyone, but there was no one special, you know.'

It was obviously time, as Ellen had suggested, to start digging into those years before she and the judge had first met, and to speak to Miss Oates, the lady to whom she had been companion.

Here at least Judge Waring's knowledge of his wife's previous circumstances was not so limited. He could, and did, provide the address in the Birmingham suburb of Harborne where she had lived.

'I don't think Miss Oates lives there any more,' Sophy said. 'But I don't know where she is now.'

'Emilie wouldn't have lost touch – she was very fond of her, and rightly so. She was a nice woman. The new address will be in her diary.'

'We haven't found her diary, sir,' Jago said. 'She might have had it with her, in her handbag, but that hasn't turned up yet, either.' The search had revealed neither, in her snug or her bedroom. A nasty suspicion remained that the diary, at least, was part of that sad heap of grey ash in the fireplace of her snug.

'The address should be in the Family Book,' Sophy said. It was where all the addresses and telephone numbers were kept. 'For Christmas cards and so on, you know.'

'Show the gentlemen the book, Sophy, will you?' Her father was already on his way to the door.

'One other thing before you go, sir,' Reardon said, as Sophy, followed by Jago, left the room. 'We've established the family were away from here on Thursday night. Just for the record, where were you all staying?'

Waring bent a long, steady look on him. 'My daughters were with Lady Malpas, at the Malpas townhouse in London. And I slept at the Judges' Lodging in Worcester, as I'm accustomed to do during the Assizes.'

Reardon knew about the Judges' Lodging. Situated in the county town, it was a large, quiet house specially intended for the accommodation of lawyers and those who were presiding over the Assizes. The hearings took place over several days and the judges and their legal associates could relax in the evenings, at the end of each demanding and difficult day, enjoying comfortable beds, well-cooked meals, excellent wine, and no doubt erudite and interesting conversations with their fellow lawyers.

The judge couldn't fail to know what Reardon was getting at. It wasn't often a man in his position came under such scrutiny, but he retained his distant courtesy and didn't bat an eyelid as he explained further. 'Several of us stayed up talking until late, after midnight it must have been. Breakfast was at eight,' he added. *And I didn't get up during the night and drive back here to Templewood to dispose of my wife.*

To which Reardon answered in his own mind: *Unless you already knew of your wife's intention to leave you – or suspected it. And knew where to find her, to look for her on that building site . . .*

The husband was inevitably the prime suspect in cases like this one, and Judge Waring owned and drove the suave, dark-green, well-polished Armstrong-Siddeley presently standing waiting outside, a smoothly fast and reliable car, which would have covered the miles to Templewood in no time. It was possible, but the odds, Reardon felt, were so against such an unlikely scenario it was hardly worth considering. Though he would never dismiss any possibility.

Before allowing the now all-too-impatient judge to escape, he asked where he might find the young fellow Alexei. Unfinished business there. The boy had sloped off before he'd told everything he knew, Reardon was sure.

'He'll be with his tutor. No doubt they've already started work.'

Why the private tutor? Reardon had wondered. The housekeeper, Maitland, had said Alexei had been a pupil at Westingbury, the public school about twenty miles away, until recently. 'No school?' he asked now.

Waring regarded him thoughtfully before answering. 'Alexei doesn't conform easily,' he said at last. 'He is very much an individual, and one-to-one tuition suits him better.'

He hadn't fitted in there, then, at Westingbury, any more than he seemed to do here. The boy appeared to occupy an odd position in the household, neither fish nor fowl. Reardon felt sorry for him, but equally sorry for his tutor. Alexei was sixteen, reputedly clever beyond his years, and Reardon thought it entirely possible from what he'd seen of him that he would be capable of running rings around a chap like Catchpole, a young man probably only too easy to be bamboozled.

Jago had followed Sophy into the large square entrance hall, where the telephone stood on a dark oak table. Opening a drawer, she pulled out a thick book, bound in rubbed leather, the yellowed pages indicating its age. 'Oates, Oates . . . here we are.'

The name Miss Edith Oates was there, with the Harborne address the judge had remembered crossed out and another substituted.

'Lapperley? Where's that?'

'Over towards Kidderminster, I think.'

'A *farm*?'

She shrugged and held out her hand for the return of the book. Their hands touched as he passed it over, and their eyes met.

She made an obvious effort not to pull away too quickly, but her colour betrayed her. She'd taken off the glasses she'd donned when searching through the address book, and now pulled them out of her pocket and put them on again. He leant against the wall, smiling, his arms folded. 'Sit down and give me a minute, if you will.' He gestured to the oak settle with a red, padded cushion running along its seat. 'I'd like to talk to you about Martin Garbutt. Can't talk to his grandad; he's only going to stick up for him.'

'Why should Martin need anyone to stick up for him?' she asked, instantly on the defensive. 'He's done nothing wrong.' But she sat down, and he seated himself at the far end of the settle, twisting round to face her.

'Bad choice of words, I'm sorry. I take it you get on with Martin pretty much then, you and your sister?'

'Well, we've known him all our lives.'

'Then you must know he's a bad lot.'

The colour rose in her face again and her chin went up. 'That rather depends on your definition of "bad lot", doesn't it? I hope you're not suggesting he'd anything to do with what happened to my stepmother? Because if you are . . .'

She half rose from her seat, but Jago held up an apologetic hand. 'Not doing very well, am I? Let's start again.'

She hesitated, then sat back and said straightaway, 'What Martin's done, in the past, what he believes . . . it's all politics, you know. His trouble is that he thinks anyone who isn't downtrodden, or exploited, or oppressed, can't understand anything. He's as stubborn as a mule over what he thinks is right, but he's *not* bad . . . and anyway, what's all that got to do with Emilie? You really can't be suspecting Martin!'

Jago thought that only her defence of Garbutt was stopping Sophy from running away from him, and as he had a strong desire to keep her there as long as possible, he risked forcing the issue. 'Your sister believes that, too?' he asked, not forgetting the sight of Martin Garbutt, less than half an hour ago, furiously digging his heels into the gravel and then roaring away on his motorbike, minutes after the red sports car with Gizi Waring in it must have left Templewood.

'Well, of course she does.'

'You told us you've known him all your life, you all grew up as playmates, you and your brother and sister, Martin and his cousin Prue, your maid. But he's out of your sister's league now, is that it?'

Almost before he'd said it, he was kicking himself. Damn! The apology was on his lips, but she didn't look offended. She was simply staring at him, with one of those clear-eyed, watchful looks of hers.

'You've no idea, have you?' she said at last. 'It's not Gizi, it's him. He thinks everyone must be looking down on him, especially Gizi nowadays, which is absolute rot, but he just won't see it, and that's just stupid because he knows she used to agree with almost everything he believes in, until . . .' She stopped, biting her lip. 'Well, anyway, it's no good, she's got that slithy tove chum of Toby Shefford's now . . . and you needn't laugh. That's a perfectly good description.'

'I'm not laughing,' he said, controlling the impulse. 'Something like lizards, something like corkscrews. Isn't that what Humpty Dumpty said they were?'

'Either will do for Fitz, as far as I'm concerned.' She was the one who was trying not to smile now.

He raised an eyebrow. 'So, who is he, this Fitz? Apart from not being a favourite of yours?'

'Gerald FitzAlban, currently my sister's obsession. Him and his sports car, and his . . .' She took a deep breath. 'No, I shouldn't . . .'

If she was referring to the chap he'd seen driving the red Lagonda, he thought she probably should. If only from the brief glimpse he'd had of the man's arrogant profile, never mind that he'd nearly run him down.

'I'm sorry,' she said as he stood up to go. 'It's just that he makes my skin crawl.'

But she wasn't sorry. There *was* something reptilian about Fitz, although she ought to have slapped Sergeant Jago's face for laughing at the way she'd put it. Instead, she found herself smiling at the closed door when he'd left, unable to help herself.

It wasn't every man who'd have admitted to knowing anything about Humpty Dumpty.

* * *

Reardon had never heard of Lapperley, where Miss Oates lived, the old lady Emilie had worked for, he said when he and Jago caught up with each other again. 'But you'd better cut along there and have a word with the lady.'

Why me? Jago managed not to say out loud.

'More in your line than mine, I suspect. I believe I'll walk over to Falquonroy and get the lie of the land as I go. Never does any harm.' He said nothing more except that he'd try to find the boy again before he set off. 'If I can locate him. No one seems to know where he is.'

'Well, the maid is in the garden, hanging out the clothes. Over there. Have you asked her?'

Prue had in fact been taking the washing in, not hanging it out, piling sheets into an overflowing laundry basket. She'd now set it to one side and was standing, hands on hips, talking to a strapping young fellow with flaming ginger hair. She was a tall girl herself, five foot nine or ten at a guess, and well made with it, but the young chap overtopped her by half a head. They were standing near the woodshed, in front of which was a heap of logs, some of them already sawn and split. They appeared to be having the sort of animated conversation which involved a good deal of head tossing on Prue's part, while he leant negligently against the shed, arms folded.

At the same moment as she turned to pick up the basket, he unfolded his arms and leant forward to pull her towards him. She was quicker, and pushed him away with one hand flat on his chest. Big as he was, he rocked slightly.

Laughing, she picked up the heavy basket and flounced away with it, leaving the young chap looking after her with a grin on his face. Her cheeks were flushed, and her eyes sparkled as she came level with the two detectives.

'Morning, Prue,' Reardon said.

'Oh, hello.'

'Who's that?' Jago asked, nodding towards the ginger-haired man, now packing up his work.

'Him? Oh, that's only Charlie Cribb.'

'Works here, does he?'

'On and off. He's Sir Julius's chauffeur, comes over from Falquonroy to do the odd jobs here two or three times a week.'

'Chauffeur?' The young chap looked more like a prize fighter with his heavy shoulders, big blunt features and a nose that had been broken at some time.

'Yes, but he comes here to see to the logs for the fires, looks after the boiler and that.'

'Sounds convenient,' Jago remarked.

'He wouldn't be here if it wasn't.'

'Spare-time job?'

She threw him an old-fashioned look, then adjusted the basket on her hip. 'Yes, well, he's a motor mechanic really, saving up, hoping to start on his own, so he's not fussy about what he does for a bit extra. There's an arrangement for him to come down here when Sir Julius doesn't need him. He's a good worker, even if he can be a dozy article at times. Now, if you'll excuse me, it looks like rain again and we've only just got these dry.' She swung off with her basket towards the kitchen.

'All right then, Jago,' Reardon said, watching her go. 'I reckon it's under half an hour to Lapperley. Half an hour to talk to the lady, half an hour back, that should more or less do it. I'll wait for you outside the gates at Falquonroy.'

EIGHTEEN

He hadn't been entirely fair, not bothering to explain, Reardon admitted to himself after Jago's departure. But part of the reason he'd packed him off to Lapperley to find out what he could was because he wanted to take another look at The Spinney. Alone. Places and things often took on a different aspect when seen once more, at another time, in a different light, especially without all the other people concerned in a murder enquiry mulling around, as they had been the last time he'd seen it.

Leaving the main gates of Templewood, he walked on until he came to the place where the hedge had been cut back to allow access for machinery during the building of the new house. Further along, the road that would lead him to Falquonroy's main gates curved then disappeared round a sharp bend.

Today's weather, uncertain from the beginning, had a sneaky breeze that was decidedly chilly, a reminder of how fickle May weather could be, a warning not to count on summer having arrived yet. He hoped the rain would keep off while he walked to Falquonroy.

Meanwhile, he stood in the clearing with PC Shay's words about the curse said to have been laid by the old witch, Mother Foxley, echoing in his ears. On a day like this, anyone susceptible to such naive superstitions might well be tempted to believe it.

All signs of police activity had now gone, everything cleared away, leaving no sign that so recently a woman had met here with violent death. Only the stakes and stringlines remained. Dr Fentiman had mentioned trees felled to make way for the proposed new house. It seemed now that it was destined to remain unbuilt, but in time trees would grow there again. The heavy scent of the bluebells beyond the stone wall had already replaced the smell of death. Nature, in the end, took little account of human interference.

He continued to stare silently at the site, frustrated for several different reasons. He contemplated again the impossibility of anyone creeping up on Emilie as she had waited here with her luggage, presumably for someone to come with a car and pick her up, then for that someone catching her unawares and tightening her scarf until she could no longer breathe. The trouble with that was that anyone approaching would have been visible – the site was open to the road, the trees in the Templewood orchard were widely spaced and those in the little copse over the high wall separating it from the adjoining property were slender birch, throwing only a gentle, dappled shade over the bluebells beneath.

Unprofitable thoughts. Interrupted when a black cat suddenly sprang up on to the wall. It stalked along the top with fastidious steps, sooty black from its ears to the tip of its held-high tail, and took up a position with its legs folded under it. Reardon was the last man to be unnerved by black cats and bad luck, witches' familiars, curses and old Mother Foxley. Naturally unsuperstitious, sceptical by nature, cynical by training, it was his job to be pragmatic about everything connected with a case he was investigating . . . and yet, he found himself almost looking around for broomsticks. Unnerved by the cat's unblinking yellow stare, and with the monotonous cooing of the wood pigeons getting on his nerves, he turned away.

'Hello-o!'

He turned to see the elegantly coiffured head of an elderly lady just visible above the wall of the copse beyond. 'I believe you're the police, aren't you? I'm Mrs Lychfield. Do come and have a cup of coffee with me, I'd like to talk to you,' she said in a pleasant, cultured voice, the sort that wasn't accustomed to refusal.

Reardon didn't hesitate. 'Thank you, Mrs Lychfield, I'll walk round.'

'No need. Hop over the wall,' she said, 'it'll be quicker.'

Nothing but her head could be seen. But just as the site sloped upwards from the road, so did the height of the wall decrease. He walked further up until he found a height that wouldn't embarrass him to hop over. He smiled to himself and vaulted it easily.

* * *

It was all very well for his new chief to say he guessed Jago would be good at talking to old ladies . . . Jago thought so himself, driving towards Lapperley. He'd always hit it off with his gran, and he liked it that old people said what they thought and saw no need to try and be clever – but this coming meeting wouldn't be just a matter of chit-chat over tea and seed cake. True, he was saved from having to tell this old lady that someone she'd been fond of had died; on this occasion Reardon had already prepared the way when he'd telephoned for an appointment. Miss Oates would already know Emilie Waring was dead. It would be Jago who'd have to break the worse news that she had been murdered.

Driving alone, he found himself thinking of Sophy Waring. Smiling at the memory of a pair of warm brown eyes and a smile that still lingered with him. So different from those other eyes . . .

They'd met at a cocktail affair given by a man he'd previously only encountered when they were both undergraduates at Oxford, someone he scarcely knew. They'd moved in different circles, and still did, and he couldn't remember now what had made him accept the casually thrown-out invitation when they'd met by chance, waiting at a central reservation to cross the road in Regent Street, a couple of years after he'd left Oxford.

The people downing cocktails at a house somewhere in Chelsea were outside the sphere of those he normally associated with: ex-public schoolboys, debs scarcely out of the schoolroom, sons and daughters of peers of the realm, or progeny of those newly rich since the war – all of them there for the sole purpose of becoming intoxicated by one means or another.

He'd had girlfriends before, of course, though not a string of them like Sam had, but this had been different. Falling in love had been a matter of minutes. Bewitched, magicked. As though, like Titania, he'd had the purple juice of love-in-idleness dropped on his eyelids and had fallen in love with the first person he'd set eyes on when he awoke – or in that case when he stepped through the door. Too many chattering people crowded into one small space, the waving glasses and wafted aroma of cigarette smoke, alcohol and expensive perfume, yet he'd seen her straight away in the far corner. And then she was there, standing in front of him.

'Hello,' she said, 'I'm Eloise.' Small, scarcely reaching to his shoulder, light as a feather, a cloud of fair hair, a heart-shaped face and green, unknowable eyes.

After that, he hardly knew what was in the glasses that were thrust into his hand that night, but he'd ended up drunk and so perhaps had she, which was why they'd finished the evening in bed . . . starting a relationship which had lasted for five months.

Those unreadable green eyes, her restlessness, unpredictable moods . . . He should have known, recognized the signs, but he'd been blinded and didn't see it. In any case, it was already too late by then.

He had left the car and was peering over a five-barred farm gate, cussing at what appeared to be an acre of thick mud and God knew what else that he must cross on foot in order to reach the farmhouse, when a woman came out of one of the barns.

She was tall and stringy, with straight grey hair cut short and held firmly in place with a strong kirby grip. She came over to him, hand thrust in the pockets of the shabby man's suit jacket she wore, her wellington boots sucking and squelching in the mud.

'Miss Oates?' he said without thinking.

'No. I'm Mrs Burridge, her sister. She's expecting you, if you're from the police.'

Of course this ruddy-cheeked woman wasn't the woman he'd come to see. Miss Oates was supposed to be some sort of invalid. He acknowledged that he was indeed from the police, gave his name and showed her his warrant card.

She wasn't impressed. 'You've come to the wrong gate,' she accused him. 'Go back to the road; the proper entrance is further along. There's a sign with the name on it. You can't miss it.'

Why did people say that, even though what you were looking for was invariably hidden – in this case by great clouds of golden blossom hanging on the tree which gave the farm its unlikely name: Laburnum Farm, so he supposed she might have had a point of sorts. The drive beyond had no such pretensions to beauty, being nothing more than a concrete strip leading straight as a die towards the grey, square-built farmhouse, no more appealing than the drive itself. At least it was clear of mud and farmyard muck.

When he halted the car near the door, he found Mrs Burridge had come through from the back of the farmhouse and was waiting for him, arms akimbo, wellingtons exchanged for a pair of flat, sensible one-bar shoes.

'Don't keep her long,' she ordered. 'She's had a big shock and she's not strong.'

Edith Oates' sitting room was a total surprise after the depressing exterior of the farmhouse. He found her sitting in an armchair by a small coal fire. She had surrounded herself with furniture that was old and graceful, with pretty china displayed against pale painted walls. She herself was small and plump, quietly dressed, pale-complexioned and grey-haired, the antithesis of her sister. Whatever her disability, it didn't seem to have aged her beyond her years, though he guessed she wasn't far off seventy.

'You must excuse me if I don't get up,' she said in a gentle voice, touching the walking stick propped against her chair. 'And please, do take a seat.' She had a nice smile, and her teeth were still good.

Drawn up in front of her was a small table laden with tea things. A romantic novel by Ethel M. Dell rested on her chair arm, the sort Emilie Waring had liked to read, and dozens more of them were neatly lined up in a bookcase against the wall.

Jago stepped on to a Turkey-patterned rug and cautiously made his way between a couple of delicate tables towards the chair directly opposite where she was sitting, before realizing it was a Victorian tapestry nursing chair which would leave him at a distinct disadvantage: too low, his knees up to his chin. Just in time, he veered towards a more upright chair with an ample Georgian seat.

Miss Oates leant forward and began to pour the tea. He wished it had been coffee, but it wasn't Reardon-strength, and she didn't drown it with milk. The biscuits were Garibaldi. Dead-fly biscuits, nearly as bad as seed cake. Squashed currants which got stuck between the teeth. He suspected Garibaldi would have hated them as much as he himself did. Out of politeness, he reached for one reluctantly.

'Tell me,' she said when they were settled. 'How is it you have been sent to tell me about poor Emilie?'

She had china-blue eyes, which gazed straight at him as she waited for an answer, and he didn't insult her by underestimating her intelligence. She knew a policeman wouldn't come to tell of the death of a friend unless there was some specific – and not very pleasant – reason. He braced himself and told her the facts, as gently as he could. She took it well. She had been pale to start with, and perhaps had gone even paler, but there were no tears. She simply leant back into her chair and closed her eyes, long enough for him to slide his biscuit back on to the plate with the others.

'Would you like me to pour you another cup of tea, Miss Oates?' he asked at last.

'That would be nice,' she answered, 'if it's still hot.'

It was, under its knitted crinoline-lady tea cosy, and she sipped gratefully. Soon a faint warmth returned to her cheeks, and he judged she was able to hear the details, or as many as he felt it appropriate to give.

'What could have led anyone to do such a wicked thing? To Emilie, of all people?' she asked in her faint, gentle voice when he'd finished.

The eternal dilemma for people who had lost a loved one. He shook his head. 'Would you mind if I asked you a few questions, Miss Oates?'

'About Emilie? No, of course not. But I must warn you . . .' She stopped and took a sip of her tea. 'Dear girl that she was, I really knew very little about her.'

'How long had you known her?'

'Let me see . . .' She thought for a while, then surprised him. He hadn't expected it to have been so long. 'She lived with us for eleven years, until she married Judge Waring, and that was about seven years ago, I believe. I haven't seen so much of her since then, though she did manage to come over and see me occasionally, on my birthday and so on.'

'How did she come to live with you?'

'Oh,' she replied, and a small smile came to her lips, 'that was one of what my brother used to call life's serendipities. It's quite a story; I don't want to bore you.'

'It's what I want to hear, Miss Oates. We have so little information on Mrs Waring before she married. Even her husband knows very little.'

She was unsurprised. 'That I can understand. It was always the way with Emilie. She never talked about her previous life. I used to wonder what it had been, to make her so . . . closed up.'

'But she was happy with you?'

'I believe I can say yes to that. When we first met, I saw a deeply unhappy young woman, careworn and even careless of her appearance, as if . . . well, let's just say that in time she gradually became a different person altogether. She first came to us when we lived in London, you know, my brother and I, and his daughter.' Her glance went towards the mantelpiece, to the two photographs prominently displayed there, one on either side of a little French carriage clock. In one was a middle-aged man with a lovely, laughing child of five or six on his knee; in the other the same child, grown up to be a beauty. A little frail, perhaps, but still beautiful.

'Lucy's mother died when she was born,' Miss Oates went on, 'so I lived with my brother, Wilfred, to help with the child. I wasn't altogether incapacitated then, but sometimes it was hard. Especially that day. It was in Kensington High Street. We had just come out of Derry & Toms, Lucy and I. She was about eight at that time but . . . don't get me wrong, she was a delightful child, but a little headstrong at times, you know, and impulsive. When we came out of the shop, she rushed away from me while I was putting up my umbrella and stepped straight out into the road without so much as looking. Straight under the wheels of a taxicab she would have been if Emilie hadn't just happened to be passing and grabbed her. They both fell back on to the pavement in a heap. Such a mess, with all the rain and everything! But luckily, no damage was done. Neither was hurt. I insisted on taking Emilie into the nearest teashop for a cup of tea. And that was more or less how it was. We talked, and I learnt that she was alone in London, presently looking for work. Lucy had taken to her, insisting she'd saved her life, and I took a chance. I asked her if she was free to come and live with us, to help me in the house a little, and with Lucy . . . the child had had rheumatic fever, you see, and it leaves complications. She was never very strong afterwards . . . and perhaps a little spoilt, because of it.' She sighed. 'Well, it was the best decision I ever made. Emilie and Lucy adored each other. She came as Lucy's nanny and was soon a family friend. She brought sunshine back into our lives, Sergeant.' Her voice was sad now.

He waited a few moments before he asked about Emilie's social life, her friends. 'Oh, she didn't go out much at all, though she did have one special friend . . . Nurse Rafferty, the district nurse. I was her patient and that's how they came to know one another. Nice woman, and I believe they still kept in touch. Both she and Emilie were so kind to us when . . . when Lucy . . . She died, you see.' Her voice faltered, but then steadied. 'After that my brother and I moved from London back to Harborne, where we'd spent our childhood. Emilie came with us. Wilfred was already retired from his solicitor's practice, and he couldn't bear to go on living in the same house. Lucy had been everything to him. He'd married late, and she was barely eighteen when she died, you know. But it was no good. They say you can't die of a broken heart, but he too was dead within a year.'

'I'm sorry.'

'I had Emilie. She stayed with me until she met Judge Waring when we were taking a little holiday in Scarborough. They wrote to each other for a while and then he began to visit and take her out. I could see how things were, and it worried me. You see, I knew I was becoming more and more dependent, and I feared the dear girl would feel she had obligations to stay with me. So, before he could ask her to be his wife, I told her I had made arrangements to come here to the farm, to live with my sister Henrietta. I couldn't let her sacrifice her chance of happiness.'

From what Jago had seen of Henrietta, in choosing to live with her it was Miss Oates who might have made the greater sacrifice.

NINETEEN

Lunch that same day at Templewood was early, what Maitland called a cold collation – a help-yourself affair as it always was on her Women's Institute afternoons, enabling her to get off in good time. Lex joined Sophy and found a letter waiting for him by his plate, an unusual enough event to make him hurriedly shove it into his pocket without opening it.

'The post's late today.' Sophy finished shelling a hard-boiled egg and gave him a speculative look. Girlfriend? No, she'd already taken a quick look at the envelope – not a feminine hand, more like a spider that had fallen into an inkwell and then trailed itself across the envelope.

The cousins were lunching alone. Pa had left after speaking to the police, and Gizi had gone off for lunch at the Thorpe-Bassetts with Dee and Toby.

'Where's Catchpole?' Sophy asked.

Lex had already polished off a bowl of leek soup and a bread roll. 'Dunno,' he replied now, through a mouthful of the mighty ham sandwich he'd made for himself. 'He went off somewhere. We've finished for the day.'

'Unusual for him to miss lunch.' The plump tutor liked his food and usually tucked into his meals with relish.

'I expect he's already had it.'

Sophy waited until he'd finished his sandwich before she said, 'Lex, you can't go on dodging the police forever, you know.'

'What do you mean, dodging?'

'Oh, come on, you know very well. They've been putting their big boots all over the place, looking for you again this morning. You'll have to face them some time.'

He said nothing, went to the sideboard and hesitated over the apple pie and the Dundee cake. Finally he came back with a slice of pie and a lump of Wensleydale to go with it. Still a growing lad, as Maitland said. Sixteen and six foot already, and gosh, good-looking enough to have girls swooning over him, if it weren't for that defiant look he always seemed to have lately. He'd always been hard to talk to, until a few months ago, when Sophy had started to think they might actually have begun to communicate, the two of them. And then had come that business when he'd left Westingbury, since when a clam had nothing on him.

The letter had made her decide to give it another go and try to talk with him. Post for Lex was almost unheard of, and when he'd seen the scrawled handwriting on the letter he'd almost leapt back as if it were a snake, then shoved it into his pocket without opening it.

A silence fell while he munched on. Sophy got up and poured herself coffee from the pot, then came back and resumed her seat.

'Why did they chuck you out of Westingbury?' she asked suddenly, not allowing herself to think what the consequence of asking such a question might be.

He didn't react as she might have expected. He flushed scarlet again, but said, calmly enough, 'They didn't chuck me out. I chucked myself.' An uncanny echo of what Sam had said about himself and his job.

'Why? What had you done?'

'Nothing.' He went on eating. 'That was the problem.'

'You mean you hadn't been working hard enough?' She was staggered. That was the last thing to be a problem to Lex; he'd been born clever and studious.

'Not your business, Sophy.'

It wasn't, but she was determined not to be put off. 'I'm sorry about Emilie,' she tried again. 'I know how fond—'

'Stop it, Sophy. I've told you, it's none of your business. And if you don't want that cake you've left, I'll have it.'

Lex's favourite spot, the place to go to if you didn't want to be disturbed, was that pool at the far end of the garden where the woods began. It was always peaceful and quiet. He sat beneath the tree near the edge of the pool, his knees drawn up, the still-unopened letter in his hand.

Even if it hadn't been for the atrocious handwriting, the spelling would have given the sender away. As it was, the letter might never have reached him at all. The address (apart from Templewood, written in laborious block capitals) was almost indecipherable, and when it came to his surname, Kyriakou, Scuddy had almost given up.

A letter from Scuddy – now there was a thing! Open it or throw it away unread? The latter was Lex's first inclination, but it seemed unfair when his former study mate had actually brought himself to *write a letter!* Besides, he owed him, didn't he?

Eventually he slit the envelope open with his thumb and, with a short laugh, began to try and make sense of the nearly unreadable missive.

Lord, Scuddy was dense – a good egg, top-hole in fact, but thick as a brick. Everybody knew that, but nobody cared because he was Captain of Games, a great left-arm bowler; he'd swum for Westingbury in the inter-schools swimming gala and was the best prop forward the school's First Eleven had had in years. An excellent all-rounder – unless it was anything involving the form of torture known as holding a pen or pencil. And yet he'd actually gone as far as to write a long (for him) letter!

Lex slowly deciphered the contents: Scuddy's arm and other injuries were now perfectly healed, he said. He wished Lex was back at Westingbury. The fellow who'd replaced him as his study mate was a blister. His feet smelled, and he farted all the time. Scuddy's spectacular fall and his short spell in hospital had resulted in nothing worse than you could get down on the rugger field after all. He was glad to be back at the old fortress. The nosh had been worse in the hospital than here, if possible, and the nurses could have stood in for prison warders. *Tomfool thing to do, leaving like that, old bean, my own fault for misjudging the jump, you know me, act first, think later.*

No word of recrimination for what had happened. Lex shoved the letter back into his pocket, coals of fire burning bright. He watched a dragonfly shimmering over the pond but saw only a narrow canyon between two buildings . . .

Opposite and below where they were sitting on the roof was the new school gym – a square, modern-style erection of one storey with a flat roof, chosen and paid for by an ex-pupil who'd made a fortune manufacturing the electric vacuum cleaners everyone must now have.

The school governors, suitably grateful, had seen no need to overdo it. The unfortunate construction, its style inconsistent with the Victorian gothic of the rest of Westingbury, had been squeezed tight up to the rear of the main school, out of sight, with only a few feet of space between the two, thus creating a narrow gully. Looking down from the chimney stacks, a favourite place for an illicit smoke, was a slightly dizzying prospect.

Lex and Scuddy had scrambled through attics and a skylight and were sitting on the slates with their backs against one of the tall brick chimneys. Scuddy tossed his fag end across to the gym with practised ease. The flat roof, a few feet away and two storeys down, had been an obvious target for the fag ends of many another delinquent before him. But so far no one had thought of jumping across.

'Dare you!' Lex said suddenly, hardly knowing why. You didn't make a dare with Scuddy without being sure you were up for it yourself. Never mind that; all at once he'd felt invincible.

'Oh, OK,' Scuddy agreed equably when it dawned on him what Lex meant. 'Both of us together?'

Together? Lex wasn't sure that was what he'd meant, but he laughed. 'Why not?'

They stood up, faced the gym and counted. 'One, two, *three*!'

Scuddy jumped. Lex didn't.

Why hadn't he? It wasn't cowardice, though he was sure everyone thought so, including the Head. Scuddy had landed safely, after all – if you counted suffering only a broken arm and bruised ribs as a safe landing. As safe as Lex had known it would be. Until he'd had that flash, that sudden insight, a millisecond before the pair of them had got to *three*. A flash in which he'd seen exactly what could easily happen and that he shouldn't have suggested it. It was just this whole thing of going against authority, simply because he could. Like walking out of the English exam after reading the infantile questions and deciding it was an insult to even expect him to bother answering. Like taking the day off to go for a long hike alone, 'forgetting' he was on the cricket team to play their rival school.

He recalled what his uncle had said about that. He also remembered Emilie's warning about jeopardizing his chances of Cambridge . . . of Greece . . . of ever finding his father. And what she had said about having to live with oneself and the consequences of what one had done.

It hadn't come to being sacked. For one thing, the Head didn't want to lose two of his star pupils, both of whom had already shown their mettle, one academically, the other a hero on the sports field. Strong measures would be taken against the two boys, of course, *pour encourager les autres.* Forsyte could wait until he was out of hospital and fit enough to face the music. As for Kyriakou . . .

Lex didn't give the Head time to dole out punishment. He swore that the whole idea had been his, admitted he'd lost his nerve, which wasn't true, simply an irresistible pressure, forcing him back. He wrote to his uncle, begging him to take him away from Westingbury.

It had taken him three months to admit to himself that his leaving had solved nothing. His uncle, dammit, was right. *And Emilie, too.* Learning to live with the consequences of what you'd done wasn't gained by turning your back on the problem.

Mrs Lychfield was waiting for Reardon after his vault over the wall. That she'd known he was from the police didn't surprise him. It was a fact of life that something about him made people recognize him as a policeman without a second glance, but he'd grown too used to that for it to bother him. Nevertheless, he'd showed his warrant card and introduced himself properly before they walked between the bluebells to the front door of the house he'd glimpsed between the tree trunks.

It couldn't have been a working farm for a long time. All signs of the unassuming grey stone house's previous existence as a farm had disappeared. Instead of a muddy, trampled yard and the vulgar stench of animal husbandry, where once barns and shippons must have stood, there was now a paved forecourt filled with the scent of roses. Mrs Lychfield's gloves and secateurs were on the ground where she had laid them when she had stopped in the act of deadheading.

'Lovely rose,' he remarked, thinking how Ellen would have appreciated the sight of golden yellow blooms climbing high against the old grey wall.

Mrs Lychfield beamed. 'Oh, isn't it? *Maigold.* Appropriate, isn't it? Always the first to flower. And such a heavenly scent. Do come in, Chief Inspector.'

Another woman of similar age appeared when they entered the house, and Mrs Lychfield asked for coffee. 'Or perhaps you'd rather have tea?'

The other woman had already disappeared, so he said coffee would be greatly appreciated. She led him through the wide, flagged hall into a room with a door standing open to the garden at the back. He thought how very like Templewood's sitting room this one was. There was actually another portrait of the judge's first wife hanging on the wall, but Isobel Waring had after all been this woman's daughter.

Armed with the background information he'd been supplied with, he knew Ursula Lychfield was a grandmother in her mid-seventies, but unlike so many other grannies, age had scarcely even begun to wither her. She was well dressed, as he guessed she always would be, even when gardening. Her hair was quite white but immaculately Marcel waved, and her eyes sparkled with lively intelligence.

The coffee was brought in and poured. 'Thank you, Agnes.' Agnes, a strong-faced woman who didn't smile easily, nodded and silently withdrew.

Mrs Lychfield had said she had something to say, but she didn't seem in any hurry to reveal what it was. She handed him a steaming cup. 'This is a terrible situation we are facing . . . If I can help in any way . . .'

'How well did you know Mrs Waring, and what did you think of her?' he asked, taking his cue for directness from her, at the same time wondering whether he should have said the *second* Mrs Waring. She might not have had all that much contact with daughter's replacement; perhaps she had even resented Emilie taking her place, so he was surprised when she said slowly, after a moment's consideration, 'I wouldn't say I knew her *well* – I don't think anyone did, not even Eliot – but what I did know of her, I liked. Very much indeed.'

He found himself rather glad to hear this. Such accolades hadn't actually been thick on the ground so far. 'It wasn't an easy position she found herself in, you know.' Mrs Lychfield replaced the delicate china cup on its saucer. She wore rings on many of her fingers, even when gardening, old diamonds and a heavy gold signet ring. 'Everyone loved my daughter; she was a very lovable person.' A shadow crossed her face. 'It's hard to take the place of someone like that, and Eliot . . . well, Emilie was a good wife to him, and I don't mean just as a hostess, a social asset. She was good for him in other ways.' She smiled a little. 'He can be rather stuffy, you know, though he wouldn't like to hear me say that, but she taught him to let his hair down on occasions.'

Like many older people, Mrs Lychfield spoke as though age gave her the right to opinions she might once have been more careful about expressing openly, though it was obvious she was fond of her son-in-law.

'You'd say she was a happy woman, then?'

She regarded him gravely as she placed her coffee cup down carefully. 'No. That's not how I saw her, not always. She had a smile that could light up a room, you know, but she could be . . . I'd almost say sad, on occasions. As if there was something never far from her mind, something that weighed heavily, though she never spoke of it.'

That was something no one else had picked up, or seen fit to pass on. 'I'm interested in anything that might have happened to her during the last week or so,' he said, while she leant over and refilled his cup. 'You'll have heard that her suitcases were found with her, I suppose?'

'Yes, indeed.' She hesitated. 'I don't think I'm breaking a confidence . . . I know I'm not, in fact. My son-in-law has told you, hasn't he, that she was intending to leave him? I find that very hard to believe.'

'Might something have upset her, to make her want to do that?'

She returned his watchful gaze, not saying anything for a long time. Then she asked abruptly, 'Where did you get that scar? Is it a war wound?'

He was taken aback, though he'd long since ceased to be embarrassed by references to the blemish which decorated his left cheek. 'I fell off a motorbike in France.'

Which was all anyone ever got in explanation of the incident when he had been a police dispatch rider in wartime France, and which had put him in hospital for months, earned him a medal and was the reason his face now looked as it did. The scar had been with him so long he had – almost – forgotten it, or so he told himself.

She nodded, as if approving, then reached out and touched his hand lightly. 'Forgive me. I let my tongue run before my discretion.' She added quietly, 'I lost my son in the war, you see, and I honour the people who fought in it.'

He was reminded that as well as a son, she had lost a husband and two daughters, the youngest being the mother of the boy Alexei, sorrow no one should be asked to endure.

She didn't let the moment linger. With another swift change of subject, she asked, 'Are you interested in gardening, Chief Inspector?'

'I'm a dab hand with a spade when necessary.'

She laughed.

'My wife's the gardener. She's making a new one out of the old one we inherited.'

'How delightful! You must bring her to see this one – we made it from the old farmyard. Do come and look.' As eager to demonstrate as any other ardent gardener, she sprang up and beckoned him into the small, charming garden outside where a venerable and crooked apple tree in full blossom bent over a scented spread of wallflowers. Seats here and there. Tulips, too, and forget-me-nots, fronting that pretty little copse which lay beyond.

He made admiring noises which she acknowledged with a gratified smile, and then she said suddenly, 'I have something I ought to tell you, though I'm really not sure . . .' She beckoned him to join her as she took a seat on one of the benches, bending forwards to tweak out by its roots an offending dandelion in a paving crack, which disobligingly snapped off. Tutting and tossing it away, she said, 'Well, the other morning, I wandered over to look at the bluebells – so lovely this year, aren't they? – and I heard Emilie's voice, coming from The Spinney. She appeared to be having some sort of argument with someone.'

'Did you see who—?'

'I'm afraid not,' she cut him off. 'They were standing directly beneath the wall, just where it's highest, so I couldn't tell who it was, you see. Without a ladder,' she added with a smile. 'But

I suppose it must have been the architect, Mr Surtees. Who else? They were always having arguments.'

'But not serious ones, I think?'

'This wasn't another silly squabble about that rather dreadful house,' she said, evidently not an admirer of the modern style.

'You heard what they were saying?'

'Not altogether, but his voice was raised, and I heard enough to . . .' She stopped, with slightly heightened colour. 'He called her . . . an interfering baggage.'

He guessed the epithet had been edited, however accustomed she was to being outspoken.

'What's more, he . . . well, he said she'd better stop, or he'd find some way of making her.'

'Are you sure it was Mr Surtees?' It certainly didn't accord with Surtees' own views of his relationship with Emilie.

'It must have been. He could be very arrogant, you know, about that house.'

He wondered if she was quite as certain as she sounded. He could also see, however, that she wouldn't be pressed further about the exchange she'd overheard and what it implied. She'd done her duty, now it was up to him.

'Thank you for your time, Mrs Lychfield,' he said, getting to his feet.

She rose too. 'I hope I haven't detained you too long, Chief Inspector.'

'Not at all, but I'm due to meet my sergeant at Falquonroy Park soon. A ten- or fifteen-minute walk, I suspect.'

'There's a shortcut through the woods. You don't need to walk all the way along the road. I'll show you.'

She walked part way down the drive with him to point out the path he should take. When he looked back as he turned through the gates, she had already reached for her gloves to tend the yellow climbing rose again.

Sure enough, as she had said, the barely detectable gap in the hedge on the opposite side of the road gave access to a path of sorts. Few people must come this way. Brambles clutched at Reardon's trouser legs, ground ivy threw trip wires over the barely discernible track and stinging nettles swayed either side to meet each other. An overpowering scent of wild garlic came from the wide swathes of starry white flowers stretching out either side.

He slipped and slithered and finally emerged in the shallow valley. The path towards Falquonroy sloped up the opposite hillside, not much different from the one he'd just come down. Annoyed to find himself hot and bothered, recalling that speculative look young Jago had thrown him outside Surtees' office when he'd spoken of his rugby-playing days, he drew a breath, then took the slope at a fair jog. He reached the top, dishevelled but no more than breathing hard. Trying to keep the grin off his face.

Jago was waiting, the car drawn up outside Falquonroy's tall, wrought-iron gates. Forbidding, but at present standing wide open, more a sign of demarcation than a barrier, they were flanked by stone piers supporting a huge pair of black marble falcons. Guardians of Falquonroy, sleek and poised, they were horribly realistic with their wings folded, ready for the swoop on their prey, curved beaks wicked and deadly. At the end of the drive, the house stretched out towards the seemingly endless, forested background.

Through the driving mirror Jago saw Reardon approaching, smoothing his hair, plucking bits off his trousers. Looking pleased with himself. 'Shortcut across the valley,' he offered as he slid into the passenger seat. 'So, anything interesting from the old lady, Miss Oates?'

'Nothing of any consequence, I'm afraid.' Jago's disappointment showed, but there hadn't been much she had to tell, after all, only the uneventful life Emilie had led before her marriage to Judge Waring. So uneventful Jago had begun to wonder if there was something he had missed.

Reardon had fared better, talking to *his* old lady. When Jago heard of the argument Mrs Lychfield had overheard, he thought he knew why Reardon was looking so chuffed: it felt to be the first thing they'd heard which might have any significance to Emilie's death, however obscure that might still yet be.

TWENTY

'Don't worry about Boo,' Dee told her mother airily. 'He only says it to get a laugh. I mean – Boo, in uniform, imagine! He's barely out of the nursery.' Boo was the same age as she was. 'Though actually everyone wants to be a Mosleyite. I might become one myself and drape a Union Jack around my shoulders. Silk, of course.'

'Dee,' said Lady Malpas, tweaking a slightly withered leaf which threatened to disfigure one of the otherwise perfect flowering plants she'd brought in from the conservatory. 'That young man Boo is a fool and I'm sorry he's a friend of yours. Please don't talk such nonsense.'

'But I just adore those uniforms! I—'

'Dee! You may think and do what you like when you're a married woman, although what Toby would say to all that I'm sure I don't care to imagine. Until then . . .'

'Oh, Toby wouldn't mind. He's too lazy to bother about things like that.'

Dee lay back on the cushioned sofa and extended a stockinged leg, the better to admire her newly varnished toenails showing scarlet through the flesh-coloured silk. 'Although,' she added rather wickedly, 'Toby would look frightfully good in a black shirt and jodhpurs, like Sir Oswald and his boys. *Très du jour!* Only he's far too busy playing games to join – especially with his fencing, and look what that's done for his knee! He'll never be a champ, like Sir Oswald. But then, Sir O's top hole at everything he does, isn't he?'

There was movement at the back of the room. Sir Julius, with some force, threw down the newspaper he'd been reading. He came to stand by the sofa. 'We'll have no talk of that man in this house, Devorah,' he said, scarcely raising his voice but with a severity that caused Dee to look uncertain for a moment. She knew her father tried to remember not to wave his hands about when he was excited, but mostly he forgot, and the rich aroma wafting from the cigar he was holding between his fingers, mingling with the heady perfume of her mother's Madonna lilies, made Dee's stomach give a little lurch. Her father rarely showed anger.

'Haven't you given a single thought to what he is, that man Mosley, or what he's doing?' he went on. 'To who we are?'

'Oh, you mean all that beastly rot about antisemitism? It's all lies, what people are saying about him, you know, and . . .'

Her voice trailed away. She thought of protesting further, but her father's face told her no. She hadn't feared her mother's criticism – what she, Dee, had just been saying was all flim-flam anyway, the sort of thing other girls said just to be thought daring, or outrageous, even if, like her, they didn't really mean it. She'd only been talking to fill the silence that seemed to be gripping everyone, ever since they'd heard the sickening news about poor Mrs Waring. Dee wasn't unnerved by much, but that was just too frightful to contemplate. Chatter about anything else, no matter what nonsense, was surely better than a silence that left them all to their own horrid thoughts about what had happened to her. But this side of her father alarmed her. She was afraid he was going to begin one of his lectures on how she should be proud of being Jewish, of the huge successes their people achieved in life, and how they were survivors in the world, despite their long, persecuted history. On and on.

'Rot, you call it?' he said. 'Just you wait until you hear what Sam Waring has to say when you see him later, my girl. You won't call it rot then.'

'*Sam?*' Dee's voice rose to a little scream. She'd always had a very soft spot indeed for her friends' big, handsome brother and had in fact once hoped . . . perhaps she still did, a little . . . 'What do you mean, see him later? Is he coming home from Berlin?'

'He's already here, and I think your other friends might be better off listening to what he has to say, too.' (He meant Toby, and also Fitz, she knew, to whom he'd taken a dislike, though they'd only just met. She was sometimes a bit afraid he wasn't too keen on Toby, either.) 'It might put those dangerous notions out of all of your heads.'

'Julius, please,' Lady Malpas warned, in her quiet way. His face had gone alarmingly red.

Dee knew her mother could always calm her father down and she saw him reining himself in with an effort now. 'Very well, Ruth, I'll say no more for the moment.' He gave Dee another stern look, then left them and went to resume his seat and his newspaper at the back of the room.

But the little exchange had left an atmosphere. Dee began to wish she hadn't started the conversation. Her father was always so touchy on the subject of their race, although he wasn't in any way *religious*. Couldn't he see that sort of thing didn't matter any longer to anyone, even to the old fogeys? Her father was so rich and successful that as a family they were accepted anywhere. It was true, her mind kept saying, that Sir Oswald was sometimes a little strong on the subject of successful Jewry, but . . .

Dee's butterfly mind skittered away from thinking through such difficult thoughts and turned to the lunch to which they'd been invited today – she, and Toby and Fitz, who were both staying on after the party. She felt suddenly pleased that she'd chosen to wear this delicious new outfit (scarlet poppies on a cream background, with a frilly jabot at the neck) rather than keep it for Monte next week.

Monte Carlo, the usual crowd, what a breeze! Then she remembered Toby didn't much like Monte, so perhaps Biarritz . . . there were the casinos there, too, which was what mattered to him. Her father would stump up for her, she was sure. Her parents, she thought with a sudden rush of affection, fusty as they were over certain things, were generous in the extreme when it came to providing spending money, parties, new clothes and other necessities of life.

The door opened. Bracewell, elderly and correct, and looking as slightly disapproving as his normally kind face would allow, announced, 'Some . . . gentlemen to see you, Sir Julius.'

The nearer the police car got to the house, the more evident it became that the additions and alterations inflicted upon the ancient edifice by time and previous generations, most of them with ambitions rather than taste, hadn't always added to its beauty and symmetry. Like the proverbial curate's egg, it was good in parts, particularly the creamy stone façade, impressively restored in the romantic, neo-Gothic style. But even that had been spoilt:

set back a little from the elegant frontage, part of the ancient house still remained, stretched out to one side, an incongruous oddity which the restoration hadn't yet caught up with. Moreover, behind the main front were glimpses of older, grey-slated roofs not in the best of condition, a crenellated tower, and even further back, the green spire of what might once have been a chapel.

The gravelled drive led straight down towards the house, then circled round a large parterre blazing with colour, before rejoining itself and thence to the back of the house. Barely had the car drawn up by the front door than the ginger-haired chauffeur who'd been talking to Prue earlier that morning at Templewood was there waving his arms.

'Sorry, sir, I'm afraid you can't leave your car here,' Jago was told as he wound the window down. 'I can park it round the back and fetch it for you when you need it.'

Rolling his eyes, Jago surrendered and followed Reardon up the stone steps. Another pair of black falcons stood at the foot of the steps, and a heavy knocker sounded like the knell of doom. After some time, the enormous oak double doors were opened by an elderly manservant. His face froze when their warrant cards were shown, but they were admitted into the entrance hall and asked to wait.

'Blimey!' Jago's head swivelled, taking in the vast and echoing space. Acres of polished marble stretched out towards a series of arches at the back. The walls everywhere were hung with gilded portraits, huge mirrors and the heads of victims of the chase; a very gracious, wide and shallow staircase divided itself before soaring up and disappearing into the ether.

They hadn't long to wait in these surroundings before someone was walking towards them.

Sir Julius Malpas was not an impressive figure – stockily built, his grizzled hair receding from a domed forehead – but his eyes were shrewd, his handshake firm, and he gave off an unmistakable authority. 'I've been expecting you,' he said, appraising them both quickly with a sharp look. 'Please, do come with me, where we can talk.'

This turned out to be a large and well-appointed drawing room. Handsome, but not overpowering in the way the grand entrance hall had been. Still big enough, though, for two chandeliers to hang from the high ceiling, its cornices elaborate. French windows opened on to a flagged terrace commanding a view of steps leading down to a wide lawn with blossom trees at the end, a fountain gently playing and tall urns of flowers, beyond which stretched the forest.

With all its size, the room felt comfortable enough. Possessions were scattered around and the smell of scented flowers mingled with the rich aroma of good cigars that lingered in the air. And a drift of Chanel No. 5 or some other expensive perfume from the young woman sitting on the sofa, surrounded by magazines.

Jago recognized her instantly as the back-seat passenger in the Lagonda which had nearly mown him down. A jolly-looking girl with a lot of dark hair, she had tidied herself after her wind-blown outing earlier that morning. Sir Julius introduced the two women as his wife and his daughter, Dee.

Lady Malpas waved them to seats and offered refreshments. They declined politely. She nodded, picked up a lacy piece of crochet work and lowered her eyes to it, with evident intention of leaving the talking to her husband.

'It's not every day we have the police here,' he began when they were seated. 'I'm afraid it's Emilie – Mrs Waring – you've come about? Yes, of course it is. Anything we can do to help in this sad business . . .'

News travelled fast, sad news faster. Half a mile of woodland and a pretty valley separated this household and Templewood, but it was already clear from what they had been told so far that the two families were as close as any semi-detached neighbours.

'It's almost impossible to believe . . . Emilie, dead?' Sir Julius shook his head sadly. 'And they said it was only a cold.'

'A cold, sir?'

'She was supposed to have been here with the rest of her family on Saturday for a dinner party we gave – our daughter's engagement celebration – but she cried off because they said she'd developed a cold.'

So, the Warings hadn't been prepared to let it be made public at that point that Emilie had (as they had then thought) absconded with her lover, and her absence had been passed off with a diplomatic lie. These friends here were visibly shocked over her death, but was it possible they actually didn't know yet that she had been murdered? The answer came when the young woman, Dee, gave a choked sound that might have been a sob. Her father reached out and patted her hand. 'It's almost impossible to believe,' he said, 'that someone should take that poor woman's life.'

To forestall questions he could see coming but wasn't in a position to answer yet, Reardon stepped in to begin with his own. 'How long had Mrs Waring worked for you, Sir Julius?'

'She didn't work *for* me, not in that sense. She was working *with* me, voluntarily. No compulsion on her at all. She heard from my wife that I could do with some assistance in matters I'm presently engaged with, and it was entirely her own idea to give me a hand. She came whenever she could spare the time, and I was very glad indeed of her help.'

Lady Malpas looked up from her crochet work and spoke unexpectedly. A matronly woman in good clothes, her grey hair pulled back into an unfashionable bun, she was a comfortable figure with a round, pleasant face and a sweet smile, which was at present wavering a little. There was no dabbing of a lace handkerchief, no tears, but her eyes were deeply sad. 'We have lost one of the dearest of friends in a most terrible way,' she said, 'and I hope and pray you'll catch and punish whoever could even have thought of doing such a monstrous thing.'

It was the most heartfelt tribute yet paid to Emilie – and all Reardon could think to do was to reassure her with platitudes about doing their best. He thought it wiser not to try. She had already lowered her eyes and returned to her work, and he turned back to her husband.

'When did you last see Mrs Waring, Sir Julius?'

'Let me see. It would have been . . . it was several days ago – yes, Wednesday. I wasn't here myself the following day. When she didn't come over on Friday, I simply assumed she must have had other commitments – she'd left a note about things she'd been hoping to complete but hadn't had time to do. Then we were told on Saturday she was feeling unwell and wouldn't be able to attend the dinner party.' He paused. 'I shall miss her and her help greatly, although as I've said, she only came here on a voluntary basis.'

'So we've been given to understand. Cataloguing, or sorting

out books in your library, I believe.' Reardon watched for Sir Julius's reaction.

'Is that what she said she was doing?'

'Not in so many words, perhaps, but it seems to have been what people assumed.'

Not giving anything away, Sir Julius said, 'She was more than happy to help, I assure you. Dedicated, in fact.'

He was a shrewd businessman, used to summing up situations and people, so 'dedicated' was probably a fair assessment. Reardon thought of the late nights Emilie had been said to keep, the number of letters she had written. Not all of them private correspondence, surely.

Sir Julius's next words broke into his thoughts, and almost as if he had followed the train of them, he asked abruptly if they had spoken to Sam Waring.

Jago looked up from his notes. 'He and I met last night for a drink, sir. We're old friends from university.' He chose his next words carefully because the way Sir Julius was looking at him made him wonder if perhaps Sam might have been indiscreet in saying even as much as he had. 'He told me,' he added cautiously, 'something of what you and his stepmother had been working on.'

'He did? Then I suggest we go into the library where we'd been working and take a look.'

Before they could move to do so, there was a token tap on the French windows and they were pushed open. Dee cried, 'Oh, there you are, darlings!' as two men stepped inside, whom Jago immediately recognized as being the other occupants of that red Lagonda.

Men of a very different stamp. The big chap in cricket shirt and flannel bags, presently leaning on a walking stick, was introduced as Toby Shefford, Miss Malpas's fiancé. Tall and broad-shouldered, looking rather bored and indifferent. Brawn and no brains, rugger forward if anyone was, intelligence not being the first quality they were noted for, Jago summed him up uncharitably.

And the other man . . . So this was the FitzAlban whose name was anathema to Sophy – the driver of that red sports car. He too was tall, but slim and fair-haired, handsome enough in an aristocratic, beaky-nosed way. Silk cravat and blazer, of course. Unlike his companion, he looked as though he'd never kicked a football in his life. Jago thought with amusement of what Sophy had called him. Despite the consciously charming smile, there *was* something cold-blooded and lizard-like about him, and as for corkscrews . . . he suspected those pale blue eyes could drill like gimlets.

'These gentlemen,' Dee was telling the newcomers, 'have come to talk to us about poor Mrs Waring.' Her big dark eyes filled again. Tears obviously came easily to her, but Jago thought they were genuine.

'You knew the lady as well?' Reardon asked the two men.

Both shook their heads.

'Sadly no,' FitzAlban said. 'We never met.'

'But *you* did, Toby,' Dee reminded her fiancé.

He turned a blank face to her.

'You remember – Mama's birthday, and those pictures she brought her as a present?' She waved a hand towards a somewhat shady corner where four small charcoal drawings were hanging. 'You said what a nice lady she was.'

'Did I? Well, if you say so. I'm afraid . . .' He looked at the pictures and frowned. 'Not too jolly a birthday present if I might say so, Lady Malpas? Gloomy sort of place by the looks of them.'

'One can't call them cheerful,' she allowed, 'but Emilie had drawn them herself. She apologized for the poor way they were framed, and we agreed they deserved better, and I should have them properly done. As you can see, they're much improved now.'

Jago had risen to his feet and crossed to examine them more closely. 'They remind me of Cornwall,' he remarked, as he had before: these were recognizably four more of that series of charcoal drawings Emilie had left behind in her snug.

Shefford threw them another indifferent glance then withdrew his attention, checking his watch. 'I say, Dee old girl, don't you think we should be pushing off?'

She jumped up. 'Yes, yes, we should.'

It appeared they were due to lunch with the Thorpe-Bassetts at Headley Court.

The name fell like discordant music on the ears of the two

police officers. Vernon Thorpe-Bassett MP, once thought to be in line for one of the great offices of state. Very well known, very rich, heir to the Bassett iron and steel conglomerate. His constituency covered not only the country villages adjacent to Folbury on this side, but also, on the other, several thrusting fingers of the industrial areas nigh on Birmingham.

FitzAlban was reminding Lady Malpas as they prepared to leave that they would be staying on after lunch to take advantage of the clay-pigeon shoot Thorpe-Bassett had recently set up. A four-day event was apparently presently in progress.

'Competitions?' Reardon enquired.

'And practice,' Shefford answered.

'Don't forget we have the Porsons coming for dinner, darling,' Lady Malpas reminded Dee.

It was FitzAlban who replied, smoothly filling in the pause that followed. 'We'll make certain she gets home in time, Lady Malpas.'

Shefford should have made the response himself, and a flush crossed his face at the implied reproof, but he didn't let it linger. Putting his arm around Dee's shoulder, he smiled. He should smile more. It transformed him. 'Absolutely. Goes without saying, Lady Malpas.'

Sir Julius watched them as they departed with his daughter, again via the French windows. 'Curious, that,' he murmured, an enigmatic remark which might have meant anything, but which his wife apparently understood perfectly.

'We haven't had the pleasure of Mr FitzAlban staying here before,' she said. 'But both the young men are to be our guests for a while longer.'

'Idle rich!' said her husband. Then he smiled, shrugged off the last few minutes' awkwardness and got down to the business which had brought the police to Falquonroy. 'Well now, gentlemen, if you want to see what Emilie was doing, come with me and I'll show you. We'd better go through the house,' he added, peering through the window at the clouds gathering for what might be another shower. 'The old library is in what used to be called the garden wing.'

TWENTY-ONE

The two detectives followed Sir Julius back into the great hall, then through the arches at its rear. A bewildering number of rooms were passed, one of them a well-appointed billiard room, through the door of which two large pictures of the king and queen could be glimpsed, graciously rubbing shoulders with a number of their subjects, sporting heroes of the past and present.

Further beyond the arches was what must once have been the old stable yard, the stables now rejoicing in their new role as garages, with accommodation for servants above. A great clock fastened to the wall creakily measured out the seconds. Their own sturdy police Wolseley stood there in the yard, next to a sleek and stately black Daimler, over which Cribb, the chauffeur, could now be seen smoothing a shammy leather as lovingly as if it were a prize racehorse.

A minute later and they were following Sir Julius through a heavy, creaking door. From here it was but a step into the ancient Falquonroy, a maze of ill-lit, variously sized and seemingly randomly placed rooms through which corridors twisted and turned. Unsafe-looking staircases rose out of the gloom at intervals, most of them roped off. A creeping chill hung in the air, draughts appeared from nowhere, and the smell of mice was overpowering. Windows unwashed for decades, or maybe centuries, made it too eerily dark to distinguish anything much at all and the ceilings were too low for tall police officers. Instinctively they ducked and raised their hands to shield their faces from gruesomely sticky spiders' webs – unless they were bats – which swung from the ceiling.

On they forged, until another heavy door was pushed open. Darkness and clammy air were instantly replaced by daylight, plus a strong smell of clean, new wood and the sounds of workmen hammering and sawing coming from a short distance away.

And there they were, in a big, rectangular room with tall

windows too narrow for the room's size in each of its shorter sides, overlooking the front and back respectively. Clearly this, what Sir Julius had called the garden wing, was that unreconstructed arm which stretched out to one side behind the front facade.

The dim room itself was undoubtedly a library – or had been once. Books in their thousands, collected over the centuries, stood on shelves occupying the whole room, but their leather spines were cracked, faded or broken altogether, some of them stacked in drunken piles or slithered sideways in mini avalanches. The sorry sight of books so ill-treated was enough to bring tears to the eyes, even while Reardon guessed most of them had probably been forever unread. It was a library in name only.

In a different context were the orderly signs of purposeful activity and intention to which the room had recently been put. Apart from a loud-ticking Napoleon-hat clock standing on the mantel, the room was empty of ornamentation and otherwise cleared of its original furniture. It now housed a long utilitarian trestle table stretching down the centre, with a few chairs pushed under it, where all the documents relating to the real business which had been occupying Sir Julius and Emilie were laid out. Also on the table was a typewriter and stacks of files in manila folders, some of them so high they were threatening to topple over.

And in the midst of all this, springing up from one of the chairs drawn up to the table, facing a pile of papers which he appeared to have been sorting, was Sam Waring.

Sir Julius showed as much surprise as his visitors to see him. 'Here again already, Sam?'

'Might as well make myself useful while I'm still around, sir.' Some agreement on the subject had obviously been reached for him to take up the slack of the work Emilie had left behind. His wide, cheerful grin and a wave of the hand encompassed the papers in front of him and the same big hand then reached out across the table to take Reardon's as Jago introduced them.

At that moment, the elderly manservant who had opened the front doors to them appeared with a tray. It was heavy and his arms trembled as with evident relief he put it down in the space Sir Julius cleared. 'Thank you, Bracewell.' There were spots of rain on the man's jacket. He had faced the rain rather than use the insalubrious way they had come, and who could blame him?

Sir Julius opened and extended a silver cigar case when they had pulled chairs out and were seated at the table, their tea in front of them. Reardon had smoked his last cigarette before the operations on his face had begun and now had no desire whatever to smoke again, and although nearly everyone smoked nowadays, including Jago and Sam, the offer of the small cigars was politely declined all round.

Sir Julius lit one for himself and began to speak, addressing the two detectives and waving his hands. The waft of rich smoke almost overcame the fusty smell of the forlorn old books. 'So you and Sam have spoken, Sergeant Jago? Then you'll already have some idea what this is all about, hmm?' he said, taking it for granted Jago would have shared the information with the chief inspector. 'Good. Then I don't need to go into too much detail.'

'As much as you feel able to tell us, sir.'

Sir Julius sat on silently for a while, gathering his thoughts before he spoke. When he began, it was hesitantly, and what he had to say wasn't quite what anyone else had expected. 'Neither I – nor my family – have ever been particularly religious.' He paused. 'But a catastrophe like this – and when I say catastrophe, I'm talking about what's happening to the Jews in Germany, as of course you know . . . Well, there are obligations, you understand, duties, commitments. We are doing what we can.'

He quickly summarized the story Jago had heard from Sam. While Sam had been working with Max Loehmann in Berlin to obtain the necessary documents and the wherewithal for emigration to Britain and other countries (sometimes legally but often otherwise, due to the fact that those they were assisting were often classed as subversives), Sir Julius, along with other wealthy and influential British Jews, had been chairing refugee committees in this country, part of a network set up as the Nazi terrorization in Germany increased.

'What was Mrs Waring's part in all this?'

Sir Julius knocked the ash from his cigar into a glass ashtray on the table. 'Helping with fundraising – a never-ending task – typing letters lobbying the government, finding offers of accommodation and other means of support when the refugees reach this country, and heaven knows what else . . . she was tireless. She even took work home.'

'Letters – to Germany?'

'And elsewhere.'

'Did she speak German?'

'Unfortunately not. That's where Sam came in.'

'Eventually,' Sam said, lifting his shoulders.

Jago knew his friend, and knew he was still blaming himself for having held back so long. It had seemed, on the face of it, as he'd told Jago, such a simple thing Sir Julius had asked of him, yet it had taken the disappearance of Fraulein Keppel, his friendship with Max Loehmann and his eventual disappearance, too, to shame Sam into action.

Sir Julius gave him a shrewd look then began again, this time with some satisfaction. 'All that noise you can hear . . . it's this garden wing being converted into accommodation for several families from Germany. The first of them should be here at Falquonroy next week and five more will follow shortly.'

'Stout decision, sir,' Reardon said, thinking not only of the fortune Sir Julius, and others like him, was expending, but also the criticism levelled by many on what they were doing.

'Not everyone thinks so.'

'*Three million unemployed and we are allowing foreigners to flood into the country and take our jobs!*' Reardon had lost count of the times he'd heard this lately, though he didn't believe it was necessarily callousness over the fate of the Jewish people. Men who had no jobs or even the prospect of one, and with hungry mouths to feed, didn't look kindly on those who were bringing dispossessed people into the country.

'And it's not enough, not by any means,' Sir Julius continued. 'Eighteen months, or closer to two years ago, when I first began, there were dozens waiting to come over here. Now there are thousands. Many of them with no hope whatever of getting out. They wait, and wait, for the documents which will let them leave to start a new life in a new country, most of them doomed to disappointment. And it's going to get worse, much worse, as long as the present insanity ruling Germany is allowed to persist.'

Sam had pushed his chair back and walked to the window

while Sir Julius spoke, as if it was too much to bear. He stood stiffly, hands braced against the window frame, his back to the room, staring out at what was not an engrossing view: nature had taken back whatever part of the gardens had given its name to this wing and now it was a wilderness running up towards the dark belt of trees, the beginnings of the forested acres beyond. He gave a jump when Jago's hand touched his arm to say they were leaving. He'd been miles away, and he was still standing there when they reached the door.

Reardon began to think, having declined the offer to be guided back through the eerie labyrinth of the ancient house to the garages, that they'd underestimated the feat of memory needed to negotiate it. They were, however, at last reunited with the police Wolseley, and Cribb, who was waiting to hand over. He stood with his hand on the passenger door and asked, red in the face, if he might have a word.

'Go ahead.' Reardon wondered what was coming as the big fellow shuffled his feet, muttering that something had cropped up that might be of interest to the police.

'Come on then, spit it out.'

By his feet sat a workman's tool bass – a heavy two-handled canvas bag carried over the shoulder, Dick Whittington style, by means of a hammer slotted through its two handles. Reardon watched as Cribb dived into it, rummaged and finally produced something which he shoved across as if it were red hot.

'Where did you get this?'

The fine tan leather was scuffed and stained, though not enough to obscure the fact that this was almost certainly the clutch handbag belonging to Emilie Waring, the one she'd presumably had with her the night she had been killed.

'I just come across it.'

'Came across it? Where?'

'By one of the garages.'

'Which garage? When?'

His face screwed up, confused by the rapid questions. 'Sunday, mebbe, I misremember exactly. Anyway, it was when I went to give the motor a bit of a polish afore we had her out that afternoon.'

'And you found it in the Daimler's garage?'

'No, no, just in front of that'n next door to it. It'd fell between the wall and that bucket by the standpipe.'

'Why didn't you hand it in straight away?'

Not a handsome man, Cribb. He looked like one who could frighten off all comers. Nor were his looks improved by his decidedly shifty appearance at the moment. He ought to have handed over the handbag to someone in charge as soon as he'd found it, and he knew it.

'What was the problem handing it in?'

'We-ell, see . . .' He swallowed and then went on in a rush. 'First off, I reckoned it must've been dropped by one of the young women staying in the house over the weekend, see. Thought I'd keep it until somebody asked about it,' he said, avoiding their eyes, 'but nobody did. They went home Monday, didn't even know they'd lost it, or didn't care if they had, more like, even though there's money in it. That's nothing to them. And afore you ask, it's still there, the money, every penny, I haven't taken nothing from it!' He paused for breath. In a more subdued tone, he continued, 'I reckon it belonged to Mrs Waring, though, didn't it?'

'You knew that, but you still held on to it?' Jago asked.

'What did I just say? I didn't know whose it was, nor even that you was looking for a handbag at all, until Prue said, not more'n a couple of hours since. She told me you thought her cousin Martin Garbutt had took it, but he never. If I'd known it belonged to Mrs Waring, I'd of brought it to you soon as I found it, honest to God I would!'

'All right, I believe you,' Reardon said, and he almost did, though he suspected there could be more to it than Cribb was owning up to. 'Whose car was parked in that garage?'

'I don't rightly know that anybody's was. There was a lot of people here at the weekend and they leave their motors anywhere they think fit, taking up space and getting in the way.'

'Right. Well, thank you for letting us have this, Cribb.'

The chauffeur nodded stiffly, held open the car door and stood back, watching them as they drove off.

* * *

Sir Julius didn't stay long in the library after the police had gone. Left alone, having abandoned his unseeing contemplation of the jungle outside, Sam returned to the stack of work Emilie had left behind. Inevitably, by its very nature, it only succeeded in turning his mind once more to those last days in Berlin. He pushed on but it was useless, and at last he gave up the attempt to forget.

He and Max had continued to meet regularly after that concert, Sam's first introduction to Schoenberg, until it occurred to him one day that he hadn't seen or heard from Max for longer than was usual. He took a tram to the district where he lived.

There was no answer to his repeated knocks on the door of his friend's apartment, but he knew someone should be in. Opening the letterbox, he shouted Max's name several times and announced who he was. Eventually the door was cautiously opened by Rosa. He was appalled at the sight of her. She was a thin, neat young woman with a naturally pale complexion, but now she looked deathly. Thinner than ever and frightened. Sam knew by now that her husband had been a university lecturer who had 'disappeared' two years ago into one of the forced labour camps, probably Dachau, which had been opened for the express purpose of detaining those intellectuals who were most likely to cause trouble to the Nazis. Rosa had discovered through the underground grapevine that he had died there, and now, she asserted with stricken certainty, Max's turn had come, and she would never see him again, either.

More than that, without Max, she was destitute. She had no money and was afraid of being turned out of the apartment, or that they, the Nazis, would come for her and her children, sooner or later. Max had been taken three nights ago and she had been terrified of leaving their rooms here and going outside. When Sam arrived, they had been eating a thin soup and black bread, the last of what there was in the apartment.

Sam was not a man who easily lost his temper, but when he did it was a spectacular affair. When he thought of all that had been happening during the time he'd been living in Germany, he felt an overwhelming urge to smash his fist into things, preferably into that gang of jumped-up Nazi ruffians who were proclaiming themselves saviours of the nation while a dark undercurrent of fear ran through the everyday life of the city, and the licensed humiliation and cruelty imposed on those of its citizens considered unacceptable went on. He had an almost uncontrollable desire to shake the dust of Germany from his feet – but to leave was impossible now, with the danger Rosa felt she and her children were in. He knew she was right to feel this: she was a clever young woman, once a teacher, and was well aware of what Max had been doing, and that Sam had lately been helping him. She had suffered so much already, and he found himself caring very much that this must stop. She had to leave Germany.

To be granted a visa for another country, however, Rosa would need to be issued with a host of documents: a passport and proof there was employment and guaranteed support waiting for her at her chosen destination – evidence that she had sufficient funds to maintain herself. None of which Rosa, wife of a known 'degenerate' and possibly suspected of being one herself, had the remotest hope of obtaining. He must do whatever he could to get her and her children out of the country.

Easier said than done without Max's help in the matter of faked documents and escape routes which avoided the German frontier crossing points into Belgium, Holland or Switzerland. Max had been obsessive about keeping the names of his contacts close to his chest. It was safer that way, but his disappearance had left Sam hardly knowing where to start. Yet he had to make the attempt. His heart almost failed him, but just walking away wasn't an option.

'You can't do it. You can't even try. You won't be safe,' Rosa had protested, her eyes full of a new terror, this time for him as well as herself.

'I'm a foreign national. They can't do anything to me.'

The claim sounded hollow even to himself. Anyone who didn't fall into line, much less tried to subvert or go against the Nazis in any way, was classed as an enemy of the state and as such liable to its punishments. He knew he was at risk, British or not. Perhaps especially so. He was too distinctive, too recognizable with his still imperfect German, his easy manners and good intentions. His brain told him Rosa was making sense, but it wasn't his brain that made him feel for Rosa as he did. How could he live with himself if he didn't try? Or live without her, he admitted at last, if he failed?

He was met with a wall of silence from those he tried to contact. It made him see, as nothing else had, that rather than being a help, he could actually become a liability, not knowing the ropes as a native Berliner like Max had known them. Rosa was right: without Max he was out of his depth. He felt like a blundering schoolboy and was almost in despair.

Until . . . 'Rudi!' declared Rosa, as almost simultaneously the same name came to Sam.

Rudi Schiller was now in his teens, six years on from the ten-year-old destitute orphan with an impudent grin who'd evaded authority and lived on the streets ever since he could remember. Max had encountered the urchin when he had spotted him thieving a bratwurst from a market stall, and then had caught up with him round the corner, wolfishly devouring it. He'd talked to him, looked out for him again, and a friendly association had developed. Streetwise, cheeky and slippery as a fish, wily and knowledgeable, Rudi knew everyone and was in awe of no one. Max later found him a job as a pageboy in one of the big hotels on the Ku'damm where, in return for his now regular food and the cubby hole he slept in, not to mention the tips he earned, he was more than happy to pass on any information Max might find useful about guests staying there. Also to act in other ways when required. The Artful Dodger in a smart uniform and a pillbox hat at a rakish angle was how Sam would always remember him.

It only needed him to tell Rudi what had happened to Max for Rudi to see that the whispered word got around to the right people. Within only a few days Rosa and the children were on their way and very soon were safely, if temporarily, installed with a welcoming family in a small town near Liège, in Belgium. Sam didn't enquire into how it had all been achieved so quickly.

He knew his own role in the escape would soon be known. It would be wise to get out while there was still a chance that he could. He tendered his immediate resignation at the bank to much disapprobation, though he couldn't help feeling that the point where his employers would be recalling the rest of their staff to London couldn't be far off.

Throwing all his belongings into the little Opel, he set off. The car had been second-hand when he bought it and he knew it may well give him trouble, but he had grown fond of it and was reluctant to leave it behind. In the event, it took him and his English passport sweetly across the border and on to home and Templewood without any trouble at all. It was never wise to underestimate German efficiency, especially in the matter of engineering.

TWENTY-TWO

So here it was, the contents of the small handbag Charlie Cribb had found, now being examined in the CID office by Jago and Reardon and anyone else who cared to stop by and have a look. Not that there was anything unusual to see, despite the fact that it was stuffed to the point where the soft leather bulged and spoiled the shape: a comb and mirror, a powder compact, a crumpled handkerchief, a purse with a few coins in it, a wallet – but most of all, a bundle of photographs crammed into its inner pocket, taking up most of the room. These were now spread out on Jago's desk. One or two people hung over his shoulder to see if there was any chance of recognition, but they were sending out no clues to anyone.

The handbag was not looking so chic now, a car wheel having passed over one corner, leaving a black tyre mark but miraculously missing the contents, including the wallet, which was stuffed with paper money. Jago whistled. Ninety-five pounds.

'That would have kept her in silk stockings for a while!' one of the onlookers remarked with a grin. Gargrave, who else? He saw his mistake as Jago threw him a sharp look. 'Sorry, I only meant . . . well, it's a lot to carry around.'

'How long do you think it would last if you'd nothing else in the world and no prospects of any more to come?' Reardon asked.

Long enough to keep Emilie living for some time, perhaps, unless she'd had other expectations as to how she was proposing to exist in the future. Something, or someone, to support her? Surtees? Reardon hadn't yet given up on the architect.

Ninety-five pounds was a lot of money, but it was an odd amount, five short of a nice round sum. Charlie Cribb would do anything for money to help set up his own business, wasn't that what Prue had said? Anything at all? He'd sounded honest enough, if not all that bright. And he had passed the bag over, however strong the temptation. Reardon didn't think he would have handed it in at all if he'd helped himself.

'Or else he'd have taken the lot,' Jago said.

Reardon turned the soft leather bag over in his hands. 'He was looking pretty shifty, and he's not telling us everything, but I don't think we're talking money. Anyone know if he has form?'

No one did. Gargrave offered to check it out. Meanwhile, people gradually wandered back to their desks while Jago stayed where he was, puzzling over the significance of the photos in front of him.

They were snapshots. A crowd of people, young for the most part, lounging about, laughing, bottles and glasses much in evidence. Taken at some outdoor summer party or event in what looked like a large garden. Spreading lawns, flower beds, water in the background. Among them was one picture he stared at long and hard. No snapshot this, but the posed, professional studio portrait of a young girl of about seventeen or eighteen.

The one missing from the frame in Emilie's bedroom? It was the right size and was held between two same-sized pieces of the thin card used to hold pictures in place inside their frames.

There was an obvious inference here, but he could see no resemblance between the photograph and what Emilie Waring may have looked like in life. Yet if he hadn't already seen and learnt who the girl in the photo was, he might have found a different answer to why Emilie had taken the picture of Lucy Oates with her when she walked out of Templewood, while leaving almost everything else of her life behind her. He'd last seen it, or an exact copy, gazing at him from Miss Oates' mantelpiece.

The police in Fort William had come up trumps!

Grinning broadly, Jago strode in to Reardon with the news. PC Murdo Grant had managed to contact Rex Surtees' friend McAllister at his mother-in-law's address, and he'd telephoned Jago with an almost verbatim report of the conversation they'd had. Yes, McAllister had indeed lent his newly purchased car back to its previous owner before driving up to Scotland – though only after much argument and persuasion. 'Who sells a car and then asks for the loan of it back straight away?' the new owner had demanded, reasonably enough, though he had in the end agreed to the request. Only because, he stressed, he and Surtees were good friends of long standing, and only after financial inducement was offered. Plus a guarantee that the car would be returned, petrol tank full, PC Grant had concluded with canny Scottish approval.

The office clock said three ten p.m. There was still time to find Surtees at his office. Another trip to Wolverhampton, but maybe Ockham's principle might just have some validity, that the obvious – and so far only, Reardon reminded himself – credible suspect would turn out to be the one they sought.

This time, Rex Surtees didn't look quite so much at ease with himself when they confronted him. His eyes were slightly baggy behind the gold-rimmed spectacles, an indication that perhaps he hadn't slept well. His hair was not quite so sleekly in place and his tie was very slightly askew, as though it had been loosened and then hurriedly adjusted before he faced the police again.

Coffee cups were laid out as before in the same room where they had previously been received, and the beverage to fill them promptly appeared, brought in by Miss Cox. That same delightful smile embraced them all and only her voice assaulted the eardrums. Surtees waited until she had poured the coffee and left before speaking.

'I know why you're here, Inspector.'

'Then you've spoken to Mr McAllister.'

He nodded and smiled, but didn't look comfortable.

'You didn't tell us the truth the last time we spoke to you, Mr Surtees.'

'Not – er – not the whole truth, perhaps,' he admitted, the smile now valiantly trying for rueful.

'Then now's the time to repair the omission.' Reardon heard himself, as pompous as Knott; it was the effect Surtees had on him. 'You were quite certain you didn't drive over to Temple Atwode on Thursday the ninth of May, but we now know that you did.' Not strictly true, but apart from Jago, who knew that?

'Yes, but—'

'Did you meet Mrs Waring at The Spinney – the building site – and later kill her?'

'What the heck – of course I damn well didn't!' He ran a finger round his collar. 'All right, I did drive over there, yes, I'll admit that. Much against my will. But I didn't kill Emilie! Why should I?'

'Perhaps if you tell us the truth this time round, that may sound more convincing.'

'Oh, God!' Suddenly, he dropped his head into his hands and the silence grew. Reardon let it carry on until at last Surtees looked up. His face was clay-coloured, but it had taken on a certain decision. 'Look here, I'll tell you exactly what happened, and then perhaps you'll believe me.'

'That would be a start,' Jago said.

He threw him and his notebook a sour look and took a deep breath. 'What happened was, she – Emilie, I mean – had telephoned me earlier in the day, asking if I would meet her that night at The Spinney and drive her to New Street station in Birmingham. She was going away for a few days and had to catch a London train. There was no one else at home, or so she said, to drive her to the station. I was taken aback, to say the least, and naturally, I asked her why me, and why she didn't just order a taxi, but she said she had to get away without anyone seeing or knowing. I wanted to know what was going on, what the big secret was, but she wouldn't say. I told her I no longer had the car anyway and she became so agitated that . . . well, in the end I agreed to see what I could do.'

'Despite the fact that you thought the request so strange? And why should she want to make use of you in particular?' Reardon asked.

'Well, of course she *was* using me,' he said, seizing the justification, 'and I thought it more than a bit of a cheek. But she insisted there was no one else to help her and by then she could hardly speak for crying. I honestly began to feel alarmed, you know? That was so unlike Emilie. She may have annoyed me at times, with all that changing her mind about my plans for the house, but she was otherwise a sensible woman, so I assumed she must have had a very good reason for asking. Probably a row with the judge, I thought, and well, anyway, I was quite fond of her.' He was becoming more fluent as he went on, looking a bit more at ease, as if he was beginning to believe his story would be accepted. 'I told her to ring me back later and I'd let her know what I'd decided, although I wasn't very happy about any of it.

I just hoped I could convince Mac to let me use the car for an hour.'

'Which of course he did.'

'After a lot of grovelling and promises to refill the tank and so on and so on.'

'Plus a certain financial inducement?'

'All right, yes,' he admitted sulkily after a moment. 'He hadn't yet paid me in full for the car and I agreed to knock a bit off the original price. I couldn't really blame him. To tell the truth, I felt a bit of a jackass, asking him at all. You don't sell a car and then still expect to be able to use it, do you?'

'You certainly went to a great deal of trouble to help Mrs Waring out. What happened when you saw her?'

'That's just it, I didn't see her, as I've already told you. When I drew up at The Spinney, she wasn't there.'

'What do you mean?'

'I mean she wasn't *there*!' he repeated loudly, almost shouting.

'What about her luggage?' Jago asked. 'Her handbag?'

'Luggage? I didn't see any luggage, or any handbag, either.' His temper was rising, along with his colour. 'You may find it difficult to believe, but I wasn't actually looking for any!'

'Did you get out of the car?'

'I didn't need to; the whole site's pretty visible from the entrance, so why should I? I could see there was no one there. I was furious with her. It had taken me ages to convince old Mac to let me have the car and I knew I was nearly an hour later getting there than I'd said I would be, though I'd reckoned there was still time for her to get a train to London. I decided she must have found some other mug to drive her, but I waited another fifteen minutes or so, just in case.'

'And then?'

'What would you have done? I gave it up and drove home.'

Reardon let the silence go on. 'You were overheard having words with Mrs Waring the week before,' he said at last. 'What was all that about?'

'Words? What are you talking about? We were always having words, never stopped, about my plans for The Spinney.'

'You were arguing,' Jago said. 'Having a row. You threatened her.'

'*What?* Who's told you that? Well, sorry, but you've got that one wrong! Seriously wrong. I had no row with Emilie, ever. We might have had a few differences, as I've said, over her ideas to better my design – but it didn't bother either of us too much.'

It hadn't bothered him because it was plain to everyone he would never have agreed to what he would regard as the ruin of *'my plans, my design, my house'*? Possibly. Yet in the end he and his partners had rid themselves of the whole project.

'Thank you for your time, Mr Surtees. We shall need to speak to you again, so please don't think of making any moves to leave for France in a hurry.'

'Did you believe him?' Jago asked as they got back to the car.

'He's plausible, I'll say that for him.'

It was as far as Reardon was prepared to go. He kept his voice calm, though he was damned annoyed – more with himself for letting his hopes rise. Any prospects he might have seen for bringing the case to a quick conclusion by interviewing the architect had taken a distinctly downward plunge. 'If he was telling the truth this time –' and Reardon was still by no means sure about that – 'where *was* Emilie when he arrived to pick her up?'

'Maybe she gave up on him and for some reason took herself over to Falquonroy. We know she must have been there at some point, because of the handbag.'

'And then walked back to The Spinney, only to get herself murdered? Walked, in those shoes?'

Not that Reardon would ever underestimate a woman's ability to trot about without any apparent discomfort, all day if necessary, wearing what to men would be instruments specifically designed to torture. It was a fifteen-minute walk along the road from Falquonroy to The Spinney, at least. As for taking the shortcut and scrambling down that path . . .

TWENTY-THREE

It did sometimes happen in an investigation . . . the break you prayed for. This time the shift of focus came via a telephone message the next morning, which Reardon received before he'd even left home for the office.

He'd been awake since five, given Tolly his run, and was just making Ellen a cup of tea when the call came, unusual enough for the phone to ring at that time of a morning to make him jump slightly, just as he was pouring. Scalding tea splashed on to his wrist and slopped into the saucer. Swearing roundly, he put the pot down and went to answer the phone.

'Another beautiful morning, Chief Inspector.' It was Rossiter, Dr Kay Dysart's husband.

'Morning, Doc.' Less enthusiastic than the pathologist himself sounded, Reardon sucked his wrist. Not expecting any surprises from the postmortem on Emilie Waring, he hadn't pressed for a quick result, although Rossiter didn't normally hang about. 'Problems?'

'Not for me,' Rossiter said cheerfully. 'Just ringing to let you know the results on the body you sent me. Sorry I haven't been quicker . . . backlogs and all that. Catching up before I'm off . . . I suppose Kay told you we're away to Torquay tomorrow for a day or two?'

Reardon remembered vaguely that she had, but he'd forgotten.

'I put your lady through as soon as I could . . . the judge's wife, huh?' The r's rolled. His Scottish accent was always more apparent on the telephone.

'What do you have for me, Donald?'

'I'll be sending the full results round to you in the course of today, but I thought you might like a preview, as it were, all things considered.'

Some note in his voice alerted Reardon, but he didn't betray his quickened interest. 'Always helps to know in good time.'

'Aye. There's always that.' Rossiter was impervious to irony.

Something was coming and he wished he would get on with it, but cautious Scot that he was, the pathologist wasn't given to quick-fire explanations. He enjoyed drawing them out.

'You're going to tell me she was pregnant, I suppose,' Reardon said at last, bringing him to the point.

'I am not.' Still not to be hurried, he said that for a start he could confirm his wife's original findings. Cause of death was strangulation, as she correctly assumed. 'It's all on my report. You'll no doubt be hoping for the time she died too.'

No, Reardon wasn't. He hadn't met a medic yet who wasn't reluctant to give this, notoriously difficult as it was to estimate how long since life had departed from a body, everything depending on such variables as ambient temperatures, body weight and a host of other elements. But he was guessing Rossiter had something up his sleeve, so he merely said, 'As far as we've been able to ascertain, she was last seen alive about six to seven p.m. on the Thursday before she was found.'

Rossiter relented. 'Then I'd estimate she was probably killed within a few hours after that.'

'And lay there for nearly three days before she was found.'

'Not quite. Near enough, but . . .' and then he came out with it. 'When Kay examined her, she thought it possible she hadn't been in that position from the time she'd died, and I was able to confirm that when I examined her properly.'

'Go on,' Reardon said, recalling Dysart's hesitation, intrigued now.

'She lay for some time on her side after she died. Meaning . . .'

Reardon listened, while Rossiter told him what he already knew: once her heart had stopped beating, ceased its job of pumping blood around her body, gravity would have caused the blood to pool and settle in the body's lowest part. Leaving a discolouration, purplish like a bruise, indicating the position she had lain in during the time when the joints and limbs were still flexible, before stiffening had set in.

'Curled into a foetal position,' Rossiter finished, 'almost trussed up, I would say.'

'Trussed? You mean she was tied up?'

'I found no ligature marks, no signs of that. What I did find was bruising on both arms, as if she'd been held. Puzzle, no?

But that's one I'll leave you with, Bert. You'll have my report in full this afternoon.'

'Thank you, and give my regards to Torquay,' he said before they rang off.

Back in the kitchen, he put the kettle on for a fresh pot of tea and ran the cold tap over his wrist while it boiled. Before it did, Ellen was downstairs, ready to get breakfast on the go. 'Who was that, ringing so early? Not an emergency, I hope?'

'Not as such, but I have to go, love. Don't bother with breakfast.'

'Rubbish! You've time for a slice of toast.' She knew that he liked his breakfast. He always said he couldn't work on an empty stomach. She began to gather things together and in hardly more time than it took to toast a slice of bread, bacon had been fried as well and breakfast was on his plate in the shape of a toasted bacon sandwich. Which he couldn't in all fairness leave behind when his stomach rumbled, and it smelled good enough to make his mouth water. He gave in, as far as picking up the sandwich, but stood up to eat it while she poured a mug of tea.

'So who was ringing?'

'Donald Rossiter,' he told her through a mouthful.

'What did he have to say?'

'Oh, he and Kay are having a few days in Torquay. Maybe we could do the same . . . take a break, I mean, when this case is finished.'

'That's not what's making you rush off. What's so urgent that you can't sit and let your breakfast go down?'

'Nothing,' he admitted at last, hooking a chair out with his foot. 'I suppose I'm over-reacting.' He knew he was. Dashing about and giving himself indigestion before he'd had time to think things through was pointless. He told her, as briefly as he could, what Rossiter had said, but he still needed another quick cup of tea when he'd finished. He'd be awash with it before the day was done, but nothing else did the trick.

Questions were bedevilling him as he walked down the hill and set off across the river bridge towards Market Street and the police station. Halfway across he came to an almost automatic halt, leaning his arms on the parapet above the iron railings. It wasn't the loveliest aspect of Folbury. Behind him the water tumbled and eddied over the weir before flowing under the bridge, while in front were the industrial premises and allotments which bordered the river at this point; the ruin of the old flour mill and the town's gasholder loomed in the distance. But it was a familiar view and it was almost routine to stop here for a breather and a few minutes' thinking time.

Today was going to be another warm one. Already there was a slight mist rising on the water; the Fol's level was still high after the winter and a wet, early spring, and the few trees visible on the banks at this point were already in full leaf, softening the harsh outline of the industrial buildings.

There was no carpet of bluebells here, however.

He closed his eyes and saw The Spinney again. Emilie with her suitcases, waiting for Surtees to arrive as daylight faded. Desperate to get away. The enormous silence of the deep, surrounding woods. The gathering dusk and the patter of rain on the leaves. Growing impatience, perhaps turning to fear as no one came and the night grew darker.

What had happened between then and when she was found by her little dog, three days later, the life strangled out of her, peacefully laid to rest with her hands folded across her chest?

She hadn't lain in that position for all of that time. The blood pooling, showing she'd been curled up just after she'd died, could possibly have been due to the way she had fallen to the ground and been left there . . . until her killer had returned and for some reason rearranged her. And because she was lying on the ground, that could have been why Surtees had failed to see her when he'd at last arrived. It was possible, but it didn't account for everything.

Reardon strode into the CID room in a grim mood, which was unusual for him. Everyone there sat up straighter. But it was Jago he wanted to see. 'In my office, Sergeant, please – there's been a development.' At his door, he swung round. 'Before you do, send someone to fetch Surtees here. We need another talk with that one and I'm damned if we're traipsing over to Wolverhampton yet again. Get him here, pronto, before he decides to do a flit for France.'

Later, it was a subdued and very different Surtees who sat

across the table in that sorry room they used for interviews at Market Street. A scarred deal table, some uncomfortable chairs and a small high window that always needed cleaning, it was a depressing room at the best of times. The sun only got to that side of the building in the late evening and in any case missed the window, so it never looked any better. A far cry from Surtees' own office where he met his clients with easy chairs and porcelain coffee cups, and not forgetting Miss Cox and her vases of lilies, even if they were artificial.

'What am I doing here? What do you want with me – *again*?' he demanded. 'Your chap wouldn't tell me anything.'

That was one reason why Gargrave had been sent to fetch him. Surtees wouldn't get a word out of the strictly cautioned DC, who in any case wasn't one for opening his mouth much, except to put his foot in it.

Rex Surtees today was hardly the up-and-coming young architect they had first spoken to. His well-cut suit seemed as if it had suddenly become too big for him. He looked diminished, older and very sorry for himself. Being brought here had thoroughly shaken him and pierced his complacency. He was due to be shaken even further, thought Jago.

There didn't seem any point in recapping what had been said at their last meeting. Surtees needed no reminders anyway. Despite his attempt at bravado, he was the picture of a man who knows he's in for it. The arrogance and slight swagger had been replaced by a look best described as hangdog. 'I've told you all I know,' he protested, nevertheless. 'What's the point of going through all of it again?'

'No point at all. You've given different stories on the two previous occasions we've spoken,' Reardon said. 'So I suggest we cut the waffle and go straight to the right one this time. Starting from the point when you said you arrived with your car at The Spinney, where you'd agreed to meet Mrs Waring – and discovered she wasn't there. You last said this was on Thursday, the ninth of May?'

'Yes, but—'

'I'll remind you again what else you said. She wasn't there as promised, you waited for fifteen minutes or so, then left and went home. Is that correct?'

'Yes – I mean no. Yes, I did say that, and I'm sorry but,

actually . . .' He was not so much pale now as ashen. 'No, that wasn't what happened, well, not exactly . . .'

Reardon sat back, arms folded. 'You lied again.'

'Can you blame me? I was hardly going to put my head in a noose, was I? You'd have had the whole thing pinned on me like a shot.'

'You knew all along that she was dead.'

'Good God, no! The first I heard of that was when you came to my office and told me.'

'When you swore you knew nothing.'

'Because I didn't! Look here, you've absolutely nothing on me!'

'Then there's no reason for all this shilly-shallying, is there? I'll ask you again what happened, and this time, I'd advise you to stop confusing things and tell us what you really know.'

Surtees fidgeted on the hard chair, put his elbows on the table, looked up at the dirty window and received no help from it. 'I need a smoke.' Getting a curt nod, he fished a tortoiseshell cigarette case from his pocket. Jago supplied a match and shoved a tin ashtray across the table.

'Any chance of a drink?'

These delaying tactics were all too familiar, but Jago went out of the room to fetch one. While he was out, Surtees attempted to speak again but Reardon silenced him until the DS returned with a beaker of water. Surtees looked as though he'd expected tea at least but he drank thirstily. By the time he'd finished swallowing, he'd come to a decision.

'All right, I'll tell you exactly what happened.' He took the last sip of water. 'I did see her. I was late getting there, like I told you. It had taken me longer than I thought to get hold of the car, but there was still time, if we got a move on, for her to get a London train. I expected her to be in a state, like she'd been that afternoon on the telephone, but she was cool as a cucumber. It didn't matter now, she said; she was sorry for dragging me out there, but waiting had given her time to think, and her plans might have changed. She'd been a coward, she said, and refused to face up to things. She was going to stay and face the music. You can imagine what I felt . . . everything I'd done . . . for nothing! I was livid, I could have—'

'Strangled her?'

The blood rushed to his face. 'You see – that's what I mean! You'd like nothing better than to think I'd killed her, wouldn't you? But I didn't. I was furious with her, who wouldn't have been? But *I did not* kill her! The last I saw of her she was very much alive.'

'And that was?'

He fished for another cigarette. His hands were shaking, and he gave up the attempt. 'All right, you're not going to believe this, but too bad. It's what happened.'

She had been tense, he said. Strung up, but perfectly lucid, and she repeated what she'd said about leaving Templewood. But it was essential that she saw Sir Julius Malpas that night. It was vital . . . something about an important letter she'd sent him . . . and she had begged Surtees to drive her over to Falquonroy Park. There would be no need for him to wait for her, because she didn't know how long she'd be. In any case, she was certain Sir Julius would see that his chauffeur got her home safely.

'You know, now that she'd stopped the hysterics, I actually felt sorry for her. She said something very odd. "*I believe Eliot will understand after all. He's a good man and I shouldn't underestimate him.*" I don't know what she meant, but finally I drove her over to Falquonroy, as she wanted.'

'Leaving her luggage where it was?'

'Luggage? I told you before, I didn't see any luggage. Believe it or not, that was the very last thing that would have occurred to me in the circumstances. Or to her, one would imagine, since she didn't mention it.'

Reardon ignored the sarcasm; he was probably right. If Emilie had indeed decided against going away, she would have meant to come back for the cases, or to have them picked up.

'I just drove her to the door at the big house and left her there – not the main door. She didn't want to use that – there was another where she could let herself in, further along the front, set back a bit. She knew where the key was tucked away.'

He must mean the one into the garden wing. One which did give access to the rest of the house, if you were prepared to stumble through that eerie, derelict part. 'You actually saw her go in?'

'Yes, and I waited until the door closed behind her before I left. And that, I swear, is the last I saw of Emilie Waring.'

They had to let him go. Jago didn't trust him, nonetheless. 'Is he still trying it on, swearing he left Emilie alive?'

'I don't know.' The man could have told the truth in the first place; instead, he'd lied, hoping they'd leave him alone and only succeeded in digging himself into a hole. At the same time, Reardon couldn't see any reason why he should be lying about Emilie having business with Sir Julius at Falquonroy. Whatever had taken her there, it didn't appear to have anything to do with him.

But whether it had or not, it was Falquonroy that was becoming the focus of attention. 'Those lividity marks are consistent with being squeezed into the boot of a car,' Reardon said. 'I think she was probably killed there.'

'And then taken back to The Spinney? Why?'

Well, it was harder to dispose of a dead body than detective story writers might have their readers believe. Digging deep enough among the roots in the wooded acres surrounding Falquonroy would have been neither easy nor quick. On the other hand, in the ancient house itself were all those hidden, secret places, rooms unused and unvisited, where a body might lie undiscovered for months, years . . . centuries, it was possible to believe. Except that the present work of restoration and rebuilding was almost finished, with homes ready and waiting to offer a fresh start in a new country for people whose lives had been devastated. And who could tell if their arrival, bringing with them their harrowing stories, might not convince Sir Julius to extend his philanthropy and open up, for others in the same situation, more of those hitherto unused places in the mansion? And in the process, exposing any dead body which might have been hidden there?

In that case, taking her away from Falquonroy made sense. The flaw there was that The Spinney could not have been a random choice. Clearly whoever had deposited Emilie back there must have had some inkling of her plans.

The night she had died, Sir Julius had been alone at Falquonroy, his wife and daughters away, house guests for the engagement party not due to arrive until Saturday. Alone apart from old Bracewell, who found carrying a laden tray an effort, never mind lugging a body around and getting it into a car. Sir Julius was himself not a young man, nor especially active, Reardon would have guessed. It had to be someone more able-bodied than either.

Cribb, for instance. If anyone would have access to a vehicle, he would. His master's Daimler, God forbid, not to mention other vehicles used on the estate that were parked here and there . . . plus any the builders might have left standing around. Charlie Cribb though, with a delicate scarf in his big hands? That didn't sit right, somehow.

'He's no good, anyway,' Reardon said after a moment's thought. 'He was still in London, chauffeuring the ladies about.' There were, of course, the other servants. 'How many would you say it takes to run a place that size?' he asked Jago.

'Half the local population, I shouldn't wonder.' Unlike Templewood, where the place was managed by Maitland, Prue and Ezra Garbutt, with only two women from the village to do the rough, plus Cribb's occasional contribution. PC Shay had made short work of questioning the two local women, who'd had nothing useful to add. Interrogating all of Falquonroy's staff would be a different kettle of fish.

So Cribb, a questionable suspect in any case with no apparent motive, was out of the running. Similarly that firebrand Martin Garbutt. For one thing, what possible connection could he have had with Falquonroy? Added to which, he had no car, though there was no doubt that he would have no difficulty in getting hold of one if he had to.

TWENTY-FOUR

Bracewell showed less reluctance to admit the two officers this time when they arrived at Falquonroy the next day. Presumably he now knew who they were, and what their business was. Reardon was relieved to find Sir Julius and his wife alone. Their daughter, Dee, was better kept out of the picture for the moment.

This morning, her parents were sitting comfortably relaxed, taking coffee in the dim surroundings of the conservatory. Sunlight filtered through the vines, palms and ferns. The air was heavily scented, the plants' musky perfume mingling with damp earth and the aroma from Sir Julius's inevitable cigar, music on the radio. It should have been a palm court string quartet, but it was theatre organ melodies relayed from the Tower Ballroom in Blackpool.

Probably lost on Sir Julius anyway. He was busy with his fountain pen and a pile of papers.

Reardon apologized for what seemed like an intrusion into such a domestic scene. 'Do please join us,' Lady Malpas said, as if it were a social occasion, crossing the room to switch off Sandy McPherson and ring for more coffee.

'We won't detain you long,' Reardon promised. 'Just a few questions, Sir Julius, about the letter you received from Mrs Waring.'

'Letter?' He frowned. 'Oh, you mean the message she left me? Hardly a letter – it was just a note on the table in the library. I suppose I might still find it if you think it's necessary?'

'No, I'm not talking about that note. This was a letter she wrote later – perhaps an apology for not turning up?'

'Well, that's what I might have expected from Emilie, but I have to disappoint you. I never received any such letter. I must ask Bracewell if he knows anything about it.'

'If anything came for you, Julius,' Lady Malpas said, 'he would have let you have it.'

Ash fell from her husband's cigar as he held up a hand. 'You're quite right, my dear, of course he would. Are you sure?' he demanded of Reardon.

'Well, it seems she'd written to you, been expecting an answer, and was very upset at not receiving one.'

'Who says that? Oh, I suppose I'm not entitled to ask.'

'Let's just say we have reason to believe Mrs Waring came to Falquonroy on Thursday, presumably in search of a reply to what she'd written.'

'Thursday? If she did, she didn't get to see me. I had a very busy schedule that day – out for most of it, followed by a refugee committee meeting that didn't end until just before dinner.'

More coffee arrived. While Lady Malpas poured, it occurred to Reardon that members of that committee were more than likely to be personal friends as well, and in the absence of his family had maybe been invited to stay on to dine with Sir Julius. And yes, he nodded when asked if there had been guests for dinner.

'How many were there, sir?'

'Three. You've already met two of them – our two house guests, Mr Shefford and Mr FitzAlban.' Not the committee then. 'They came a day ahead of the other weekend guests, with that other young fellow, Boo.'

'Boo?'

'Oh,' Lady Malpas said, 'don't take any notice of that. His name's Algernon Bouvier-Summerson, a rather foolish young man, I'm afraid. That's what they all call him, Boo.'

'Understandably,' Jago said, then wished he hadn't, but it caused a smile all round.

So, the three men had arrived at Falquonroy while Lady Malpas and her daughter, Shefford's fiancé, were still in London? That was a surprise.

Sir Julius seemed to guess what Reardon was thinking. 'I see an explanation is needed. It's quite simple.' All the same, he seemed to find a pause necessary to gather his thoughts before giving one. 'Our daughter Devorah – Dee – is twenty-two. She's our only child, born late in our marriage. We – or perhaps *I*,' he amended, with an apologetic glance at his wife, 'have been rather more indulgent with her than is wise. Don't misunderstand me, she's a good girl, but sometimes impulsive and easily persuaded.

At any rate, for reasons not necessary to go into, I've begun to think I've been remiss in not getting to know this young man she's engaged to a little better. Not that . . .' He stopped, looked down at the cigar that was now burning his fingers before stubbing it out in the ashtray Lady Malpas held out in anticipation. 'I've made provision for my daughter, of course I have, but Shefford has no money – run-down family business somewhere up north – and it's high time he stopped playing games and pulled himself together. If a man hasn't anything better to do by the time thirty's behind him . . .' He watched his wife as he added, 'I've already been looking into the possibility of a position for him in one of my concerns.'

This seemed to be news to her, but he spoke before she could say anything. 'Let me finish, my dear. As I say, Mr Reardon, I wanted a good talk with Shefford. That weekend seemed an ideal time – invite him ahead of the party, when Dee and her mother were still in London, spend the evening alone together and get things straight between us. Unfortunately, it didn't turn out quite like that. He'd twisted his knee – *fencing*!' It came out as if something that went round a garden had no business to be calling itself a sport.

'Very popular, lately,' Jago murmured.

'And we know why.' He looked as if he'd found a blowfly or something equally disgusting in his spoonful of ice cream, a look that clearly said *Oswald Mosley*. 'The injury means Shefford can't drive at the moment, hence Mr FitzAlban's offer to drive him here, with the other fellow cadging a lift as well . . . and an end to my idea of a confidential talk.'

For reasons not necessary to go into, he'd said. Was he, despite his evident wish for it to seem otherwise, having second thoughts about allowing his daughter to 'marry out' as it was known? He had previously stated quite categorically that he wasn't a practising Jew, but given the unstinting work he was doing on their behalf, the money he must be contributing to see his plans carried out, not to say offering to open up his home, it was unlikely that race was an unimportant issue with him. Were his doubts about Toby Shefford merely concerned with what he clearly regarded as an idle life?

'I take it there were just the four of you on Thursday then. No other guests, Sir Julius?'

'That's right. I could wish there had been more of us. I find the conversation – if it can be so called – of the young people nowadays very difficult. I don't understand their jokes, and that night, with the three of them . . . I was a very unmannerly host, I'm afraid. After we'd dined, I excused myself and saw them on their way to the billiard room, did a little work in my study for a while, then took an early night. They stayed up late. I heard them going to their rooms in the small hours. Very noisy. Rather tipsy, I'm afraid.'

'Can you be more specific about the time?'

'Not really. But I had to be up early the next morning and once wakened I don't get off to sleep again easily, so I wasn't best pleased.'

'Are the gentlemen available for us to speak to?'

'Not at the moment. Bouvier-Summerson's left. Someone gave him a lift back to London. The other two are staying on but they're off again today to Headley Court.'

'Not to worry. We'll catch them later.'

The slight nod Reardon gave Jago was a signal for their departure, but before he was on his feet, Jago had slid his hand into his inside jacket pocket for the envelope found in Emilie's bag. It seemed to have found a permanent home in his pocket.

'Sir Julius, could I ask you to take a look at these and see if you recognize anyone? You too, Lady Malpas, if you don't mind.'

But although the snapshots were given a carefully considered examination, like everyone else who had seen them, they shook their heads. No, there was no one there they could identify. No one, including the studio portrait of Lucy.

'They were taken some time ago . . . ten years perhaps?' Lady Malpas asked as she handed them back to Jago. She smiled at his surprise. 'Look at those young women! Shingles have been out for years – and as for those hemlines . . . above the knee!'

Jago grinned back. She was an astute lady. Despite her old-fashioned bun and her own undatable, sensible frock, she was well up to current fashion trends. Although any mother of a thoroughly modern miss such as Dee Malpas would have to be blind, and possibly deaf, not to be, he thought.

* * *

So there had been more people at Falquonroy that night than had been supposed – three more, in fact. Did he really believe, Reardon asked himself, that they were likely suspects, any of them? A half-drunk trio who'd happened by chance to be there on the night Emilie Waring died, and who had no connection with her? FitzAlban had never even met Emilie, and Shefford so briefly he barely remembered her. The one they called Boo, now back in London, seemed even more unlikely.

All the same, they may have seen or heard something that might have seemed irrelevant to them. They would all have to be questioned, but Reardon decided the two who were still here could be left shooting clay pigeons for the time being. 'We wouldn't want to interrupt their practice, would we?'

Jago rolled his eyes. Trying to hit a bit of pot thrown into the air from a machine? He'd seen better stuff in fairgrounds. Practice, Shefford had said. For what? The Glorious Twelfth? That annual grouse and game slaughter in August for which the gentry flocked to their shooting lodges on the moors? If that was it, no doubt Vernon Thorpe-Bassett, MP and clay pigeon shoot organizer, would be among their number.

They drove on in silence for a while, Jago's thoughts soon going back to the exchange with Sir Julius and his wife. 'We're having no luck with those photos,' he remarked.

Reardon threw him a quizzical glance. 'Got the bit fairly between your teeth there, haven't you?'

'I suppose I have. They might mean nothing, but from what Miss Oates told me, Emilie thought the world of Lucy, so it's understandable she'd take them with her when she left Templewood. But why cram them into that little handbag along with all that other stuff?' Several of them had become creased, dog-eared and fuzzy at the edges. 'Why not put them in the suitcase out of harm's way?'

'If we can believe Surtees, she was hoping to see Sir Julius. Maybe she thought they'd mean something to him.'

'She'd have been disappointed then, wouldn't she?'

He'd hoped for more than blank looks at the sight of those pictures. He wished too that he'd had them before he'd talked to Miss Oates. He might have had better luck with her. Then it struck him that perhaps it wasn't too late for that. He'd no wish to upset the lady unnecessarily with reminders of the beloved niece she'd lost, but if there was any chance she might recognize one or two of the people in the photos, or even the place where they were taken, it was surely worth a try.

Reardon, after a moment's thought, surprised him by agreeing. 'Nothing lost.' He looked at his watch. 'There's still time this afternoon, if you get off straight away.'

There was no answer when Jago telephoned Miss Oates. After a moment's thought, he took a chance and decided to go along to Lapperley anyway. She was housebound, and he thought it extremely unlikely that the sort of person he'd judged her to be would refuse to see him simply because he hadn't made an appointment.

This time he found the correct entrance to the farm the first time and drove past the graceful, golden laburnum and straight down the unlovely concrete drive to the front door. His knock was answered by Mrs Burridge, wearing her hat and coat: the former an unforgiving pudding-basin affair and the latter a brown, soldierly looking garment strongly reminiscent of the British Warm worn by army officers during the war.

She recognized him immediately. 'You're the young chap who came to see my sister,' she asserted sternly.

He acknowledged that he was. 'I'd very much like to see her again now for a few minutes, if I may. I hope I'm not disturbing you; I can see you're going out.'

'No, I've just come in. From seeing my sister. If you've come to bother her again, you'll be disappointed. She's in hospital.'

'I'm very sorry to hear that.' And he was. He'd liked the old lady and was concerned for her, not to say disappointed that this second visit was going to be a waste of time. 'Nothing serious, I hope?'

Her sister shrugged. 'I dare say she'll be all right. She's taken like this sometimes, and they know what to do for her in the cottage hospital.' The worried look in her eyes belied the offhand reply, and she went on stiffly, 'She's not to be bothered, though. I won't have that.'

'I wouldn't dream of it.'

'What was it you wanted?' She hadn't asked him in, and he was still standing on the doorstep.

An idea came to him. He wondered if he dared. Henrietta Burridge was not a woman to be trifled with. He took a deep breath. 'Mrs Burridge, I don't want to be a nuisance, but I think you might be able to give me the help I need yourself.' It could be a long shot, but he'd nothing to lose.

She stared at him for some time before answering. 'It's about Emilie Logan again, isn't it?' That was how Emilie had been known to her of course. Emilie Logan.

'In a way. But it's also about your niece, Lucy.'

He was prepared for a brush-off at the mention of her name, but she said nothing and after further scrutiny she held the door open wider. A few minutes later they were seated in the kitchen, Mrs Burridge divested of hat and military overcoat, but looking no less severe in a stiff striped cotton blouse and brown serge skirt. The kitchen was warm, the deal table ruthlessly scrubbed. Copper pans shone, and newspapers were spread on the floor by the door to catch any stray farmyard muck or mud that dared to put in an appearance. A pair of large-size leather slippers warming in front of the kitchen stove was the only sign there was a Mr Burridge who might conceivably be allowed to enter the house – after leaving his gumboots outside.

'Well, then. Edith told me you were asking about our Lucy,' she said, going straight to the point when they were seated on either side of the table.

'Yes. I was sorry to hear that she died so young. It was heart trouble, I believe?'

'Her heart, you think?' Her mouth twisted. 'Well – it might have been troubling her, but she didn't die of it.' She was no fool; she had her reasons for being willing to talk to him, and he didn't want to lead her, so he let her take her time before going on, which presently she did.

'Lucy wasn't strong, that's true. She caught the rheumatic fever as a child, but she grew better as she got older. Better in her health. But Wilfred, our brother, he was too soft with her, and having no mother . . . She was a lovely child, you know, but spoilt. He let her have her own way too much, even when she started running around with that fast crowd – though she was far too young. Made excuses for her because, well, you know, she was such a joy to be with, though if I'm honest she could be a right handful as well! I didn't see so much of them as they lived in London at that time,' she added, as if that explained everything, and perhaps it did. The implication being that if she had been there, Lucy would have been kept better in hand. 'It was only her beloved Nanny Logan could do anything with her,' she went on, 'although even she wasn't always listened to – never mind that Lucy thought the sun shone out of her.'

'How well did you know Mrs Waring – Mrs Logan as she was then?'

'Not well, I'll admit that. As I say, they lived in London and we're busy people here, too busy to take time off for visiting. But they came up to see us sometimes, Christmas and so on, Nanny with them, and I liked what I saw of her. She seemed a sensible sort, but even she couldn't prevent what happened to Lucy.'

'It wasn't her heart, you said. Might it,' he asked carefully, 'have been anything to do with . . . drugs?'

The huge iron kettle she'd set on the stove started singing and without answering she went to make tea. While she was there, she bent to check something in the stove and when the door was opened a rich smell of oxtail stew cooking in a slow oven was released into the kitchen. Bringing the brown earthenware teapot to the table, she set it beside two oversize mugs. No china cups and saucers this time, but no Garibaldi biscuits either.

'No, it wasn't drugs,' she said, sitting down again. 'Edith and Emilie between them would have noticed that, but still, you can't keep these flighty young women under lock and key nowadays, can you? She was nearly eighteen by then and had her friends, not all of them girls of her own age.'

'A boy?' he asked, as gently as he could, having seen the way things were going and guessing what was to come.

'He was no boy!' she responded fiercely. 'He was a *man* – a young man, yes, but well old enough to know better. Old enough to give her money to do what was necessary – and then make himself scarce when the worst happened.'

She fished in the pocket of her skirt for a handkerchief and blew her nose. Henrietta Burridge was by no means as unfeeling as she made out.

Sounds came from outside: the lowing of cows, a clanking of

pails. She looked at the clock. It was coming up to five and Jago thought he might not have much more time before they were interrupted by Farmer Burridge coming in for his tea.

'Who was he, this man?'

'I never knew his name. Her friends clammed up and we never found out. Oh, my brother tried to find him, but perhaps not hard enough, you know? I don't blame him. He wasn't a well man and the whole thing had taken the stuffing out of him. It all became too much and in the end he just lost the will to carry on. He couldn't bear to stay in the same house though, and he and Edith – and Emilie Logan – moved away from London, back up to Harborne where we'd all grown up. He didn't live long after that.'

Before he left, Jago again produced the photographs, his purpose in being there, and showed them to Mrs Burridge. He'd no desire to distress her more, but her reaction was only of surprise. 'Where did you get these?'

'Mrs Waring had them in her handbag.'

She nodded. 'Yes, she would have kept pictures of her Lucy. Where were they taken?'

'I don't know. You don't recognize the place? Or any of the people?'

She dutifully examined each snapshot again, but they clearly meant nothing, apart from the studio picture. Lucy might have been in some of the snaps, but it was hard to distinguish particular features in any of them. 'I'm afraid not. Lucy's friends were strangers to me. She was leading her own life by then, as I said.'

And unspoken between them, almost unbearably, was how little time there had been left of that life.

TWENTY-FIVE

Reardon sent for something to eat at his desk the following day while he took time to make inroads into clearing away some routine stuff. The criminal world's activities didn't stop, not even for the murder investigation of an eminent judge's wife.

He'd almost finished when Sergeant Longton came in. 'Grass widower is it then? No sandwich maker?' he asked pityingly as he set down a paper bag and a large mug of tea. Longton was unmarried and lived with his mother, food provider par-excellence, as his girth testified.

'Only until next week, George.'

The French pupils for the student exchange with Maxstead had arrived yesterday. Ellen had been persuaded by Miss Henshall to stay over at the school for the first week of their six-week visit, tasked with what seemed to Reardon to be the daunting prospect of settling half a dozen sophisticated little Parisiennes from a fashionable lycée into a boarding school in the remote British countryside. 'All in a day's work,' Ellen said. But he was happy for her, knowing she would revel in it; she loved children, even adolescent girls. Both of them, he and Ellen, had their own way of coping with the sadness of not having children of their own.

He finished signing the pile of crime sheets, reached out for the sandwich and took a bite. It might have been cheese, but he wasn't sure. It was definitely white bread, slightly dry. Marge, not butter. Not even any pickle.

The telephone rang.

He knew who it would be. Knott, very edgy about keeping the investigation low key and under wraps for as long as possible. The press, amazingly, hadn't yet got wind of a murder in such a quiet place. When they did, and learnt the victim had been Judge Waring's wife, they'd be overrun.

It wasn't Knott.

'What can I do for you, Mr Catchpole?' He wondered why the tutor should be ringing him, unless it was something to do with the elusive Alexei.

Catchpole dithered nervously before eventually getting to the point. 'There's something I should have told you, something you ought to know.'

Reardon sighed, but prepared to listen. People did this all the time. Thought they knew better than the police by keeping something back, although nine times out of ten it was only some trivial thing they feared being brought to light. There was, however, always the possibility that it might turn out to have some significance, and the man's agitation was obvious. 'I think it could be important,' he was saying.

'Then you'd better come in and see me. Soon as you can.'

'It won't be today; the bus has already left.'

'Isn't there another?'

'Not until tomorrow, gets into Folbury at ten fifteen.' A pause. 'I think you'd want to hear this.'

Reardon looked at his watch. 'Stay where you are,' he said with resignation. 'We'll be right over to see you.' He hung up, looking at yet another journey out to Templewood and asking himself why people chose to live in the back of beyond, especially at lunchtime. He hesitated, looked at the sandwich then threw the inferior offering into the bin and went to find Jago.

The first thing evident when their car drew up at Templewood was the motorbike parked just inside the gate leading to the bothy. 'Young Garbutt's here. Good, we can catch him before we meet the tutor.' Reardon had unfinished business with Garbutt.

'Isn't Catchpole expecting us?'

'He can wait. He hasn't been in any hurry so far to tell us whatever it is that's suddenly so urgent.'

There was no answer to the knock on the half-open door of the bothy or to their shout. Jago stepped inside, came back and reported no one there. Across the garden, Prue was sweeping the flagstones outside the kitchen door. 'Seen Martin around?' he called.

'Helping Grandad, down by the potting shed,' she answered. 'And Catchpole's waiting in the schoolroom.'

'Garbutt first,' Reardon decided. 'He might well be off again by the time we've finished with Catchpole.'

The potting shed, when they found it, stood next door to a fair-sized greenhouse. Both Garbutts, Ezra and his grandson, were pricking out tender young plants from a seed tray into pots set on a wooden table standing outside. The old man's stubby fingers worked quickly but gently, touching the leaves with the sure yet delicate care dictated by a lifetime's experience. Martin's movements were slower, by no means as deft.

'A word or two, please, Martin,' Reardon said. 'We won't disturb you for long.'

Garbutt senior regarded them steadily from shrewd blue eyes, rubbing the loose soil off his fingers, while he decided whether this was any of his business. 'I'll be leaving you to it then, and getting on with me tomatoes,' he said finally. He nodded and went into the greenhouse, though not before throwing out a warning to his grandson. 'Just watch your lip, young 'un, right?'

Martin seemed to be in a slightly better mood today, less truculent. His face actually creased into what might have been a slight smile. You could see he might be quite an attractive man. 'What do you want now?' he asked, almost resigned.

'Well, to begin with, Martin, I believe you said that you and Mrs Waring weren't acquainted.'

'No, I didn't. I said I just never had reason to talk to her much.'

'But you did talk to her last week . . . in fact, you had a row with her, at The Spinney site.' Reardon thought it worth a try.

His head jerked up. 'I'd no row with her, then or ever. Where'd you get hold of that idea?'

'You were overheard. What was it about?'

'I just told you – we didn't *have* any row! Least of all at Old Foxley's. Haven't set foot in there since me and Sam used to knock on her door and run away when we were kids . . . or not until that once, when the pup found Mrs Waring.'

'Someone heard you calling her an interfering old . . . baggage.'

Reardon used Mrs Lychfield's euphemism deliberately, emphasizing it enough to make it obvious that was what it was, and bringing the blood to Garbutt's face.

'Who said that? I wasn't there, I tell you, with or without Mrs Waring.'

'Let's stop messing around, Garbutt. The truth is you didn't get on very well with her, did you?'

His gaze dropped to the plants resting on the table. He had big hands, black with dirt under the fingernails from the pricking out. He still held a dibber, and his fist was clenched around it. There was a lot of held-in emotion there, but he was simmering down and sounded tired, in fact. He said, more quietly, 'I didn't know her well enough to get on with her or not. But I wouldn't ever have slagged her off like you just said, even though she did interfere – in what she didn't begin to understand. Least of all would I have threatened her.' After a moment, he admitted reluctantly, 'I suppose she meant well, but it was nothing to do with her.'

'What was nothing to do with her?' Extracting information from him was a tooth-drawing exercise, but Reardon had kept his patience with people more disinclined to answer his questions than Martin Garbutt could ever compete with. In the end, he was the one who would give in. And he did, as if, all at once, he needed to get the weight off his chest. Or maybe the chip off his shoulder.

'She'd no idea what she was talking about! Me and Gizi – all the Warings if it comes to that, Sophy and Sam included – know each other, we grew up together. Everything's always been all right between us, or it was until . . . well, never mind.'

'Until you began to fancy Gizi? And Mrs Waring warned you off?'

He didn't flare up again, simply stared at Reardon. 'You just don't get it, do you? Me? Gizi wouldn't look twice at me.' It wasn't the right answer. He clearly wouldn't have objected if Gizi had given him some encouragement. 'Not when there's the likes of that chinless wonder around, that FitzAlban!'

Recalling Sophy's opinion of FitzAlban, Jago said, 'What have you against him?'

'That upper-class toff?' He laughed. 'Look here, me and Mrs Waring – we were on the same side as far as he was concerned. All right, she did want me to lay off Gizi, I'll admit that, but not because she thought I was after her. She knew I was on at her to give that bloody FitzAlban the push, and she also knew if you try to make Gizi do something, she'll just do the opposite. Well, I know that, don't I, but I don't intend waiting to see if she might come to her senses over that swine before it's too late and she's made a mess of her life. Somebody has to try and make her see sense. I've told her what I think of him, and I'll go on doing just that,' he ended defiantly.

'What exactly have you told her about Mr FitzAlban?'

'Nothing she doesn't know already. And is prepared to put up with – marry him, give him the heir he wants, as they all do, that lot. All for a tin-pot title and the high life and . . . and all the rest of it. She won't listen, just tells me to mind my own business. Her stepmother was right. She's contrary by nature, can't help it and won't try to be anything else. I did hope, now Sam's come home, he'd make her see sense, but he has his own problems. And if her father knows what's going on, he doesn't seem to care. For all I know, he very likely thinks it would be a good match.'

'You don't give Judge Waring much credit. He's a man of the world, a judge, for heaven's sake, not easily taken in. Men like FitzAlban are open books to him.'

Garbutt threw a scornful look. 'He doesn't know everything.'

His boot dug into the gravel again, apparently his default gesture when he was angry beyond words. When Jago had seen it before, it had been done viciously, as if grinding the driver of the Lagonda into the ground might not be a bad idea, either. This time, however, it lacked the same conviction, as if his unaccustomed eloquence had used up any spare energy. 'Yes, well,' he said at last. 'But she's being a damned pain in the neck, Gizi, all the same.'

'So what was it about Emilie – Mrs Waring?'

'I was just narked with her. She wanted me to keep away from Templewood, not even a visit to my grandad, she said. What was that to her?'

As Gizi's stepmother, Emilie had evidently felt otherwise, but Reardon didn't point it out. 'So there was no row with her that day?'

'How many times do I have to tell you?' Garbutt said dispiritedly. 'No, there wasn't.'

Someone hadn't been telling the truth about that conversation Mrs Lychfield had overheard and Reardon didn't think it was Mrs Lychfield. These last few minutes, Garbutt had been frank enough, up to a point. He was the type to lose his temper and lash out . . . but to row with Emilie Waring, then bide his time before enticing her somewhere where he could choke her to death? Hard to imagine. On the other hand, Garbutt's temper was dangerously inflammable . . . and he was nobody's fool, whatever else he might be.

Catchpole was not alone when they eventually located him in the old schoolroom. Also seated around the battered old central table were his pupil, Alexei, still looking stubborn and unco-operative, Sophy and a somewhat bored-looking Gizi, who was sitting with her chair pushed sideways towards the table, in an attitude of couldn't-care-less-but-at-least-here-I-am. A real family gathering, if Sam had been there. Or their father, the judge, for that matter.

An odd lethargy hung about the room, and not only because it was so warm. Although Lex and his tutor worked here every day, the old schoolroom had the forlorn, unused air of nursery days left behind. A big blackboard and easel stood near a shelf holding a balding, once-loved teddy bear, an armless doll and a wooden fire-engine with its red paint chipped. In one corner was a highchair the children had sat in as babies, and in another a sad rocking horse with a mangy mane, well overdue for transport to the knacker's yard.

All the same, Reardon was suddenly not displeased that Catchpole had dragged them out here. Better for everyone than the sad, cold little interview room at Market Street police station, which to say the least didn't have an atmosphere conducive to persuading anxious people to spill secrets. Secrets? He was guessing by now that's what they might be about to hear. But Catchpole didn't seem able to start.

He appeared to have lost the initial impetus which had caused him to telephone and kept rubbing at the crease between his brows. He had his jacket off and a large mug of black coffee stood at his elbow. Just lifting it to sip from seemed like an effort.

'Mr Catchpole?' Reardon prompted.

The tutor blinked and heaved a sigh that seemed to come from his boots. 'Sorry. Not sleeping well. Bad headache.'

His glasses had done their trick of slipping down his nose again and he slid them up, then raked a hand through his thin sandy hair, looked down and ran a nervous finger along a gouge in the scarred tabletop. Then he braced himself, took a deep breath and announced baldly, 'Emilie was my sister.'

TWENTY-SIX

The announcement had the effect on everyone sitting around the table of robbing them of speech, or even movement, except for Gizi, who sat up straighter, her eyes narrowed and sharp.

Brother and sister! This stodgy, dull and physically not attractive young man and Emilie as she must have been, with her bright hair and the smile that people remembered. His sister. Not a would-be lover then, as Reardon had half surmised.

'Go on, Mr Catchpole.'

It took several more moments before he could. 'That's how I came to get the job of tutoring Alexei, when they were looking for someone.'

'And you were free?'

'I'm taking a sabbatical from my teaching post. Radwell,' he added, naming a minor public school, one presumably willing to grant such concessions to its staff.

'Did Judge Waring know who you were?' No one else had – the astonished faces of the others had showed that.

'He does now.' Brushing the question aside, he said, 'Emilie, I suppose I should call her, though she's still Emma to me, was my big sister, Emma Catchpole. It's a long story.'

'We've plenty time.' But not that much, Reardon thought, as more long moments passed. 'The beginning's a good place to start.'

'What? Oh. Yes.' Then the words came, jerkily at first, but very soon he could hardly keep up with himself. 'Well, she was nine years older than me, you know. Our mother died when I was three . . . but Emma always took care of me. Father was strict with us, a churchgoer, demanded good behaviour all the time. That didn't mean he wasn't a good man,' he added hastily, 'and we were happy enough, just an ordinary family, no problems.'

'Where was your home?'

'Oh, near Hitchin, in Hertfordshire. But Emma only lived there until she was sixteen. Until she . . . ran away.' His voice had become gravelly with emotion. 'All because she fancied herself in love with the man who was her teacher at the grammar school, her art teacher. The man we learnt later who'd been stringing her along ever since she was *fourteen*!'

Now he'd got so far, he couldn't stop. Philip Atterfield, he went on, had kept his affair with Emma going by promising he would marry her when she left school. 'But Father found out. You can imagine the ructions. She couldn't marry without his consent, but a man who could seduce a girl young enough to be his daughter was beyond redemption in his book. And our Emma was always impulsive, headstrong. Self-willed, Father used to say, and sometimes a bit silly, as girls are at that age. There were terrible rows . . . Father threatening to lock her up . . .'

The sun had moved from behind the swooping branches of that huge conifer in the garden and a blade of golden light came through the angle of the opened casement and rested on his bent head. That might well have been all he had to say, but he began again. His glasses were smeary and behind the pebble lenses, his eyes were suspiciously bright. 'Ours was a small village – and you know how it is. Gossip spreads, and rumours were already going round. They reached Atterfield. He knew he was in trouble, left the school of his own accord and disappeared. For another teaching job, as we later found out.'

'And . . . Emma?'

'She followed him, of course. She knew where he'd gone and she left a letter saying she was going to live with him, married or not . . . It almost killed Father. You can imagine . . . *I wash my hands of her . . . she's no daughter of mine . . . she's made her bed, and she must lie in it.*'

'Where did they go?'

'To a small woollen town in the north, called . . . Wykedge.'

The pause before he gave the name, searching their faces, said he expected it to register. Jago raised his eyes from his notes and met Reardon's.

'The Wykedge murders,' Reardon said. The name Atterfield had already given him an inkling of what might be coming, and Jago too would have studied the case during his training at

Hendon. Both his name and Wykedge had gone down in police history.

'Of course you remember it, being police. Decades ago, and it hasn't gone away, little wonder.' Catchpole reached into his pocket for his handkerchief and wiped it across his face like a towel. Underarm sweat patches had spread visibly across his shirt. But he wasn't going to let it stop him from liberating himself of the whole story now that he was into the swing of it.

The Wykedge murders, permanently recorded in police annals, would not be forgotten easily by the general public either. The case had become notorious, a sensation: the rape and murder of two young women, both fifteen years old, by a man who had been their teacher. He had been discovered when he was caught in an attempt to rape a third girl. The sensational trial, the over-blown banner headlines in the newspapers, the pictures of a handsome man with an open, smiling face, one any young girl would trust, thinking she was unique in being singled out by him, beguiled by his flattery. Two young girls, their lives brutally cut short. Emma herself had perhaps been lucky in escaping with her life.

Atterfield had got the sentence he deserved and paid the ultimate penalty: the noose had tightened around his neck. 'But even that wasn't enough for Wykedge,' Catchpole went on bitterly. Feelings had still run high in the town and questions were asked: why had the authorities been so remiss as to allow a teacher with a questionable reputation into one of their schools? How was that allowed to happen?

'Wartime,' Reardon said. 'They were hard pressed for teachers with so many men joining up. As I remember, accusations were thrown at the police too, because people thought it had taken too long to find the murderer.'

The strain of recalling the appalling story had finally brought Catchpole to a halt. He stared out of the window at the cloud of pink cherry blossom against the blue sky, as if he could find nothing more to say. At last, he managed it. 'You can't begin to imagine what it was like for her, what she felt she must do.'

Reardon, who had encountered not dissimilar situations before, had no such difficulty. He could almost have written the next part before Catchpole went on.

Emma too had become another target for the people of Wykedge's need to find someone to blame. In the town she imagined had become her home, she found herself now shunned. She'd always known that she had never really fitted in, that she was not one of them: she spoke with a different accent they considered la-de-dah; she didn't wear a flowered crossover pinny and scrub her front steps, preferring to take a pad and pencil and go out sketching up on the moors. And of course, the fact that she and Atterfield had not been married – perhaps the worst sin of all – had come out during the trial. Whatever the reasons, she found people avoiding her in the streets and even refusing to serve her in shops. Before long, graffiti began to deface the outside of her house, a window was broken by a stone thrown at it. Hate mail was pushed through her door, saying she *must* have known what was going on, been a party to it, that she couldn't live as the wife of a murdering rapist and not know something was deeply wrong.

If enough people tell you, often enough, that you are bad, sooner or later you can come to believe you are, her brother said bitterly. Bit by bit, Emma convinced herself that what they were saying must have some basis of truth. She *had* known, deep down, or at least had strong suspicions, that something had become strangely amiss with the man she called husband, hadn't she? Never for a moment had she suspected he was capable of a double murder – which might easily have been three – but something, at any rate, had been very out of kilter with their life together and she ought to have acknowledged it. And because she hadn't, two young girls had been robbed of any future they might have had. She grew up suddenly, if late. She had made the biggest mistake of her life, and must accept part of the blame for what had happened. There was nothing she could do to repair that now . . . but she was no longer the careless, laughing, headstrong girl she had been, and maybe there was still chance to make another life somewhere else. Not, certainly not, in Wykedge.

Home? Not when her father had refused to let her name ever again pass his lips. Somewhere then, where no one knew, or cared who she was.

In the end, she had departed the town quietly, taken a train to the big city where thousands of other lost souls regularly sought anonymity. London, where Emma Catchpole became Emilie Logan, and where she'd found work wherever she could to support herself.

Reardon had asked for no interruptions, and no one had attempted any. It seemed that even now they could find nothing to say after what they had heard.

Gizi had shrunk further back into her chair while the tutor had been speaking, crossing her arms as though she was cold despite the sun pouring into the room. Alexei had the same frozen look, his young face becoming a mask as he stared at the wall above Reardon's head. He was finding this hitherto unknown version of Emilie and her past a bitter pill to swallow.

Suddenly Gizi stood up. With a tremulous smile that failed to hide how shaken she was, she spoke to Catchpole. 'Thank you for telling us all this about Emilie. She was . . . very brave, wasn't she?'

Reardon thought it was brave of *her* to say that, an admission that she'd misjudged her stepmother, and was sorry now that she had. 'May we go now?' she asked.

'We,' she said, looking at Sophy and including her. Sophy, her face still blank with shock, looked uncertainly at Reardon.

'Sergeant Jago and I need a few more words with Mr Catchpole, but none of you have to stay,' he said.

Alexei went first. Without another word, he scraped his chair back, stood up and walked from the room. The others followed.

It was the name *Wykedge* going round and round in Sophy's head, like a gramophone record with its needle stuck in a groove, that sent her to Papa's study, where she paused outside the door.

There was a tall, narrow window in the passage, with a sill wide enough to sit on. Sinking on to it, she stared at the door, trying to make sense of the thoughts that were going round in her head.

It wasn't forbidden territory, Pa's study, certainly not to her. Even in a house this size, with all its hidden nooks and crannies, it was annoying how often someone would come across you and interrupt, in whatever quiet place you thought you'd found to write undisturbed. But Pa had never minded her taking her 'scribblings' into his study, perhaps even in the faint hope, who knew, that she might pick up something from among all the law reports, the tomes on jurisprudence and forensic science on his shelves and be inspired to follow in his footsteps. Not a chance!

What *had* interested her was the set of printed and illustrated volumes of notable and usually sensational murder trials, going back many years. The author, whose name wasn't familiar (probably some journalistic hack, writing for popular consumption), had included sketches and sometimes lurid photographs which Sophy had devoured eagerly when she was at that age to find such things exciting.

But now she slid off the windowsill and stood uncertainly outside the door, her hand on the knob. She understood at last that faint, elusive sense of recognition she'd felt on that first encounter with Emilie in Scarborough, and which had haunted her from time to time ever since.

For a long time, she stood there, horribly undecided. Then, abruptly, she walked away.

'Mr Catchpole,' Reardon began when the door had closed and he judged the tense silence which followed had gone on long enough, 'you still haven't been entirely open with us. There's more, isn't there?'

He well understood how painful the revelations had been for the man, but they were police officers, not here to offer a shoulder to weep on. There were still very large gaps not accounted for in the final sad stages of Emilie's life. He changed tactics and said, sharply now, 'You've kept this to yourself all this time. Why are you telling us now?'

Catchpole looked up at last through his smeary glasses, took them off and began polishing them with the end of his tie. Without them, his face looked naked and raw with grief. 'I don't know,' he admitted miserably. 'Unless I've become so used to secrecy it's become a habit.' After a moment, he said, 'What hurts most, you know is . . . losing her like that, after parting not . . . well, to be truthful, not on the best of terms.'

'You'd quarrelled? Why was that?'

'It wasn't a quarrel – or not exactly, and it was my fault. I was tense and feeling very irritated with her, I'm afraid. She was being so unlike herself, irrational and impatient, and she wouldn't tell me what was wrong.' He stopped, losing the thread. Time passed. 'I – I'm sorry, where was I?'

'Begin with where you took her luggage down to The Spinney.'

'How did you know I did that?'

A guess, or perhaps a process of elimination, but Reardon wasn't about to tell him so. 'You knew she was leaving.'

'Not *leaving*, precisely. Just going away for a while, she said. She had things to think over and needed time to herself. I could only think there must have been some marital trouble. She said no, of course not, but she still wouldn't say what it was. She needed to go quietly, without fuss, so she'd arranged for someone to pick her up from The Spinney and drive her to catch a train.'

'Did she say who that was?'

'No, but I suspected it was that wretched Surtees. The architect. They were very pally, God knows why . . . I couldn't think who else.' He shrugged helplessly. 'And there was that letter as well.'

'What letter was that?' Reardon asked sharply.

'It was one she'd written to Sir Julius. She'd expected him to reply, but he hadn't, and it was making her very edgy.'

'Didn't you think it odd that she'd write to him when she was seeing him practically every day?'

'Yes, I did.'

'Had she posted it?'

'I wouldn't have thought so. More likely she'd have given it to one of the servants to take across to Falquonroy. Or handed it to that fellow Cribb for all I know. He always seems to be hanging around here. It must have been urgent . . . she was very agitated because Sir Julius hadn't sent a reply or even telephoned. I couldn't think what the devil was the matter with her – I think she hardly knew herself. I couldn't get anything sensible out of her.'

He was virtually repeating what Surtees had said. Who perhaps hadn't been lying after all. And perhaps Catchpole was not quite so innocent as he was making out.

'Anyway,' he continued, 'though I was still annoyed with her, it ended with me agreeing to give her a hand with her luggage, carry her cases down to The Spinney. We went there together. I thought of hiding somewhere to see who the "someone" was who was supposed to be giving her the lift, but she stood at the site entrance and watched me walk back up the road.'

'You didn't think she might be in any danger, leaving her alone in a lonely spot at night?'

'Danger? Around here? Strangers wouldn't know about The Spinney and those who do know wouldn't go near. Haven't you heard it's supposed to be haunted?'

TWENTY-SEVEN

It was after six. Reardon was clearing up in his office, while Jago still sat at his desk, contemplating what was spread out in front of him. Everyone else had gone home.

The two of them had spent the last hours going over what had emerged that afternoon, and by now they'd both had enough of tossing around the 'what ifs' and 'might haves' and getting nowhere. Trying to see what significance, if any, the disconnected threads of Emilie's life had to the puzzle that was her death. What had happened to her in Wykedge had clearly shaped the rest of her life. She'd embraced a quiet, uneventful existence, looking after the little girl, Lucy. It was probably why she'd tried to stop Gizi ruining her life by attaching herself to the wrong man, as she herself had once done. Above all, it said why she'd worked so unstintingly with Sir Julius and his refugee committee . . . Emilie had known what it was like to be persecuted.

But what relevance had any of this to her death?

The CID room where Jago sat stayed silent, while from the rest of the station, carrying on with its usual business, came only the normal evening murmur, the lull before the pubs closed and any trouble kicked off.

Presently Reardon appeared, jacket over one shoulder. 'I'm off home and so should you be,' he remarked, nodding towards the photographs spread out as though they might be tarot cards possessing some psychic, occult significance. He rested his hand momentarily on Jago's shoulder. 'Pack it in for tonight. Things always look better in the morning, as Grandma used to say.'

Jago threw his pencil down and stretched. Reardon looked as knackered as he felt himself. He was probably right about these photos, though he must know that when something was bugging you and wouldn't go away, it was useless to try and ignore it. 'OK,' he said. 'I'll call it a day soon.'

Reardon left. The door closed behind him and Jago heard,

'Night, George,' and the avuncular response from Longton, who was probably hoping for a quiet night and maybe even the chance of a snooze behind the front desk.

Reardon took his time walking home. There was no hurry. There would be no Ellen waiting for him, nor even Tolly, with his crazily joyful greeting.

For the first time since they had moved in, the house didn't say welcome, despite the savoury smell coming from the still very slightly warm earthenware stew pot sitting on the table. Brought over of course by Maisie, Joe Gilmour's wife, who always thought any man left alone for more than half a day would starve, and didn't yet have her husband home from hospital to cook for. She'd also left one of her famous Bakewell tarts, tidied up and set a place for him at the table. One knife, fork and spoon.

A folded paper was propped against the stew pot. When he opened it, he saw the crayon drawing of a stick man with orange hair lying on a bed with his outsize bandaged leg in the air and a label on his chest saying 'My Dady'.

Underneath was written, in unsteady capitals, 'Love from Ellie' with the rest of the paper covered in kisses. He laughed. The house suddenly didn't feel quite so empty.

After changing into something more comfortable, he put the hot pot into a low oven as instructed and walked along to fetch Tolly from their neighbour who looked after him on the days when Ellen was teaching at Maxstead, and at any other time his owners could be persuaded to leave him. Old Horace and the Jack Russell were bosom pals and great company for each other, but Tolly's inexhaustible energy needed a good brisk workout at least twice a day, which the old man wasn't up to nowadays.

'He's had a walk around the houses at lunchtime,' Horace said after the usual cup of tea and friendly chat, but Tolly sat commandingly beside where his lead hung, his eyes fixed unwaveringly on Reardon. He was up for a *real* walk and Reardon wasn't going to get away without taking him for one. 'Come on then, mutt,' he said.

This time, he didn't try to prove himself by jogging up the slope; he took it at the usual pace. Tolly left him behind, and when he caught up, was already racing around looking for non-existent rabbits. Reardon chose a perch on one of the foundation stones of the old mansion which had once stood there, looking down at the spread of the town below him, now familiar territory, for whose law and order he was partly responsible.

The area of Folbury known as the Old Town, with its ruined castle and ancient houses, had taken on a picturesque, almost romantic aspect in the dying light of what had been another glorious day, hopefully the start of a more settled period after this last spell of uncertain weather, it being neither one thing nor the other.

The town's industrial spread towards Birmingham was mercifully hazy in the deepening dusk, while Maxstead, Ellen and her little French *mam'selles*, Templewood, Falquonroy and the forested acres surrounding them lay behind him. Although less than fifteen miles away, it could have been another country.

He sat on the stone, chin in hand like Rodin's *Thinker* and tried, unsuccessfully, to let his thoughts drift. He'd warned Jago not to get obsessive over those photos and here he was, doing the same – or something very much akin. He'd known it was useless advice, knew how it could be like an itch that couldn't be scratched, like that shadow he himself kept glimpsing from his eye corner, that elusive something he'd just missed and couldn't catch.

The light was rapidly fading. After a while he stood up, whistled for Tolly and walked back down the hill for his supper and a good night's sleep.

After Reardon had gone home, Jago still hung around the office. Frustrating as it was, trying to make sense of what was in front of him on his desk was infinitely more appealing than the prospect of a lonely evening in the digs found for him, after coping with his landlady's idea of supper. She'd already learnt that his appearances could be erratic and didn't bother to start cooking until he appeared. He'd pick up some fish and chips somewhere later on. He brought a desk lamp over to give further light while he pored over the pictures for the umpteenth time.

He told himself he was imagining the faint sense of déjà-vu the scene called up. Nothing more than wishful thinking. Lucy might have been in several of the snaps as well as the portrait, but they were too far away or out of focus to be sure. People lounged about on the grass or perched on conveniently low walls, mostly with drinks or bottles in their hands. A tennis court in the background, an ancient spreading cedar. Glimpses of shining water, young men in boaters and shirt sleeves, the girls in short, sleeveless summer dresses.

The one he'd come back to yet again wasn't much clearer than the rest, smudgy and not square on because the amateur cameraman had been trying to capture four or five men horsing around in a boat, in an apparent attempt to topple one of them into the water. One of them leant out, stretching to retrieve a lost oar floating on the water before it sank.

No use! He tossed the magnifier down impatiently. Reardon was right. Obsessions didn't pay.

Then it happened: the glass he'd thrown had landed partly on that last picture, showing a white streak almost out of the frame. From another angle, and now magnified, the streak was revealed as part of a column; if the camera had taken in more, it would have shown it as one of several others, all supporting a white, classical cupola.

A white folly, built on an island in the river. Henley-on-Thames! Not regatta time, when the river would be closed to all but the boats competing in the annual races, a fashionable, social event of the summer season, but a party being held at one of those large, expensive riverside houses whose gardens ran down to the Thames.

He blinked to clear his vision and stared harder, not wanting to believe what he saw, but in the end he looked at his watch, hesitated, then on impulse, his heart thumping, reached for the telephone and requested to be put through to a London number that was engraved on his heart. It rang on into an empty silence he might have predicted, given that this was just the time people were gearing up for the London party scene. Not yet in its swing but getting towards it. At last the ring tone stopped, a receiver was lifted.

'Eloise?' he said.

'I can't, Tom, I'm sorry.' Her voice was still huskily seductive, but with new undertones of fear, as palpable down the line as if he were standing next to her.

Fear hadn't been what she'd shown when the package had changed hands, that day at the house in Henley. Secrecy, excitement, flushed cheeks . . . he hadn't been meant to see any of it, but he had. He'd seen the exchange, and it had been the source of the enormous row between them on the way home, the eventual cause of their separating. *How dare he accuse her?* He was just trying to frighten her, telling her that drug-taking was illegal, and she could face severe penalties, even a prison sentence – if she didn't kill herself with it first. It was just an occasional relaxation. Everyone used coke, didn't they? *She was not addicted.* It *wasn't* a habit she needed to kick. To prove it, she'd hurled the God-knows-what-it-had-cost packet out of the car window into the gutter, to be shovelled up by the next road sweeper driving along.

The incident was only the trigger that shattered a relationship never destined to last. In fact, he'd already begun to suspect, though not able to admit that, sex apart, they had nothing in common. His eyelids were now wide open, the fairy-dust blown away. He tried to talk to her sensibly, to make her see what she was doing to herself . . . but she wouldn't listen.

The silence had now become so intense he thought she'd rung off, until she said, 'I'd help if I could, Tom. God knows I've reason to thank you. You might not have realized, but you made me see sense. I haven't touched . . . anything, since I left you. Hugo and I . . . he mustn't know! We are . . . we have a baby daughter who matters very much to me, to both of us.'

He understood now the fear he'd sensed when she'd picked up the telephone and heard his voice. He'd always known there was a rich husband somewhere in the background, who hadn't mattered except as a means of providing the necessary for the lifestyle she'd felt she needed. Now it seemed she'd gone back to him after she and Tom had parted.

'He doesn't need to know. I only need a name.'

'It won't help, Tom. I only knew him as Pete, and he's dead now, an overdose. It was another reason I stopped.'

He knew he had no right to ask for more, but he braced himself for a last question. 'That house at Henley . . . What was it called? Who did it belong to?'

'I don't actually think I ever knew. You know how it was.'

Only too well. Any place where there was rumour of a party, amusement, plenty to drink, mindless activity, outrageous behaviour.

Probably owned, he thought, by one of those privileged families, along with their ancestral home, a hunting lodge on the grouse moors, a townhouse in London, perhaps a villa on the Riviera. Acquired on a whim, its main attraction being the Thames and the annual regatta week, one of the big social events for the leisured upper classes. Left empty or possibly leased out for the rest of the year.

Wait a minute, though,' Eloise was saying. 'It might have been Orwell House, or something like that, but I can't be sure. Does it matter?'

He thought it must. Drugs had certainly changed hands there that afternoon, a fact not necessarily known to the owners of the house – but who was to say what relevance that could have to those old photos, when in any case Lucy hadn't died of drugs, and it wasn't her death they were investigating, it was Emilie's. He was in danger of making the facts fit a theory. But the question of why Emilie had been carrying those photos around was still unanswered.

Reiterating promises that he wouldn't be bothering her again, hoping she would believe him, he thanked Eloise and rang off, not much wiser as far as obtaining the information he'd sought, but feeling strangely uplifted. It took him a few minutes, and then he understood that a drearily familiar weight had lifted from somewhere inside him. Knowing Eloise's life had changed for the better had finally sent packing that nagging fear that he was in some way still responsible for her.

PART FOUR

TWENTY-EIGHT

If only to confirm what Sir Julius had said about his Thursday-night guests, Reardon still needed to talk to them. But chasing them all over the place wasn't high on his agenda; a request had been made for them to present themselves at Folbury police station as soon as was convenient. Soon evidently didn't mean the same to them as it did to him. He had to send for them, and at last, the day after Catchpole had stunned them all by what he'd said, the pair had come in together, leaving the Lagonda right outside the police front door in Market Street, attracting much attention from small boys and holding up the traffic.

They entered, FitzAlban looking patronizingly amused, Shefford his seemingly normal, disconnected self, still walking with a slight limp but by now needing no help from a walking stick. Reardon couldn't quite see what they might have in common, except perhaps a general air of superiority. They were only here together perhaps through the accident to Shefford's knee. Reardon, who had little time for the likes of either of them, wondered why he'd let them pussyfoot around for so long.

'Thank you for coming in, gentlemen. This shouldn't take up much of your time.'

'Why have we been asked here at all?'

'Oh, just to get the picture straight, that's all, Mr FitzAlban. Only a few details to confirm what Sir Julius has told us about last Thursday night. The ninth, that is. The night Mrs Waring disappeared.'

'Sorry to disappoint you, Inspector, but nothing happened, not as far as we're concerned.'

'After you dined, Sir Julius left you to take an early night, I believe?'

'While we went to the billiard room, that's right. Where we spent the rest of the evening until we went up to bed.'

'And you saw or spoke to no one else?'

'Only the butler, who brought us some replenishments.'

'Can anyone confirm this?' Jago asked.

'Old Boo was there as well, but you'll get no sense from him. Silly ass at the best of times, Boo, and no chance of him remembering anything of that night. He was three sheets to the wind.'

'Pissed as a newt!' That singularly disconcerting smile appeared on Shefford's face, and what might even have been a gleam of humour in his eyes – though it was hard to read anything from them – brown, so dark as to be almost black. 'Took both of us to get him upstairs and into bed. Hell of a job.'

There wasn't much else to be got from them. What they had said confirmed Sir Julius's account of events, although there was still Bouvier-Summerson, this 'Boo'. The general opinion, as Jago pointed out, seemed to be that he was a bit of an idiot (even Lady Malpas had thought so, and Reardon would back her any day) but that didn't mean he wasn't a dangerous idiot. All the same, Reardon hoped he wouldn't have to be sought out and questioned.

When he arrived at Market Street the following day, Reardon was told that he'd just missed a telephone call. 'Lady wanting to speak to you or DS Jago, sir. She didn't give a name, but she's left a London number to call back.'

After only three rings the phone was answered by a brisk, competent voice. 'Nurse Rafferty speaking.' Emilie Waring's friend, who had been holidaying and hadn't been expected back until next week. 'You're wanting to talk to me about Emilie Waring,' she said when he'd identified himself. 'I got the message.'

Even without the good old Irish name, the soft Celtic inflexion and a comfortable warmth in the words coming over the wire would have left no one in doubt as to where she came from. Scarcely pausing for breath, she lost no time in launching forth. 'I can't tell you what a shock it was to hear about Emilie from Miss Oates. She was one of my long-term patients when the family lived here in Finchley – Miss Oates, I mean – and that's how I met Emilie and how we became such good friends. We've kept in touch – in fact, I had this letter from her just before I went away. I think you'd like to know what it says, but it's too complicated to discuss over the telephone. Not to worry though, it's all arranged. I still have a few days left from my holiday entitlement so I'm coming up to your neck of the woods. Miss Oates has kindly offered to put me up, so you and I can meet then. I'll bring the letter with me.'

'I thought Miss Oates was in hospital?'

'She's back home with her sister now. I've spoken with them and I'm to stay over with them for a day or two. I'm ready to set off any minute, to make good time, so it's lucky you caught me. I have a motorcar,' she announced with a hint of pride. 'Don't worry, I'll come and see you as soon as I get there.'

She ended the call. All done and dusted, temperatures taken, medicines dispensed, hospital corners folded in tightly. Patients settled but left slightly punch-drunk. The meeting with Nurse Rafferty should be interesting.

Jago put his head round the door. 'If you're not busy?'

Reardon saw the familiar envelope and waved him to sit down. 'Don't tell me you've been able to identify someone?'

'No, but I've recognized where these snaps were taken. It's a place on the Thames, near Henley. Big house, extensive garden going down to the river, a lot of money being thrown around.' He drew a breath. 'I – er – went there once, with a friend.'

What Reardon would make of that last, Jago hoped to avoid finding out, but Reardon wasn't probing further. He merely nodded towards the pictures, now laid out yet again. 'And what do you think this place – Henley, you say – has to do with Emilie's murder?'

'I don't know if it has. Except that I couldn't think why else she would want to keep these particular snapshots in her bag.'

Reardon gave them another close look. 'What was going on there with that lot, then? They all look pretty squiffy. Drink? Drugs?'

'Anything's possible,' Jago said carefully, reminding himself again that as far as they knew drugs had nothing to do with Emilie's death. 'I think they must have been a wild crowd.'

'Hmm. Lady Malpas thought these snapshots were taken, when . . . ten years ago?'

'At least. But some of these people are very likely to be still hanging around. Throwbacks from the twenties, old flappers and superannuated deb's delights, mixing with the younger ones. You know how it goes.'

Reardon's eyebrows lifted. Maybe in London, but this was Folbury. 'You think Emilie was carrying the photos around because she'd found out the identity of the man who was responsible, indirectly or not, for the death of a young girl so long ago? Is that it?'

'If she was, he's not anyone I've been able to identify on these.' Jago slid the photograph back into the envelope. 'You think I've been wasting my time, sir,' he made himself say when Reardon's silence had lasted a little too long. He'd already resigned himself to being told that, and was relieved when Reardon gave a faint smile.

'I do not. Not if there's a chance of it being a pointer in the right direction, though it's not coming to me yet just how that could work out. At any rate, if you know now where they were taken, we've more to go on than we've had up to now, which is damn all. Carry on with it,' he added encouragingly, 'and we'll see where it takes us.' He reached for his pen and the papers in front of him. 'By the way, this friend of Emilie's, Nurse Rafferty, is back from holiday. She'll be in later, so keep yourself available.'

Jago seemed undecided whether or not to say something else, but left without doing so. He would keep last night's meeting to himself for a bit longer. He wasn't yet sure if it had any relevance. And his friendship with Sam was a slippery area just now.

Sam had braced himself to telephone Jago the previous night. If he was free, perhaps they could drive out to a small pub he knew, a few miles out of Folbury?

He drove the Opel as he did most things, with determined concentration, but that evening he couldn't entirely keep his mind on it. They'd hardly got going before he found himself saying, 'Emilie, Catchpole's sister, for God's sake! Who would ever have thought that? I could kick myself for not being at home the other day. Or maybe it's Catchpole I should kick, for not waiting until I got back before making his big announcement.'

'I don't suppose you were uppermost in the poor chap's mind.'

'*Poor chap*? If he'd spoken up sooner, maybe she would still be . . .'

'You don't think that.'

No, of course he didn't. Well, not really. His thinking was all to pot since he'd left Germany and come back home – like making that sudden rash decision to take the train to London. For his own self-respect he needed desperately to find himself another job and he knew people there he could contact, so he'd gone on impulse, ignoring what Pa had said about strings which could be pulled to find suitable work here in the Midlands. He might have saved himself the journey. The trip hadn't been a success.

Inaction never sat easily with Sam, and these last few days at Templewood had left him with little to do except worry, getting him nowhere. Sir Julius seemed grateful for the offer to help with the work Emilie had been doing, but it took up too little of the space in his mind. He'd also played furious tennis with Lex, both of them taking out their frustrations by attempting to hit the ball into eternity. It was time he got to know his young cousin better, he'd decided, but Lex had been no more forthcoming than usual, too inclined to relapse into moody silences to be approachable. It had only ever been Emilie Lex would talk to, hadn't it?

By the time they arrived at the Red Bull, the sunny day was sliding down towards a lovely evening, full of the promise of a long summer yet to come. They took their drinks and sandwiches outside, to the back, where a couple of wooden tables stood on a patch of grass leading down to a wide, gently flowing stream. It was peaceful; the only other occupants were a sooty black mother coot with a dazzling blaze of white on her head, sailing along with a family of chicks behind her, and a blackbird warbling his evening serenade from the trees dipping above the water.

Sam brushed away the breadcrumbs he'd been throwing to the line of fluffy little chicks, laughing at their implausible ruffs of bright orange feathers, came back to the table and flopped on to a seat.

They sat in silence while Sam fidgeted and fiddled with his beer glass, until at last he began with what he hadn't yet felt able to speak about to anyone else: Rosa and those final days in Berlin.

She was still in Belgium, he finished, incredulous and almost angry that she was afraid to make the ultimate decision to cross what she saw as the point of no return, that narrow strip of water separating Britain from the rest of Europe. Or scared to make the equally difficult choice – not about marrying him, but about living the rest of her life amid the stiff-necked English, notoriously suspicious of foreigners, especially those they considered Huns. He wouldn't allow himself to believe she might be making excuses; he knew she truly did feel it was safer to stay where she was, where she might more easily get home to her beloved Berlin as soon as the madmen who had Germany under their heels were ousted. She couldn't, or wouldn't, yet admit that any return might never be possible.

Jago had suspected much of this and understood Sam's dilemma, but before he could think of something useful or relevant to say, Sam gave a deep sigh. 'Well, that's enough of me,' he said abruptly. 'You were asking about that damned fascist and his crony?'

Jago recognized the change of subject for what it was. Sam was annoyed with himself for nearly admitting that he needed . . . what? Support, advice, help? He let it go for the moment. 'FitzAlban and the other one are fascists then, are they?'

The word was speedily becoming almost commonplace as the worst possible insult to apply to anyone nowadays, though not necessarily in a specific sense. Sam, however, had spoken in capitals.

'Not Shefford, I would think, but FitzAlban, oh yes!'

Jago had no problem with believing that, based on nothing more than his instinctive dislike of the man and his attitude. Though he didn't actually see him as one of the black-shirted, jack-booted Biff Boys, so nicknamed for their ruthless ability with the batons they carried and used to good effect at any sign of provocation from the Lefties. Which was never far absent, it had to be said. BUF meetings, large or small (and they were still cropping up here and there, this part of the world not an exception) were guaranteed to be rough affairs.

'Too right he is! And if that's not enough, my half-witted sister, if you can believe it, is mad on him . . . on his money at least. And his title.'

'So he has a title?'

'Not yet. His father's Earl of Kyneton, but it's his elder brother, Viscount Udall, who's the heir. Fitz is still only an Honourable.

Though not for much longer, from what I hear. Udall's drinking himself to death; it's a bet he won't last the year out. They say he'll go before their father – who's ancient, by the way, never seen anywhere now – then it's Fitz who'll be the viscount, Lord Udall. Meaning Gizi,' he added bitterly, 'will eventually be a countess, if she marries him.'

You were inclined to forget, with Sam, the posh public school he'd attended, the sort of people he'd known and mixed with before Oxford, the friends he still had.

'Where does he live, this brother?'

Jago had been half expecting, and perhaps hoping, to hear him say Henley-on-Thames. Sam, however, didn't know, but thought it was Eaton Square or somewhere. 'I can find out for sure. Why, do you want to talk to him?'

'Not if I can help it!' Meeting and talking with an older, possibly inebriated, version of FitzAlban was a pleasure it wouldn't be difficult to forego. 'Another fascist, is he?'

'Shouldn't wonder; he's been into nearly everything else. But I suspect he's ceased to bother about politics or whatever else is going on now. I don't see him strutting about in jackboots.'

'Everything else, you say. *What* else?'

He shrugged. 'Just the usual story . . . drink, women, gambling, you name it.'

'Splash their money around, do they, the FitzAlbans? Where does it come from?'

'Old money, I suppose. Like a lot more . . . sugar plantations, slave trade, dark satanic mills and all that. Wasn't that how most of it was made? Grinding the faces of the poor – you should hear Martin Garbutt on the subject.'

'I already have.'

Sam rolled his eyes. Jago wondered how much else he might be prompted to recall. 'Gambling, you said, drinking. What about . . . narcotics?' he asked, again ignoring his resolve to dismiss them as having nothing to do with the case.

'Drugs?' Sam threw him a very sharp look. 'I damn well hope not, for Gizi's sake.' He hesitated. 'You may be barking up the wrong tree about drugs, but make no mistake – not wearing a black shirt and jackboots doesn't mean a thing as far as FitzAlban's concerned! He's thick as thieves with Mosley and his gang, and if you need convincing, he was at the last Nuremberg rally in Germany. I saw his photograph in the papers over there, with Mosley and those deluded Mitford women, worshipping Adolf Hitler as if he's the Messiah.' He pushed his hands through his hair. 'OK, I'm fixated, but you can see why I'm so bothered about Gizi. I'm damned sure,' he went on moodily, 'that he's actually got her halfway to believing what they're spouting, like a lot more of that set she's tagging around with.'

Jago had come across them in London often enough, these fashionable-to-be-fascist types, just as likely to call themselves Bolshevik or whatever else when the next charismatic leader came along. He wondered how they'd react if they came across real fascism.

And then, regardless of any break between what he'd been saying previously, as though his anger at FitzAlban had recharged him, Sam began in a rush, 'I've something to ask you. I might as well. I'm in a quandary. I've come to see I must go over to Belgium to persuade Rosa to come back with me, but . . .'

'You have? What took you so long?'

'All right, you may well ask. But it won't be easy,' he said miserably. 'I stopped off there, where she's staying, on my way home. That's why it took me so long to get here. Two days trying to persuade her to come with me, but convince her I couldn't . . .'

Sam's self-confidence had been eroded, doubt clouded his face; usually so sure of himself, he needed someone to back him up and assure him he would be doing the right thing.

'What's the problem?'

'Which one would you like first? But chiefly – oh, how the devil can I bring Rosa to live here, after all that's happened to her with those thugs, when my sister's halfway to being a damned fascist?'

'You have another sister, don't forget!' Jago didn't miss Sam's stare at the quickness, the sharpness in his tone, but it didn't stop him. 'Don't be a fool, Sam. If Rosa's the woman you say she is, Gizi's shenanigans won't stop her from coming here to marry you . . . if that's what you want, of course.'

'*What I want?*' Sam repeated, then quite suddenly, he laughed. That was all it had taken. As though a tap had been turned, his natural energy was almost visibly flowing back into him. 'Why the hell do you always have to be so damned right, Tom Jago?' He gave another laugh and then threw Jago a look that set his ears burning. 'Sophy, huh? Well, what d'you know?'

TWENTY-NINE

Nurse Rafferty was almost laughably as Reardon had imagined her. A very comfortably built, middle-aged woman with brown hair beginning to go grey. Blue Irish eyes. A very firm handshake, a kind face with a warm smile, and no signs of tiredness after driving over a hundred miles squeezed into the little Baby Austin that was obviously the apple of her eye. Settled with a cup of tea and a couple of custard creams, she was as garrulous as she had been on the telephone, eager to get what she had to say off her ample chest.

'Who could possibly have done this to someone like Emilie? She was lovely – all she wanted to do was to help other people, you know? Look at those refugees she was working for! The thing about her was she took everything to heart, and you can't do that, can you, not everything? If I did that in my work I'd be worn to a rag, I can tell you. And not everyone appreciates what you do for them – just the opposite! I've worried about her for years!'

'What is it you've come all this way to tell us, Nurse Rafferty?'

'Well. As I told you, there's this letter I've had, but it goes back further than that.' She paused long enough to give both officers an assessing glance. 'Mrs Burridge tells me that you know about their niece, Lucy, and what happened to that poor child?'

'Yes, we do. It's a tragic story.'

She sighed. 'I see that sort of thing all the time, I'm sorry to say. I dare say you do, too. And doesn't it always fall on the woman?'

Jago said, 'I'm afraid so. In Lucy's case, it seems they never knew the name of the man responsible.'

'That's the truth. Her father was destroyed entirely about the whole thing. Blamed himself for not keeping a better eye on her, but what father wouldn't? You know how these girls can be. If she was determined to go off the rails, he couldn't have stopped her, not Lucy! But she'd been brought up properly, and I think it was because she was too shamefaced, guilty, you know, to say a word to anyone, anyone at all, when the inevitable happened to her. So, she just went ahead and tried to stop it. And no one ever knew who he was, the devil who'd caused it all, and naturally, he wasn't going to come forward! Myself, I reckon he was married and saw no cause to stir up trouble for himself. Her father tried hard enough to find the man, though what he would have done if he had, I'm sure I don't know. Anyway, he never did find out, mostly because all Lucy's so-called friends had mysteriously lost their memories of any affair that had been going on. In the end it was too much for the poor man and he gave up. Then, months later it was, Emilie accidentally let it slip to me that she was sure she'd discovered who the snake in the grass was. Though as soon as she'd said it, mind, she could have bitten her tongue off. She wouldn't let his name pass her lips.'

'That seems strange. Can you think of any reason why she wouldn't tell?'

'I can. She admitted that she'd known him once and owed him a favour. Whatever trouble he'd caused, he'd once helped her, she said, and anyway it was too late: what was done couldn't be undone, and it wasn't going to bring Lucy back. Which was true enough.'

'When was this? When did he do her this favour?'

'I've no idea, but she said she'd never forget it.'

The nurse munched the last biscuit and finished off the tea before she went on, looking steadily at Reardon. 'Maybe I'm speaking with hindsight, but there were things about Emilie, you know, that I could never make out. I always suspected that something must have happened to her, years ago, that she had . . . well, maybe there was something in her past life she was ashamed of, is the best way I can put it. I don't know what it was – she never would talk about where she'd come from, or what she'd been doing before she came to live with the Oates family. Ask her and she'd shut up tight as an oyster! She couldn't even bring herself to tell *me*, her best friend.'

That had hurt. Nice, warm-hearted woman that she was, but patently the sort to whom gossip was as natural as breathing, she evidently didn't know herself as well as Emilie had. However well-intentioned towards her friend, Emilie's secret wouldn't have remained so for long. Reardon didn't feel it necessary to enlighten her.

'I've missed her so much since she left London,' the nurse repeated, 'and now, to think . . .' Her eyes filled with sudden tears, but she blinked them away, fished in her capacious handbag for a handkerchief and blew her nose. Putting the hanky resolutely back, she drew out an envelope and held it out. 'Anyway, this is it, the letter I promised. I think you'd better have a read of it.'

The envelope and the two sheets of lavender-coloured, deckle-edged notepaper, faintly violet-scented, were familiar.

'Another cup of tea?' Jago asked their visitor as Reardon began to read. She must be dry with all that talking.

'Oh, thank you, I could murder another cuppa!' She didn't seem to notice the word, unfortunate in the present circumstances.

After Jago departed, Reardon was mercifully left in silence to re-read the letter and think it over. It began with the usual conventional phrases, but then went on:

> *Now for some news, Eileen, which I'm afraid may be very sad and upsetting for you to read, but I really have to unburden myself to someone and I can think of no one better than you, my dear. I have come across him again – You-Know-Who! And I must and will do something positive about it this time, though I feel ill simply at the thought! I desperately need to speak to someone about it, yet if I do, my life here will be over. You've never met my husband, Eliot; if you had you would know him to be a man of strong moral principles. His judgements are not confined to the offenders who come before him in court! How could I possibly face him with my personal history, see his regard for me, his belief in my integrity shaken? It means only one thing – that I must leave here! The least I can do is not let other lives be ruined as mine almost was, once.*

The letter, which ended abruptly with simply her signature, had begun with rather flamboyant handwriting, though easy enough to read, but by the end it had become sprawling and hard to decipher. The blotches made it easy to believe tears had done that. Heartfelt and yet wasn't it just a shade overdramatized? Reardon counted the exclamation marks. Wasn't there, too, a distinct flavour of those romantic novels she'd loved to read?

Jago came back and Reardon passed the letter over to him. He read it while the nurse drank the fresh cup of tea he'd brought her.

Reardon's mind was still on what he'd read. Running away, though understandable, would seem to have been Emilie's default reaction to stress. At sixteen, she'd run away from home. She'd fled Wykedge too, though with every excuse. And had apparently been preparing to flee her last refuge, Templewood, where she had been happy. He was now inclined to think it more than possible she'd been hoping, by seeing Sir Julius before she actually left, that he might have persuaded her not to go. In the end, however, according to Surtees, it had been her own decision to stay and brave out whatever it was. *To face the music*, she'd said.

Well, that was what it seemed like, but it didn't feel very satisfactory.

The nurse was gathering her handbag to her bosom, preparing to leave. 'I'm sure I don't know what anyone's meant to make of a letter like that at all. It makes no kind of sense to me, but if it helps, I'll leave it with you and be on my way. I'd be grateful if you let me know how things turn out. And thank you for the cup of tea.'

'Just a moment, Nurse Rafferty. You've been very helpful, and we won't keep you much longer, but a little more of your time, if you don't mind.'

She sat down again readily enough, looking enquiringly at him. Reardon tapped the letter. 'One thing that strikes me about this is how afraid she was. Very much afraid, to make the decision to leave everything behind, as she was preparing to do.'

She sighed deeply. 'I know. That's just what upset me so much. She was so happy here, so it must have been bad, whatever it was. Emilie wasn't frightened of anything!' The tears sprang once more to her eyes. 'Except dogs.'

'She was scared of dogs? That's odd,' Jago said. 'Judge Waring had just given her a little bulldog puppy.'

'Goodness, are you sure? Emilie? A *bulldog*?'

'A puppy. She was very fond of it, I understand.'

She didn't believe him. 'She must have had some sort of therapy. That's all I can say.'

'Therapy?'

She said cautiously, as though not really understanding it herself, 'I've heard tell you can be sort of desensitized, or something of that nature, of these . . . phobias, isn't that the name for them? Though I've never had experience of one myself.' After a moment's thought, she added uncertainly, 'Perhaps she wasn't scared of that dog because it wasn't a very *big* one, you know?'

Jago escorted her off the premises, and after seeing her bounce away in her Baby Austin, returned to find Reardon still pondering the letter Emilie had sent to her friend. Jago said, 'At least we know now what it was she was so anxious to see Sir Julius about. She'd met him again – the man responsible for Lucy dying, directly or indirectly.'

Reardon was less sanguine. '*Come across*, is what she actually says here.' He pointed to the phrase on the page in front of him. 'She didn't necessarily have to have *met* him. She might easily have found his name somewhere among the papers she and Sir Julius were working on . . . otherwise, why would what happened to a young girl he never knew matter to him?'

After a moment Jago said, 'He has a daughter, too.'

THIRTY

About the same time as Nurse Rafferty reached Folbury, Alexei came to a halt by the gates at Falquonroy, standing uncertainly between the pair of great black falcons. He drew in his breath and then, after a minute, began the walk down the drive. He had braced himself for what he was going to do, shamed by what he'd learnt when Catchpole had revealed the extent of Emilie's sad story. He'd found courage from somewhere, and the prospect before him didn't seem as intimidating as it had been in his imagination. Even if it was, he admitted at last, it had to be faced.

He'd no desire to advertise his presence by enquiring at the great front door of the house. Instead, though he wasn't familiar with Falquonroy's layout, he cautiously made his way to the back, hopeful of getting to the garages; if the motor wasn't there, he'd be wasting his time.

But there the garages were, and there in front of them was the Lagonda, standing near the newly washed, gleaming Daimler. And there, in one of the garages with its door open, was the man he wanted to see, rummaging around towards the back among a random assortment of equipment for keeping a motorcar in spanking order.

Lex hadn't made much noise, but FitzAlban had heard the sound of footsteps and swung round. With a clumsy haste amazing in such a lazily elegant man, he hurried out, slamming the door behind him.

When he saw who it was that had disturbed him, acute irritation crossed FitzAlban's face. Only for a moment. The look was quickly wiped off, that mocking smile of his summoned up as he stepped away from the garage door, drawing out his cigarettes and lighter.

'Here's a surprise. Didn't expect to see you around here, Alexei old sport.' He held out a hand, which Lex ignored.

'What have you done with that letter I gave you?'

'Remind me, what letter was that?' Smiling still and selecting a cigarette from the silver case, FitzAlban flicked his lighter. Sobranies or not, they weren't offered to Lex this time.

'You know jolly well which one I mean . . . the one I handed to you and asked you to give to Sir Julius.'

'Sorry, I don't remember you giving me anything, old boy, a letter or anything else.'

Alexei couldn't believe what he was hearing. Or rather he could, quite easily, because it was exactly what he'd been expecting; it was just that he didn't *want* to believe it. He'd known perfectly well that he shouldn't have handed the envelope over so casually, asking for it to be passed on, ignoring Emilie's strict, urgent instructions to give it personally to Sir Julius and to him only. His stupidity had been gnawing at him ever since, knowing he'd done it only because he was furious at being regarded as a mere convenience, and not told the reason for it. It was only a letter after all; what did it matter?

Only since Emilie's disappearance and its terrible follow-up had he begun to see it might matter a great deal, after all. 'You haven't forgotten, you can't have!' The blood rushed to his face.

Fitz blew rich, expensive tobacco smoke into the air. 'Really? I've no recollection of you giving me any such thing.'

'You're a bloody liar, FitzAlban!'

All at once, the handsome, smiling man looked neither smiling nor handsome. His pale, cold eyes had narrowed. He threw down his cigarette, where it sizzled in a small puddle left by Cribb's recent Daimler-washing, and went out.

An uncontrollable impulse made Lex step forward, his fist drawn ready to punch the man, but Fitz was quicker. With a strength surprising in one who looked as though lighting a cigarette was the only form of exercise he ever took, his hands tightened on both of Lex's arms. Lex was wearing only a thin shirt, and it hurt. He was younger and fitter than the other, but FitzAlban was showing no intention of letting go. Lex struggled, but couldn't wriggle free. He brought his knee up. It didn't land where he intended, so he kicked out with his foot, and this time it connected hard with FitzAlban's shin. He swore an ugly oath and let go of the boy's arms in order to circle his neck with both hands, shook him like a terrier with a rat, then gave him a great shove. Lex staggered backwards, lost his balance and fell, banging his head and sprawling ignominiously on the ground.

'Had enough? Or would you like some more?' FitzAlban, stepping over him, got no further.

'Now then, sir. Shouldn't do that if I was you.'

Charlie Cribb stood there, shirt-sleeved, muscular, crimson of face under his red hair. Embarrassed, but not looking like anyone to be ignored. FitzAlban took a half step back.

Lex staggered to his feet. He wasn't really hurt, or not very much. His self-respect was, but nothing else. The tussle hadn't lasted all that long, although if Cribb hadn't appeared at that moment . . .

FitzAlban was adjusting his jacket, smoothing back his hair. 'What the hell are *you* pushing your nose in for, Cribb? Go away. This is none of your business.'

They faced each other. Cribb shrugged his big shoulders. 'Saw this young fella going round the corner a few minutes since and wondered what he was after, that's all. As well I come back to see, seems to me.'

Lex saw some communication he couldn't interpret pass between the two men. Cribb stood his ground as the other faced him, glaring, then, 'Damn your eyes, both of you!' FitzAlban spat out, and without another glance at Lex, turned on his heel and stalked away.

Cribb laid a hand on Lex's shoulder. 'You all right, son?'

'Yes, thanks. Or I will be. Much obliged, Cribb.'

He was very glad indeed of the intervention, but he was in fact more humiliated than hurt, as well as confused by what had passed between the two men. That hadn't been at all how anyone like Cribb should be speaking to one of the gentry. 'Thanks again,' he said.

'You're welcome.' The chauffeur didn't give any indication as to how much he'd heard, and Lex wasn't going to enlighten him. He was beginning to feel peculiar, seeing things. Not hallucinating, though. That bang on the head might have shaken his brains, but what he was really seeing was another thing he should have done days ago.

Even as he was trying to make sense of it, there came a laboured, croaky whirr, the sign that the big old stable clock was preparing to strike the hour. For a split second he stood transfixed, colour flooding back into his face. He swung round. 'Thanks again, Cribb. Must go. I've a bus to catch!'

The clock had scarcely begun its first strike before he was gone.

'So that's where the letter ended up?' Reardon seemed slightly bemused by this turn of events. 'Why ask *FitzAlban*, for God's sake? And where is he, the lad?'

'Gone back to Templewood,' Jago said. 'He was on pins not to miss the return bus back – it's the only one until tomorrow, so I let him go. There wasn't any more he had to say, anyway.'

Reardon wished he could have spoken to Alexei himself, though he knew Jago wouldn't have failed to get all the necessary details. 'I hope you put the fear of God into him. Why didn't he tell us before?'

'The longer he left it, the more scared he got?'

'What did he think we were going to do . . . hang, draw and quarter him?'

'I imagine it's more a case of feeling ashamed of himself. Emilie had asked him specifically to give the letter to Sir Julius and no one else, but he was sulking, thought he was being treated as an errand boy. He's only sixteen. FitzAlban's the one who ought to be strung up, going for him like that.'

'And what's all that about the chauffeur?'

'Cribb? Alexei felt sure there's something odd going on there. He thought FitzAlban might have been scared of him.'

'Scared of Cribb? For God's sake, why?'

'I don't know, but Lex seemed to think the way FitzAlban reacted when Cribb appeared on the scene was suspicious. He may be only sixteen but he's a bright lad.'

'Not as bright as he should have been. If FitzAlban did get hold of that letter, it's goodbye to knowing what Emilie wrote in it.' He thought for a while. 'Anything come up yet on Cribb's background?'

'Gargrave's been looking into it. He should have something by now.'

'Send him in to me when he has. But give me time to ring the super first.'

* * *

Knott was getting more and more tetchy at what he saw as the lack of progress and today, when he telephoned, was no exception. 'And if that's not enough to worry about,' he said after the expected huffing, 'the bloody BUF are cooking something up again . . . How are you getting on with Jago, by the way?'

At least Reardon was able to reassure him that the new sergeant was fitting in well. He had slid into the absent Joe Gilmour's role easily and seemed to be on friendly terms with the rest of the team. 'I'll be sorry to lose him when Gilmour's back,' he said, a sly hint at Joe's hoped-for promotion to DI, and the need thereafter for a replacement DS in the department.

'You're lucky to have had him at all,' Knott returned sharply. 'If this other business I've just mentioned with the fascists had blown up earlier, he'd still be here, working on it with us.' With that, he rang off.

But Reardon was still thinking more of the encounter between Alexei and FitzAlban than worrying about Knott's headaches over the BUF or how the case was going. And yet, early days though it still was, the super had a point.

Patience, which didn't come naturally to Reardon, was something he had been forced to cultivate over the years, but it was hard to summon when he was still struggling with that scrap of something overheard somewhere, that glimmer of insight which had lodged in a corner of his mind and was still eluding him. It was making him tetchy.

A tap sounded on the half-open door. Gargrave, holding a couple of sheets of paper. 'What's that you've got for me, Gargrave?'

'About Cribb, sir.'

'Well, don't just stand there. Come in.'

Gargrave did so and passed the papers over, still standing smartly to attention while Reardon gave them a quick scan.

Cribb's family background was all too familiar: a violent father in and out of prison while he'd been growing up; a string of 'uncles' to live in and fill the vacant position; a mother who couldn't cope with five unruly offspring. Behaviour problems at school, a bit of a tearaway after he left. A police record of juvenile misdemeanours.

'Like father, like son,' Gargrave remarked.

'Until he got that apprenticeship,' Reardon pointed out, tapping the sheet of paper.

Eventually the young Charlie Cribb had been befriended by some well-disposed garage owner with an optimistic nature, who'd trained him as a mechanic. After that, no more trouble with the police. 'Looks as if he's a reformed character now he's grown up. Since he went to work for Sir Julius anyway. Good work, Gargrave.'

'Thank you, sir.' Gargrave preened his feathers. He had his hand on the doorknob when Reardon checked him.

'Just a minute. Don't go yet.' Something about the DC had reminded him of what he'd been thinking just before he'd knocked. 'Sit down, Gravy.'

Barely hiding his gratification at the invitation and the friendly use of his nickname, Gargrave moved the usual overspill of papers to one side of the only chair and perched on its edge.

'You were in the West Riding Constabulary before you came here, right?' Reardon asked. The accent had struck a chord.

'Yes, sir.' The DC had transferred to the Midlands to marry a girl who had changed her mind about him (not without good reason, was the opinion of more than one at Folbury police station) and he'd been looking to escape, one way or another, ever since. Preferably via promotion, which he sought assiduously. Which they all did, naturally, but not as irritatingly as Gravy.

'You'll know of a place called Wykedge, then?'

'Wykedge? Where the murders happened, sir?'

'That's right. What can you tell me?'

'Well, not a lot really. I – er – wasn't above eleven or twelve when they happened,' he ventured to remind Reardon.

'Of course you wouldn't be.' *Nobbut a lad, eh?* He almost said it, but you tended not to make jokes, even such lame ones, with Gargrave, who'd been born going on thirty, and hadn't managed to acquire a trace of humour since. 'Well, it's not the murders especially I'm interested in. What else can you tell me about the place?'

'I don't know it all that well, to be honest, sir. We only used to go there to visit my auntie and I haven't been back up there lately.' He hadn't left it behind entirely, though. His accent broadened even as he spoke. 'One-horse mill town, hills and moors all round, wind to blow you off your feet.' He seemed to recall Reardon had a reputation for actually reading books. 'Brontë country,' he added brightly.

Reardon acknowledged that even Gravy couldn't have been unaware of the famous sisters. He wasn't thick; in fact, he was a competent officer when given the kind of work he thought was his due. It was his pushy personality that grated, and though Reardon tried his best to ignore that, Gravy didn't make it easy.

'Not your favourite place, then?'

'I suppose there's worse. But a lot of folks have lived there all their lives so there must be something. Not the sort of place you'd want to go for a holiday though, sir,' he added, in case that might have been Reardon's intention.

He was obviously dying to know what the sudden interest meant; encouraged by Reardon's nod, he went on, 'It's mostly just mills, a lot of small ones plus the big one, Branxholme Spinners and Dyers. Used to employ most of the town at one time.'

'Used to? They're not a going concern now, then?'

'It's not the original family firm, they went bust and it's all part of that big consortium now – you'll know the one I mean, sir, Asquith and Barrett's knitting yarns? You might have seen all the adverts for A & B Wools, knitting patterns and that. I've a cousin still works there, and my Auntie Phyllis used to do home knitting for them, testing out the patterns, you know.'

Reardon's reading matter wasn't the kind that included that sort of advert; nevertheless, the name did ring a faint bell. He nodded a carry-on to Gargrave who'd stopped himself in case the chief thought he was saying too much.

'That's all I know, but I could find out more, sir, if you like. I could ring my auntie; she'd know more than me.'

'She has a telephone?' Reardon was momentarily diverted. Private telephones were rare in small places like Wykedge, mainly confined to doctors, the police and suchlike.

'She's the postmistress, sir.'

The postmistress. Might just as well broadcast it over a loud-speaker system. The last thing they needed was speculation and rumour spreading like measles all through Wykedge, especially rumours of police once more showing interest in the town. They could do without Auntie Phyllis.

'Branxholme, you said. Was that the name of the original owners, before the consortium took over?'

Gargrave, who was after all no fool, and like all the others had been kept up to scratch with names of all concerned in the current investigation, was quick to cotton on to where Reardon was going with this.

'No, that's the name of the mill. Once owned—' But almost before he could get out the name that was on his lips, Reardon said, 'I thought as much. Thank you, Gargrave. All that's been very helpful. But keep it to yourself for now, eh?'

He knew he could trust the DC to do just that. Whatever his faults, Gargrave knew to keep his mouth shut when the boss told him.

A telephone call to Falquonroy informed them that Charlie Cribb would be occupied for most of the day with duties for Sir Julius, so the chauffeur's arrival at Market Street, having driven from Falquonroy in the little runabout they used on the estate, was unexpected. He had to be back within the hour, he told them, but luckily, Reardon was available.

'I don't reckon I'll be wasting your time, sir.'

'You've saved us a journey,' Reardon said. 'Follow me.'

He led Cribb to where they could talk, signalling Jago, presently engaged on the telephone, to follow.

Cribb was looking very smart, in a decent dark suit, collar and tie. Sir Julius evidently didn't think a uniform as such was necessary. The only concession to chauffeurly livery was the peaked cap he was holding, twisting it round and round as he stood stiffly, avoiding looking directly at Reardon.

'Please sit down.' Reardon gestured him to one of the hard, uncomfortable chairs which were all that was on offer. Comfort wasn't deemed necessary when dealing with the offenders most likely to be sitting on them. He hoped Jago wouldn't be long. He thought he was right about why Cribb was here, and Jago was the person the boy Lex had spoken to about the scrap with FitzAlban. He did in fact follow them in almost immediately, flushed and with his thick hair tousled as if he'd run a hand through it, his habit when excited or thinking hard.

Cribb was still hesitating, still uncomfortable. 'It's about that fight young Lex was involved in, isn't it?' Reardon prompted.

'The lad's told you about that, then? I thought he might be headed here when he scarpered so quick. But no, it's not that, not directly, any road.'

'It's not about the letter?'

'Letter? I did hear mention of some letter, but I don't know nothing about it.' Again, he fell uncomfortably silent.

A few more painful moments, Jago shifting impatiently, and then Cribb blurted, 'What I told you last time, about that handbag I found. I might have given you the wrong impression.'

Reardon sighed. 'You were lying.'

'No! No, only there's a bit more to it. I . . . I should've told you what happened on Thursday night at the park.'

'Thursday? So you should, Mr Cribb, so you should. It's not too late. Spit it out.'

'Just a minute,' Jago put in. 'You weren't there at Falquonroy on Thursday. You were still with Lady Malpas and the young ladies in London, and didn't return until Friday morning.'

Cribb shook his head. 'The mistress and Miss Dee had been staying down there for a couple of weeks, see, but Sir Julius couldn't spare me for all that time. He reckoned they didn't need a car in London, with all them taxis and that. I set off very early Friday morning to go down and bring them home.'

'I see. Well, carry on,' Reardon said.

Bit by bit the story emerged.

The room in which Cribb slept had, in Falquonroy's glory days, had been the one given to the head groom. It was above the largest of the stables, looking out over the yard. He'd been wakened during the night by a light shining below.

'It looked like somebody had forgotten to switch off, see. Sir Julius is very partickler about not wasting the electric, but there's been gyppos around lately and Sir Julius . . . he'd have my guts for garters if that motor of his went missing or got messed up. It weren't the Daimler though. They was in the next-door garage.'

'The gypsies?'

'Nah, them two young fellers, Miss Dee's young chap and

him that has the Lagonda . . . treats it like a baby, I'll give him that, and Sir Julius has given him permission to garage it at night, on account of the gyppos. But the pair looked guilty as hell when they saw me there. "'Ere, what you up to?" I asks. They tried to pass it off with a laugh and I could see they was pie-eyed, both of 'em. Miss Dee's chap was that unsteady he near toppled over. I thought he might be going to throw up, so I stepped back pretty damn quick. Put my hand on the Lagonda's bonnet . . . and it was hot. The other feller, him they call Fitz, saw I'd noticed and started to say they'd just been having a look at the ins and outs of the engine. As if I'd come in with the last load of coal! As if I couldn't make a fair guess what'd been going on.'

'Which was what?'

'That there Doraleen, that was what. Right tart she is. Used to be a housemaid at the Park. Lives over to Sawbry now and comes in to help out sometimes. Like she did last week, getting ready for that do they had on Saturday.'

'You thought they'd been visiting this young woman?'

'They wouldn't be the first! That's what I thought then, anyway. And that Fitz pulls out a fistful of notes, shoves a tenner at me and taps his nose. "Not a word, right?" he says.'

'Nice little backhander,' Jago said.

'If he was that free with his money, I wasn't going to say no, was I? A tenner's not to be sneezed at!'

No one could argue with that. How many ordinary folk had even *seen* a ten-pound note?

'I wouldn't have said nothing, but since I heard what had happened to Mrs Waring . . . well, I can put two and two together as well as the next. There's promises and promises,' he said, standing up. 'Any road, that's it. I have to go now. Except,' he added, pulling a crumpled ten-pound note from his pocket and tossing it on to the table in contempt, 'you can give this back to that bastard. I don't want no truck with his dirty money.'

Reardon stood up too. 'Thank you for coming in, Cribb. Very helpful, but mum's the word, right?'

Reardon had picked up the despised ten-pound note and was thoughtfully smoothing out its creases when Jago returned from escorting the chauffeur out, eager to talk about what had just passed, but also still full of the telephone conversation he'd been having when Cribb had walked in.

Detective Sergeant Ted Rowley was an ex-Scotland Yard colleague, now transferred to C Division which, among other things, dealt with vice and drugs. He had started his working life in the Thames Valley police, and though that was a few years back now, Jago had thought he might be able to tell him something about Orwell House, Henley-on-Thames.

'I think you might mean Audley House, not Orwell,' Rowley had said when Jago had first contacted him. 'It used to belong to one of the nobs, years back, though I don't recall who, and I think it's changed hands since. Who owns it now, I don't know. Leave it with me and I'll find out.'

Jago had been happy to do that. Rowley was a first-class detective and he had every hope that what he would come up with would justify his own so far unsupported suspicions. Rowley had been as good as his word.

'So, let's hear what he had to say, then,' Reardon said.

THIRTY-ONE

Sophy sat on the garden swing by the goldfish pool, the soft evening dusk gathering round her like a caress on her skin, inviting her to relax, which felt like the last thing she could do just now.

After toying with her supper, she'd tried first to read, then to write up her journal, then she'd tried opening the rough draft of her novel. But to try to write about a fictional murder enquiry now felt crass, sickeningly insensitive, when there was one only too real going on all around. She'd shoved both aside, gone out into the garden, nothing to do, left out and feeling sorry for herself.

Gizi had gone out earlier with Deedie and those two men, looking simply beautiful in her newest dress, a delicious wisp of soft blue-green silk threaded through with fine, silvery metal threads. A diamanté slide catching back one side of her shiny black hair. Lips scarlet as holly berries against her pale skin. Laughing and full of high spirits, determined to enjoy herself. And where, Sophy had wondered waspishly, after they'd dined with the Thorpe-Bassetts, were they expecting to find around here the sort of smart London party they were dressed for?

The four of them had roared off in the red car, leaving her behind. Cinderella longing to go to the ball, even though she knew it wouldn't have been any fun with those companions, and there would certainly have been no Prince Charming to dance with and no glass slipper.

'Why don't you come with us, darling?' Gizi had coaxed, waiting for the car to pick her up.

'Too busy,' Sophy replied. *No fear!* she thought. Playing gooseberry to the four of them: Toby and Dee, Fitz and Gizi.

Of course, if she were honest, the real reason she was feeling so down in the dumps had nothing to do with all that – or only marginally. It was that telephone call from Jane Gilchrist. While she, Sophy, had been dithering about accepting the offer from Jane's brother, Piers, to work for him, it had suddenly gone up in smoke, along with his proposed venture. He'd decided, Jane told her, that running an art gallery wasn't quite *him,* and was looking for something less boring to do.

Sophy had put down the receiver, furious with the wretched Piers, though more with herself for ever having thought she'd be satisfied with a job demanding nothing more than 'being decorative and nice to the customers'.

She wished Sam were here to talk to, but he was off and away again, determined not to come home until he had his Rosa and her boys with him.

Leaning back now, she closed her eyes, aware of the still garden, the small, secret sounds coming from the undergrowth, the rustle of leaves in the trees. A goldfish plopped from under one of the lily pads on the pool. She swung the seat more.

Several miles away, Gizi was feeling confused and for some reason failing to work out just what she was doing sitting on a hard, uncomfortable chair in somewhere stiflingly hot, a place she could only imagine must be some kind of church or parish hall. They'd been hustled through the door too quickly for her to have seen it as anything more than a makeshift sort of building with a corrugated-iron roof and a cross on its apex. Inside, rows of chairs, unoccupied as yet except for a very few people, though others were entering in ones and twos. A low platform, with seats behind a table. A microphone. Vernon Thorpe-Bassett MP strutting about, for whom the central chair was evidently waiting.

Men at the back of the stage began to hoist a huge flag. As it went up, red emblazoned with a big white lightning flash, it became all too horribly recognizable. This, Gizi realized with a sudden outrage that momentarily lifted her confusion, was a BUF meeting! FitzAlban and his lapdog Toby Shefford had brought them here. *How dare they?*

She'd hardly been aware of Fitz suggesting they went on somewhere, as the four of them had piled into the Lagonda after a very early meal at the Thorpe-Bassetts. Not paying attention for one reason and another (but mainly because she was preoccupied with that snatch of conversation she hadn't been meant to overhear earlier) she hadn't listened to any plans they were making. If she had, she would never, not in a million years, have come here, especially not wearing this dress, or anything remotely like it. As she and Deedie had been escorted to seats in the front row of chairs, she'd noticed the other women already there, working women wearing awful hats and shoes, no coats over their cheap cotton frocks because it was such a warm night. She could feel their eyes boring into her back, making her cringe with embarrassment. Despite the heat of the room, she was glad of the flimsy little jacket that was slung around her shoulders. Her silk dress was not only shamingly expensive and too fashionable in this context, it was also very nearly backless.

She tried to squint along the row, but two strange men had been seated between her and Deedie, who was looking straight forward so that only her profile and her hands clasped tightly together in her lap were visible.

Something told Gizi she ought to stand up, there and then, drag Deedie with her and leave, but by now she was feeling weirdly lethargic. There had been bubbly before – and wine with – their dinner, but she was used to that. Perhaps it was the magic powder Fitz had given her and showed her how to snort. Something she'd done only once before and wasn't sure about, though she understood why people used it – that, and the other stuff Fitz could provide, for a price. It made one feel so good – until the euphoria began to wear off.

A bell rang. She *wasn't* going to stay here! In something like panic, she half rose from her chair but there was no escape – the man sitting next to her put a heavy, restraining hand on her arm and shushed her. The meeting had begun and the Hound, Thorpe-Bassett, was speaking, his red face polished and his hands eloquent as he made his points. Scattered applause began, enthusiastically joined in by Fitz who was sitting beside him, he who supposedly had no declared political affinities! Clearly, it was no longer possible to believe anything he said. She closed her eyes and tried not to listen. The heat pressed down like a lid under that corrugated roof.

'*My dearest, darling Pamela . . .*' Had she really heard that, from Fitz, who didn't like Pamela, just as she'd come out of the

Thorpe-Bassett cloakroom and seen them sitting close together on the little green settee just along the corridor? Or had she simply imagined it?

Pamela Thorpe-Bassett: tall, blonde, nose in the air . . . with a promised inheritance of money by the ton. She wasn't here in this hall tonight, of course she wasn't! There was going to be trouble, as there always was at these meetings, as the Perfect Prefect had obviously been aware there would be.

The applause started again, some foot stamping. All those on the platform stood, arms raised and extended in stiff salute. The Hound's face had grown redder, its beam spread as he went on expounding the manifesto of the British Union of Fascists. Promises which were beginning to sound repetitive, tired and frayed round the edges – and not just to her, apparently. The Hound was having to raise his voice against the heckling and booing that was now rising.

The 'stewards' – fit young men in black shirts and breeches tucked into shiny knee boots – began prowling the aisle for any action which would give them the opportunity to use their clubs. The catcalls and the applause began to merge; Gizi's ears rang. It was so hot . . . '*My dearest, darling Pamela* . . .' Her head jerked up with a great start as the doors burst open with a sudden violent crash. Uniformed police were rushing into the hall. The Biff Boys were walloping anyone they could with their weapons. The excitement had become a melee of people shouting, women screaming, chairs being turned over, police pushing in from outside, people frantically trying to get to the door. A familiar face – what was *he* doing here? As if she didn't know!

She hardly had time to decide whether she was glad or sorry to see him before her chair was suddenly knocked from under her. The floor came up to meet her. Her head met it with a crack, and she saw stars. And then, nothing.

The sudden sound of an approaching car made Sophy twist round on the swing to see the Lagonda roaring up the drive. Back already? It came to a violent stop, and the driver leapt out, leaving his door hanging open, and strode round to the passenger side. In a moment he was supporting, almost carrying, a slim figure in a silvery blue dress. Sophy was already on her feet and running towards the car as the driver – who wasn't Fitz – surrendered her and stepped back. 'Take care of her; she's had a shock and cracked her head, but I don't think it's anything to worry about,' he said, already striding away. 'I've got to get Dee home now.' Sophy saw Dee's white face as a blur in the back window.

'Martin! What's happened? Are they all right? What are you doing with Fitz's . . .?'

'He won't be needing it where I hope he's going!' Jumping back into the car, he threw over his shoulder, 'He took her to a bloody fascist meeting!'

Emitting a belch of exhaust fumes, like some angry dragon, the car was gone.

Gizi had detached herself from Sophy and was weaving an unsteady path towards the swing. She came to an even more unsteady halt by the edge of the pool. In the moonlight her slender, silvery figure swayed; she could have been some exotic fish which had leapt from the depths. The ruined aquamarine dress shimmered down her thin body like moonlit water. There was a long, diagonal rip across the bias-cut skirt. Her black bob was no longer smooth and tidy. She had lost the diamanté hairclip, and the matching swansdown-trimmed jacket that went with the dress was also missing. She was shivering, her bare arms goose-pimpled as she crossed them over her chest.

Sophy ran towards her and guided her on to the swing before she should fall into the water. Alerted by the noise of the car, someone came out of the house. Maitland, thank goodness, with a shawl she drew round Gizi's shoulders, her expression saying grimly, *I knew it would come to this, sooner or later*, though the words remained unspoken. Instead, she said, 'Come on, upstairs now! Bath and bed for you, lady.'

'Give me a cigarette and I'll be all right,' Gizi said.

Her evening bag was still fastened with its fancy clip to the bracelet round her wrist. With trembling fingers, she tried unsuccessfully to twist open the clasp. Sophy took it from her, found the case and a lighter. She put the cigarette in her sister's mouth and flicked a flame.

'Cigarettes aren't what she needs,' Maitland said sternly. 'Get her some brandy, Sophy.'

Sophy sped indoors and was back in a trice, with brandy filched from Papa's tantalus on the sideboard. She sat beside her sister and held her hand over Gizi's cold fingers, in case the heavy glass fell to the ground.

Gizi sipped and waved her cigarette in the other hand while the smoke curled round a face still devoid of colour. Maitland stood in front of her, hands on hips, watching like a hawk. In a while, assured that she wasn't going to faint, she went off, murmuring about seeing to a hot bath and hot-water bottles.

She refused to go to bed. Reclining against the sofa cushions, a Madame de Récamier in a black silk kimono receiving her admiring audience was more in Gizi's line. Even though the audience in this case comprised no more than Maitland and Sophy.

'Well, the Tin Chapel!' Maitland sniffed. 'What else did you expect?'

'Is that what they call it?' Gizi was diverted, already showing every indication of overcoming the shock of the evening. 'How too apropos!'

'Appro or whatever, it was only supposed to be there till the Methodists raise enough money to build a proper church. Meaning it's very likely to be permanent. Hired out in the week, dancing class, Girl Guides and Brownies. And Blackshirt bullies now, it seems!'

'The things you know, Maitland!' Gizi sank back on to her cushions as Maitland left them, but as soon as the door closed, the smile left her face. She considered Sophy, curled on the other end of the sofa, and after a moment she said, 'I suppose everyone will be delighted now that it's off with Fitz and me.'

'Nobody will be delighted at anything if you're unhappy,' Sophy said sharply. Then came an uplifting thought. 'Is it really off?'

Gizi began to pleat a fold of her kimono, staring at the ruins of the beautiful and expensive blue silk dress she had chosen to wear with such delight a few hours ago, now a discarded heap thrown into a corner. 'I'm not in the least unhappy. Truly. Just furious with myself that I didn't see it coming.'

Could this really be true? Sophy sat up, uncurling her legs and finding room for them alongside Gizi.

'He always said politics meant nothing to him and I believed him.' Gizi examined her nails. 'Actually, I still do. He's only going along with that fascist thing because of dear Pamela, *pretending* to be a fascist – which is even worse than being a real one to my mind.'

Sophy was so much in agreement with this last that it took her a moment to realize what else Gizi had said. 'The Perfect Prefect – and Fitz? I don't believe it!' She could have laughed, but Gizi wasn't joking.

'Well, I do mean it! He's been whispering sweet nothings in her ear, as he does – even in Deedie's, when she'll listen. And in mine – once. But I don't have a rich papa, do I?'

Sophy searched her sister's face for signs of distress but saw there only the angry self-reproach Gizi had confessed to. 'Not that I care,' she added with a tinkly laugh. 'I wouldn't have the Honourable Gerald FitzAlban now if he was the last man on earth!'

After a moment, Sophy said, 'Not now, perhaps. But you would have, once, wouldn't you? You wanted nothing more than to marry him.'

Gizi took time before she answered. 'All right, perhaps so. Not for reasons you'd approve of, of course.' She reached out a slender, scarlet-tipped hand and stroked Sophy's instep. 'Darling Muffin, Fitz won't marry anyone for other than money – or to get another little FitzAlban to carry on the name. Everyone who knows him knows that.'

Sophy didn't understand immediately, but then of course she did. She might have admitted it all along if she hadn't been too blinded by her instinctive dislike of the man to see him objectively.

'He only offered to drive Toby here to wangle himself into the Thorpe-Bassett good books, you know.'

Sophy saw that Fitz's perfidy still rankled. 'Martin was right about him, wasn't he?'

'Oh, I dare say!' One of Gizi's scarlet nails had suffered a chip to its varnish. She began to pick at it. 'But Martin has to be right about something occasionally, doesn't he?'

Sophy remembered the time, not so long ago, when Gizi had wholeheartedly shared those somethings that Martin thought were right. 'Yes, he does. Like being there to rescue you tonight.'

'My knight in shining armour! And in Fitz's car, too!'

The thought was suddenly too much for them. The last tensions of the evening melted away as they began to laugh.

THIRTY-TWO

Across the valley at Falquonroy Park, the stable clock had just struck eight, sending its notes echoing over the roofs to the far corners of the big house. Dusk was beginning to suck the light from the sky, but the sun hadn't yet disappeared entirely. Against a glorious orange and red-gold backdrop, dramatically purple-streaked, a huge murmuration of starlings wheeled in a perfectly synchronized, virtuoso performance before settling to roost in the trees behind.

The radiance from the sky outside didn't do much to lift the darkness of the old library. Without the benefit of gas or electricity in this part of the house, light was dependent on the oil lamps placed along the length of the table. Long shadows leapt to the high ceiling, lent mystery to its corners, so that the tumble of books on the shelves seemed to crowd in towards the centre, enclosing the lighted tableau at the long trestle table. On one side sat Reardon and Jago, opposite was FitzAlban.

Reardon had asked for the old library as somewhere to conduct the police business, not only because it would be less disturbing for the household, but also because he felt comfortable there. Perhaps it was the books.

FitzAlban was here alone. After they'd done with him, Shefford, at the moment with his fiancée and her parents, would be next. Reardon wondered if the engagement would still be on after Sir Julius had had his say. Shefford would not easily be forgiven, if ever, for taking his daughter to that fascist meeting. Why the two women had been taken there at all was a question still to be answered. Unless it had been intended to show the hoi polloi that the BUF was supported by the local bigwigs and must therefore be a Good Thing. Quite possibly they'd all been a little too drunk to consider the implications.

That particular meeting at the locally known Tin Chapel had, sure enough, been the source of the trouble Knott had been anticipating, but in the event had turned out to be nothing but a damp squib. Certainly not the 'fun' Knott had vowed Jago would be sorry to miss. Simply another attempt to revive the party's declining popularity, it had ended neither in triumph nor mayhem, as their meetings had once tended to do, but ignominiously – a whimper rather than a bang. A few cracked heads, some arrests on both sides. Names had been taken and passed on, more than sufficient reason for another, now overdue talk, Reardon felt, with Dee Malpas's fiancé and his friend, taking them one at a time.

The latter, his gaze lighting on the ancient books and dusty cobwebs, had ostentatiously shaken out an expensively monogrammed linen handkerchief and flicked dust, imaginary or otherwise, from his chair before sitting down. His immaculate tailoring appeared to have suffered not one whit after the last disorderly hour or so. He frowned impatiently, but Reardon was in no mood to be hustled, and it was unsettling him. 'Look here,' he said, 'this isn't on, don't you know. As far as I'm aware, there is nothing illegal about holding a party meeting. The BUF is a perfectly legitimate organization.'

'That's so . . . at present.' A situation unlikely to last much longer, Reardon hoped. Restive as people everywhere were for drastic change to fair working and living conditions, German-style authoritarian rule, emphasized by the wearing of quasi-military uniforms, wasn't likely to be tolerated for long by those who had fought and suffered and still remembered the armageddon of the Great War. 'However, we're not here to discuss the meeting, nor your political views, Mr FitzAlban. It's simply a matter of a few questions we need you to answer on other matters.'

'Correct me if I'm wrong, but don't you think I'm the one who should be asking the questions? Such as what right have you to keep me here? And also, by the way –' with increasing heat – 'who the devil took my motor away without my permission?'

'It was returned.'

'That's hardly the point! Someone drove *my car* away from where I left it outside the hall!' Reardon knew it was Martin Garbutt who had taken and used it to get the two young women away from the scuffle in the Tin Chapel as fast as possible. He didn't feel FitzAlban was owed, or deserved, an explanation. Unable to believe any oaf out here in the sticks would have the effrontery to lay a finger on such a possession, let alone know how to drive it, he'd left it unguarded, right out at the front of the building. And then had the effrontery to be outraged at its appropriation.

Reardon ignored the needless interruption. 'Your politics don't concern me at the moment.' Not entirely true, but FitzAlban wasn't in any position to know that. 'We're investigating the death of Mrs Waring, as you're well aware, and that's what we're here to talk about just now.'

For a moment FitzAlban made out he hadn't understood. 'The judge's wife? Then why me?' A puzzled frown. 'I don't see how I can help you there, never having made the lady's acquaintance.'

'Of course, it was Mr Shefford who knew her.'

'Well, I don't know about him *knowing* her. Didn't he say he only met her once, briefly? Memory like a sieve, old Sheff, but even he wouldn't have got that wrong, surely.'

Reardon wasn't deflected. 'DS Jago here has something to show you. We'd like you to look at these photographs and tell us if you recognize anyone, or where they were taken.'

FitzAlban let his glance slide over the pictures Jago spread out before shaking his head. 'Sorry, not anyone I know.'

'What about the place?' Jago asked.

'Nor that either.'

'That's rather odd. You don't recognize your old family home?'

'My family home, as you put it, is nothing like this. It's in Norfolk, if it hasn't fallen to the ground by now,' he returned, not without bitterness. 'No one's lived there for years . . . my father's bedridden and now lives with my aunt, his sister, in Derbyshire, and my brother and I have our own places in London. Where is this?' He jabbed out a finger.

'Take another look. It's the garden of a house near Henley-on-Thames, which I think you know very well.'

'Henley?' This time he peered more closely. 'Good grief, I believe it may be Audley House! Well, if it is, yes, it *was* in the family's possession, though never somewhere I visited much . . . it was mostly leased out, until it was sold, fairly recently.'

To a rich American, according to Jago's ex-colleague, DS

Rowley. An utterly respectable person, a family man who seemed to be keen on settling in Henley, sending his children to neighbouring schools and taking an interest in local affairs.

Jago produced the studio portrait which until now he'd held back. 'And this young lady?'

'Who is she? I wouldn't have forgotten a beauty like that if I'd ever met her, but I assure you I haven't.'

'Her name was Lucy Oates. She died when she was eighteen.'

'Sad, but no, I'm afraid not.'

'Very well, then,' Reardon said. 'Let's forget that for the moment and talk about the fight you had with young Alexei Kyriakou.'

That did at last get a reaction. 'Fight?' he repeated sharply.

'Unwarranted attack, if you prefer it.'

'I prefer nothing of the sort, if you're referring to the slight scrap I had with the boy.'

'He asked you to pass a letter on to Sir Julius, but you denied ever having been given it.'

'No, Inspector. I said I didn't *remember* any such letter. I still don't.'

'You're saying both Mr Cribb, the chauffeur who witnessed the fight, and young Alexei, are not telling the truth?'

'I would imagine that's not beyond the bounds of possibility in either case. But that young pup's view of the situation is almost certainly coloured by what he seems to have felt for Mrs Waring. I'll admit I lost my temper when he squared up to me, but one can hardly ignore being called a liar. And as for *Mister* Cribb,' he added with a curl of his lip, 'I wouldn't set too much store by what someone like him says if I were you.'

'Hmm.' Reardon flicked back through his notes, taking his time, while FitzAlban began to fidget. A tie that didn't need to be adjusted, a foot starting to tap of its own accord. After a minute or two, Reardon said, 'Let's go back to Thursday night. When you last spoke to us, you said that after Sir Julius left you, you played billiards for some time, and then you and Mr Shefford helped your inebriated friend upstairs and afterwards went to bed yourselves.'

'That's correct.'

'And during that time, you saw no one else?'

'Except for the butler, Bracewell, when he brought us another bottle. As we said.'

'As you said, yes. But Mr Cribb spoke to you and Mr Shefford outside, in one of the garages at a point much later than that.'

His eyes flickered, but he said easily enough, 'Oh, that! Well, Shefford's thinking of buying a new motor himself, and as we told the chauffeur, we'd slipped out for me to explain the finer points of the engine to him. A bit of an ass, old Sheff, I'm afraid – mechanically speaking, that is.' He smiled tolerantly, inviting a shared masculine amusement, which wasn't returned. 'Always been like that, old Toby. Some people are.'

'You've known each other for a long time then, you and Mr Shefford?'

'We were at school together. He was my fag.'

Curious, Sir Julius had remarked the other day as he'd watched the pair of them departing with his daughter for that lunch at Headley Court. Which was fair comment in Reardon's view. Despite the old-school-tie stuff, nothing suggested the two men were destined to be soulmates. In fact, although FitzAlban's remarks about Shefford were made in the jokingly insulting way of long-standing friends, Reardon wouldn't have sworn to it that they were actually jokes.

He resumed. 'So, you came back downstairs after you'd put your friend to bed and went outside to look at your car.'

'Yes. Didn't seem to be able to get it through to Sheff how the finer points worked, so I took him outside to demonstrate.'

'But surely Bracewell had seen to it that the place was all locked up by then? That's a butler's job, isn't it?'

'Oh, the back door in the kitchen corridor doesn't need a key, there's just a big iron bolt. Makes for a short cut from the garage I was told to use if I wished.'

'And no one else was stirring when you went out?'

'Only the chauffeur, as you've pointed out. He showed his face after a while. We disturbed his beauty sleep, apparently.'

'He noticed your car engine was warm.'

'It would be, wouldn't it, if it had been switched on? As it had been.'

Reardon knew he was unlikely to get much more than this

sort of thing for now. And he'd had more than enough of Mr FitzAlban. 'All right, you may go.'

'You've finished with me?'

No, my friend, we haven't finished with you, not by a long chalk. 'For the moment,' he said. 'We'll need to speak to you again after we've seen Mr Shefford.'

Not for the first time FitzAlban wondered, as he walked away from that last, distinctly uncomfortable fifteen minutes, why he'd ever thought of using Shefford. If it hadn't been for him and that Waring woman, the police wouldn't have been sniffing around, asking awkward questions. He needed to talk to him as a matter of urgency, before the police did. There was no knowing what Sheff was likely to say – enough to blow the lid off the whole shebang probably. He was sometimes more trouble than he was worth . . . always had been, if the truth were told, ever since he'd been a grubby little squirt and Fitz a lordly senior ordering him about. The thing was, he was useful. He didn't know the meaning of guilt. He would do anything he was paid to do without ever asking if there might be consequences.

Thinking of consequences, FitzAlban knew what a dangerous game he himself was playing. One which could lead to severe penalties. If he were ever found out. He didn't intend that to happen.

The rich are always with us. That was what people thought – and indeed some of them still were, though the FitzAlbans were not among them. Like others of their class, they were feeling the pinch, to put it mildly, the state the country was in. The general public, of course, didn't believe this, but it was true. Swingeing death duties, increased income tax rates, failed investments. Not to mention a disinclination to abandon self-indulgent lifestyles.

But Audley House? What was the police interest there? Since the American had bought it, he'd had nothing to do with the place . . . though he had of course recognized one or two people in those old photos they'd shown him – that girl, especially.

He had to see Sheff before the police did.

But Shefford, when he was sought, was nowhere to be found.

* * *

Where he'd sloped off to, no one could hazard a guess. None of the vehicles used on the estate were missing and he was nowhere in the inhabited part of the house. Ideas of searching further, in those derelict rooms, attics, passages and other intimidating spaces, especially in the dark, were soon abandoned. He'd turn up. He was, after all, a grown man and entitled to time alone if he wished.

'Oh, how can he be so tiresome?' Dee was cross, rather than worried, and when Shefford then, after all the disruption, appeared the next morning at breakfast time as if nothing had happened, she didn't throw herself into his arms. She hadn't forgiven him for going off without a word, still less for hustling her and Gizi into the meeting at that frightful place they were calling the Tin Chapel. It had been a shock to come face to face with reality, to find Toby and Fitz were, if not in uniform, at least in sympathy with Thorpe-Bassett and the fascists. It made her feel ashamed of trying to provoke her parents with those silly, off-the-top-of-her-head remarks about Mosley, and threatening to drape herself in a Union Jack, which she hadn't really meant in any case.

'Where have you *been*?' she demanded of her fiancé when they did eventually meet again.

'Walking.'

'*All night*?'

'I found somewhere sheltered to bunk down for a while. It wasn't all that cold.'

With a shock, she saw he didn't care at all that she might have been worried. She'd always known her newly betrothed was marrying her for the money she'd bring, but she'd assumed he had affection for her too. Now she wasn't so sure. Or even how much she had for him.

Her mother was looking distressed. 'Go and have a bath, Toby my dear, something to eat.' Her father, coldly angry, said nothing. He would want an explanation, but he'd expect Toby to offer it without it being demanded, as a gentleman should.

That's put the kibosh on it, Shefford thought as he limped (his restless night not having done his knee any favours) to face the police in the old library. It was all up with Dee – her old man would see to that. And, he thought pessimistically, there was more trouble to come. Your luck didn't change if you were Toby Shefford. Unless you changed it for yourself.

That was what he'd decided at some point during last night. Hadn't he?

Bloody Fitz! What had he been saying to the police? Nothing that was going to get himself involved, that was for sure. Sliding out of it, leaving him, Toby, to their mercies. Well, he was clever, but not as clever as he thought he was.

He believes I'm a fool, and no doubt I am, though not in the way he sees it. We've never liked each other, so why do I bother with him? Damnfool question! Liking didn't come into it when it was a matter of survival. That's how it had been, ever since he'd got himself into that scrape over . . .

Well, we shall see.

The morning was a grey one once more, muggy and threatening rain. The old library had lost its mystery and simply looked dusty and neglected, not unlike Toby himself. He slouched opposite the two detectives at the long table, sullen and uncooperative, looking as though he'd been dragged three ways through a hedge. He'd eaten a huge breakfast, but he hadn't bathed and, never tidily put together, he looked a mess. He was sweating heavily, and he'd pulled off his jacket and was in his shirt sleeves, one of which had lost a cufflink or a button and was flapping loose.

They'd seated him facing the light, looking towards the dark forest that began its endless stretch at the back of the house. All those trees made him feel claustrophobic and the room itself didn't help. That big, ugly clock on the mantelpiece had a loud, intrusive tick. One of the oil lamps lit against the gloom had burnt out and its acrid smell was everywhere, despite the open door. He thought he could hear the scratch of something small and verminous behind the skirtings, and those useless piles of crumbling old books gave him the pip.

'What am I supposed to have done wrong?' he demanded. If it's about that meeting, forget it. You don't imagine I'm one of that gang of fascists, do you?'

'I'm glad to hear you're not,' the inspector said drily. 'And I won't ask you what you were doing there in that case. We're not here to talk about that. Not just yet.'

'What do you want with me then?' A large fly which had been making suicide attempts against the windows gave up and began whizzing around the room before deciding to target him. He brushed it away impatiently.

Suddenly, Reardon said, 'What can you tell us about Wykedge, Mr Shefford?'

The name, hitting him like a missile from another universe, threw him into a momentary panic. He had to wait until his heartbeats went back to normal before he could reply. 'Wykedge?'

'It's your hometown, isn't it?'

'It was. Never been back there since I was eighteen, thank God.'

The persistent fly landed on his face. He raised his arm irritably to brush it away, his unfastened sleeve flapping back down his muscular arm.

'Nasty scar you have there, Mr Shefford,' the younger detective remarked, his eyes on the ugly, knotted blemish stretching from wrist to elbow as Shefford dragged the sleeve impatiently down.

'What? Oh, that's nothing. Bad-tempered Alsatian got me when I was a boy.'

He waited for someone to carry on with the questions, but neither detective did. Reardon was staring at those stacks of old books, his pencil tapping his teeth. The sergeant was scribbling something in his notebook. He tore the page out and passed it to Reardon. The chief inspector read it, folded it and put it between the pages of his own notebook. Then, as if Wykedge had never been mentioned, he said, 'So what was all that about, you disappearing last night? Where did you go?'

'I just walked.' Repeating what he'd said to Dee. Wondering why it mattered to everyone else. 'I think better when I walk.'

'You had something special to think about, then?'

He wasn't at all sure that thinking was the right word, but it was beyond him to explain what had been going through his confused mind. He could only shrug.

When no reply was forthcoming, Reardon scraped his chair back. 'We'll leave you to consider that for a minute or two. We'll be back shortly. There's water over there in the jug if you need it.' They left the room.

What the devil was going on? Toby pushed his own chair back and went to stare outside. In the strange way a reflection can sometimes be seen, even in an undarkened window, there appeared to be a ghostly image of his own scowling, troubled self, looking back at him. His hands were clasped tightly behind his back, perhaps in an effort to stop them shaking. What had that been about? Good God, *Wykedge*!

Walking, as he had done last night, was what he used to do in Wykedge, on the moors above that grimy little northern town he hated so much. As a child, and later as a youth, he'd roamed the moors alone, his lips and tongue stained blue from the bilberries he'd picked, drinking clear, cold water from the becks that tumbled into the valley below. Except for the peewits' shrill call, silence surrounded him as he lay on the coarse grass between the whin bushes and the heather, with a bird's eye view of the dozens of smokestacks and the dominant family mill below. Watching the lorries piled high with huge square bales of raw wool as they trundled under the Shefford & Sons stone archway.

A lonely boy, he would go back to the big old house where he lived, without parents, brothers or sisters, without supervision. No one but his uncle – when he was there, that was, and with the servants when he wasn't, which was often. Preston Shefford was usually too busy finding pleasure in London. Squandering on wine, women and horses the money his grandfather, his father and his brother had rejoiced in making. Leaving the business to the devices of the mill manager, who did his best, but which even Toby had come to know wasn't enough.

It wasn't in Toby's nature to question whether he was happy or not. He lacked the imagination to query why his life was as it was, or to challenge whatever happened to him. Such as eventually being sent away to a 'good' school (made possible by a legacy from his grandfather) where he excelled at sports if nothing else, where he picked up better manners and haughty attitudes, lost his local accent and tried to forget Wykedge and his origins.

THIRTY-THREE

The library door opened, and the two detectives came back, motioned him to resume his seat and took their own places opposite. The sergeant held a clutch of photographs in his hand and now arranged them on the table. 'Recognize anyone?'

He barely looked at them before shaking his head.

'Let me tell you something that might help. I've been puzzling over these pictures, trying to find a face that would fit. But it wasn't a *face* I should have been looking for, was it? It was that scar you pulled your sleeve over.'

Embarrassment, Reardon had suggested, out there behind the closed door. He knew about scars and, though he'd had to learn to live with the one on his own face, which couldn't be concealed, he knew they could be a source of mortification, even shame, to some people.

Jago pointed now to the picture showing those young men, laughing and fooling around in a boat that looked ready to capsize, one of them precariously standing up, another kneeling with his sleeve rolled up and an arm outstretched to retrieve a lost oar from the water. His face couldn't be seen but plainly visible on his bare arm was what Jago had previously taken to be a shadow or a camera fault, but was now clearly visible as the scar that ran up Shefford's forearm.

'Matches, doesn't it? Unless someone else got the same nasty dog bite.'

Shefford shrugged, admitting nothing, and Jago placed the last photo, which he'd withheld, in the centre of the others. 'Do you know who this is?'

Time ticked loudly by. The first scatter of rain hit the window. And the pesky fly finally found the open door. 'It's Lucy,' Shefford said at last. 'Lucy Oates.'

The admission brought some change in him, an awareness that almost saw him sloughing off the don't-care slouch. He sat up straighter and for an instant something that spelt disquiet seemed to spark in those dark, obsidian eyes.

'I need to smoke,' he said suddenly, groping in his pocket for cigarettes, making a business of it but giving up the search in the end. 'Lucy—'

'We'll come back to Lucy later. First, we need to talk about Wykedge. You knew Mrs Waring from there, didn't you?'

'How . . . how do you know that?'

Connections, coincidence, sixth sense, intuition. A casual mention by Sir Julius of Shefford's run-down family firm 'somewhere up north' lodging in Reardon's mind; his chat with Gargrave, what Catchpole had told them and what they had gathered of Emilie's life afterwards . . . facts unrelated until logic or intuition, whatever you liked to call it, linked them together.

'I didn't actually *know* her,' Shefford said at last. 'We only met once.'

By the time he left school, Toby's home circumstances had changed. His uncle Preston, hard up and now crippled by arthritis, had been forced back up north, wheelchair-bound, looked after by a grumbling old family retainer, raging at life's unfairness. Toby himself had determined never to set foot in Wykedge again, but return he did, just once, when he was eighteen, for his uncle's unregretted funeral.

Since leaving school, he'd had nothing more to support himself than his grandfather's legacy, which his spendthrift uncle fortunately hadn't been able to touch. If he had hoped anything might be left to him after that man's dissolute life had ended, he was disappointed. There was nothing, except debts which there was no chance whatever of anyone repaying. After a dolorous meeting with the solicitors charged with settling affairs, he went out on to the moors in a towering rage. He walked until he felt ready to drop before turning back towards Wykedge.

The great arch of Shefford & Sons was visible when the commotion arose, shattering the silence: a woman's screams, the deep barking and snarling of a large dog. Without conscious thought, he found himself running in the direction of the noise. A huge grey-brown Alsatian was standing over the body of a woman lying spreadeagled on the stony path, as if she'd tripped while running away from the animal. Her mass of red-gold hair had come loose from its pins, and she had lost a shoe.

He guessed she'd probably taken a wrong turning and found herself on the path leading towards the small farm, or small-holding, further along, when the beast had bounded towards her and knocked her to the ground. It had a fold of her rucked-up skirt clamped in its jaws and its forepaws were on her chest. There was a tearing sound as she frantically tried to pull away. Toby stood over the animal and with all his brute strength, which was considerable, brought the side of his hand down on its nose. It let go of the woman with a yelp and turned on him, clamping its teeth on his arm. The woman scrambled to her feet and began to kick it, but its teeth only sank deeper. Skin and flesh tore as Toby tried to pull away.

A short, red-faced man appeared, shouting the dog off. At its master's voice, it went still, but not until he got near enough to give it a great cuff did it release Toby and back away, cowering. The woman dropped to her knees on the grass beside him and took hold of his arm, regardless of the blood.

Far from being apologetic for the behaviour of his dog, the farmer was irate. ''Appen that'll learn you to do your bloody courting somewhere else!'

'And happen you'll teach your bloody dog better manners!' Toby retorted, matching the rough accent even while gritting his teeth against the burning pain now beginning in his arm.

'If the daft bitch had stood still and not run, he wouldn't a gone for her.'

Toby thought this was possibly true, but he could hardly say so. The woman was hurling her own rejoinder. 'If you'd kept that . . . *wolf* tied up, this would never have happened!' Victim turned rescuer, she appeared to be quite unharmed herself and bent over Toby, who was trying not to show the pain he felt. 'And can't you see this young man needs a doctor?' she called back over her shoulder.

Even light-headed as he was now feeling, Toby noticed the 'young'. She couldn't have been that much older than he was. He admired her spirit, which echoed what he was feeling. If he hadn't been incapacitated by that damned dog, he'd have knocked the bloody man's teeth down his throat before now. The fellow was, however, now hesitating, something in his better nature at last asserting itself. 'Stop where y'are, and I'll get me car, get you down to t'doctor's.'

'No need. I only live down there.'

He threw Toby a closer look. 'Branxholme? Oh aye, I might a known you was a Shefford! Well, suit yersen! I reckon there'll be a telephone there you can use.'

Toby was attempting to tear off his already ruined shirt with the woman's help. Wincing, he let her bind it round his arm to help staunch the blood. The farmer watched for a minute or two, then decided to wash his hands of the pair of them, whistled for the dog, turned away and stomped back to his farm.

Still furious, the woman shouted something after him, words that shouldn't have been in a young lady's vocabulary. She didn't act like a lady, though. Or indeed dress like one. Her accent wasn't local. 'But he's right,' she said, 'you do need a doctor.'

'Oh, I'll live.' Toby's arm was damned painful, but the bleeding seemed to have stopped and he was already struggling to his feet. 'Unless I get blood poisoning, or gangrene. Or what d'you call it, hydrophobia?'

She summoned up what was almost a laugh. 'No, I'm serious, you should see a doctor.'

'As he said, there's a telephone.'

She rubbed the blood from her hands as best she could on the rough grass, retrieved her shoe and bent to pick up her scattered belongings: a satchel and what had spilled from it – what looked like a sketchbook and various other things, including pencils and charcoal sticks. She had a light jumper in the bag too, which she tied around her waist by the sleeves in an effort to hide the rips the dog had made in her skirt. Watching her deft hands as she finally gave up the attempt to tidy that mass of red-gold curls, he noticed she wore a wedding ring.

She insisted he should lean on her as they made their way down the hill, though he didn't feel the need. Although she was small, she seemed strong. At the mill gates where she left him, she gave him a curious look from a pair of blue, almost violet eyes, but simply thanked him for coming to her help and said goodbye. He didn't even have her name.

The breezy young doctor, not long out of medical school by

the look of him, who came in answer to his telephone call, told him to cheer up, the damage looked worse than it was. 'Flesh wound only. Lucky it wasn't an artery.' The injury was swabbed with antiseptic, stitched up and he was given instructions for its further care. The young medic gave a rueful laugh at his own handiwork. 'Sorry it's so rough, I'm no needlewoman!'

No one could have argued with that, though to be fair, the wound was long and jagged with no clean edges to fit neatly together. Toby made a good guess that the scar was likely to be with him for the rest of his life. All for a silly woman who hadn't known better than to stand still.

THIRTY-FOUR

He'd been allowed to tell the story without interruption and now reached out for the water he hadn't yet touched and drank thirstily, let his eyes close and his head sink to his chest, as if all that unaccustomed talking, on top of a rough night, had exhausted him.

'Mr Shefford!' He opened his eyes and with the inspector's look fixed on him, slowly straightened up. 'So you met again, you and Mrs Waring, and you recognized each other?'

'I remembered *her* straight away. Though she wasn't Emilie Waring when I first saw her.'

'No, she was Emma Catchpole, common-law wife of the murderer Philip Atterfield.'

He hadn't expected them to know that. He swallowed hard and reached again for the water. 'All that stuff hadn't happened then. I left Wykedge within days of meeting her and I haven't been back since. I'd forgotten all about her until her husband killed those girls. Until the photographs in the papers, the talk, the nasty rumours that she'd shielded her husband . . . I realized then who she must have been.'

'Where and when exactly did you next meet her?'

'Only a few weeks ago, here at Falquonroy. Lady Malpas's birthday tea party. Could have knocked me down with a feather when I realized who I was seeing! The last time I'd seen her she was a sparky young woman with wild hair and a temper. And now there she was, so – well, so . . . respectable. Classy. The wife of a *judge*, for God's sake! But I was ninety per cent certain I knew her.'

'What made you so sure?'

'When I saw those drawings she gave Lady Malpas. Hardly works of art, but they were Wykedge, right enough. I knew she'd recognized me too, but she wasn't saying anything, so I kept my mouth shut. I guessed she wouldn't welcome any reminders of that part of her life any more than I did.'

'You're saying that was only the second time you met? Which is what, how long after you first met in Wykedge?' Toby didn't answer, just began fumbling again in his pockets for his cigarettes. 'Aren't you forgetting the time she lived with the Oates family, when you were friendly with Lucy, the girl you've just identified from the photograph?'

Cigarettes forgotten, he froze, absolutely still. 'What? *What* did you just say? She lived with the Oates family? With Lucy?'

'She was Lucy's nanny. Surely you must have known her then?'

'Mrs Waring was once a *nanny*?' As if such a person couldn't possibly have been the judge's wife, mistress of Templewood, close friend of Lady Malpas. 'Not – good grief, not *Nanny Logan*?'

'It was the name she was using at that time.'

He was thunderstruck. 'I knew Lucy's old nanny was still with them, but I never met her. Or any of her family, come to that!' he said bitterly.

Easy enough to see why he hadn't. A young woman like Lucy would have been very careful indeed to keep the louche young fellow Shefford must have been even then well away from their certain disapproval.

'So how did the situation with you and Mrs Waring resolve itself?'

'I've just told you.'

'You mean you simply carried on pretending you'd never met previously?'

'Something like that, yes. Why not? Our first acquaintance wasn't anything either of us wanted to resume.'

'If that was the case,' Reardon said, as Shefford again groped for his cigarettes and matches, and this time found them, 'how do you explain the argument you had with her, just after that birthday party, down at The Spinney? I mean that building site next door to Templewood.'

'I know where The Spinney is, but I've no idea what you're talking about.'

'No? You were overheard having a fierce quarrel there with Mrs Waring. Threatening her.' This time, he knew he was talking to the right person.

'I can't imagine who gave you that idea.' He shook out his match without seeming to notice it had burnt right down to his fingers. 'All right,' he admitted at last, 'she'd sent a note by one of the servants asking me to meet her there after breakfast. I very nearly didn't bother, but in the end, I slipped out. Curiosity, I suppose. I'd no idea what was coming and when it did, I couldn't believe what I was hearing.' He paused to draw smoke deep into his lungs. 'She actually told me – no, ordered me, dammit! – to break off my engagement with Dee! It was so ridiculous I just laughed, but she was serious. And by the way, let me correct you – if any threatening was being done, she was the one who was doing it! If I didn't find some way of backing out, she would . . .' The match stub was flicked away. 'Well, she was obviously mad as a hatter and I was damned if I was going to call it off with Dee. She's the best thing that's ever happened to me.'

For a split second Reardon thought he'd been mistaken in thinking Dee meant very little to him, but then Shefford spoilt it. 'Marrying her would get me out of Queer Street once and for all and I wasn't going to let anyone put a spoke in that.'

Queer Street. A curiously old-fashioned term coming from Shefford, meaning he was in serious money difficulties. 'The gee-gees?' Reardon asked. It nearly always was.

'And the rest.' He shrugged. 'So, I decided to ignore what she threatened, call her bluff. Even if my past did come out, it's no worse than . . . Well, I'd hardly be the first man to have had an unsatisfactory affair. I don't suppose Dee thinks I'm an innocent either,' he added cynically.

'What exactly *was* she threatening?'

'Only that she'd go to Dee's father with all that stuff about me and Lucy! Her being pregnant, losing the baby and . . . everything.'

He wouldn't meet Reardon's look. Shame, or because he was anxious not to give more away? 'You've met old Julius; you don't need me to tell you that would have been enough for him. He doesn't like me to begin with, and no way would he have let his daughter marry me once he'd listened to that old tittle-tattle.'

Was that all Lucy's tragedy was to him . . . old tittle-tattle? Something he'd been able to put out of his mind as nothing but a silly, youthful mistake? Reardon swallowed his disgust as Shefford went on, not troubling to conceal his bitterness. 'Especially if it came from Emilie Waring. He'd have believed anything she said. You could see he thought the sun shone out of her. The thing was I still couldn't imagine how she could have known about . . . about Lucy and me.'

'She had that photograph of you, the one in the boat,' Jago said. 'The one showing the scar.'

It took him a while to process that. 'I might have guessed. Lucy. That girl couldn't keep a secret to save her life! She swore she'd told no one about us but she must have told her precious nanny. And I guess she noticed this when we met,' he said, touching his wrist where the scar began.

Reardon let him brood over it until unexpectedly he burst out, 'Look here, *she* was the one who was against having the baby – Lucy, not me! She didn't want to get married, either, even if there'd been any question of that, which there wasn't. We didn't have a brass farthing between us. And she said her father would kill her if he knew she was pregnant, and probably kill me first.'

'How did she manage the termination if you'd no money?' Reardon had seen enough of these sorry situations, God knows, to be aware they didn't come cheap, even some back-street operation which he supposed that one had been.

'We scraped it together,' he said sulkily at last, adding with a sort of defiance, 'You think that was wrong, what we did! Well, it wasn't why she died. Not directly, anyway.'

'What do you mean by that?'

'Well, we knew someone, a doctor, just qualified. He'd got himself into a spot of bother. He needed cash and he agreed to . . . to do the necessary. He assured us it would be all right, it was simple, nothing to it, but he botched the job. Leaving Lucy . . . I tell you, she was in agony!' For a fleeting moment, genuine guilt showed itself. 'She . . . if she hadn't taken too much she'd still be here.'

'Too much of what?' It was Jago who jumped in at that. 'Coke, was it? That doctor gave her cocaine?'

'No! Good God, no, he was appalled when he heard what had happened – in an absolute panic. He knew questions would be asked . . . couldn't sign the death certificate fast enough.'

'Then it was *you* who gave it to her! Where did you get it?'

He hadn't actually said what had been administered to Lucy, but whatever it was had killed her. It had taken more than aspirin to do that. He and Jago stared one another out. Shefford must be kicking himself, knowing he'd gone too far with the truth of how Lucy had died, and that he'd put himself on dangerous ground. Not yet ready to admit it, however.

Reardon broke the impasse by asking, 'How do you make your living, Mr Shefford?'

'What?' It wasn't clear from his expression whether he'd understood, or merely thought the question impertinent.

'What do you do for money?'

'Money? Oh, I have that wonderful thing called an annuity – the sort that wouldn't,' he said sourly, 'keep a sparrow alive.'

'But you managed to "scrape together" enough for Lucy's abortion. Where did that come from?'

He didn't like that ugly word falling between them. 'How do you think? Borrowed it from a friend – if it's of any interest.'

'The friend being Mr FitzAlban, by any chance?'

'And if it was? Isn't that what friends are for?'

Especially a well-heeled friend, one of those whom Sir Julius had despised as the idle rich. With enough money to own the sort of car FitzAlban drove. Yet FitzAlban had not an hour ago admitted, with some bitterness, that his family home in Norfolk was crumbling. And that Audley House had been sold.

Audley House. No suspicious activities there had ever come to the notice of the police, DS Rowley had reported to Jago when he rang back. It was only when he had learnt that the owner previous to the American had been Lord Kyneton (family name FitzAlban) that alarm bells had begun to ring for him. FitzAlban had been a name of interest to C Division for some time.

Jago had been quick to sense the need to tread softly when Rowley guardedly mentioned this: if by his enquiries he'd unwittingly stepped into one of C Division's hush-hush, ongoing investigations, scuppering it with intrusive questioning was definitely not the way to go. But the little Rowley was prepared to say hadn't totally disappointed him and they both knew this could in fact turn out to be a mutually rewarding exercise.

'Where does the FitzAlban money come from?' Reardon was asking now.

'Not the sort of question one asks of people,' Shefford replied coldly. He didn't actually add 'in polite circles' but it was there. FitzAlban himself couldn't have done it better.

Jago had no such qualms. The gut feeling he'd had all along was being justified and he was elated. 'We believe FitzAlban's dealing in drugs, Shefford. And you've been helping him. That was where you got the cocaine for Lucy.'

It was after all the most likely explanation for a relationship that didn't seem to have any other reason. Not friendship that kept the two men together, but a mutual dependency: FitzAlban wanting someone like Shefford to dispense the drugs he obtained, and Shefford's desperate need for money.

Shefford hadn't replied. Reardon let the moment sink in and switched tactics. 'You're thinking about buying a car, we've been told. Is that right?'

Shefford's lips twisted. 'Thinking's as far as I'm likely to get.'

'But enough to make you go out to the garages last Thursday, in the middle of the night, for Mr FitzAlban to demonstrate some point about car engines.'

'If that's what he says. I don't clearly recall. You know how we were that night. Old Julius keeps a good cellar and we'd done it justice. I suppose we might have gone out at some point; I vaguely remember Fitz yakking on about motors, as usual. He thinks I'm a bonehead where engines are concerned. I dare say he's right. We don't all aspire to be Malcolm Campbell.'

The point wasn't pursued and he looked relieved. Indeed, he laughed shortly when Reardon asked him why he'd come to Falquonroy ahead of the other guests the previous Thursday.

A royal command's not something to be ignored!'

'Meaning?'

'Meaning Sir Julius wanted to talk to me. And that I was in for a pi-jaw – all that guff about the excellent proposition he'd put to me, to work for him.' He rolled his eyes.

'But you never had that talk, because of having your friends with you. Take us through that evening again.'

'Again? I keep telling you I can't remember that much, I was fuddled.'

'Your memory does seem confused. But try. To begin with, you were all very drunk . . .'

'Not as much as you might think. We'd had one or two, but we weren't plastered. Except for Boo. It never takes much before he gets ridiculous. Should've seen him on Boat Race night!'

'And on Thursday?'

'Oh, well, after the old man had left us, he began fooling around at the billiard table, grabbing the balls from the baize and chucking them at George and Mary. Their Maj,' he elucidated, in case they didn't get it, or hadn't seen those two stately portraits of the king and his queen in the billiard room. He was talking too much, trying to skirt the main issue. 'Even the servants, or most of them, had all gone to bed by then, and before the silly blighter woke the entire household, we hauled him upstairs to his room and on to his bed – hardly got his feet off the ground before he passed out cold. After that we needed a snifter, I can tell you, and we went back downstairs.'

'And found Mrs Waring had arrived.'

That at least stopped him.

'I have to tell you, Mr Shefford, we have a witness who saw Mrs Waring enter the house.'

He still said nothing. Not asking who, as if it didn't matter, though Surtees was a name unlikely to mean anything to him anyway. But all at once he struggled to his feet and stood gripping the edges of the table. 'I need some time,' he said at last and shoved his chair back clumsily, so that it almost fell over. Reardon made a sign to Jago to leave him as he went to stand, hands thrust deep into his pockets, head down, in the same position by the window they'd found him in when they'd re-entered the room.

Reardon took a minute or two himself to do some refocusing, until his patience ran out. 'Mr Shefford!'

He turned slowly. His face was drawn and without colour. He'd lost that sulky, what's-it-to-me expression. 'All right,' he said at last, 'since I've already told you so much . . . Confession's good for the soul, they used to tell us at—' He broke off. 'Shouldn't Fitz be here as well?'

'We've already spoken to him. And we will again, I assure you.'

He nodded, with a curious expression crossing his face.

Between them, the two detectives had heard plenty so-called confessions: someone's need to get the weight off their chest; self-justification; the hope of mitigating their sentence. Occasionally, it was due to genuine sorrow and remorse. In Shefford's case, it was probably something of all of them except the latter. He might even, Jago thought, throwing a meaningful glance at Reardon, be one of those sad nutters who falsely confessed, even to murder, totally innocent but desperate for attention, spouting all kinds of impossible rubbish.

But Shefford didn't look like a nut case. He seemed calm, and actually smiled. *That smile!* That disarming one Reardon knew now not to trust, and probably with good reason, because some odd and disturbing vibe had crept into the gloomy library as it darkened still further, the threatened downpour came down in earnest and the rain began hitting the windows.

Shefford closed his eyes for several minutes, then began to speak in a flat monotone, the words coming as if what he was saying had recalled what had been playing itself out behind his closed lids ever since it had happened.

After putting the drunken Boo to bed they had together descended that grand staircase (wide enough to take four abreast, sufficient to accommodate farthingales, crinolines, Georgian girths – a coach and horses one was tempted to think – and where indeed a wild young Falquonroy of yore had reputedly ridden his horse to the top, tried to come down again and killed both horse and himself), and he and Fitz had found her standing at its foot.

There she was, dwarfed but by no means intimidated by the great hall. Spotlit in the circle of light created by the few lamps always left burning overnight, their light unable to reach as far as the distant corners.

It was Fitz who broke the silence which had taken their tongues at sight of her. 'You're Mrs Waring, I believe?' Socially adept, extending a hand, his saurian smile. 'Gerald FitzAlban. I'm very pleased to meet you. Heard a lot about you from your lovely stepdaughter.'

'I've heard about you, too.' Cool response. No move to take

the proffered hand, while questions erupted through Toby like rising yeast. What the devil was she doing here, all dressed up, paying calls this time of night? What did she want? Who had let her in? A dirty torn remnant of spider's web clinging to the shoulder of her smart jacket answered that one: she'd braved it and come in via the garden wing, through those ghastly passages leading to this part of the house.

'Have you any idea what time it is?'

What did that matter, her look said. She'd come to see Sir Julius. She couldn't leave it any longer. She'd been trying to get hold of him all week, but he'd been so busy, run off his feet. Not even responding – which was totally unlike him – to the letter she'd sent him, begging some time for a very private and important conversation. 'I intended going away, you see, leaving Templewood, and I was desperate to see him before I went. And you know why, Toby Shefford – you know what I'm talking about.'

She was getting above herself, speaking to him like that, with a hint of the temper he'd once, long ago, sensed in her. All the same, he was not about to admit that he knew only too well she was intent on carrying out those threats she'd already made, spilling the beans about his affair with a dead girl, ten years ago. And what was all this about her going away? 'You obviously didn't leave.'

No, she admitted, though if things had gone as she'd planned, she would have been long gone by now. She'd arranged for someone to pick her up that night from that place, The Spinney, take her to where she could get a train somewhere a long, long way from here.

It sounded too much to him like something she'd made up on the spur of the moment, but not apparently, to Fitz, leaning against the newel post, arms folded, following the exchange with interest. 'Running away, Mrs Waring?' he asked softly.

Impertinent question. She didn't bother to answer, just continued speaking to Toby, her face now very miserable. 'It might still come to that,' she said sadly, 'but I pray not. I've been a fool, but I've begun to see sense. I had a long wait, you see, down there in The Spinney, time to realize that I couldn't go away without speaking to Sir Julius, even though it would mean the whole truth would come out. It's bound to, you know. *Everything*. Isn't it?'

Her look challenged him, but she was quite right, of course. Sir Julius was the last man on earth to leave stones unturned. Any whisper of that old affair with Lucy, and he wouldn't rest until he'd got right to the bottom of it, the association with Fitz, drugs and all. Every detail. Fitz done for as well as Toby.

'I still can't understand *your* problem, why you must leave.'

'Can't you? Can't you see it's not just about Lucy and you, it's me as well? He'll want to know how I recognized you, where we'd met . . . and that means . . . oh God, that means Wykedge, don't you see?'

'Wykedge?'

'All that lying stuff the papers wrote . . . the hate it stirred up against me, hinting I might have stopped those murders if I'd come forward earlier. Everything I've since tried to keep to myself for all these years will start again, things I couldn't bear my husband knowing, perhaps believing there could have been some basis of truth in them. Oh, he could – I even persuaded myself of that once! He's a good man, my husband, but he expects so much of one. But it doesn't do ever to underestimate him and I'm daring to hope he might understand if I speak to him. Perhaps it's foolish to hope; maybe I will have to leave after all, I don't know. In case I do, I have to talk to Dee's father before she gets home tomorrow.'

'You *don't* have to. If you don't say anything, he'll never know.'

An abyss of misunderstanding yawned between them. She didn't answer. She looked drained and tired. Finally, she said, 'If you can accept that, I can't,' and began to move towards the stairs. 'Let me pass.'

Fitz intervened smoothly, 'I'm afraid you're out of luck, Mrs Waring. Sir Julius is having an early night; he's already in bed.'

'Then I'll wake him up.'

'She was already halfway up the stairs,' Shefford said, 'trying to push past us. Then she tripped and fell, right across the stairs. Both of us went after her, trying to save her.'

'To save her?' Reardon said. 'I don't think so. She was going to let the cat out of the bag, and you weren't going to let that happen, neither you nor FitzAlban, were you? He had as much reason as you for hiding the truth, perhaps more.' *Because he knew what was in that letter Alexei had handed to him and what it would mean for them both.*

'I tell you, we did try to save her! What exactly happened next – it was all so quick, it's a bit of a blur I don't really remember . . . but I know how we struggled and tried to pull her to her feet. Grabbed at her, snatched at her clothes, anything. But she was . . . oh God, it was unbelievable! A few minutes, seconds, and she was *dead*.'

Did he really expect them to believe that was how it was? He lifted his arm and the flickering lamplight lit the twisting scar and showed a line of sweat on his brow as he wiped his sleeve across. But the panic was leaving him. 'It was an accident. I swear it. She was never meant to be hurt.'

'That's not how it happened,' Reardon said. 'There were bruises on both of her arms, as well as evidence of deliberate strangulation. Someone held her down, while someone else tightened the scarf that throttled her.'

'She must have bruised herself when she fell; it was all an accident, I tell you!'

'Then why didn't you rouse someone to get help?' Jago asked.

'What was the point of that? She was already dead, there wasn't anything to be done. It was an *accident*.' Repeated like a mantra, it was as if the more he said it, the truer it would become.

'But you still felt it necessary to get rid of the body.'

'We had to. What if she'd already told someone else what she was going to say to Sir Julius? What would it have looked like then? We had to get her out of sight, at least until we thought what to do. As it was, anyone could have heard the noise, come along at any minute and seen us, though no one did.'

'You used the Lagonda. FitzAlban actually allowed *that*?'

'How else were we to get her away from Falquonroy? It was hard enough manoeuvring her body out of the house.'

That would have taken some doing, for sure. Through the arches at the back of the hall, along that cloistered walk, through the iron-bolted back door to the garages. All the time, trying not to make a noise, hampered by the weight of a dead body, however small.

'Why take her to The Spinney?' asked Reardon.

'What? Oh, I don't know. Because she'd just mentioned it, I suppose.'

'Taking a gamble, weren't you? When she'd told you someone was coming to pick her up from there?'

'If they were already there, we would have just driven past.'

Emilie hadn't told them, then, that Surtees had actually arrived, taken her over to Falquonroy and driven off home to Wolverhampton. The riskiness amounted to craziness. On the other hand, if suspicion was to fall on anyone when the body was found, and if Emilie had been telling the truth about someone meeting her there, then that person would have been the first suspect. Skewed thinking. Reardon wondered if they'd thought at all.

'Look, you have to believe me, we never meant her to *die*!' Shefford was sounding desperate, unaware that he was half admitting blame. We only wanted to hurt her a bit, to frighten her. Make her see what she was doing.'

In a world inhabited by civilized people, women were not made to feel afraid, certainly not by having their own scarves tightened around their necks until they died, accidentally or otherwise. Yet between them these two men had done just that. They had killed her. They had taken her down to The Spinney and arranged her still-gloved hands (and which of them had thought of that?) piously across her chest. In their haste, they had let her handbag slip away, unnoticed. It must have given them a few uneasy moments when they remembered it, when FitzAlban had to go searching for it.

Jago looked at Reardon and Reardon looked back.

They were wondering the same thing – which one of these two men had actually killed Emilie Waring? Shefford, prepared to do anything to save his engagement to Dee Malpas, with its promise of a future free from money worries? Or the other one – who allegedly hadn't even known Emilie? Whether he had or not, FitzAlban must have been aware that Emilie could not be allowed to go to Dee's father with what she knew about Toby Shefford, and its consequences for himself.

Both men were implicated, but over the last half hour Reardon's opinion of Shefford's intelligence, as well as his capacity for cruelty and revenge, had undergone a drastic revision. He regarded him steadily, for what seemed like forever. The heavy shower stopped as abruptly as it had begun. He stood up. ‘Toby Shefford, I am arresting you—’

A low rumbling noise had arisen somewhere outside and the rest of what he was saying was drowned as the rumble erupted into an ear-splitting roar. All three men swung towards the front window as the red Lagonda hurtled past. Totally out of control, it veered crazily round the parterre and down the drive. The noise when it met one of the great stone gateposts could have been the crack of doom.

And in less time than it took to count, the once sleek, beautiful machine was nothing more than a meaningless heap of twisted metal and broken glass. In the following, noiseless split second, nothing moved. Then, as if in slow motion, the huge black falcon on top of the gatepost slowly toppled over and crashed down on to the wreckage below.

EPILOGUE

Someone is playing Mama's piano. A haunting echo, the golden stream of rippling, baroque notes flows out from the living room to where Sophy sits in her favourite spot in the garden, reading a letter from America. She listens for a minute, then leaves the swing and goes to investigate, the letter still in her hand.

What is *he* doing here? Tom Jago, of all people, at the piano! That's who he is now to the family – Sam's friend Tom, not Detective Sergeant Jago. He lifts his hands from the keyboard when he sees her, slightly abashed. 'Oh, hello, Sophy.' He closes the piano lid carefully and stands up. 'I'm sorry. Can't think what came over me.'

'Don't be, it's lovely to hear it played again. Scarlatti? Why aren't you a professional musician? You could be.'

'Kind, but untrue. You didn't hear the wrong notes. In any case, my Methodist upbringing predisposes me towards work that will actually allow me to eat.'

Sophy laughs and goes to the window seat. There's plenty room now on the long seat for him to join her there, which he does. Dear old Juno has recently died, and Towser hasn't yet reached the reclining stage, if ever he will. Sophy can hear his barks now, above Sam's voice and the children's noisy cricket game.

'And so you went to Oxford instead,' she says when he's still not offering to say why he's here. 'And then became a London policeman.'

'So I did. And as I'll be on my way back there in less than an hour, I came to say goodbye.'

'I thought we said that the other day.'

'I know we did. But the chief's pinched some time to visit Mrs Lychfield, so I cadged a lift for the chance to say it again.'

'Oh.' He's looking at her in a way that brings warmth to her cheeks. Then she does a double take. 'Inspector Reardon? Granny?'

'He needs to check the name of a climbing rose she grows on the wall of her house.'

'Ah. If he's another gardener, they're friends for life.'

'It's Mrs Reardon who's the gardener. He just goes along, or so he says.'

There's an awkward pause. The shouts and children's laughter are dying down. Presumably the cricket game's over. Sam has been teaching the rules to Rosa's boys and some of the other children who've also now arrived at Falquonroy from Germany.

The skies over Europe may be darkening with the clouds of war, but here at Templewood, Sam's beloved old home, which will belong to him one day, and where he and Rosa are beginning their married life, the world is still bright. Two months previously, Sam had sped towards Belgium in his Opel, the nightmare possibility in his mind that Rosa might still be afraid of what the future with him might bring. He need not have worried. Their relatively short separation had brought with it a realization that life without Sam wasn't possible for Rosa. When he arrived, she was ready, almost as if she'd been waiting.

They'd driven back to Templewood and married in almost indecent haste, and now Rosa is painstakingly learning from Maitland how to run a house very different from anything she has ever known – and to smile more often. While Sam seeks another position that won't entail moving away, they are both working tirelessly for the Jewish Refugees Committee, continuing Emilie's work on the never-ending task of helping as many people as possible to escape from Germany.

As for Rosa's sons, the change is miraculous. They've lost that unchildlike caution, the fear at the back of their eyes. They are swiftly becoming ordinary small boys. They wear shorts and jerseys, not stiff, correct suits. They're allowed to run wild in the woods, climbing trees with the local children, making friends, learning their language – in all its variations. 'It is a bugger, this English grammar,' Dieter had declared yesterday, scowling over some impenetrable homework.

'You haven't yet said you'll be sorry I'm going back to London, Sophy,' Tom says now. He's smiling, so he must be teasing.

'Well, I'm going to be there too.'

'Really?' The smile widens enormously, then fades a little. 'You'll be staying at the Malpas townhouse, I suppose?' Dancing and dining out, parties, his tone implies. Which isn't what he'd like to hear.

'No. I'll be working, Tom. I've got a job.'

'Have you indeed? Something I've missed?'

'I've only known since yesterday.'

She'd told no one about the proposal to work for Jane's brother in Highgate. Or not until it had come to nothing, when Granny, who always knows if something's amiss, had wanted to know why she was looking peaky. Sophy had told her, confessing how much she longed for some independence, and then things had moved quickly. It turns out that one of the girls Granny had come out with all those years ago had defied tradition and thrown away any chances of marriage by going on to study at Holloway College. She had later become part-owner, with her suffragist friend, of a small, exclusive bookshop off Charing Cross Road. Sadly, her friend had died, leaving her bereft, but sole owner of the bookshop.

Granny had characteristically kept in touch with Harriet, Miss Proudie, who was at last admitting that at her age she was in need of an assistant. The flat above her bookshop was somewhat cramped, but there was a spare room. Both the job and the room were Sophy's if she wanted them.

Sophy does, desperately, though she isn't sure how she'll find living and working with this rather formidable-sounding, eccentric woman. Miss Proudie's bookshop, Granny tells her, has become a well-known meeting place for an interesting (but still, to Sophy, intimidating sounding) circle of writers, artists, poets, intellectuals. But it's a challenge and she's prepared to give it a go. One of Miss Proudie's friends is Virginia Woolf.

'You'll love it, I guess,' says Tom, when she's told him about it, and hopes he's right. At least it might give him a chance to see her occasionally.

'By the way, Gizi's coming home,' she says, suddenly aware of the letter still clutched in her hand.

Soon after the shock of Toby Shefford's arrest, Gizi and Dee had been waved off at Southampton, starting a five-day voyage of utter luxury on the fabulous new French liner *Normandie* before arriving in New York, and thence travelling on to Boston for an extended stay with Papa's sister.

Aunt Eleanor is married to Uncle Waldo, a wealthy American financier who is also a senator. He's from one of the old Boston families, with a large house on Beacon Hill and a prominent place in Boston society which, Sophy has gathered, is stiff-necked and snobbish, although both Gizi and Dee have been overwhelmed with invitations. The young bloods there are apparently falling over one another to claim an English rose as a bride – and since most of them appear to be filthy rich, the appeal is mutual. Dee, determined not to let what happened with Toby ruin her life, has already met someone 'very interesting'. Like everyone else, she is trying to put Toby, Emilie's murder, and the horrific circumstances surrounding it, back into the past, though no one is finding it easy.

Gizi, however, is at this precise moment on her way home, though not to Templewood. 'She says she's going to find work in London,' Sophy tells Tom.

After a moment, the ludicrous idea of Gizi actually *working* strikes them both and they begin to laugh, but Sophy soon sobers. 'I don't think she means work in that sense.'

He gives her a sharp look and says bluntly, 'What she really means is, she's going to hang out with . . .'

'Don't! Or don't let anyone else hear you say that, much less Papa. Not unless she allows him to marry her, which is what she ought to do, and what he wants, of course.'

Martin Garbutt is now living in London. He has found paid work that suits him down to the ground, employment at the TUC's London headquarters, a safe, settled job at last. Yet everyone who knows Martin will never believe he can stand aside from the political upheavals going on down there, the mob violence still causing havoc between fascists and antifascists, particularly with the heavy Jewish population of London's East End. Sophy hasn't forgotten the time, not long ago, when Gizi had fervently shared Martin's ideals and aspirations, long before her infatuation with what she once imagined FitzAlban could offer. If Pa hears the pair of them are together, sparks will fly. Not that he has anything against Martin, quite the opposite. He admires him for standing up for what he believes in, always has, but since the time Martin went too far, getting himself sent to prison, to Winson Green, Pa has kept a wary eye on him. It's no use telling either of them, Martin or Gizi, to be careful, of course.

But Pa isn't here, at Templewood or indeed in England, at present.

'I intend, very shortly, to announce my retirement from the Bench,' he had announced one day at lunch, as calmly as if he were telling them he was going to take a walk.

That's the kind of announcement to render one speechless. Judges are notorious for carrying on working until they topple off their perches, but Pa hasn't reached that stage yet, not by a long way. 'Meanwhile, I have it in mind,' he'd continued, 'to travel. France, Italy. And Greece. We can go together, Alexei, if you'd like to come with me, actually see some of those ancient places you've been reading about.'

Would Alexei like to go! He is there with Papa now, until he goes up to Cambridge. He sends postcards of the Acropolis, of Delphi, of Ephesus and the temple of Artemis, saying he's having a stupendous time. The remote chance of finding his negligent father seems to have been postponed, forgotten, even perhaps abandoned.

Sophy has her own ideas about why Papa feels he can no longer be a judge. Not for an instant has she ever doubted his assertions to the police that he hadn't at any time pressed his wife for details of her past. Pa would never lie – and forcing Emilie to relive the worst time of her life would have been unthinkable to him. Perhaps because he had known about it anyway. As Sophy had known when she remembered those printed volumes with details of the trial, the photographs. She'd known then why Emilie's face had appeared familiar, that Pa had probably recognized her when he had first set eyes on her, when she had bumped into him in Scarborough. He hadn't lied, of course, simply omitted to explain. Which still must have come perilously close to obstructing the police with their enquiries. The truth of how Emilie died has emerged, albeit in a different way to what it might have done had Pa been more forthcoming, but Sophy can't believe that all this would have escaped Tom Jago, much less his boss, Chief Inspector Reardon. She has schooled herself to believe that if the police, not to say her father, can live with that, she must put the thought of it to rest too. Maybe, in time, she can do this.

A motorcar is coming up the drive. 'Here comes the chief.' Tom stands up, slightly flushed, his hair mussed up where he's run his hand through it and he starts to speak hurriedly, as if he's run out of time. 'Look, Sophy, we must see each other when you're in London.'

He takes both her hands and pulls her to her feet, too. They face each other uncertainly. He hesitates, leans forward and kisses her gently on the cheek. Another uncertain moment. 'Sophy?' And then he throws caution to the wind, drops her hands, and folds his arms right round her, fiercely tight, almost lifting her off her feet. He bends his head, she raises her face, and this time, the kiss is anything but gentle.

Reardon takes the wheel of the police Wolseley as they head back to Folbury for Jago's train. He is thinking of the first time they had driven the other way, into Temple Atwode through that green tunnel of trees. He had been bemoaning the absence of his right-hand man, Joe Gilmour, just when he needed him most, in what was destined to be a sensitive investigation. And not least, wondering why the devil he was having to make do with the young Cornishman who'd been wished on him.

Now, driving away from Templewood, Falquonroy and all that had happened there, he feels sorry to be losing him, though he knows Jago isn't sorry to be going. His heart is in London, on his successful transfer to the Murder Squad at Scotland Yard.

Reardon is pleased for him, if that's where his sights are fixed, though it's not something he would ever want for himself. Murder is comparatively rare around Folbury, and he's relieved that his part in detecting the last one is over. Leaving him free to concentrate on less stressful casework and not allowing the memory of Emilie Waring's death to linger. It's what he's been trying to do for weeks. But inevitably, in view of where they've just been and to whom they've been speaking, thc conversation turns back to the murder of the judge's wife.

The final, decisive report has just come in from the experts who have for weeks been examining and puzzling over the

Lagonda wreckage. Nothing, they've finally concluded, has been found which would account for the inexplicable way it had behaved before that final, fatal crash into the gatepost.

'What else did we expect?' Reardon asks.

And Jago says, not for the first time, 'We both saw Shefford's face, and how he looked after the crash.'

The way Shefford had looked in those few seconds is something neither of them is ever likely to forget. A look that said he was not such a fool with engines as he claimed.

Nevertheless, they both know that any suggestion of him having tampered with the engine would have no chance whatever of being taken seriously by anyone. FitzAlban had seen to it that his beloved motorcar, that pampered, beautifully engineered, pedigree beast, had been regularly and meticulously maintained. Unlikely as it seems, it must be accepted that some as-yet inexplicable fault had developed.

It's been suggested (and the super, Knott, is inclined to go for this, despite evidence to the contrary) that the crash was not due to some mysterious fault in the car's engine, but to the driver himself – FitzAlban, after all, has been found to have had a dodgy, drug-dealing history. Knott may have a point, though he should know better than anyone that dealers, as often as not, avoid using the drugs they've no compunction in peddling to others. That appears to have been true of FitzAlban, but in any event, his body was in a condition that left looking for traces of drugs superfluous.

Shefford had at last admitted to having acted for FitzAlban in passing on narcotics, hoping for it to be taken into consideration. If you have no money to your name, have a gambling habit and are massively in debt, how else are you to repay a friend who had once got you out of a deep hole, other than by doing him a few favours, he asked.

And how long would you endure feeling beholden, before gratitude turned to resentment, bitterness or the need for revenge? Reardon had felt like asking.

Well, unlike FitzAlban, who escaped – in the sense that he will never be brought to justice, or not in this life at any rate, if that's how your beliefs go – Shefford will be spending a very long stretch of his life in prison, whatever transpires.

A sombre prospect, but what of the lost years of Emilie's life?

Reardon draws the car up to the station approach. They shake hands, Reardon claps Jago on the shoulder and wishes him well. He watches him stride easily away, unhampered by the holdall slung over his shoulder, and smiles. He'll be back, if Reardon is any judge, the way he and Sophy Waring had looked at one another before the car left Templewood.

Meanwhile, if the nursery garden is still open when he gets there, Reardon has a golden rose to buy for his wife. He has a brochure in his pocket for a small hotel in Ambleside, too. He had promised Ellen some time away when the case was finished and now, if somewhat late, he's ready to suggest the Lake District. Long walks over the hills, the still, calm lakes . . .